TUSH

TUSH

JAFFE COHEN

CARROLL & GRAF PUBLISHERS
NEW YORK

TUSH

Carroll & Graf Publishers
An Imprint of Avalon Publishing Group, Inc.
245 West 17th Street, 11th Floor
New York, NY 10011

AVALON
publishing group incorporated

Copyright © 2006 by Jaffe Cohen

ISBN-13:978-0-7394-7176-0

Interior design by Maria E. Torres
Printed in the United States of America
Distributed by Publishers Group West

TUSH

Book 1
Prophesy

Chapter One

The fan letter was so moist and puppy doggish it might have licked the adhesive flap and jumped into the envelope by itself. Like many such letters, it was filled with exclamation points and underlined words, as though enthusiasm alone might compensate for its misspellings. With Venus transiting his ascendant that morning, Joel Eisenberg had already guessed there might something in his mailbox reeking of cologne and the possibility of romance. It was ten years to the month since his astrological guru, the late Yris del Coro, had predicted he would meet his Twin Flame, and even more tantalizing than the possibility of hot sex with a young admirer was the chance of meeting his one true love. Joel sat down on the steps of his building and read the letter eagerly.

June 3, 1997

Dear Joel,

You don't know me from Adam, but I know you from your <u>wonderfly</u> informitive book <u>When You Dish Upon the Stars</u> and from your many hilarious appearances on Howard Stern's radio show. (How did you do it?) When I think of you, the word that comes to mind is <u>genious</u>! You and your book have helped me so much breaking up with Vinnie (who is a Scorpio) because I know now that being mean is his nature and that he will <u>never</u> change! What else can I say but <u>thank you</u>! What I learned from your book does not lessen the pain (Vinnie was my <u>first</u> love! Ouch!). But you have given me faith that the universe might have something else <u>wonderful</u> in store for me and I can't <u>wait</u> to find out what it is!

Joel became aware that he was getting an erection. Pulling the chocolate muffin out of his mouth, he shifted his weight, leaving more room in his pants for the possibility of continued swelling. The letter continued breathlessly.

I know you must be very busy with your various career activities but do you give any <u>private</u> consultations? I would <u>love</u> to meet you. In case you're interested I was born October 2, 1971 at 3:10 PM in Knoxville, Tennessee. I am 25 years old, better than average looking and my phone number is as follows: 212-357-EAZY.

Yours truly,
Lucas Allison

Joel's grip tightened on the powder-blue note paper; his heart was beating faster than the wings of a hummingbird. *"Better than average looking"*? Scooping up the rest of his bills, bank statements, and coupons, he ran up the stairs to do the young man's chart. While waiting for his Zodiac program to open on the desktop of his computer, he reviewed what he had already guessed about Lucas.

This man/boy, a Libra ten years younger than he, most likely took it up the kazoo and was probably a blond. The handwriting alone gave him away. It was a round, childlike scrawl, the primitive, upbeat markings of a former cheerleader or the head of the glee club. Joel was almost drooling as he typed in Lucas's birth information. In a moment the chart appeared on his computer screen: first the house cusps, then the signs, and finally the planets themselves.

With Venus conjunct his sun, there could be no doubt that Lucas was a cute little seductress with an unconscious daddy fixation. Even better, with Saturn conjunct his Mercury, Lucas would also be a little slow and easily impressed by a fast-talking native New Yorker. Neptune on his ascendant, however, was a little worrisome. Lucas might be one of those guys who went through life posing as if they were available—maybe even thinking they were available—when in actuality they were never as user friendly as they liked to pretend.

Setting aside any negativity, Joel lay down on the floor and began to masturbate, occasionally opening his eyes to glance at Lucas's chart and mumbling the placements of Lucas's outer planets: "Neptune in Sagittarius. Pluto in Virgo. Uranus in Libra. Slap that Uranus!" He came very quickly, and at the same moment there was a surge of electricity in the apartment. Lucas's chart flickered and disappeared momentarily from the screen. *How odd,* Joel thought, not sure whether to take this as a sign from God or merely a notice from Con Ed that he hadn't paid his electric bill.

He reached up, grabbed the phone off his desk, and dialed the number in the letter. He wasn't just going to read this young man's future: he was going to become it. The phone had barely rung once when a light baritone shouted on the other end, "I told you *not* to call. It's not *fair* to either one of us."

Joel knew he'd reached the party he'd been seeking.

"Lucas, this is Joel Eisenberg," he said, attempting to clear up the confusion.

There was a pause—just enough time for Lucas to experience the lowest depths of his capacity for embarrassment—which, apparently, weren't all that deep. "Oh, my god!" he bounced back. "I'm *so* glad you called."

"I received your letter," Joel said nonchalantly.

"It's *only* gotten worse. I thought you were my boyfriend calling—or rather my ex-…"

"You mean Vinnie?"

"How'd you know his name was Vinnie?"

Joel momentarily considered claiming telepathic powers, but decided it wouldn't be necessary. "You mentioned him in your letter."

Lucas sighed deeply. Even his sighs were italicized. "I think I'm going to *kill* myself."

"Sounds like I called just in time."

Joel heard the irritating beep indicating Lucas was getting another call—a sound that made him nostalgic for the busy signal. It beeped again.

"Are you going to get that?" Joel asked.

"It's probably him again," Lucas whined. "Should I talk to him?"

"I'll call back later."

"No. *Hold on.*"

Joel heard another beep as he was put on hold. Taking a deep breath, he considered how best to dispose of what was left of Lucas's current love affair. Within seconds, Lucas returned.

"Oh, god, Vinnie wants to come over. What should I tell him? I mean astrologically speaking, what's going on?"

"The moon's in Scorpio," Joel guessed without checking his ephemeris. "Vinnie's feelings about his family are very strong right now."

"How'd you *know* that?"

Emboldened by his lucky hunch, Joel kept talking. "And there's probably some kind of crisis. Is his father in some kind of trouble?"

Joel paused briefly, waiting for Lucas to murmur his assent, but the young man was silent. "His sister?" Joel ventured.

"Not really."

"His brother?"

"You're getting warmer."

"His brother-in-law?"

"Oh, my god. How'd you know that?"

Joel knew that he was home free. "I saw two words in my mind," he answered. "*Brother* and *law*. I just put them together."

"Wow! You're amazing. His brother-in-law *just* got arrested for tax evasion. So, what should I do?"

"I really don't feel I should be butting in," Joel demurred.

"No, *please*. What should I do?"

Joel sighed. "Vinnie should probably be with his family now. They live, where—in Brooklyn?"

"Ridgewood, Queens. Near the Brooklyn border."

"Tell Vinnie not to come to your apartment. Do you understand? Tell him to stay away. Tell him to go home to his mother's house."

"*Stay right there,*" Lucas demanded. "Don't hang up."

Joel heard another beep while Lucas applied what he hoped would be the coup de grâce to his boyfriend's devotion. In those few seconds, Joel thanked God for how many guys named Vinnie came from large, close-knit Queens families with serious legal problems. When Lucas came back on the line, they made an appointment for an astrological consultation the very next day, which might include, as Joel so delicately put it, some "bodywork."

"*Great,*" Lucas responded. "Should I wear comfortable clothes?"

• • •

The next day Joel woke up excited and masturbated again, knowing that the need to wipe off his stomach would be a good excuse to get out of bed. He then considered doing a major house-cleaning but, after an exhausting twenty seconds with the DustBuster, he settled for straightening a pile of papers and closing the venetian blinds so the shadowed stripes would visually thin out the mess. Knowing that he would eventually ask Lucas to lie on the floor for his "bodywork," he stacked a down comforter and a few large pillows alongside the couch.

He then switched on his computer in order to retrieve Lucas's chart from cyberspace. Joel would need to stock up on a few key concepts and catch phrases, so he began thumbing through some texts and rereading Dane Rudyard's definitive description of the Libran archetype. Working as an astrologer had at least marginally improved his sex life. Only seven years before he'd been slaving away as an assistant teacher at a daycare center—not a sexy career by BoyBar standards. Even worse, Joel was living in gay Manhattan without being particularly handsome. He wasn't exactly homely: he was a perfectly pleasant looking, slightly plumpish Jewish male with glasses and a bald spot. In the less demanding world of heterosexuals, he might have rated a solid seven; but in the highly competitive arenas of Chelsea and Fire Island, his percentile rating plummeted. The pain Joel felt over not being found attractive by other gay men far surpassed any torture the heterosexual world could ever have inflicted.

Like many people who aren't particularly successful or beautiful, Joel was drawn to astrology, a system in which there are no losers, only difficult aspects and tough transits. Joel found East West Books on Fifth Avenue and read everything he could about the ancient Babylonian art of divination. He discovered that Cancer was his zodiac sign because, looking from planet Earth, it was the constellation directly behind the sun at the time of his birth. He learned that all the other planets were also located in signs and they all affected one's personality. Mars was symbolic of one's aggression; Venus showed how one might relate to others; Mercury colored the way one thinks. Astrology continued to get more interesting the more Joel studied, and by the time he got his chart done by the cranky but charismatic Yris del Coro, he was well on his way to giving readings of his own.

Joel had been very lucky to get an appointment with the great lady, who just happened to be the aunt of one of his co-workers. Yris was considered an enlightened being by her many devotees— mostly working-class women who waited years for a chance to kiss the hem of her skirt. How thrilling and scary it was to walk into her Hell's Kitchen apartment and be told that he would soon become a famous astrologer in his own right. He was a little less thrilled to be told that he would have to wait ten whole years to find true love. Swallowing his disappointment, he immediately signed up for a class with the Puerto Rican prophetess, who grudgingly took him under her wing. Yris became Joel's astrological spirit guide. Whenever he was in doubt about what to say to one of his clients, he closed his eyes and channeled her voice.

The inner Yris was often right, and their psychic connection only got stronger after the old lady died. At night she came to Joel in his dreams—often to scold him for being a fool—and she would nag him to improve himself whenever he sat down at the altar he had created for the very purpose of invoking her spirit. Over the years Joel had begun to depend on Yris for more than just astrology; he found himself praying to her whenever he felt needy or out of sorts, such as when the D train was running late or the line was particularly long at Duane Reade.

But even without Yris del Coro's telepathic assistance, Joel would have made a good astrological counselor. Two decades of struggling to seduce handsome men had polished his ability to figure out what a person wanted to hear and proclaim it as the truth. Most people, he'd discovered, were so desperate for some kind of cosmic order that, if he were willing to risk making a fool of himself by guessing wrong 60 percent of the time, he would be considered a genius for the 40 percent when he was right. Starting with a few friends, he was soon getting so many referrals for readings that he was able to quit his job at the daycare center. Before long he had a roster of clients that included a group of wealthy women from the Upper East Side who had nothing better to do than come down to Greenwich Village and be told that they were morally and spiritually superior to their powerful husbands. He also discovered a knack for writing that set the stage for a magazine column and a surprisingly successful book. This had led to TV appearances, and—thanks to Howard Stern—a weekly gig on the most popular radio show in New York. In the early nineties, he had become so well known that he was commonly referred to as the "Richard Simmons of astrology."

But regular comparisons to the exercise queen were not exactly an aphrodisiac for cute guys. After striking out in every gay bar from the West Village to West Hollywood, he was forced to do what most other semifamous shlemiels have done: he hired a callboy from an escort service. Unfortunately, like his mother Roz, who always vacuumed before the maid came over to clean her house, Joel masturbated several times before the prostitute arrived. When he did show up at Joel's hotel room, instead of performing his job, he found himself being advised to pursue a more respectable career in massage therapy.

Bottom line: Joel was more interested in the possibility of a sexual encounter than actually having one, and nothing he did in bed could ever beat the moment when the hottie said, "OK, go ahead." One day, while making a point about the lower chakras to a young client with a big, round heinie, he impulsively asked the guy to lie down on the floor and unbuckle his pants. Surprisingly his client obeyed, and Joel spent the next two hours massaging his tush in the guise of healing his psyche. Only after his client left was Joel able to set the scene for the perfect sexual experience. After lighting some incense, dimming the lights, and putting on a CD of rhythmic Hindu chanting, he jerked off without the inconvenience of somebody else in the room.

His private readings became pretexts for copping a feel from clueless cuties in tight pants. That was very often the extent of his sex life because he chased after tush the way a dog chases after cars, having no idea what to do once he caught one. AIDS had made fucking somebody without protection unthinkable, and his one attempt at putting on a condom had resulted in it shooting across the room like a rubber band. As for rimming, he'd always been a picky eater with a greater than average aversion to bad smells and questionable textures. Once or twice, when the tush was extraordinarily shapely and the area was spotlessly clean, he'd laid all scruples aside. In most cases, however, he'd merely fingered the orifice with one hand while jerking the guy off with the other.

In any event, Joel's clumsy lovemaking techniques rarely resulted in a second date, much less meeting his Twin Flame. So at the age of thirty-seven he was getting desperate for someone who would warm his feet at night and remind him to call his mother on the weekends. The wiser part of him knew that it was highly unlikely he would ever achieve this kind of domestic bliss with somebody like Lucas Allison, but just in case—and to kill the time while waiting—he began digging through his desk drawer in order to find a cassette labeled "Yris del Coro/June 24, 1987." Joel fast-forwarded to the section in which he asked questions about his love life.

"In ten years' time you will find the love of your life."

"You mean like my soul mate?"

"Your soul mate? Phooey! Soul mates you meet every day on the street. No. The man you will meet is your Twin Flame. You have only one Twin Flame for all eternity."

"Wow."

"When God made your soul, he also made your Twin Flame. In every lifetime you meet him and he'll show you what love is. Listen to me. In ten years you will go on a journey to the north. But when you get there, you will feel like you've gone south. Do you understand?"

"I think so."

"And when you get there, you will meet a man."

"Will it be love at first sight?"

"No. This man will be in love with someone else."

"Figures."

"There will be many trials and much pain but eventually you will meet your Twin Flame and you will never again be alone."

"And how will I know I've met him?"

"There is only one way to know your Twin Flame. He will give you his heart. Now let us talk about other things...."

Joel turned off the tape. Lucas *was* in love with someone else, just like Yris had predicted. And he did live on 116th Street, which meant that a journey north to visit this Tennessee boy's apartment would be like crossing the Mason-Dixon line. As for the third requirement, "He will give you his heart," only time would tell. Still, Yris's prophecy might just be some kind of cosmic code. The journey north might only be a mythic journey.

"The only real issue is whether he shows up at all," Joel said to himself impatiently. It was already 2:20 and Mr. Better-than-Average-Looking was starting to look like a no-show.

Joel ran to his bedroom to sit in front of his altar and invoke his spirit guide. Throwing his old bar mitzvah tallis over his shoulders, he sat cross-legged on the floor and lit several candles. After taking a moment to center his ch'i, Joel scribbled "MAKE LUCAS COME SOON" on a slip of paper and placed it in front of a framed photo of Yris del Coro. Then he picked up his prayer beads, wrapped them around his fingers, and began to wail, *"Nam myoho renge kyo,"* again and again. As he chanted, he sifted through some of his previous notes. "UNDRESS BRENT" had already been granted so he crumpled it and tossed it over his shoulder. "GET MORE MONEY FROM YOUR PUBLISHER" and "FIND A HIGH-POWERED TV AGENT" were still works in progress so he refolded them and stuck them back on the altar. After a few minutes of vigorous chanting, Joel finally began to hear the voice he'd been seeking.

"Hey, stupid." It was Yris del Coro, whispering deeply inside his brain. "Be patient. True love is closer than you think."

"Why do I always have to be patient?" Joel grumbled. Blowing out the candles, he began pacing around his apartment. He glanced at the kitchen clock. It was 2:34. *What if Lucas doesn't come?* Joel thought. At 2:36 he collapsed in his chair and began pounding on his desk, wondering if there was an astrological reason why Lucas was late. Maybe Mercury had gone retrograde or the moon was Void of Course, he mused. Joel tried to check his ephemeris but his fingers were too impatient to find the requisite table. He groaned, throwing the book aside. Falling to his knees, he put his head to the floor. Bypassing Yris del Coro altogether, he resorted to some old-fashioned Jewish pleading to the G-d of his ancestors. "Adonai, please. Let me have this one. He sounded so cute on the phone."

Just then the buzzer sounded and Joel flew across the room to the intercom.

"Yes?" he said breathlessly, crossing his fingers.

"It's Lucas Allison. I am *so* sorry I'm late!"

"No problem!" Joel called back. Then he pressed the buzzer and ran to the bathroom to wash the smell of desperation from his mouth. While gargling he completely forgot to thank the Old Testament God for answering his prayer, although he did briefly remember to congratulate Yris for accurately predicting that Lucas had been very close by.

Chapter Two

Lucas Allison had woken up that morning with every intention of getting to Joel's apartment on time. Unfortunately, his audition for *Mamie,* a new musical based on the long, sad life of Mamie Eisenhower, had been scheduled for noon. In no way had he imagined waiting an hour and forty-five minutes to sing eight bars of "Mama, a Rainbow" from *Minnie's Boys.* In no way did he imagine the F train would be running on the E track and he'd have to wait fifteen minutes for a train. And in no way did he imagine that he'd be so enthralled by Bernadette Peters singing "Broadway Baby" on his Walkman that he would completely miss the Fourteenth Street stop.

"Joel Eisenberg is going to hate me," he said to himself, trying to calm down. The first lesson he'd learned in acting class was that he could stuff his anxiety into the deep recesses of his abdomen as proficiently as he could pack a tiny gym bag for a whole weekend on Fire Island. At 2:36 Lucas pressed Joel's buzzer and, in the seconds it took the astrologer to answer, he managed to take a few deep breaths, just enough to suck the oxygen out of the Astrodome and regain a small measure of what was, for him, composure.

While racing up the five flights of stairs, he considered what he wanted to ask Joel. The anxiety over his relationship with Vinnie had already been jostled off the front burner of his mind by some thoughts he'd had during the audition. Lucas was preoccupied with those as he turned the corner onto the fifth-story landing and beheld a rather sweet-looking man with a worried grin. Completely abandoning his previous idea of maintaining an aura of dignified calm, Lucas bounded forward and fell to his knees, having guessed correctly that some kind of lowly prostration would please his host immensely. "Oh, my *god!* You must *despise* me."

Looking down, Joel saw a head of thick, dirty-blond hair pressed against his thigh and two big, brown eyes staring up at him. The headphones of a Walkman were holding back Lucas's hair and reminded Joel of the way high school girls would keep their bangs out of their faces in gym class. Then, just as suddenly as he'd lowered himself, Lucas jumped up and chirped something that sounded like his name.

He's a cutie, all right, thought Joel. *An item. A snack. Small— maybe only five foot five. A mini-hunk that could be easily folded and carried into a bedroom.*

"You have *no* idea how *excited* I am to meet you," Lucas was now saying.

"Come in," Joel said demurely. Standing aside to let his guest squeeze past him in the doorway, Joel caught a glimpse of Lucas's big round butt vacuum-packed into jeans that fit him as tightly as plum skins. Joel also noticed that Lucas had the slightly turned-out stride and raised elbows of a gay man who had once studied ballet.

"What are you listening to?" Joel asked, pointing at Lucas's Walkman and trying not to seem like he was fishing for information.

"Bernadette Peters's Carnegie Hall album," Lucas replied as he scanned Joel's apartment. "She's a goddess!"

TUSH   17

• • •

Lucas, meanwhile, discreetly sized up Joel's place. It wasn't quite where he suspected a "successful author" to be living. The old wood floors were buckled more steeply than the Berkshires, and thousands of dust particles floated in the striped sunshine streaming through the unwashed venetian blinds, as if the place hadn't been cleaned in decades. Nevertheless, Lucas found the apartment charming; it reminded him of the backstage storage area of the Forestburg Playhouse where he'd once played a waiter in *Hello Dolly*. Amid the clutter he noticed a down comforter and a few pillows piled next to the desk. Lucas had no idea why someone would stack bedding on the floor, but he was pleasantly reminded of another theatrical venue: the crowded attic set from his high school's production of *The Diary of Anne Frank*.

"You mind if I catch my breath?" Lucas asked as he crossed the apartment in two strides, pulling off his Walkman and flopping down on Joel's futon couch.

"Not at all," Joel replied. "Would you like some soda or juice?"

"Just water," Lucas replied, "if it's not too much trouble."

"Tap?" Joel asked.

"Not really. But I can learn fast."

"I mean, is tap water OK?"

"Oh! I'm sorry," Lucas said, slightly embarrassed. "Tap water's fine. I just came from an audition."

"I figured," Joel responded with a laugh, starting to believe that Lucas was every bit as dim-witted as he'd hoped. Returning to the living room with the two glasses of water, he made an attempt at light conversation. "Since you're a Libra, I should have cleaned up a bit."

"Why's that?"

"Librans like things lovely. When Aquarians come over, I mess the place up even more."

"This is just how I imagined you'd be living," Lucas lied, and gulped down the water. Setting his glass down, he leaned back on the couch and pushed his basket forward, adding, "I'm *really* comfortable here," causing Joel to wonder if he was flirting or just being polite. With Librans there was such a fine line between the two, and right now that line was running along the inner seam of Lucas's pants. But he knew he'd have to be careful. Scorpios and Capricorns knew when they were asking for it; Librans, a strangely prim and proper sign, often didn't.

"Want to see your chart?" Joel asked, popping up and crossing the room to his desk.

"Oh, my god! Yes," Lucas replied. "You *have* to help me with Vinnie."

Hiding his displeasure at the sound of his rival's name, Joel sat down in his office chair and motioned for Lucas to sit beside him. He pointed to the zodiac chart on the computer screen. "The natal chart is a map of the solar system at the time and place you were born. These symbols on the outside of the circle are the signs of the zodiac. The zodiac belt consists of those constellations of stars on the same elliptic as the solar system…."

Joel knew that Lucas wouldn't understand a word he was saying; he barely understood it himself, but he knew that the better part of spiritual seduction was establishing one's esoteric knowledge, like a cantor singing in Hebrew or a priest performing Latin Mass. It also served to dull his listeners' resistance. Sure enough, as he pointed out the Moon's Nodes and The Arabic Part of Fortune, Lucas's eyes started to glaze over. In truth, the zodiac chart looked like nothing more to Lucas than a pecan pie sliced into twelve pieces. It reminded him of his waiting job at Café Raffaella, and he began to shift despondently in his chair.

"I suppose you're wondering what all this has to do with your life?" Joel finally asked, leaning back in his chair and pressing the tips of his fingers together.

"Yes. Yes!" Lucas replied, snapping to attention.

"When did you study jazz dance?" Joel asked.

Lucas almost fell out of his chair. "How did you know that?"

"Your moon is squared Mars," Joel replied, knowing full well that 90 percent of the gay men in his neighborhood had moved to New York humming "The Music and the Mirror" from *A Chorus Line*.

"You're so right," Lucas continued ecstatically. "Is that what I'm supposed to do?"

"Yes—and no. There's something else you could do better."

"What?" Lucas cried.

"I'll tell you later. First I want to talk about your biggest problem. You came here wanting to talk about Vinnie, but I want to talk about you."

"Me?"

"Yes, you. Librans always want to talk about somebody else's problems because they have no idea who they are or what they really want."

"Right," Lucas responded only vaguely aware of what he was admitting about himself.

"Your biggest problem isn't Vinnie. It's that you keep doubting your talents."

Lucas gasped.

"You see this symbol?" Joel asked. "With Saturn transiting your seventh house, you need to forget about relationships for a while."

"You're absolutely right. I was just thinking that on the way over."

"What you need more than anything else…"

"What?"

"You need to sing."

Lucas leaped from his chair. "Oh, my god! You knew that from the chart?" he asked.

"Mars in Taurus on the mid-heaven," Joel replied.

"This is amazing. I swear to god. I was just thinking that. I want to be just like Bernadette Peters."

"Really?" Joel replied.

"She's my inspiration. She does everything a singer isn't supposed to. She makes faces. She rips her throat apart when she sings. When I was younger, I sang all the time. But when I came to New York and I saw the competition, I just gave up."

"You shouldn't have."

"I may not have the biggest voice. Hell, I don't always stay on pitch, but I can act the shit out of any song. And that's what I want to do. I want to be just like her. I want to be emotionally naked onstage. I want to bare myself to the world."

"You'll soon get that chance," Joel replied, reaching for the down comforter from beside the stack of pillows. "Would you mind lying down on the floor? I want to show you something."

"Right here?" Lucas asked.

"Right here," Joel replied, unfolding the comforter and spreading it on the floor with one expert flick of his wrists. Lucas lay on his back and looked up expectantly.

"Roll over," Joel demanded.

Lucas rolled over.

Joel began chanting. *"Nam myoho renge kyo. Nam myoho renge kyo."*

"What are you doing?" Lucas asked.

"Asking my guru for guidance," Joel assured Lucas. He repeated the mantra several more times before clearing his throat and meditating for a few moments in silence. "Now we can begin," Joel whispered as he laid one hand on the small of Lucas's back. "The fact is you have all the basic talent of Bernadette

Peters. It's just that your energy is constricted. Do you know what chakras are?"

"No," Lucas replied.

"They're energy centers in the body," Joel lectured, running his fingers up and down Lucas's spine. "According to the Hindus, there are seven chakras ranging from the base of the spine through the top of the head. The reason you feel constricted is that your astrological energy is split in two. Libra is an air sign and Taurus is an earth sign representing physical energy. With both these energies prominent in your chart, there's a split between your intellectual center, which is located here," Joel scratched the top of Lucas's head, "and your physical energy, which is located here." With almost ceremonial courtesy, Joel very lightly let his hand rest on Lucas's fabulously shaped behind.

Lucas sighed.

"So that's why we need to shake this energy up a little."

Joel pressed a little harder on Lucas's butt and started moving it gently back and forth.

Lucas moaned.

"How does this feel?"

"Great!"

Seeing no reason to hold back, Joel climbed on top of Lucas's legs and began moving both hands up either side of his spine. "We need to get the energy from the lower chakra up to the higher. This will relax your voice and help you to sing better."

"Where'd you learn to do this?" Lucas asked.

"I took a few courses," Joel lied. "Does this feel good?"

"Oh, yes," Lucas sighed.

Grabbing Lucas by the back of his belt, he said, "Pull your pants down to here." He drew a line with his hand about six inches below the base of his spine. Lucas reached below him to undo his belt buckle, raising his butt that much higher in the air. Joel waited patiently for the lovely music of the zipper being pulled down and the clanking of the belt buckle as it grazed against the floor. Reaching beneath the couch, he found a bottle of massage oil where he'd left it the night before, squirted some into his hands, and rubbed his hands together hungrily. A few delicious inches of Lucas's crack were now visible. Joel began rubbing Lucas's ass and, with each circular swipe of his hands, he managed to push Lucas's pants down a little further until his whole heinie was completely visible. Lucas moaned as Joel kneaded his tush like two big mounds of dough.

And this last delighted moan was all Joel needed to brazenly lift up Lucas's knees, just enough to pull off his pants. Then, placing both hands on Lucas's thighs, he pressed down hard and slowly let his hands slide upward, back to those two lovely mounds of flesh. He paused there just long enough to savor his victory. *This ass is mine,* he told himself. Like Sweeney Todd wielding his barber's razor, he might have cried out triumphantly, "At last my arms are complete again!"

Chapter Three

Joel Eisenberg had two compelling desires in life. One was to find true love, and the other was to find some really great tush. While he never had a very clear picture of the former, he did know what kind of ass he liked: large, high, and wide. Joel was an ass-aholic and a connoisseur of cans. A hairy chest hardly mattered. Testes were untempting. When he fantasized about men, they were always lying on their stomachs, facedown and moaning with pleasure. Deep down, Joel hoped that his ultimate tush would come attached to his soul mate, although Joel pursued love and sex in two very different ways. Up until this point, Joel had merely waited for a lover the same way Jews waited for the Messiah, praying fervently but otherwise doing nothing to hasten his arrival. When it came to tush, however, Joel had always gone to extraordinary lengths.

At the age of eleven he'd begged his mother to buy him a pair of binoculars with which to spy on his next-door neighbor. In high school he raced through the halls just so he could be at his gym locker when his favorite lacrosse player stripped down to his jockstrap. At the age of thirty he flew all the way to Houston, Texas, just to get a bag of peanuts from a particularly wide-assed flight attendant. Most of his waking hours were nothing more than a constant effort to gaze upon a goodly pair of glutes, with minimal attention paid either to its owner's character or intelligence. But Lucas Allison was a guy with a fabulous ass who—if Yris del Coro was correct—might also be his one and only Twin Flame. That tantalizing combination made Joel a little more foolhardy than usual as he tried, during the following weeks, to make him feel as he did— that the two of them were destined to be together.

From the very beginning, Joel had a hard time turning Lucas into his honey bunch. After nearly an hour of massaging the actor/singer's behind, he left the room for a pee break, and when he returned Lucas had sat up and put on his clothes. Joel was even more disappointed when next they got together and his Libran companion recommended an outdoor café and resisted Joel's suggestion to return to his apartment for further "counseling." Joel might have cut his losses, but the next day Lucas called and invited him to his studio apartment to watch a video of his high school's production of *Joseph and the Amazing Technicolor Dreamcoat,* a temptation too great to resist. Joel got as far as getting Lucas to strip down for a "chakra shake-up," and who knows what might have happened if Lucas's roommate hadn't suddenly returned home and suggested they all watch a particularly dreary episode of *NYPD Blue.*

Even worse, Lucas turned out to be a first-class mooch. If Joel suggested they take in a Broadway show, he'd get stuck for not only the price of the tickets but the cast album and an overpriced T-shirt, too. Being the older and less handsome of the two, it also fell upon Joel to pick up the check whenever they met for lunch. In spite of all this frustration—or because of it—Joel found himself falling head over heels for Lucas. Just the possibility of getting his hands on some great ass was more than enough to blind Joel into thinking that Lucas might one day return his affections.

Day by day, though, he could feel the young actor becoming less and less interested in him. So when Lucas's office temp job ended for the summer and he suggested going to Provincetown for the Fourth of July weekend, the astrologer jumped at the opportunity to bind Lucas to him by taking him out of town, where they would spend the night together in a room he had paid for. He was further intrigued by the possibility that this trip to Cape Cod might be the "journey to the north" that his spirit guide had predicted. Later that day, filled with hope, he sat down at his computer, did Lucas's transits, and was happy to see that the actor would be experiencing a Venus transit at the time of their trip and would be more receptive than usual to having his bountiful butt massaged.

And so it was that barely four weeks after they met, the astrologer and his client were seated side by side on the Bonanza Bus hurtling up Route Six to the very tip of the Cape. In spite of the bucolic scenery floating past the bus window, Joel was in turmoil. In order to leave town for the week, he had been forced to cancel several readings with, among others, the wife of a fabulously wealthy investment banker and the owner of a prestigious art gallery in Chelsea. He needed the money from these consultations because as Joel was finally beginning to admit, his heyday as a minor media icon was long past.

Joel stared out the window and reminisced sadly about the very brief period during which he'd been one of the most famous gay men in New York. It had been five years since his book had made it to number seventy-eight on the *New York Times* bestseller list, and four years since his last appearance on the *Howard Stern Show*. That had been the year a closeted gay executive at NBC got him an agent and flew him to Hollywood, where he played an embarrassing parody of himself on a particularly odd *Nash Bridges* Christmas special. A month later his agent managed to get him cast in a supporting role in a pilot starring Tim Valentine, a twenty-year-old TV icon who'd become world famous as the oldest son in a family of wacky orphans. Unfortunately, the pilot stank. He stank. Tim Valentine stank. The show failed to make the fall line-up and soon there were no more TV offers for either Tim or Joel. A previously planned cable show was given to Christopher Lowell instead, his agent dropped him, and now his literary agent was also starting to lose patience. The only thing that might revive his career would be another best-selling book, but Joel had yet to come up with an idea that would make the public sit up and take notice. He'd packed his laptop and planned to write in Provincetown, but he sincerely doubted he would get anything accomplished.

Joel glanced at his current distraction, and he wondered if he was simply avoiding his work. Even if Lucas were the Twin Flame Yris had predicted, would he ever want to be his partner in bed? *He's just so damn handsome, so completely out of my league,* he thought. *Yris del Coro was just an old phony. Nobody knows anything. Life is only chaos. There is no god.*

As awful as Joel was feeling, he would have felt even worse if he had known what Lucas was thinking while he pretended to sleep in the seat next to Joel's. The week before, he'd met a hot guy named Oscar Gonzalez who danced naked on the bar at Splash, and one night of sex with this luscious Latino had accomplished what all of Joel's well-meaning advice had not: it had completely erased Vinnie from his mind. The following day Oscar had left New York for Provincetown to perform with a radical gay theater troupe, and Lucas might have forgotten him altogether if not for a postcard he'd later received picturing a sturdy lighthouse on which Oscar had scrawled, "This is what my cock looks like whenever I think of you."

So Lucas had a plan: as soon as he found Oscar, he would slip
away from Joel for the remainder of their trip. A traditional Capricorn or an honorable Aries might have felt more of an obligation
toward the man who was picking up the tab. But Lucas, the well-
balanced Libran, had weighed the pros and cons and come to a very
different conclusion. Joel had long since toppled from his astrological pedestal; he was now just an older guy who desperately needed
to get laid. Although Lucas had no intention of providing this
service himself, he hoped that by bringing Joel to Provincetown and
introducing him to some of his friends, he'd be increasing the odds
for getting the astrologer some nookie—and out of his hair.

"We're almost there," Joel murmured.

"Whuh?"

"We're almost there," Joel repeated. Lucas removed the magazine from his face and looked where Joel was pointing. The bus had
just pulled around a bend in the highway and both men were getting their first view of Provincetown's picture-perfect skyline. A
few miles up the highway a row of houses hugged a scimitar-shaped
seacoast, above which rose the 250-foot Pilgrim Monument. As they
approached, the forests gave way to sand dunes glowing gold in the
late afternoon sun. A few minutes later the bus pulled off the
highway onto a side street and they were driving down leafy lanes
past saltbox houses fronted by lush English gardens. They neared
the center of town, and the bus stopped in a parking lot at the base
of MacMillan Wharf. Lucas leaned across Joel to look out the
window and get a better view of some local gays, a trio of shirtless
hunks hanging out in front of a food stand.

"We're here," Joel announced apprehensively. "Are you excited?"
He struggled to pull his knapsack from the overhead compartment.

"Oh, yeah," Lucas replied, whipping off his shirt and following
the boys with his eyes.

"You know those guys?" Joel asked.

"Not yet," Lucas replied in a hungry tone that made Joel feel—not for the last time—a little nervous about having put any of his eggs in this young actor's very firm little basket.

A few minutes later, Joel was cursing the day he had decided to come on this trip. As he tried to hurry Lucas to their guesthouse, it became apparent that the same Venus transit that was supposed to make him more pliable was also making him more attractive to everyone in Provincetown, including children, lesbians, and dogs. Worse, he seemed to know every cute guy in town. In front of the Taffy Emporium they met Joey G. from his step class. Across from town hall they bumped into Edmond, who'd worked part time with him for a catering firm. Next to Adams Pharmacy they were dragged into a conversation by Hoyt and Graham, both of whom had been on the gay swim team with him. And, although Lucas—the polite Libran—would always make a point of introducing his companion to his friends, they invariably took one look at Joel and closed ranks, refusing admittance to any merely average-looking guy who might dare to try to break into their exclusive circle of cuties.

In the meantime, Lucas was on the lookout for Oscar's theater troupe, which they found hanging out in front of the Unitarian Meeting Hall taking a break from rehearsing its next show, *Shut Your Von Trapp!*, a bawdy burlesque based on *The Sound of Music.* This group of freaks and misfits was called The Loose Sphincters and its producer/director/star was Rudy Cantwell, a local institution who ruled over the drag theater scene as absolutely as Stalin had dominated Russia. Oscar was nowhere to be found, but Lucas knew one of his castmates well enough to fish for information. He was a pretty young man named Keith Antonelli with whom Lucas was acquainted from an acting class in Manhattan. "Oh, my gawd!" the two young thespians exclaimed as they came within sight of each other, and hugged like they were the closest of friends when, in fact—being the same type with similar tastes—they were quite guarded around each other, and Keith wondered why Lucas seemed so eager to engage him in conversation.

Like Oscar Gonzalez, Keith had come to Provincetown to express himself artistically in a radical gay environment and had fallen into the hands of Rudy Cantwell. He had also succumbed to the director's sexual advances and had assumed the official role of Rudy's summer fling. It was easy to see why this young man had caught the director's eye. He was tall and slender with a perky rear end, a bow-shaped mouth, and large luminous eyes. In spite of his beauty, however, he didn't look very happy to Joel. He spoke to Lucas with the tired, slightly distracted demeanor of a restaurant waiter being forced to recite the dinner specials one last time before the kitchen closed for the evening.

Joining his cigarette break were two other cast members, both of whom were introduced to Joel by their drag names: Aida Lott, an enormously fat actor in baggy overalls, and Ida Dream, a well-built little black man and one of only three African Americans in town that summer. Like most drag performers, they were miserable off-stage without their wigs, and they took out their frustrations by making vicious comments about every passerby. All three of the Sphincters—Keith, Aida, and Ida—lived in a state of constant pre-emptive warfare, quickly disarming anyone who might possibly find fault with their sexual orientation, their taste in clothes, their skin color, or their weight. They were also stoned on pot and Joel sensed right away that they didn't like him.

"So tell me all about the show," Lucas asked Keith.

"Well, Aida's playing the Baroness. Ida's playing the Mother

Superior, and I'm playing Rolf—you know, 'I am Sixteen Going on Seventeen.' I'm actually playing a guy for a change. And there's this whole love triangle with Liesl and Maria. It's too complicated to explain."

"And Rudy wrote the show?"

"I helped a little bit. I was the one who gave him the idea that Maria should be a lesbian."

"Wow! So you're also writing?"

"Yeah. Provincetown's pretty great that way. Everybody does everything here. One of the guys in the troupe—Patchouli—he's learning how to paint."

"Patchouli?" Lucas asked.

"That's what we call him because he's, like, into essential oils. His real name is Oscar."

"Oscar Gonzalez?"

"You know Oscar?"

Knowing that Joel was listening, Lucas decided to reveal as little as possible.

"Yeah. We … we, uh, met in New York last month."

But Joel had already become suspicious. He wanted to pull Lucas away to question him, but just then a handsome coffee-colored man came bounding out of the Unitarian Meeting Hall, threw his arms around Lucas, and lifted him high into the air.

"You came. You came!"

To everyone's surprise, Oscar Gonzalez pressed Lucas up against the fence and planted a big wet one on his lips.

"Oh, my god!" groaned Aida Lott, rolling her eyes and stamping out her cigarette.

"Get a room," bitched Ida Dream.

"Stop!" Lucas squealed as Oscar continued to kiss him.

But nobody was more alarmed by this sudden display of affection than Joel. "We really have to go," he urged. "Or we'll lose our reservations."

Oscar whispered something into Lucas's ear.

"Not here," Lucas replied.

The Latino whispered something else.

"What are you, crazy?" Lucas protested.

"Lucas," Joel interrupted. "We have to be at the guesthouse in three minutes." Lucas reluctantly tore himself away from Oscar.

"Nice meeting you guys," Joel muttered as he pulled Lucas down the street.

"See you later," Oscar called after Lucas.

"How am I gonna find you?"

"I'll find you!" Oscar yelled back. "If I don't see you at the A-House, I'll see you in front of Spiritus."

For the rest of their walk together, Lucas was silent.

"Who was that guy?" Joel asked.

"Which one?"

"The one that just kissed you."

"Someone I met."

"In New York?"

"I forget."

"You forget?"

"I don't want to talk about it," Lucas said.

But the excitement of seeing Oscar again simply couldn't be contained. Wanting to smooth ruffled feathers, he slipped his arm through Joel's and started humming like he was Judy Garland in the final scene from *Easter Parade*. For Joel, the thrill of having Lucas's hand resting in the crease of his elbow temporarily eased his misery—even though he strongly suspected that his friend's affections would be nothing if not fleeting.

Chapter Four

During the second half of the twentieth century, gay men and lesbians started buying up real estate in the historic fishing village of Provincetown and quickly made it a prime destination for homosexuals on vacation. One of the many guesthouses catering to queer customers was the historic Fore 'n' Aft, located in the west end of town, just beyond the gift shops and just before all the two-hundred-year-old houses being converted into condos.

Skipping up some newly painted steps, Joel and Lucas pushed through a mahogany door and approached a front desk that had been decorated to suggest high camp on the high seas. Nailed to its facade were an antique ship's wheel and two hand-painted lobster traps complete with plastic crustaceans. Behind this desk was the one decent piece of art in the room, a well-crafted painting of a lonely seaside cottage, as well as an even lonelier looking desk clerk named Raymond Hennigan, whose complexion was the color of driftwood. Seeing two new customers, Raymond somehow managed to lift his head and smile wearily. Joel gave him their names and the clerk automatically handed him both keys.

"You're in Riptide," Raymond rasped to Joel, who took the keys and handed one to Lucas, who was already murmuring little cries of appreciation. Lucas loved everything about the decor. He loved the seaweed-stained ropes wrapped around the banisters. He loved the miniature lifeboats hanging from the ceiling. Thinking it clever that every room had been named after something oceanic, he read each plaque aloud. "Hurricane. Typhoon. Shipwreck."

Joel was less impressed. "Someone oughta declare this place a disaster area," he quipped.

But nothing could have prepared Joel for the peculiar ambience of Riptide. Pushing into the room, he dropped his luggage and gasped. Every square centimeter was covered with nautical knick-knacks: lifesaver ashtrays, a swordfish mounted over the headboard, and fishnets hanging from the ceiling stuffed with starfish and crabs. But, because this was a gay resort, the walls had been painted bright pink with a lavender trim, two colors that hadn't gone to sea since Ann Miller guest starred on *The Love Boat*.

"It's very Long John Silver Lamé," Joel joked rather desperately.

"I love it," Lucas blurted out as he wandered over to the window to check out the view of the street.

"Yeah. I read an article once that these two colors actually encourage the body to produce estrogen. You could develop breasts just from sleeping under this bedspread."

"Where'd you read that?" Lucas asked, distracted as he turned around and stared at the bed. There was only one king-sized problem in the middle of the room, even though Lucas had suggested that Joel reserve a room with two beds.

"So what side do you want?" Joel asked nonchalantly.

"You decide."

Joel lay down on the side closest to the door. "This is OK for me."

Lucas paused for a moment and then, holding his breath, he took a flying leap onto the other side of the mattress, the way one might dive into a pool of icy water.

"Nice mattress," Joel commented.

"Would you pass me my magazine?" Lucas asked.

Joel reached beside him for Lucas's well-worn copy of *Entertainment Weekly*. His brain was working feverishly as it considered all the different ways he might get Lucas to roll over and pull down his pants. If only he could be honest and spell it out. S-E-X. What he really wanted more than anything else was simply to kiss Lucas, but one sideways glance at his companion's boyishly beautiful profile and Joel completely lost his nerve. Meanwhile, Lucas laid down his magazine, stared at the ceiling, and started thinking about Oscar.

"What do you think of Libra dating a Pisces?" he asked.

"Not good," Joel replied immediately. "They'd both be bottoms." Joel wasn't willing to admit that Lucas might combine well with anyone but himself. He also suspected that Lucas was still thinking about the Spanish guy he'd just met on the street. "Why do you ask?"

"Some … friends of mine just started dating."

"Anyone I know?"

"Not really."

"What's that smell?" Joel wondered if some of Oscar's essential oil had rubbed off on Lucas. "Did you just put on cologne?"

"Nope."

The tension in the room was now thicker than liver paté and Lucas was starting to worry. Recently his friend Chad had refused to blow a real estate mogul on Fire Island and he'd been sent home on the late-night ferry with barely enough money to get back to the city. *But Joel would never do that,* he thought. *He's spiritual, and spiritual people* enjoy *spending money on their friends.* Just to be safe, he cleared his throat and announced, "Listen, I think we need to set some boundaries."

"Boundaries?" Joel winced. The very word set his teeth on edge. "What kind of boundaries do you want to set?"

"Well … for instance … I don't want you to think we came up here as boyfriends. I mean, just because you're paying for the room."

"I know."

"Because I will pay you back. Eventually."

"OK."

Lucas was a little taken aback by the speed with which Joel was concurring. Just to make sure the astrologer knew exactly what he was saying, he sat up and spelled it out. "I just want to make sure you're not … well … expecting anything."

"Fine."

"And you're … OK with that?"

"Whatever you want."

"Listen, Joel. I'm not saying that I *never* want to have sex with you. All I'm saying is I *really* like you. And I *really* respect you. And I'm *really* sensitive about guys who *just* like me for my body."

"I don't like you *just* for your body," Joel answered.

Dissatisfied with this explanation, Lucas took a deep breath and managed to blurt out, "I just want you to be my friend whether or not we have sex. You think you can do that?"

Joel hesitated, but only for a second. "Oh, sure," he answered, trying to sound casual.

"So if *I* meet someone in Provincetown, or if *you* meet someone, we're *both* free to do whatever we want."

Joel stopped to consider the implications of the statement. He knew that Lucas was still thinking about Patchouli. He also knew that Lucas was starting to view him as an obstacle to his happiness and that he was just waiting for the right moment to ditch him.

Absolutely," Joel said, hoping he sounded sincere. "You're free to do whatever you want."

Lucas went back to reading his magazine. In spite of having done what he knew he had to do, his Libran mind hadn't found the delicate equipoise it sorely needed. He prided himself on his fairness and he did so hate to disappoint Joel, who was already becoming like an old friend. Oscar Gonzalez, on the other hand—the man he wanted to fuck—was still very much a stranger. Oscar had whispered to him on the street that he needed to fuck him. But there'd also been a time when Vinnie had needed to fuck him. Lucas suddenly remembered his ex-lover's late-night booty calls and the desperate notes stuck between the slats of his gym locker. It had only been a month ago before, but Vinnie's passion for him had so evaporated that it might as well have been another century. If Lucas faced facts, the guys who *needed* to fuck him often quickly changed their minds and wound up needing to fuck somebody else.

And why wouldn't they? Lucas thought. *What do I have that's different from anyone else on the street?* Lucas did a quick inventory. He wondered what he had to offer his future husband but an untrained singing voice and a big bubble butt. Would he ever achieve any of his goals? Would he ever be cast in a Broadway musical? Would an audience at Carnegie Hall ever break into applause at the mere mention of his name? Rolling over on his stomach, he buried his face in the pillow and moaned.

"Are you all right?" Joel asked.

"Not really," Lucas replied.

"Would you like a back rub?" Joel asked.

"Not now," Lucas answered softly. "Just hold me."

Hardly believing his good luck, Joel snuggled next to Lucas, positioning his erection so as not to alarm his friend. And as Lucas breathed softly in his arms, he struggled to understand what else besides the Venus transit was suddenly making Lucas so needy. Was Saturn aspecting his moon? he wondered. He decided it didn't matter. "Lucas?" Joel said softly. There was no response.

Joel heard him snoring. He carefully moved a little closer and looked at the magical landscape of Lucas's rolling hills. He held his hand an inch over his thighs, just close enough to feel the heat rising from between the young man's legs. Joel wanted the moment to last forever, but waking up early and the long bus ride were taking their toll. A few hours later, Joel woke up and found a sleepy puddle of drool on his pillow. Lucas, however, was no longer in the room, and there was a note on his pillow.

J.—
Gone to see wassup in town.
—L.

Chapter Five

Joel ran down the steps of the Fore 'n' Aft hoping to find Lucas, bring him back to their room, and have another go at his tush. Unlike the other tourists on Commercial Street, he didn't stop to read a menu on a single restaurant door or pause to admire how beautifully some of the older guesthouses had been repainted. If he hadn't been so desperate, he might have noticed the sounds of the sea: tiny waves lapping against a nearby shore, a foghorn, a ship's bell. He might have looked down an alley and seen the moon reflected off the bay. He might even have forgotten Lucas and found somebody else, a Pisces or a Scorpio, perhaps—someone with whom he would have been more compatible.

Joel turned a bend in the street and was confronted with a mighty stream of men coming toward him. Due to legislative fiat, the bars must close at one in the morning in P-Town, an hour earlier than elsewhere in the Commonwealth of Massachusetts. In order to keep the party going, die-hard Provincetown revelers stagger down Commercial Street and gather on the brick patio in front of Spiritus Pizza for one last chance to snag a warm body for a night of hot sex. Rather than fight the current, Joel slipped into a nearby doorway from which he observed the hordes as they spilled into the street and blocked traffic. Tall men. Short men. Bare-chested men. Men in sweaty T-shirts. Men in button-down shirts and men in black leather harnesses and chaps. There were extroverts laughing loudly and introverts silently scanning the terrain like birds of prey. There were the jaded for whom it was nothing more than a nightly routine, and there were the awestruck like Joel who had never experienced anything quite like it. He'd been to plenty of gay-pride rallies, but never before had he seen such a huge number of homosexuals gathering out of doors in a small-town environment. It was like everybody in Mayberry had been driven out and replaced with queers from Chelsea and the South End of Boston.

Joel was so overwhelmed by the scene that it took him a while to realize that nobody was paying him any attention. Not a soul recognized him from his TV appearances or his book tours. Not a single fan approached him with any of the usual questions about astrology. Soon the lack of attention began to feel like a lack of oxygen—he couldn't breathe. "I have to get out of here," he muttered to himself as he tried to escape the crowd, nearly swooning from the odor of boozy breath and the putrid smell of steroids. Less than midway through the mayhem, he found his way blocked by a tall, muscular man in a black leather jacket. Standing nearby were the three actors he'd met that day, Aida Lott and Ida Dream, now wearing their wigs and dresses, along with Keith Antonelli leaning against the wall and quietly staring at his fingernails.

"Joel Eisenberg!" the man in the black jacket exclaimed in a voice that sounded like it had been steeped in a vat of irony for at least two decades.

"I'm sorry. You're …"

"Rudy Cantwell. But how would you know me? I'm just a star on the stage while you've been on TV."

"Oh, well, thanks," Joel said, happy to at last have been recognized. Rudy leaned closer. He was by far the most masculine drag queen Joel had ever seen, with a dark brow, a thick jaw, and a heavy beard.

"Your friend Lucas was just here," he whispered conspiratorially. "He and Oscar just left."

"Oh," Joel said disappointedly.

"Don't look so forlorn. He had the most marvelous things to say about the horoscope you did for him. He also said you give a really great butt rub. Not that your reputation hasn't preceded you."

Joel's heart leaped into his throat.

Rudy looked him in the eye and explained. "We may be off the beaten track, but every fag in the world comes here sooner or later. Darlings!" Rudy suddenly announced to the crowd in a loud stagy voice. "I want you all to meet Joel Eisenberg—the world's greatest ass-trologer!"

Several men turned around and clapped.

"Look, everyone. It's the ass-trologer!" some loud drunk in the crowd bellowed at the top of his voice.

"Welcome to Provincetown, my dear. It's where our darkest secrets quickly become public knowledge." Turning to the crowd, Rudy waved regally, like Evita. "Good night, queens! This party's over."

"Good night, Rudy," a few drunken locals called back.

Then he grabbed Keith Antonelli's hand, pushed his way through the mob, and disappeared from sight. Aida Lott and Ida Dream, like two ugly ducklings, got in line behind them.

Joel froze. He'd been on TV. He'd been on the radio. Every week he'd faced the possibility that millions might find him ridiculous and unlikable. He was nevertheless woefully unprepared for Provincetown's particular variety of scorn. This was, after all, New

England, and he'd just been labeled with a scarlet letter—an A that stood for "ass-trologer." Sticking out his chin, Joel turned and marched through the crowd, feeling every inch like Bette Davis in *Jezebel* arriving at the ball in a bright red dress.

Emerging from the throng, he took a deep breath and trudged the quarter mile back to the Fore 'n' Aft. The front door felt heavier as he pushed his way into the lobby; the stairs were steeper and more difficult to climb. His key to Riptide barely fit in the lock and when he tried to push open the door, he was stopped by a chain. Lucas had latched the door from the inside.

"Lucas?" Joel cried.

"Come back later!" his roommate yelled back.

"What are you doing in there?"

"Later!" Lucas replied.

"Let me in!"

There was a thump as Lucas jumped out of bed and a strange voice demanded angrily, "Where are you going?"

Lucas opened the door a crack. Joel could see his left eye and a bit of his naked shoulder.

"Come back in fifteen minutes," Lucas whispered. "Please?"

"No," Joel answered in disbelief.

"You told me I was free to do whatever I wanted."

"Not when I want to sleep."

"Go back outside and meet somebody."

"I don't want to meet somebody. I want to go to sleep."

"Who is that?" asked the stranger.

"Nobody," Lucas called over his back.

A moment later, Joel saw Oscar's face peeking through the crack; he could smell the patchouli oil.

"Can't you see we're busy?" Oscar said angrily.

"This is my room."

"It's Lucas's room. ..."

"No, it's mine," Joel countered. "I paid for it. I paid for the whole thing."

Oscar suddenly pulled back from the door. When he returned, he stuck out a handful of twenties and said, "Get another room. Please!"

Before Joel could make up his mind whether or not to take the money, Oscar simply tossed the bills on the ground, slammed the door, and locked the bolt. Joel held up his fist to bang the door, but he stopped himself. He knew he and Lucas weren't meant to be. He looked at the money at his feet and moaned, for he knew that picking up the cash meant forfeiting Lucas's heinie forever. Joel sighed as he scooped up the bills. Then he realized it was only eighty dollars, barely half of what he would need to get another room.

The only room Joel could get at the Fore 'n' Aft that night was a tiny cubicle on the first floor with a dumpster just outside the window filled with the garbage from a nearby fast-food stand. It took a while for Joel to get used to the rancid smell of fried clams and coleslaw, but finally he fell asleep and dreamed about Yris del Coro. There she was in her tiny kitchen stirring a pot of refried beans, just as she'd been when they had met for his first reading. Her face was perspiring and her glasses were kept from slipping down her nose by a rhinestone chain.

"¡Ay ay ay! You see what happens when you don't listen to me?"

"But I did listen to you! Lucas was everything you said my Twin Flame would be. I went north just like you told me. And it does feel like south because it's summertime and Provincetown is on the beach."

"Sí. But would this man ever have given you his heart?"

"Maybe. I don't know."

Yris shook her head.

"Why not?" Joel asked.

"He had no heart to give. Only a big rear end."

"But I like a big rear end."

"*Dios mío!*" Yris screamed and threw her hands up in the air.

"And what good would it be to find my Twin Flame if I'm not attracted to his butt?"

Yris put down her ladle and took off her apron. "*Ven conmigo,*" she said. "I want to show you something."

Taking Joel's hand, she led him out the door of her apartment onto a sun-dappled country road that wound through a forest. Turning a bend in the road, Yris pointed to a lighthouse standing atop a sandy hill. It was glowing white in the light reflected from the ocean several hundred feet below.

"I want to give you one more clue. In order for you to meet your Twin Flame, you must first find a man who paints houses."

"A man who paints houses?"

"Now I want you to see one more thing." Yris led Joel to a well surrounded by a low stone wall. "I want you to lean over and look inside. If you do, you will see your future."

But as soon as he bent over the well, Yris ran up behind him and shoved him in. As he plunged into the abyss, he tried to grab the sides of the well, only to discover they were soft and fleshy, for they had been built not of mortar or stones—but of thousands of tushes. Each brick was a slippery buttock. Unable to maintain a hold, Joel plunged into the darkness, bouncing off butts, surrounded on all sides by his favorite body part.

Joel's eyes snapped open. He sat up in bed and turned on the light. His heart was pounding. Leaning back in bed, he noticed a painting of a lonely lighthouse glowing orange in the sunset, probably done by the same artist who'd painted the sea shack in the lobby. It was also the exact same building that Yris del Coro had shown him in his dream. Joel climbed out of bed to take a closer look. It was quite a lovely painting, by far the classiest and most expensive item in the room. "Oh, my god," Joel whispered to himself, suddenly remembering the earlier part of his dream. "My Twin Flame will be a man who paints houses." Leaning closer, Joel examined the name of the artist signed precisely in the bottom left corner.

Dennis Fairchild.

What a lovely name, Joel thought. *Is this the man I've been searching for?* "Dennis Fairchild," he repeated to himself. In a flash he realized that his guru had been guiding his entire life, carefully engineering his every thought and action, in order to lead him to that very spot in front of that very painting. His ordeal with Lucas had been nothing but a test, and by finally letting go of that bubble-butted idiot, he'd passed that test with flying colors. Overwhelmed by the desire to offer his gratitude, Joel grabbed the corner of his bed for support, got down on his knees, and bowed his head. *"Nam myoho renge kyo,"* he chanted, and with each repetition he was able to convince himself that his desire for Lucas Allison was being cleansed from his heart.

Chapter Six

When Provincetown became a destination for tourists, it also became a home for visual artists who were able to make a living creating canvases that were little more than enlarged postcards, a particularly tedious task since most tourists only wanted pictures of the quaint little fishermen's cottages that lined Provincetown's streets. Faced with the prospect of rendering gray saltboxes for the rest of their lives, most of these artists took to working with a brush in one hand and a quart of vodka in the other. Every generation, though, a handful of hardy souls managed to stay reasonably sober while painting off their mortgages.

In 1997, Dennis Fairchild was the most successful of this group. He'd risen to the top of his profession by taking that standard Cape Cod house painting one step further: he limited his subject matter to only one quaint little house per show, rendering it at different times of the day, somewhat like Monet had done with the cathedral at Notre Dame. Unexpectedly, Dennis's minimalist approach spoke to a deeply ingrained aspect of the Puritan psyche that abhors fuss and only wants to think about one thing at a time. It also helped that Dennis was skilled enough to create effects of light that reminded people of Edward Hopper, only without all those depressed people mucking up the foreground. Over the years, Dennis had become a star of the regional art scene, and his devoted followers eagerly awaited each exhibition, anxious to buy yet another Fairchild to hang alongside their *Misty Tuesday Morning* or their *Stormy Sunday Night*.

But even Dennis Fairchild had a breaking point. By 1997, he was bored to tears and, almost out of spite, he had decided to try something different. Rather than painting one more pretty house, he searched for—and found—the ugliest building on Cape Cod: an abandoned gas station just this side of the Bourne Bridge. Feeling it necessary to warn Dennis's collectors that the artist was offering something different for the first of his two summer shows, the gallery owner, Duncan Deeds, had nonetheless cleverly named the exhibition "Bourne Again." Keeping his fingers crossed, he was waiting to see if the people accustomed to Dennis Fairchild's more precious fare would now buy a painting of the kind of building they usually preferred to ignore.

The jury was still out as Joel entered the gallery to meet the man he now believed to be his Twin Flame. In spite of all his chanting, he'd woken up that morning filled to his eyeballs with rage against Lucas. Quickly changing his mind about trying to find Dennis Fairchild, he jumped out of bed and ran to MacMillan Wharf to catch the next bus out of town. Unfortunately, he'd already missed the morning bus, so he'd bought a ticket for that afternoon and then decided to kill a few hours by strolling east, away from anywhere he might run into Lucas and Oscar. It was there in the Gallery District that he'd come upon the Duncan Deeds Gallery and seen that Dennis Fairchild, "the man who painted houses," was actually having a show at that very moment. Believing this might be another sign from his spirit guide, he'd pushed his way inside.

Weaving his way through the crowd, Joel was impressed that so many people had turned out. He was also a little daunted that his intended boyfriend was such a star in his own right. He'd always imagined that his lover would live in the shadow of his own career rather than the other way around. If he'd known anything about the art business at all, he might have been relieved that there were so few red dots stuck on the walls—a sure sign that business was less than brisk.

Midway through the gallery he bumped into a crowd of patrons clustered around someone who was gesturing toward the art and speaking in an authoritative tone of voice. Joel stood on his tiptoes hoping to catch a glimpse of the artist and to his great dismay discovered a sixty-year-old dandy with white frizzy hair and a mottled complexion. He was wearing a clownish bow tie and suspenders. To make matters worse, the artist was surrounded by a rapt audience of young male beauties and taking every opportunity to caress their shoulders and fondle their pumped-up chests.

Joel's heart sank. He had assumed that his Twin Flame would be a hottie; the last thing he wanted was for him to be as homely and desperate as he was. For decades he'd been unsuccessfully trying to nab a looker from the A-list—*maybe God wants me to lower my standards,* he thought. Craning his neck, Joel took another glance at Dennis Fairchild, who was now practically drooling as he conversed in awkward French with a dark-haired beauty with a smooth, olive complexion. Joel shook his head. There was no way he could even think of dating such a *miskayt* in a world filled with the likes of Lucas Allison—*that little son of a bitch*. Although Joel almost never touched alcohol, all of a sudden he needed a drink.

Again feeling bitter about the night before, Joel weaved his way to the back of the room. Beneath a window overlooking the bay, he found a long table on which had been placed several trays of finger food and some bottles of cheap champagne. A handsome young man wearing a white shirt and black pants stood beside the table.

"Could I have a glass of champagne?" he asked.

The waiter appeared startled, as if he had been daydreaming, and turned a pair of spectacularly blue eyes on Joel.

"Of course," he answered with a wry smile. He poured a glass of champagne and handed it to Joel, who slyly let his hand graze the waiter's fingers. Joel's heart began to beat rapidly and his pants suddenly felt a little tighter in the crotch. *My, my. My Twin Flame turned out to be a toad,* he thought to himself, *but the afternoon doesn't need to be a total waste.*

Eyeing the waiter discreetly, Joel noticed that there was something extraordinarily dignified about the young man; he had an almost regal bearing. Perhaps he was from Belgium or Scandinavia, and Joel imagined him serving Swedish meatballs somewhere in Stockholm. Then again, there was also something proudly New England about him—he wouldn't have looked out of place in a three-cornered hat serving drinks at the Boston Tea Party. He exuded the confidence that said: if you're looking for the most fascinating guy in the room, look no further.

Joel was dying to hear his voice, but unable to think of an opening line, he moved away and leaned against a nearby wall. From that vantage point, Joel was able to see that the beauty of the boy's rear end more than matched the beauty of his face. It was a wonderful rump: large and plump—perhaps too large for some, but certainly not for Joel. It was almost—womanly. *He might be as old as thirty,* Joel thought, *and in a year or two he might even lose some of his boyish charm. His ass might get too fat, like two big scoops of vanilla ice cream just about to melt.* Joel wanted the chance to lick off a piece of the young man's creamy white ass before it slid any closer to the floor. But first he had to get him to talk. Introducing the subject of the stars might get him back to his room for an "ass-trology" reading. An opening statement like, "What's your sign?" could break the ice—but it might also stop the conversation cold.

Two elderly women with pastel-colored sweaters draped over their bony shoulders stood in front of the refreshment table. "If this artist wanted to make some dreary comment about life, he should have written to the *Globe*," one announced as she reached for a cracker topped with goat cheese.

"I agree," the other woman replied, snatching up a sliver of quiche. "We drove all the way from Mystic this morning and I must say, I'm terribly disappointed."

Joel couldn't help noticing that the waiter had rolled his eyes. He seized the opportunity.

"True art lovers," he mumbled sarcastically as the two women clacked out of the room. The waiter nodded and chuckled in sympathy but said nothing. For a few moments the two men stood side by side in complete silence. Joel yearned for one more sound. Throat clearing. A yawn. A sigh.

How his heart rejoiced when the waiter unexpectedly turned to Joel, looked him right in the eyes—an action no less piercing than laser surgery—held out his hand, and said, "Hi."

Trembling silently, Joel shook his hand. It was thicker and stronger than he would have expected, like the hand of a Romanian gymnast. "I'm Joel Eisenberg," he said.

The waiter smiled revealing a set of perfectly white teeth.

"I'm a writer," Joel continued.

"A writer?" the waiter answered, obviously surprised. "What do you write about?"

"This and that," Joel replied. He decided to avoid any mention of astrology for the moment. "I know a little bit about art," he lied. "Back in New York some of my closest friends are gallery owners." He paused to let it sink in that he was from the greatest city in the world.

Sure enough, the waiter asked, "You're from New York?"

"Manhattan," Joel answered to erase any remaining doubt. "The Village," he added, although he was afraid he was gilding the lily.

"What do you think of these paintings?"

Joel paused. If he praised the artwork too highly, he might appear unsophisticated. If, on the other hand, he demeaned them, he might seem too critical. He decided to gamble. "Thank god somebody in this town has had the nerve to paint something other than a Cape Cod house."

"You don't find them a little disturbing?"

"That's why I like them," Joel exclaimed. "A pretty picture of a pretty subject is only illustration. If you want art, you have to paint something ugly."

"Hmm."

"Are you allowed to leave this table?" he asked.

"Sure." The waiter nodded.

Joel walked up to "Rainy Thursday Afternoon," in which a couple of rusty old gas pumps stood stiffly next to each other like two figures on a wedding cake.

"This is a self-portrait," Joel pronounced, praying to the goddess of gab to keep him from embarrassing himself. "You see these gas prices up here and this nozzle stuck below? Whoever painted these gas pumps is someone with dollar signs on his mind and a penis up his ass."

The waiter laughed. "You don't say."

"But what's most interesting is that he's standing next to somebody just like himself."

"You mean the other gas pump?"

"Exactly. This is the self-portrait of a complete narcissist, and whether he knows it or not, he's miserable."

"Miserable, huh?"

"Sure. Look a little closer."

The beauty leaned forward giving Joel the opportunity to take in the contours of his bubble butt and appreciate how the seam of his pants accentuated his crack. Inhaling deeply, he detected starch in the waiter's shirt. It was a clean, all-American smell that made him shiver with lust.

"What am I looking at?" the waiter asked.

"You … uh … see that dark space between the two pumps? That represents the artist's solitude. This guy's very lonely and frustrated."

The waiter turned and looked at Joel as though he might be on to something. "How do you know all this?" he asked.

"I'm kind of a psychic."

"Really?"

"Actually I'm a professional astrologer. I was on TV."

"Really?" The waiter turned to Joel and looked him up and down with renewed interest. His smile was just this side of wicked. "What would you say about me?" he asked.

Joel was caught a bit off guard and gave his stock answer. "I would have to do your zodiac chart."

The waiter lifted up his chin in playful defiance. "Can't you read my aura?"

"Seriously," Joel said laughing. "When's your birthday?"

"Guess," the beauty challenged.

Joel hated to be put on the spot like this, but he decided to take a stab. He said the first thing that popped into his mind.

"You're a Gemini."

"And why do you say that?" the waiter responded, giving nothing away.

"I think you're a little older than you look."

"That's true. But I'm definitely not a Gemini. Guess again."

"Scorpio?"

"How come?"

"You're very seductive."

"Nope."

Joel leaned back to get a better look at how the beauty stood, how he proudly held his head. "Oh, my god, you're a Leo."

"Nope," the waiter said, shaking his head.

"You're not?" Joel felt utterly demoralized.

"Three wrong answers. Care to shoot the moon?"

"Just let me do your chart."

"Nope."

Before Joel could ask again, the handsome young Frenchman he'd seen earlier in the front of the room slid over to the waiter, grabbed him by the arm, and kissed his cheek.

"Dennis!" he cried. "Duncan has been looking all over for you."

"I'm afraid I have to get back to business," the "waiter" said regretfully. And indeed he did, because a moment later the white-haired dandy whom Joel had seen speaking to the crowd grabbed his other arm.

"Come, darling. No more hiding out by the refreshment table."

"Any offers yet on *Full Moon in September*?" Dennis Fairchild asked as he was pulled away by what Joel now realized were his art dealer and his latest boyfriend from Paris.

"Not yet, my dear."

"Keep guessing!" Dennis called over his shoulder to Joel as he was led from the room.

"I thought ..."

But Dennis was no longer the least bit interested in what Joel was thinking. Nose held high in the air, he marched to the front of the gallery where several worshipping patrons were waiting to make his acquaintance. Joel watched his tantalizing tush disappear into the crowd. It moved from side to side, not exactly swishing, but purposefully, as if it had a mind of its own—as if it were promising Joel that they would meet again.

Chapter Seven

"Nam myoho renge kyo. Nam myoho renge kyo."

Several days later, Joel was still living in his cubicle beside the Dumpster. This afternoon he was chanting himself into a frenzy in front of the temporary shrine he'd built to replicate his altar back in New York. Instead of his bar mitzvah tallis, he'd draped a beach towel around his shoulders. Instead of many little notes about Lucas Allison, there was only one large piece of paper on which he had printed, in big bold letters: DENNIS FAIRCHILD. TWIN FLAME. NOW!

"Nam myoho renge kyo. Nam myoho renge kyo."

After meeting Dennis at the gallery, Joel threw away his bus ticket to New York, paid for another week at the Fore 'n' Aft, and began preparing for his next encounter with the artist. Wanting to look his best, he signed up for a training session at the Province-town Gym with a muscular lesbian named Delores, a former coal miner who approached the job of whipping Joel into shape with the same grim efficiency she'd once used to extract coal from the ground in West Virginia. Later that afternoon, Joel went shopping

at Martinique's Boutique, where Martin, the proprietor, was happy
to help him find clothing items to "accentuate body parts worth dis-
playing and to camouflage those unsuited for public scrutiny."
Knowing Joel's flabby ass had only limited appeal, Martin steered
Joel to some baggy shorts and boxers made popular that year by
rappers and hip-hop artists. As for Joel's upper body, the slight pro-
tuberances on his arms could have been mistaken for biceps, so he
was encouraged to purchase a tight sleeveless shirt that Martin gaily
referred to as an "elegant spandex blouse."

"Nam myoho renge kyo. Nam myoho renge kyo."

That night he ran down to Spiritus Pizza and waited for Dennis
Fairchild to show up at the meat market. As long as the crowd was
sparse, he'd been able to convince himself he was a fine piece of
kosher brisket. At 1:05 somebody may have cruised him. At 1:10
Lou Lustig, the portly publisher of the *Provincetown Poop* showed
up, and it turned out that he and Joel knew each other from New
York, where Lou had once worked as a publicist. At 1:15 haughty
old Rudy Cantwell and his troupe descended and Joel managed to
hold his head high, even when Lucas appeared holding hands with
Oscar Gonzalez. It was only when the crowd turned into a mob
scene that Joel started to feel inconspicuous and unwanted. And
when Dennis Fairchild finally made his appearance at 1:30, arm in
arm with Jean Paul and a coterie of Eurofag fashion models all of
whom had cheekbones higher than Mount Rushmore's, what little
was left of Joel's self-confidence evaporated completely.

"Nam myoho renge kyo. Nam myoho renge kyo."

Not daring to approach his Twin Flame in such stellar company,
Joel retreated into a doorway and watched Dennis laughing with
Jean Paul and his gorgeous friends. Compared to the rest of this
group, Dennis was a little too short and his nose was a little too pug
to be considered a classic beauty. Yet wearing only jeans and a

simple blue work shirt, he still somehow managed to outshine the Frenchmen—the Sun King holding court at Versailles. One by one, Dennis's friends and admirers walked over to congratulate him on the new direction his art had taken. Complete strangers adjusted their positions to get a better view of him, and any idea Joel might have had for getting the artist alone withered and died. At two o'clock the astrologer admitted defeat, slunk home to the Fore 'n' Aft, masturbated, and wiped up the mess with his brand-new shirt.

"*Nam myoho renge kyo. Nam myoho renge kyo.*"

But the evening hadn't been a total waste. Lou Lustig had insisted on interviewing Joel for the *Poop.* The last thing Joel had wanted was local publicity, but he quickly discovered that Lou had a tendency to give out more information than he elicited. It also turned out that he hated Rudy Cantwell. So in exchange for a few barbed comments about the evil impresario, Lou was quite happy to give the astrologer all the information he might need about Dennis Fairchild: whom he dated, where he lived, and when he might possibly be home.

"*Nam myoho renge kyo. Nam myoho …*"

Joel suddenly stopped chanting for, sure enough, the unmistakable voice of Yris del Coro started to come through. Grabbing a pencil and paper, he scribbled down the first thing that came into his mind.

Idiot! Stop chanting. Go to where he lives and find out his birthday. If you do his chart, you will discover everything you need to know.

Yris was right, of course. *I can do this,* Joel told himself. *I can get this guy. I can find out his vulnerabilities. I can discover his inner demons. I can make myself his indispensable counselor, and my reward for saving his soul will be unfettered access to his ass.* But then Joel began to wonder if he was crazy. If Lucas Allison had been an Olympian feat, Dennis Fairchild was scaling Mount Everest.

Objectively speaking, there was absolutely nothing about this arrogant little prick that needed Joel in the least. Grabbing a pillow, he pressed it to his face and screamed with frustration.

In the bathroom, Joel squirted some Vaseline Intensive Care into his hands, yanked down his pants, grabbed his cock, and whacked off: the fourth time he had jerked off thinking about Dennis's big, round tush but, as Joel had long since discovered, a thing of beauty can be a joy forever.

Afterward, he cleaned off his stomach with a warm rag, pulled up his pants, ran out the door, and scampered into the street. It was another hot day. Most of the town was at the beach, so he was able to make good time as he raced east on Commercial Street.

Passing the Gallery District, Joel started checking the houses for commemorative plaques. According to Lou Lustig, Dennis Fairchild had recently purchased what the Library Association referred to as the Smuggs House, a rambling, clapboard structure that had been built by a randy nineteenth-century whaler to house his Portuguese mistress and his six illegitimate children. Although Captain Smuggs had been reviled in his day as a loud-mouthed, drunken pirate, his domicile had become famous in 1926 when his granddaughter, Florence Smuggs, wrote a best-selling autobiography called *Lost and Found at Sea*. For years tourists had walked past this building as though it were Mount Vernon and its original owner had been the father of the town. By the time Dennis purchased it in 1990, however, it had been inhabited for two generations by Bohemian artists and sculptors who'd hung sheets in the windows and filled the yard with painted bathtubs. According to Lou, the town's historians had been thrilled to have a successful, clean-cut fellow like Dennis move in and start fixing the place up. What Lou had failed to mention, however, was that Dennis wasn't living there alone. Sharing his home for the seventh summer in a row was an ugly old drag queen named Sue Veneer who cooked, cleaned, and took care of the artist's dog.

Although Ms. Veneer had once been one of the most successful performers in town, she'd long since fallen on hard times. The best one could say about her nightclub act was that her impersonations were nearly as good as the originals. The worst was that she mostly imitated vocalists who didn't sound all that great to begin with—such musically challenged legends as Carol Channing, Lauren Bacall, and Cher. Whenever Sue Veneer did attempt to re-create a truly gifted singer, such as Judy Garland or Billie Holiday, she generally chose a period of the woman's life when barbiturates or heroin had sufficiently ruined her voice, making it easier for someone as tone-deaf as Sue to imitate. Her brief heyday had been the late seventies, when a man had only to slip on a sequined gown to be considered controversial. When Rudy Cantwell came to town in 1988, his brazen vulgarity was more in keeping with the times, and it wasn't long before he stole the older star's venue and exiled her down the street to the Seaview Lounge, where she barely eked out a living each summer honking out standards and cajoling her audiences into leaving tips in a jar on top of her piano. Although she professed to be unfazed by her diminished status, there were nights when she was so sour that her stage makeup seemed to curdle under the lights like cottage cheese left in the sun.

How she'd come to be Dennis Fairchild's housemate was a village tale with many versions, including the story that Dennis had made a Faustian bargain: for letting Sue live in his house, he would stay eternally young and beautiful while the old drag queen aged horribly. In truth, Dennis had offered the room to Sue Veneer when she was still one of the biggest stars in the town, and her presence there meant the house was filled with music and laughter. Over the years, though, as Sue's status diminished, Dennis only tolerated her presence in his house because she turned out to be a much better homemaker than she was an entertainer. Cursing like Joan Crawford, she kept that old house spotless. Chirping like Julia Child, she cooked delicious gourmet meals.

Most important, Sue Veneer walked and fed Bunny, a little French bulldog who'd been given to Dennis by his ex-boyfriend James, an older man who'd wanted to see if Dennis was mature enough to pay attention to any living creature who wasn't a sexy guy or an art buyer with deep pockets. Sure enough, Dennis found Bunny amusing for about two weeks and then grew bored with her, as he grew bored with anyone who didn't flatter him. After Dennis and James broke up, Dennis would have given Bunny away except that his ex-lover persisted in calling every month to ask about her welfare. The little dog was the means by which Dennis kept James on a tight leash in case he should ever want to revive the romance— and Sue Veneer was the means by which he would never have to be bothered with her.

"Pghh. Pghh."

Sue Veneer looked down to see Bunny standing beside her and snorting. "What do you want?"

Bunny tilted her head to the side as if to ask, "What do you think I want?"

"Gimme a second," Sue replied as she sat up and scrounged for a roach in the ashtray near her bed.

If she was going to walk Bunny on that same old stretch of beach, she'd have to get stoned first. She also wanted some relief from her worries. The night before only three people had paid to see her show at the Seaview. Two of them had been Filipina women attending the Gay and Lesbian Southeast Asian World Conference;

they stared at her, dumbfounded throughout her entire set. The owner of the lounge wanted to have a serious talk with her that afternoon, and Sue had the awful feeling that he wanted to cancel her show and use her time slot for a karaoke night. What would she do then? Maybe she should simply go back home and live with her mother on Long Island. The old woman was getting a little dotty and she would probably welcome having her "daughter" back in the house.

"Pghh. Pghh."

"Aw, baby," Sue Veneer cooed as she scooped Bunny into her arms and ran her fingers through the thick folds of skin around Bunny's neck. "I love you to death. I do. I do. You're the only pure soul in Provincetown and I'll never leave you. Never."

Determined to hold her head high in the face of adversity, Sue slipped on a housedress, walked into the kitchen, and started making corn fritters for breakfast. As she dropped the corn into the pot of boiling water, she stared into the steam and found something else to worry about. Dennis Fairchild's fall exhibition at the Duncan Deeds Gallery was only six weeks away and he hadn't yet made a single sketch or stretched a single canvas. In fact, he'd done nothing in his studio but lie on the floor and stare at the ceiling. Sue had seen Dennis in this mood before. For several years he'd been a reluctant painter, complaining about the solitude, the stench of turpentine fumes, and the awful pressure of living up to his own reputation. For years he'd been saying that he'd like to give it all up, travel the world, and enjoy civilization's artistic treasures without feeling compelled to add to them by actually doing any work. Sue had even heard him musing with Jean Paul about the two of them moving to Paris where they would buy and sell antiques. Sue's eyes suddenly darted upward to the bedroom above the kitchen. Would Dennis fly off to France with Jean Paul? she wondered. And if he did, what would become of the house? In all likelihood, he'd rent out the property, and the new occupant wouldn't appreciate a pot-smoking drag queen living in the room behind the kitchen. "One way or another, I'm fucked," Sue Veneer muttered to herself. "Completely fucked." Grabbing a bowl from a high shelf above the sink, she began cracking eggs, breaking them cleanly and whipping the shells into the garbage. "Dennis will not leave town this summer. As soon as he and Jean Paul wake up, I will feed that Frenchman one corn fritter and then throw him out in the street. Dennis just needs a little encouragement to paint. He owes it to himself to keep painting. He owes it to his public. Hell—he owes it to me."

Tap. Tap. There was someone at the door.

"Ah, crap!" Sue said under her breath as she threw open the door, fully intending to shoo away the intruder. What she saw standing before her only increased her ire: a bespectacled man in an unbecoming spandex shirt poking his head in the door and smiling nervously. Wiping her brow, she dug her wrists into her waist, pursed her lips, and glared at the man in a withering manner that would have made Bette Davis proud. "What do *you* want?" she bellowed.

"I'm sorry," the intruder stammered, "but I didn't see a front door."

"This *is* the front door."

"Oh." It occurred to Joel that he might have come to the wrong house. "Is this where Dennis Fairchild lives? He asked me to stop by."

"He's not awake. Good-bye." Sue tried to close the door but Joel reached out and prevented her from slamming it shut.

"He said if he were sleeping, I should come in and wait for him."

"No, he didn't. Dennis never allows anyone in the house until noon."

"Are you his maid?"

Sue bristled and again tried to close the door. Again Joel blocked her.

"I don't think you understand. My name is Joel Eisenberg and I met Dennis at his opening the other day. We talked about astrology and he asked me to come over to do his chart."

"Listen, honey, my good friend Ida Dream's told me all about you. And if you think you're gonna impress anyone around here with that shit, you're barking up the wrong fruit tree. So, if you don't mind ..."

Sue Veneer tried one last time to close the door. Just at that moment, though, Bunny, who hadn't been fed yet, stood on her hind legs, clawed at the tablecloth, and pulled the egg batter onto the floor.

Sue Veneer turned around and screamed, "Bad girl! Bad girl!"

Sue began chasing Bunny about the room. Taking advantage of the diversion, Joel stepped adroitly into the house just in time to have Bunny scurry between his ankles and accidentally nudge him even further into the room.

"Get out of the way!" Sue yelled.

But the more Joel tried to wiggle away, the more the dog circled his legs until he tripped sideways and fell into a chair. Bunny, who was still seeking protection from Sue, heaved herself onto his lap and started licking Joel's face.

"Bad girl!" Sue screamed. "Bad girl!" She then lifted her arm with every intention of striking the naughty dog, but something in her heart melted at the sight of Bunny cringing in Joel's lap. Turning around, she grabbed the edges of the sink, gritted her teeth, and yelled, "God, I hate my life!" Then she closed her eyes and slowly counted to ten.

For a few moments, nobody said a word. Sue wet a rag and cleaned off the floor. Bunny, meanwhile, was becoming intoxicated by the smell of Joel who, after sleeping three nights in a room beside the Dumpster, reeked deliciously of cheeseburgers and fried clams. She began vigorously licking his arms and hands.

At first Joel was repulsed by Bunny's sloppy, wet tongue, but he had a hunch that being kind to the canine might gain him entry into the house, so he bent over and cooed, "Budgy, budgy, budgy," into her ear. Meanwhile he was sizing up the house for clues to Dennis's sign. The kitchen reminded him of a boring vacation he'd once taken as a child to gawk at the Amish in Pennsylvania Dutch country. The stove was cast iron. The garbage pail was an old barrel and the walls had been carefully treated to appear like they'd been aging for three centuries. Could his Twin Flame be a history-loving Capricorn? Perhaps if he were clever enough he could pry the information out of the cranky old queen who seemed to reside in this kitchen.

"Beautiful house," he murmured as he ran his fingers across the broad-beamed table and looked around the room. Behind him was a wall of china cabinets containing everything from some expensive-looking crockery to several brightly colored boxes of Cream of Wheat. He stretched his neck to get a better view of the front parlor. "Is that the living room?"

Sue nodded grudgingly.

"Can I look around?"

"Absolutely not," Sue replied as she rinsed out her dirty rag.

"By the way," Joel suddenly announced, "when I met Dennis at his art show we had a fascinating conversation. I really think you can discover an artist's zodiac sign by analyzing his art."

"Really," Sue said, bored.

"For instance, Picasso was a Scorpio, so it makes sense that his most famous painting is about war."

"Hmm."

"And Michelangelo was a Pisces. That's why he's most famous for his religious paintings."

"Really."

"And Van Gogh was an Aries. That's why all his paintings have all those swirls of energy."

"You don't say," Sue mumbled.

"So, Dennis must be ..."

Sue had had enough. She turned and glared at Joel. "How stupid do you think I am? You're obviously trying to guess Dennis's sign so you can get him alone and give him a little back rub. Well, baby, I've seen a lot of clumsy attempts to seduce Dennis, but yours is one of the dumbest. So, if you don't mind, I'm having a bitch of a morning and you're only making it worse." Sue marched over to Joel, grabbed Bunny off his lap, and pointed to the door. "Get out!"

But Bunny was still loving Joel's smell and wasn't ready for him to leave. Wrenching herself around, she opened her mouth and nipped Sue in the face.

The drag queen was stunned. Bunny had hardly ever shown that kind of aggression, and never toward her. Losing her temper, she tossed Bunny away. The poor thing landed in the sink. Frantically trying to climb out, the dog grabbed at the dish rack and knocked it off the counter. The crash of dishes frightened the dog silly and she ran right out the door. Sue followed in hot pursuit.

"Where's she going?" Joel asked.

"How the hell should I know?"

The two ran into the yard just in time to see Bunny dart into the street and hear car tires screech. Sue Veneer gasped as a Volvo station wagon braked only inches away from Bunny's head. Tail between her legs, the little dog skulked back onto the sidewalk. Sue was in shock. "Oh, my god!" Bunny looked up at Sue and found her even more terrifying than the Volvo had been. "Don't you ever do that again!" Sue screamed, waving her finger. Bunny ran past her and around the back of the house.

"I'll get her," Joel offered, and chased after what was now his only friend in Provincetown.

Chapter Eight

Joel followed Bunny around the house just in time to see her push her way into a small shack on the far end of the property. He was surprised to see curtains in the windows. *Somebody actually lives there?* he thought to himself. Unbeknownst to Joel, Dennis Fairchild had yet another employee living on his property that summer, a handyman named Bill Doyle who'd been hired that winter to restore the main house to its original nineteenth-century shabbiness. In short order, Bill had chipped the floors and stained the walls to look like they'd been untouched since the War of 1812. He'd done such a good job antiquing the interior that Dennis had asked him to fix up the backyard shed so that Bill could live there that summer and work on the exterior of the house. In no time flat he had relined the chimney, replaced the gutters, and painted the entire house white—in spite of not having drawn a sober breath since 1994. He was one of those sad souls without whom Province-town could not have survived—a functioning alcoholic who lived there year-round and not only lent his labor to the town, but also spent his hard-earned cash in the town's many drinking holes.

"Pghh. Pghh."

Bill opened his eyes to find Bunny licking his face.

"Aw, jeez."

As usual, Bill had been dreaming about Mitchell Savitt, his ex-lover, who had died three years ago from AIDS. For one blissful moment he'd mistaken Bunny's kisses for those of his former lover, who sometimes visited him while he was sleeping.

"How'd you get in here?" he asked the affectionate dog.

"Pghh. Pghh."

"Anybody home?" came a voice from outside his door.

"Who's there?" Bill called across the room.

"I'm looking for a dog. A little bulldog."

"Hold on."

Bill staggered fully dressed off the couch where he'd fallen asleep the night before. Squinting through the screen door, he saw something that sobered him up completely. The man peering through his door looked enough like his former lover to have been his twin.

"Mitchell?" he asked incredulously.

Joel looked behind him, wondering to whom he was referring. "No. I'm just looking for a dog."

Bill rubbed his forehead to see if he could still be dreaming.

"If this is a bad time ... I could ..." Joel started backing away from the door.

"No, don't go."

"But you're still sleeping."

"No, it's all right. Come in."

Bill held open the door. With trepidation Joel stepped inside and saw Bunny seated on the floor beside the couch. He moved carefully around Bill, whose expression, an odd mixture of bewilderment and adoration, unnerved him. He wanted to grab the dog and get out fast, but as soon as he bent down to pick up Bunny, she ran across the room into a dusty kitchen alcove, scurried beneath a table, and pressed her body against the wall. Joel got down on his hands and knees, reaching for the dog and giving Bill the opportunity to check out his ass.

The handyman couldn't believe how much Joel reminded him of Mitchell—they had the same stooped posture and the same trace of a Long Island accent. They were the same height, had the same color and texture hair, the same bright blue eyes and rosy complexion. Joel also had that same uniquely Jewish mixture of fear and aggression, the ability to be both pushy and apologetic at the same time. "I'll get her," Bill offered graciously as he got down on his knees next to Joel. "Bunny!" he called, and the little bulldog immediately ran into his arms.

Just then, Sue Veneer rapped on the door and pressed her ugly face against the screen. "Bill? Is Bunny in there?"

"I got her," Bill yelled back as he stood up and went to the door. Joel, meanwhile, crawled further under the kitchen table to avoid being seen.

"Would you mind watching her for a few minutes?" Sue asked. "I need to go to the A&P."

"No problem."

"Also, have you seen this little guy with glasses snooping around?"

Bill glanced back at Joel, who was cowering beneath the table, holding his fingers to his lips, and shaking his head.

"Nope," he answered Sue.

"Well, if you do, give him the old heave ho. We don't need anyone hanging around the property while Dennis is still sleeping. You stay here, baby," Sue cooed to Bunny through the screen. "Mommy'll be right back." Joel listened as Sue climbed on her bicycle and rattled up the lane onto Commercial Street.

"You can come out now," Bill announced.

"Thanks," Joel replied as he stood up and brushed off his knees. "I just didn't feel like dealing with her."

"I understand. Listen, do you know …" Bill couldn't finish his sentence.

"Who?"

"I'm sorry it's just that …"

"What?" Bill was staring wide eyed at Joel, and the intensity was making him uncomfortable. It wasn't that Bill was all that unattractive. He was pretty well preserved for someone in his late forties: a full head of hair and decent biceps. He had the kind of looks prized by younger, more effeminate men who yearn to be fucked by a real man—one who doesn't pluck, moisturize, or do anything to smooth out the gullies in his forehead or the crow's feet around his eyes. Joel could appreciate all this, but he'd also seen from beneath the table that Bill didn't have much of an ass, which was for him an absolute deal breaker. After an awkward moment, Joel began inching toward the door. Before he could slip away, however, Bill reached out and grabbed his arm.

"Wait. Do you have to leave so soon? Can I get you a cocktail or something?"

Joel startled. *A cocktail?* he asked himself. *At ten in the morning?* Looking around the room, he noticed that every available surface was covered with beer and liquor bottles and the kinds of food alcoholics bring home to make their houses look more like the corner bar: ripped bags of pretzels, popcorn that had gotten stuck in the carpet, and half-eaten cans of nuts. Joel grimaced and shook his head.

Bill realized his mistake. "How 'bout a cup of coffee?"

"No, thanks," Joel demurred as he put his hand on the doorknob.

"Are you … are you staying here in town?" Bill asked anxiously.

"Um … well …"

"Can I see you again? What are you doing tonight for dinner?"

Joel winced as though he had a scheduling problem.

"How about tomorrow?" Bill asked.

Joel hesitated. Of all people, he knew how painful it was to be rejected, and he was loath to inflict that pain on somebody else, however unappealing he might be.

"I … I guess."

"Great! Where do you want to eat?"

"You pick it."

"How about Napi's?"

"Sounds good," Joel said, pushing through the screen door and stepping into the yard. Bill followed after him.

"Wait. Do you know where it is? It's on Standish and Bradford."

"I'll find it."

"How's eight o'clock?"

Joel frowned.

"Nine? Ten?"

"Fine." Joel started to walk down the lane. He was anxious to shake Bill so he could get back inside the house and snoop around.

"Wait! What's your name?" Bill asked.

"Oh … um, Joel. Joel Eisenberg."

Bill stared longingly at Joel, who felt a cold breeze between his legs as the handyman undressed him with his eyes. "See you tomorrow."

Bill watched Joel leave, astonished how Joel even had that gay-Jew walk, sucking in his stomach to appear thinner and leaning forward as though the weight of the world was on his shoulders. He wondered if Joel, like Mitchell, had a dark trail of curly hair snaking up from his groin to his chest.

Chapter Nine

Joel hid himself behind a corner of Dennis's house and waited for Bill to go back inside his shack. He had noticed a rear entrance and was determined to snoop around before Sue Veneer got back from the store. Seeing that the yard was empty, he slithered along the side of the house until he reached an open door into a mudroom. Assuming that Dennis's bedroom and studio were on the top floor, Joel began tiptoeing up the steps, praying they wouldn't squeak. He passed through another vestibule and slunk into a long dark room filled floor to ceiling with antiques. *So he's quite a little pack rat,* Joel thought. *Maybe he's a Cancer, like me.*

Though the shutters were closed, Joel could discern an old writing desk and an Empire couch waiting to be re-covered and restuffed. On the wall behind it there were several old portraits of sea captains. In front of these was a long mahogany table with claw legs that seemed to be buckling beneath the weight of a number of cardboard boxes filled with art books and ancient maps, along with the dusty models of old ships and rusty tools of an indeterminate age. Moving along carefully, Joel saw a poster for an ocean

liner circa 1910, several magazines from the 1920s, and a half
dozen restored photographs of hatchet-faced old maids. *He's a
Capricorn,* Joel decided. *Why else would he keep so many ugly old
artifacts?*

The door at the end of the parlor opened into a small storeroom
filled with empty canvases, brushes, and turpentine. Stealing
through another door, he entered the artist's studio—a brightly
sunlit room. In addition to the skylights overhead, there were several large windows on both sides covered with sheer, white curtains
that flapped in the breeze. In spite of the ventilation, the place
reeked of paint fumes. Joel breathed in deeply. However toxic the
fumes might be, this was Dennis's aroma and he found it deeply
erotic. All his senses were aflame. He'd have to work fast.

Hanging behind an old desk was a cork bulletin board on which
Dennis had pinned some postcards and letters. Joel ran up to it and
greedily searched for a birthday card or a calendar with a special
date circled. There were some Polaroids of run-down houses, road-
side diners, and abandoned factories—research, perhaps, for the
kinds of buildings he now wanted to paint. Joel's palms started to
sweat. He hated to think of himself as a spy, but his passion to know
Dennis was every bit as powerful as his passion to fuck him. Every
scrap of paper was like an aphrodisiac—even the electric bill and
junk mail made Joel's heart tingle with excitement.

Taking extreme care not to make any noise, he slid open a desk
drawer. He found a photo of a man of about forty, prematurely gray
and wearing an old flannel shirt. His facial features were classically
noble, albeit a trifle sharp. "Love always, James," the photo had
been inscribed in a large bold script that managed to be beautiful
without being the least bit effeminate. *Was James a boyfriend? But
what about the Frenchman? Perhaps this is an ex, which would explain
why it has been hidden in a drawer,* he thought.

Joel remembered Yris del Coro's prediction: his Twin Flame would be in love with another man. Encouraged, he reached deeper into the drawer and found a pile of letters, all in the same handwriting and addressed to Dennis from a place called Greenville, New Hampshire. He also found a yellow legal pad on which the words "Dear James" had been written at the top and then mysteriously crossed out. *An aborted attempt to respond?*

Turning, Joel noticed two doors on the far side of the studio. The one on the left was closed. Joel guessed it led into Dennis's bedroom, where he hoped the artist was still sleeping soundly. The door on the right was open—it was the artist's bathroom, which would contain a veritable treasure trove of information that Joel could use when he finally got to do the artist's chart. Unable to resist, Joel tiptoed into the john and began snooping through Dennis's medicine cabinet. The painter had an awful lot of ointments and pills for sore joints and muscle aches. *Is Dennis a hypochondriac,* Joel wondered, *or merely a Virgo?*

Closing the cabinet door, Joel came face-to-face with himself in the bathroom mirror. Nothing twists a face more than a guilty conscience. Taking a moment to center himself, he bravely confronted his reflection, squared his shoulders, and mouthed the words, "I am completely good." Unable to believe himself, he tried again, more forcefully, this time saying, "I am completely good, even though I sometimes do the most horrible things."

Something in the glass caught his eye and distracted him. They were Dennis's blue jeans, hooked on the wall where he had put them after removing them the night before. Joel approached them reverently, reached out, and let his fingers graze the cloth. He knew what he was aching to do but he'd have to act quickly. Just one sniff, he told himself. Only one. Taking the seat of Dennis's jeans in his palm, he rubbed the faded fabric between his thumb and forefinger, pressed the fabric to his nose, and inhaled deeply. They smelled of bleach. *Of course, Dennis bleaches them—so they hug his beautiful bottom more tightly.*

Then he smelled leather. His hands came upon an object in the back pocket. But did he dare remove a wallet from a stranger's pants? Why not, he reasoned. Hadn't the pants miraculously appeared before him? Hadn't this wallet been handed to him by a Higher Power? Wasn't this exactly what his guru had wanted for him? While mentally offering his immense gratitude, he gingerly slid the wallet from the pocket, opened it, and discovered Dennis's driver's license. The artist's birthday was emblazoned upon it in boldface: February 13, 1967.

"February 13, 1967," Joel whispered reverentially, like Bernadette in the presence of the Holy Virgin. Replacing the pants on the hook, he wiped his sweaty palms on one of the artist's towels and quietly but happily made his way back down the stairs. "An Aquarian." He ran back home to consult his ephemeris. *No wonder I couldn't guess,* he thought. *They're completely unpredictable.*

Chapter Ten

Like many of Provincetown's most famous citizens, Rudy Cantwell's past was shrouded in mystery. One rumor had it that he'd been born Richard Cantor in Williamsburg, Brooklyn, and his father was a Hasidic rabbi. Another suggested he was the child of Cuban peasants and he'd worked as a child prostitute in Havana. As for his playwriting talent, the Boston critics agreed that Molière and Shaw had nothing to worry about. His satiric targets were poorly chosen and his aim was scattershot. In terms of his acting ability, it was barely sufficient, and although he always played the leads in his plays, a more resourceful supporting player would almost always walk away with better reviews.

What Rudy did have in great abundance was a shamelessness that, over the years, had come to be confused with star quality. In spite of these limitations, Rudy was much appreciated by the locals for his long history of writing and producing the kind of outrageous queer theater that Provincetown liked to call its own. Whether or not one appreciated his stagecraft, his fans heartily agreed with his company's artistic manifesto: most of the world's problems would be solved if every straight man simply bent over and took it up the ass—a thrilling theatrical concept that managed to be written into each of his plays.

But today, Rudy Cantwell was having serious doubts about being able to continue spreading the gospel of spreading one's cheeks. The night before he'd received a disturbing call from Reverend Debbie Levitzky, the Jewish lesbian minister of the Unitarian Congregation, during which he'd been abruptly informed that the elders of the church had read his most recent script and unanimously decided that, even by the loose standards of their liberal faith, *Von Trapp!* was too filthy to be performed in their basement.

"Damn it!" Rudy shouted. He banged the old wood railing just as his boyfriend Keith ambled out the door with a cup of coffee.

"Everything's gonna be OK," Keith reassured Rudy.

"It's June, darling. Where else can you sit a hundred fifty people except for Sue Veneer's ugly old face?"

"I hear she's losing her show at the Seaview. Maybe we can do it there?"

"Have you seen their carpets? It looks like the Holiday Inn in Bridgeport. I need the Meeting House!"

"Calm down."

"Where else can I re-create an Alpine nunnery, the Von Trapp family castle, the city of Salzburg? Fuck! Fuck! Fuck!"

Keith calmly held the hot coffee in his hands while Rudy stamped his feet on the deck. Luckily, Keith had already smoked a joint that morning, so he was feeling unperturbed about the show's cancellation, even though it would mean the loss of his own starring role as Rolf.

"Maybe you could make the script less dirty."

"Absolutely not. My fans demand that all my shows be disgusting."

"Is there any way the elders will change their minds?"

"No way. They're still pissed at me for making fun of their elevator drive. Excuse me! But do you really need to spend thirty thousand dollars because one fat old dyke can't climb the stairs?"

"Can you make a donation?"

"With what money?"

Keith handed Rudy his coffee, then came up behind him and hugged him while he drank it. "You know who they love? Dennis Fairchild. He gave one of his paintings to the silent auction this spring and they got five thousand to fix their organ."

"I'd like to fix their organ."

"I've got it!" Keith exclaimed. "Ask Dennis to be in *Von Trapp!* Make him one of the nuns. I'll bet the elders change their mind if he's in the show."

"Dennis Fairchild is not an actor."

"Sure he is. Look at him posing every night in front of Spiritus." Keith snapped his fingers theatrically. "Honey, as soon as that girl gets up in the morning, she's onstage."

Rudy shook his head and scowled.

Keith went back in the house, brought back the cordless phone along with Dennis's phone number, and placed them both on the railing. "Give Dennis a call. You've got nothing to lose."

Rudy shot Keith a dirty look. He was the only one with the right to say that about him. Keith mumbled an apology and hugged his honey. "Baby," he purred. "Did you mean what you said last night? That you wanted to spend the rest of your life with me, and that I'd co-star in all your shows and get billed just below the title in letters seventy-five percent as large as yours?"

"Sixty."

"I love you. Do you love me?"

Rudy mumbled his assent. Keith had been hoping for a more stirring declaration of his lover's feelings but he was in too much of a rush to get to his job waiting the lunchtime shift at the Lobster Pot. Stuffing another joint behind his ear, he ran down the alleyway along the wharf and jumped on his bike.

Rudy, meanwhile, was concentrating fiercely on his predicament. As a double Scorpio, he knew all there was to know about revenge, and the thought of all his enemies joining together to kick him when he was down was truly frightening. He also knew that if he were forced to sit out the season, someone younger and more outrageous might steal his thunder by staging a show even more repulsive than his. His goal had been to use Provincetown as a stepping-stone to off-Broadway and secure himself a chapter alongside Charles Ludlum in the history of ridiculous American theater.

He looked at the phone where Keith had left it. *Maybe I should call Dennis,* he thought. *Having the artist on my side will certainly get the elders to reconsider their decision. But will Dennis want to be in this show? And would he want such a small role? There's no guarantee he'll be any good … but would it matter? Townies would turn out in droves to see the two of us onstage for the very first time. Keith is doing a great job playing Rolf, but Dennis Fairchild would certainly look great in the part. Why, he has Hitler Youth written all over his smug little face.*

Rudy stood up and started pacing across his apartment. Not only could Dennis play Rolf—Rudy would make the part even bigger. The entire show could be rewritten to include a love triangle between Rolf, Liesl, and Maria. That's just what the show needed, he thought to himself.

"I'm a genius," Rudy purred, forgetting completely that it had originally been Keith's idea. He reached for Dennis's phone number. With Dennis in the role, he could get major donations to buy more material for new costumes. *The show will look spectacular. The Nazis will be pure Tom of Finland. The nuns' habits will be slit up the side and open in the back, and the week before the opening they could give an outdoor preview in front of the Pilgrim Monument. The Nazis could chase the Von Trapps up the hill, and they could all show their asses!* The Board of Selectmen might fine him two hundred dollars for gross indecency, he calculated, but the free publicity would be worth ten, twenty, thirty times that amount. And if he played his cards right, he might even make the front page of the *Boston Globe.* The *New York Times* might even include him in their annual summer roundup of regional theaters.

Dennis Fairchild had to play the part. Keith would just have to step aside for the good of the company.

Rudy picked up the phone and dialed. When an answering machine picked up, he barked, "Dennis. Rudy Cantwell here. Call me back."

Chapter Eleven

At that very moment, Dennis Fairchild was strolling along the beach looking for seashells and purposely trying to upset Jean Paul, who was sitting alone back at their blanket and fuming because he'd been abandoned on their last day together. All morning Dennis had said barely a kind word, and Jean Paul, like so many jilted men before him, was coming to the conclusion that Dennis Fairchild was not only reserved, but also cruel and unfeeling.

In Dennis's mind, however, he was doing Jean Paul a favor. The Parisian was a bit nelly for his taste, and he'd long ago concluded that he didn't want to make the effort to maintain a long-distance relationship. Rather than being cruel, Dennis believed he was acting standoffish out of the goodness of his heart. In his early twenties he'd discovered he was unusually fascinating for someone so sexy, and that if he shared too much of his inner life with his bedmates, he'd be stuck with some lovesick slave knocking on his kitchen door, disturbing his privacy, or—worst of all—making dumb conversation in front of Spiritus while he was trying to reel in his next bedmate. It was so much kinder, then, to keep postcoital conversation to a minimum and, if the tryst turned into an affair, quietly let the man down easily when he decided he'd had enough.

But Dennis had more pressing thoughts on his mind that day. His Labor Day Show was two months away and he'd soon have to decide whether to go back to his usual subject matter. The thought of painting one more pretty house made him want to vomit. Even worse, Sue Veneer had only just informed him that her run had been canceled and that she'd be going back to Long Island to live with her mother. Sue's company was expendable, but who would care for Bunny the rest of the summer? Who would walk her, feed her, and keep her from whining all night long? There were days when he simply wanted to give the damn dog back to James, but that would mean losing an argument with his ex-lover, one thing he simply wouldn't consider.

"Nam myoho renge kyo. Nam myoho renge kyo." Meanwhile, the man who was dying for the chance to solve all of Dennis's problems was quietly repeating his mantra as he lay flat on his stomach in the dunes behind Jean Paul. Using the information from Dennis's driver's license, Joel Eisenberg had figured out the transits to Dennis's natal Neptune and predicted correctly that the artist would be at the beach that afternoon. Stealthy as an Apache, he'd wound his way through the dunes, and when he'd found Dennis and Jean Paul, he ducked behind some tall grass for cover. His goal was to drive a wedge between the two lovers. Grabbing his knapsack and pasting a smile on his face, Joel scampered down the dune and marched over to where Jean Paul was seated.

Getting rid of this slack-jawed Parisian will be like shooting fish in the proverbial barrel, he thought. It helped immensely that he'd called Lou Lustig earlier that morning and managed to get some great dish about Dennis's continental conquest.

"Bonjour!" Joel chirped as though he and the Frenchman were the oldest and dearest of friends.

Jean Paul, who had been checking his face in a compact, turned around and was unpleasantly surprised that a total stranger was disturbing his privacy.

"Do I know you?" he asked with great hauteur.

"We met at Dennis's opening. Joel Eisenberg."

The two men shook hands. There was a puzzled crease in Jean Paul's forehead, which made Joel believe he was hardly the brightest object in the City of Lights. But he was so cute. If Joel wasn't already stalking the king of beasts, he might have taken a bite out of this tasty gazelle.

"Is Dennis here today?" Joel asked.

"Oui. Il fait un promenade," Jean Paul answered, hoping that speaking in French would discourage any further dialogue.

"He went for a walk?" Joel answered, thrilled for having remembered something from his two years of high school French.

"Yes," Jean Paul answered with a sigh.

"May I join you?" Joel asked sweetly.

Jean Paul answered with an existential shrug of his shoulders and reluctantly moved aside. In truth, he very much wanted to be left alone for a few final magic hours with Dennis, and this rude stranger was threatening to ruin the rest of his afternoon by plopping himself down on his blanket like a sack of *pomme frites.*

"What a beautiful day," Joel exclaimed. "Do you mind if I use your suntan lotion?" he asked as he grabbed the tube and squirted a big glob of it onto his arm. "This is really the best time of day to be at the beach. It's funny, but when I was a kid I used to go to the beach and wonder who was on the other side of the ocean. I guess it was you."

"I only go to the beach in the south of France."

"Really? And you're from ..."

"Paris."

"Paris! That must be such a beautiful city," Joel prattled.

"Oui."

"I really hope Dennis gets a chance to visit you this fall. You know, he'll be dying to travel in September because he'll be going through a Jupiter transit." Joel sighed and maintained a knowing silence.

After a moment, Jean Paul cleared his throat. "A Jupiter transit? What is this?"

"It's an astrological term."

"L'astrologie?" Jean Paul said, definitely perking up. "Like a ... how you say? A horoscope."

"Exactly."

"You make the horoscope?"

"I'm a professional astrologer."

"Un astrologue? I am very interested in *l'astrologie."*

"Really?" Joel replied, feigning surprise. Lou Lustig had already told him that Jean Paul was fascinated by the subject.

"So tell me," the Frenchman exclaimed. "Dennis ... you think he wants to come to Paris?"

"Oh, yes."

"What else can you tell me? Can you tell me anything about me?"

"When is your birthday?"

"The twenty-ninth of November."

"A Sagittarian! Very good. Very compatible with Dennis."

"Oh, yes. We are very comfortable with one another."

"He's an Aquarian. So you have a lot of fun together. Very good sex."

Jean Paul blushed slightly.

"But ..." Joel paused and frowned.

"Is there a ... a problem?" Jean Paul asked, alarmed.

"No, not really. Except ... well, with you and Dennis, there is no ..."

"Tell me."

"There's no glue to hold you together."

"And you know this from *l'astrologie?*"

"Also from here." Joel pointed to a spot in the middle of his forehead.

"Ah," Jean Paul concluded. "You are psychic then? *Très intéressant.*"

Joel closed his eyes to remember the rest of what Lou Lustig had gleaned by talking to Etienne, one of Jean Paul's less than trustworthy friends. "Hmm," he murmured as though being visited by a spirit. "I'm being told there is somebody else for you. Somebody back in Paris. A builder, perhaps. No, he doesn't actually build buildings. But he designs them. He draws buildings."

"He is an architect."

"Yes. Yes. An architect! I see him near a window ... drawing on a big table. And he's a Capricorn?"

"*Oui.* A Capricorn"

"And what is his name?" Joel asked.

"Charles."

"Yes, Charles. This is the man for you."

"What more can you tell me?" Jean Paul asked.

Joel turned and looked Jean Paul in the eyes. Whatever he hadn't learned from Lou Lustig, he would now be able to read in Jean Paul's trusting face.

"Oh, I don't usually get such strong messages, but because we're near the ocean.... Did something happen between you and Charles? Some misunderstanding about money?"

"Money?"

"Yes. He thinks you took his money. No, it was an object. There was some kind of argument about an object. Did you take something that belonged to someone in his family?"

"*Non. Non.* It was given to me," Jean Paul exclaimed defensively.

"Was it …" Joel made a circle motion with his hand. "… like a plate? Not a plate but a … a bowl? I see a bowl! Did his grand-mother give you an antique bowl before she died and the rest of the family thinks you stole it?"

"*Non. Non,* I didn't steal it. Does Charles think I stole it?"

Joel closed his eyes. Up until now, everything he'd said had been told to him by Lou Lustig. This was his chance to be creative.

"I see someone telling Charles that you stole the bowl. You need to go back to town and call him right away."

Jean Paul's face flushed with anger. "Who? Who is telling him this?"

"There is another man with him. Pierre? Paul?"

"Philippe. It is Philippe!"

"Yes. Philippe. Philippe is with him now. They are on a couch."

"A red couch?"

"Yes! A red couch. And there are two glasses of wine on the coffee table. And the candles are burning."

"*Mon dieu!*"

"This Philippe is very clever. But Charles is undecided. If you call him now, he will be happy to hear your voice. But if you wait until tomorrow…"

"I will call him now." Jean Paul scooped his towel back into his knapsack and leaped to his feet. "*Merci beaucoup.* Philippe! Ugh!"

"I'm so sorry. …"

"*Non.* It is better that I know this. You and I, we will talk later. And please," Jean Paul called over his shoulder as he scampered over the dune, "tell Dennis I will see him back in town, but do not tell him what we have just said to one another."

"I won't," Joel replied honestly as he watched Jean Paul leave.

Feeling exhilarated, he hugged his knees to his chest. Rudy Cantwell had been correct; Provincetown was a place where one's best-kept secrets are public knowledge. Joel imagined himself on the Cape, building his practice by regurgitating gossip as though he were channeling spirits. There was something in Provincetown's salty air—stories, secrets, gossip—and Joel was confident he might sniff them all out, like the lead beagle on a fox hunt.

Joel turned and carefully examined Dennis's possessions: a pair of work boots standing side by side like soldiers and a sleeveless T-shirt, not balled up but folded. Most intriguing was an artist's sketch pad with two charcoal pencils perfectly aligned. Joel picked up the pad and thumbed through some studies for landscapes. They were wilder and rougher than Dennis's finished paintings. He could have lingered over them all day, but he had to do some research. Carelessly tossing the sketch pad aside, Joel rummaged through his own knapsack and pulled out a dog-eared copy of *Your Life is in Your Hand: An Introduction to the Art of Palmistry*.

As Joel brushed up on the lingo, he smiled to himself: a lovely palm reading, he thought, would literally be the ticket for getting his hands on Dennis Fairchild. With the artist's sensual Taurus moon, he would melt beneath his touch. With his Mercury in Capricorn, he might also be something of a hypochondriac. And with all those tubes of Bengay in his medicine cabinet, Dennis would probably have a few sore knuckles and an incipient case of arthritis. With the moon pro-gressing into Aquarius, it was only a matter of minutes, he believed, before he got his paws on the artist's beautiful behind. Joel suddenly felt a slight tingling on the skin behind his ears, and without even turning his head, he knew the artist was returning from his walk.

Chapter Twelve

Dennis stopped dead in his tracks about fifty yards down the beach from his blanket. Where he expected to find Jean Paul, somebody else was sitting upright and reading a book. He pivoted to make sure he'd come back to the right spot. The driftwood marker and the sandy promontory were just where he expected them to be, so he ambled a little closer to identify the intruder and was only somewhat surprised when it turned out to be the astrologer from New York, the one who'd bragged about knowing some gallery owners.

Since meeting Joel at his opening, he'd found out a little more about him. At the deli, Ida Dream had cheerfully told him how Rudy had read his beads on the street, and that his nickname around town was "the ass-trologer." Knowing this didn't deter Dennis from wanting to be friends with Joel in the least. As a year-round resident of Provincetown, he was already a little bored by the same old stream of muscular tourists and lovely young houseboys who were currently pouring into town. He'd already had his summer fling with Jean Paul, and now he was ready for something different—a harmless kook, perhaps. *Liars do sometimes tell the truth,* Dennis told himself. *Maybe he does have some connections in the art world.*

"Hello," Dennis said warily as he approached Joel.

"Jean Paul had to go back to town," Joel replied, believing that Dennis seemed happy to see him.

"How come?"

"He didn't say. How was your walk?"

"Great."

Dennis was suddenly taken aback. Now that he was closer to Joel, he saw that the astrologer had not only parked himself on his antique bedspread, but also thumbed through his sketchbook and carelessly tossed it aside. While trying to decide whether to voice his concern, he pasted a broad smile on his face and just stood there, hoping that Joel would understand why he was upset and apologize for his rudeness.

But Joel Eisenberg hadn't a clue. He only saw Dennis's dazzling smile. Carelessly scooping up Dennis's charcoal pencils, he tossed them aside and patted the blanket. "Would you like to sit down?"

"It *is* my blanket," Dennis replied with a trace of annoyance.

"Help yourself then," Joel said with a chuckle, believing that Dennis was trying to be funny by showing a little attitude.

Dennis dropped to his knees, gathered his pencils, and put them back *exactly* where he'd left them. In choosing a spot, he was careful not to accommodate Joel in the least, claiming the entire middle of the blanket as though Joel weren't there. But his ploy backfired; Joel, a bit woozy from seeing Dennis without a shirt, merely assumed that the artist wanted to sit as close to him as possible.

"I looked through your sketchbook," Joel announced proudly. "I think you're quite talented and you could really go somewhere with your art."

Dennis rolled his eyes. Maybe Joel was unaware that he was already one of the wealthiest artists on the Cape.

"Do you always pretend to be the waiter?" Joel asked.

"I wasn't pretending to be anything."

"I thought you were trying to get some honest feedback. Oh, by the way," he continued, "I didn't mean to suggest that you were lonely and miserable."

"I think the phrase you used was 'complete narcissist with dollar signs in my head and a penis up my ass.'"

"I was exaggerating for dramatic effect."

Dennis shrugged. "Everyone's entitled to his opinion."

Joel smiled to himself. Nothing pleased him more than Dennis's having remembered what he said. Inserting words into someone's mind—however insulting—was the only foreplay he knew. He coughed to indicate some embarrassment. "Anyway, they're still beautiful paintings and if you ever do show in New York, it's exactly the direction you need to go in."

"Any chance of that happening?" Dennis asked nonchalantly. "You're the psychic."

"Funny you should want my opinion, Mr. Aquarian."

Dennis looked at Joel suspiciously.

"How'd you know?"

"Every now and then I meet people who are so unique I can't guess their signs right away and they're almost always Aquarians."

"Not bad," Dennis replied, fairly certain that Joel had simply read his biography back at the gallery.

Having "guessed" Dennis's sign correctly, Joel had the good sense to keep quiet. The next move would have to be Dennis's. *Nam myoho renge kyo* he prayed over and over to his guru. *Please let him be interested in me. Just give him the slightest interest in getting his palm read or his chart done and I'll do the rest. Please. Please!* Voicing a loud "hmm," he furrowed his brows dramatically and turned another page.

Dennis, meanwhile, was already intrigued by Joel—although certainly not sexually. Physically, Dennis considered Joel to be interesting looking, and he was already considering asking him to pose for a portrait. Unfortunately for Joel, Dennis was a typical gay man: when choosing men to fuck, he was almost always looking to trade up in the looks department. Dennis knew he was adorable, so what he required in a sex partner was nothing less than godlike. Joel was hardly godlike. On the other hand, Joel would be more than welcome in Dennis's large posse of offbeat acolytes and acquaintances, many of whom had varying degrees of crushes on him, all of them completely harmless. Joel might be fun to have around for good conversation, Dennis thought, but there was something even more specific that Joel might provide.

"What are you reading?" Dennis asked.

Joel turned the book over and looked at the title as though he himself had forgotten. "Just a book about palm reading."

"Do you also read palms?"

"Yep," Joel answered, flipping the book over and turning a page. Adrenaline was suddenly coursing through his veins.

"Can you read mine?" Dennis asked.

Joel answered nonchalantly, "I thought you didn't want me to tell your future."

"Please," Dennis repeated in a voice tinged with sarcasm. "Am I going to be rich? Will I find my soul mate?"

"All right." Joel groaned as if he were making a huge sacrifice. "Give me your other hand. Your left hand is your potential. Your right hand is what you've done with it so far."

"Here it is," Dennis announced. "A blank slate."

Joel took Dennis's left hand in his own, closed his eyes, and took a deep breath. Then he cradled it and delicately bounced it up and down. It was a surprisingly heavy hand, bony and muscular. With his eyes still closed, Joel began rubbing the fleshy mound at the base of Dennis's thumb. He pushed it and he smeared it around, like he was tenderizing a quarter pound of brisket.

"Are you reading it in braille?" Dennis quipped.

"Breathe," Joel ordered.

"I am breathing."

"Breathe with me."

To Joel's surprise, Dennis followed his command. The two men inhaled together and Joel could slowly feel the tension in Dennis's body begin to relax. "Keep breathing," Joel demanded as he massaged his fingers and cracked each of his knuckles. Bit by bit he could hear Dennis's breathing get slower as the artist relaxed.

"Is this OK?" Joel asked.

"Sure," Dennis replied.

"How about this?" Joel asked as he rubbed even harder, going so far as to push his knuckle into Dennis's palm.

"Great," Dennis replied, making Joel wonder if Dennis might be a bit of a masochist. Joel rubbed as hard as he could and he was soon rewarded for his efforts with an appreciative little sigh escaping from between the artist's lips.

"I'm ready to read your palm now," Joel whispered sweetly as he pulled Dennis's hand toward him and examined it as carefully as a hungry fat man might read the menu at his favorite restaurant. At last he found a crease that would suit his purposes. "Uh-huh. See where I'm moving my finger? This is your love line. And this is where it intersects with your … um … health line. You have a little arthritis, don't you?"

"A little bit."

"Has it been bothering you lately?"

Dennis nodded.

Joel closed his eyes and remembered Dennis's unfinished letter to James. "Hmm," he said. "There's a stiffness here in your Mount of Mercury. Have you been trying to contact someone recently?"

Dennis nodded as he wondered to whom Joel had been talking behind his back.

"Your indecision about taking action is manifesting as a blockage in your fingers."

"So, should I write the letter?" Dennis asked.

Joel shook his head and sighed. "I don't think so," he said. "You see all these little crosses on your love line? These exes are your exes," Joel quipped.

"I have a lot of exes," Dennis admitted.

"Hmm. Are you hoping to rekindle this relationship?"

"Maybe," Dennis answered cagily, for he wasn't about to say anything that would wind up bandied about on the street.

"I don't think you should," Joel pointed again to Dennis's hand, "because there are no more exes beyond this point."

"So?"

"I think you need to accept the fact that this man is … well, I hate to say it … but I think he's out of your life for good."

"Oh." This was hardly what Dennis wanted to hear.

"Now close your eyes," Joel suggested.

Still curious, Dennis played along, and Joel felt confident enough to complete his seduction by channeling Dennis's spirit guides. He'd once seen an old Italian woman do this at a psychic fair and he was pretty sure he could imitate her mannerisms. He started by hyperventilating. "Ah-phew. Ah-phew. Ah-phew."

Dennis opened one eye to peak. "What are you doing?"

"Some entities are trying to speak through me. I'm clearing out a space for them. Keep your eyes closed. Ah-phew! Ah-phew! Ah-phew!" Joel continued even louder than before. Then he groaned, shook his body, and groaned some more. Opening his mouth, he spoke very slowly in a smooth tone of voice more befitting a spiritual entity. He was careful not to stammer. "This is a very lucky day for you," the entity told Dennis. "Very fortunate. Somebody is entering your life and there will be a huge release of energy. He's someone who will help you."

"In my career?"

Joel took a few more deep breaths. "At first he will help you in your career. Then he will help you in your love life. But you must be ready to receive him."

"And he's coming into my life today?"

"That's right. But first your energies must be balanced in your mind and your body."

"My body?" Dennis asked, starting to have some idea where this conversation might be leading.

"Ah-phew. Ah-phew. Ah-phew. Your kundalini energy is having a hard time rising into your *saraswara*."

"My sara-swhat?"

"Lie down on your stomach," Joel suggested.

Dennis hesitated, but he found Joel's seduction so hilariously hokey. Twisting on the blanket, he lay down, curling his arms beneath him and hugging himself like a small child. Joel very gently took Dennis's arms and splayed them beside him.

"What are you doing?" Dennis asked.

"Shh," replied Joel as he allowed himself a moment to survey the wonderful terrain that had just appeared beneath him. Shivering with lust, he took a few more breaths to calm himself. "Ah-phew. Ah-phew. Ah-phew."

Then, strangely enough, the entity inside of Joel started saying almost the same thing Joel had said to Lucas the previous month. "Chakras are energy centers in the body. There are seven of them ranging from the base of the spine through the top of the head. The main reason your joints ache is that your energy is clogged. With both the earth element and the air element prominent in your essence, there's a split between your intellectual center, which is located here," Joel scratched the top of Dennis's head, "and your physical energy, which is located here." With almost ceremonial courtesy, Joel very lightly let his hand rest on Dennis's fabulous behind and left it there while he took a few more breaths.

"Ah-phew. Ah-phew. Ah-phew."

Unlike Lucas, Dennis didn't moan appreciatively when his butt was touched, and Joel had the feeling the artist wasn't quite convinced. But Joel had no time for trivialities, not with Dennis's creamy soft skin laid out before him like a buffet. Putting one hand in the middle of Dennis's back and one hand on his delicious derriere, he began to rock the artist like a cradle. "Ah-phew. Ah-phew. Ah-phew." Still moving like he was in a trance, he squeezed some suntan lotion onto his hands and ran them up the length of Dennis's spine. The artist finally made a sound. He moaned. The astrologer had guessed correctly; Dennis's sensuous Taurus moon meant the quickest way to his heart was through his aching back. Dennis was the best of all possible things: a massage whore.

Dennis was preparing to stop Joel if he went too far, although at that moment he wasn't even sure where he'd draw the line. The beach was empty, and he'd certainly been blown by less appetizing strangers than Joel amidst the cover of dunes and tall grasses. He was even getting a bit of an erection as Joel started rubbing one of his buttocks. But Dennis was thinking about something Joel had just said.

What if James and I never get back together again? Would that be so horrible? Without worrying about James, I can screw whomever I want. I might even meet this other guy—the one Joel was talking about, the one who's going to energize my life. I could get rid of Bunny once and for all.

Bunny?

Dennis suddenly remembered something Sue had told him about Joel. She'd said the dog jumped in his lap and cried all afternoon after he left. This was amazing because Bunny had never before warmed up to a stranger. Dennis started to consider having Joel move into his house to take care of his dog. It would certainly be fun to have a semicelebrity from New York in his house, one with just enough cachet to enliven his parties without overshadowing the host. He might even get a few free massages. At the very least, he couldn't be any worse than Sue Veneer had been.

"This is great," Dennis found himself murmuring.

"Thanks," Joel replied as he slid his hand over to Dennis's other buttock.

"Ever think of doing this for a living?" he said with a moan.

"Sure," Joel replied.

"What are you doing the rest of the summer?" Dennis asked.

"Working on a book."

"You could always write here in Provincetown. I heard you and Bunny really hit it off."

"Oh, yeah," Joel answered rather absentmindedly because he was so intent on drinking in the sight and feel of Dennis's ass.

"You liked her, then?"

Joel hesitated. He really would have preferred Dennis to stop chattering so the artist could fully experience the bliss radiating through his fingertips.

"She was great," Joel finally replied.

"Why don't you stay the summer?"

"I'd love to," Joel replied as he straddled Dennis's legs.

"I mean, how would you like to stay at my place and take care of Bunny?"

"That would be fabulous," Joel answered as he pushed down on

Dennis's thighs and began inching his fingers toward Dennis's crack. "How does this feel?" Joel asked.

"Great," Dennis replied.

Joel started to push his hands up Dennis's shorts. The artist suddenly sat up and started putting on his shirt.

"How's this? Sue Veneer is leaving tonight. You want to come over and talk about it?"

"Talk about what?" Joel asked.

"The dog. I just asked you if you wanted to move in and take care of Bunny."

"Oh ... sure ... what time should I come?"

"Sue is leaving at ten. Anytime before that."

"OK."

Essential business settled, Dennis quickly gathered his belongings and, before Joel's hands could stop tingling, he climbed over the nearest sand dune and disappeared from sight.

Chapter Thirteen

Three years later, Bill Doyle still felt guilty for Mitchell's AIDS diagnosis and death. For the five years they had been lovers, it was he who had always wanted to fool around outside the relationship; it was he who had gone to the baths for quickies on the way home from work; it was he who had always wanted to initiate threesomes. Mitchell had always wanted their relationship to be monogamous, and he'd only strayed once, fucking an Australian cab driver in an attempt to make Bill jealous. Unfortunately once had been enough. He seroconverted. None of the new drug cocktails seemed to work, and six months later he was dead from a rare brain cancer that had been that year's big killer.

Bill was devastated. Their friends said he started drinking in order to forget Mitchell. More accurately, he drank to remember him. Whenever he started drinking, his ex-lover's spirit seemed to show up and talk to him inside his head. In the beginning Bill thought he was losing his mind, but over time he started talking back, as though it were the most natural thing in the world to argue with a dead person. He managed to keep most of these conversations in his head, but there were times, increasingly frequent, when the exchange was so compelling that Bill would forget where he was and yell something aloud on the street.

Tonight he'd thrown back a few screwdrivers while getting ready for his date with Joel. They hadn't been very strong but they were potent enough to summon Mitchell just as Bill was pulling a black silk shirt out of the closet.

"Is that what you're going to wear?" his ex-lover whispered in his ear.

"What's wrong with it?"

"It's ten years out of date and its frayed at the sleeves."

Bill examined the shirt and tossed it to the floor. Going to his dresser, he pulled out a powder-blue alligator shirt that would show off his eyes. Looking at himself in the mirror, he decided he needed another drink.

"You really want to be drunk on your first date?"

"I was drunk on my first date with you."

"I was drunk, too. That's how you got a second date."

Bill chuckled at the memory. "If I didn't know better, I'd think you were trying to destroy my confidence."

"I just want you to make a good first impression. Not everybody is going to look at you and see the dashing figure you were ten years ago."

Bill suddenly felt a little scared and dizzy. He sat down on his bed. "What am I doing? I'm wasting my time."

"That's not true, baby."

"I'm trying to replace you and it ain't gonna happen."

"You wanna know a secret from beyond? This is the guy for you. It's the only way you're gonna get over me."

"You won't be jealous if I date someone who looks like your twin?"

"The dead don't feel jealousy. Come on. Look at yourself in the mirror. There's the man I fell in love with. Go on. Wink at yourself."

Bill reluctantly winked in the mirror.

"There you go. Tonight you're gonna get some major man pussy. Go on, growl."

"Grr. Grrr."

"Now go gargle so he won't smell the booze on your breath. Remember, he's a Jew."

A few minutes later, as he was walking down the street, Bill started to grow excited about meeting Joel Eisenberg. Something inside him suspected that Mitchell was right and this nervous little astrologer was somehow intended to be his next boyfriend—not that this new romance was guaranteed to be easy. Bill had already learned about Joel's reputation as an ass-trologer with a wicked crush on Dennis. Passing the bar at the Bradford Inn, he considered popping in for a quick Scotch, but remembering Mitchell's warning, he kept walking. To satisfy his craving, though, he scurried up the steps of the Portuguese Bakery, where he bought a generous assortment of saltwater taffy, peppermints, and fudge. Rushing out the door, he got his legs tangled in the leashes of a large family of shih tzus.

"Watch it!" Bill exclaimed as he righted himself—and bumped right into Joel Eisenberg, who was rushing in the other direction.

"Joel?"

"Bill? Oh, Bill. I'm sorry …"

"I was just going to Napi's."

Joel suddenly remembered the date he'd made. He gasped and then immediately wished that he hadn't.

"Our date? Did you forget?"

"No, no. I was just running to your … to your cabin to tell you some … some friends of mine showed up unexpectedly at the hotel. I … I haven't seen them in a long time so …"

"Some friends?" Bill asked trying not to sound too suspicious.

"Yeah," Joel answered, pretending to be bereft at not being able to spend the evening with Bill, "we'll have to do it some other time."

"Sure," Bill said hiding his disappointment. It was obvious to him that Joel was lying.

Joel had never seen someone so crestfallen at being denied the pleasure of his company. This unusual sensation of power gave him a chill. He started to back away in the same direction he'd been heading.

"Wait!" Bill called. "Aren't you going in the wrong way? I thought your friends were at the hotel."

Joel panicked. He knew the lie he was about to tell would be even less believable than the one before, but he had no other at the ready.

"Um … no. I have to meet them on … at …"

"Somewhere on the east end of town?" Bill offered.

"Right. Right. But … call me. OK? I'd love to … I'd love to get together."

Bill shook his head and, holding out the bag, offered Joel a candy.

"Oh … uh, no, thanks." Joel rubbed his belly. "I'm trying to lose …"

"I guess you better get going."

As soon as Joel left, Bill tossed the bag of candy in the garbage. "What was I thinking?" he muttered to himself as he went back to the Bradford Inn and stepped up to the bar.

As Bill Doyle was ordering his first drink for the evening, Sue Veneer was in her room taking another hit off her joint. Her plan to go back to her mother's house on Long Island had been fast forwarded by the fact that her friend Brenda happened to be driving to Boston that night and had offered Sue a ride. Once there, she could spend the night and catch an early morning Amtrak to New York.

Sick of feeling sorry for herself, Sue stood up and marched across the room to her full-length mirror to give herself a good talking to. Gazing at her face, she attempted to focus on her big blue eyes so she wouldn't have to notice her crow's feet and her sickly pallor. "I am beautiful—as a *man!*" Sue announced to herself with every intention of believing it. But as the seconds ticked away, she had a hard time taking herself seriously. "Hey there, gorgeous," she suddenly exclaimed in her best Barbra Streisand.

"Stop it," Sue scolded herself. "Just stop it." Throwing out her chest, she tried another affirmation. "I don't need the love of an audience in order to feel good about myself." But as soon as these words were out of her mouth, Sue couldn't help singing Lauren Bacall's opening number from *Applause*.

Sue closed her eyes and tried to think of another affirmation, one that would help her face her future with a modicum of excitement and joy—a future in which, for the first time in eighteen years, she wouldn't be summering in Provincetown. "I am not Sue Veneer," she announced bravely into the mirror. She felt a deep sense of well-being infuse her soul. She was now ready to exorcise her demons one by one. " I am not Marlene Dietrich," she continued. "I am not Marilyn Monroe. I am not Patsy Cline. I am not Ju-ju-ju ..."

This last admission was, by far, the most difficult. Taking another deep breath, she lowered her voice and looked herself square in the eyes. "I am not Judy Garland!" Now she was prepared to face the ultimate truth. Very slowly, enunciating each syllable, she declared, "My name is Kenneth Hoodwin. I was born on August 8, 1949, in North Shore General Hospital. And I am a muh-muh-muh ..."

But she couldn't finish the sentence without bursting into tears. As she collapsed on her bed, Bunny waddled in from the kitchen and crawled onto her lap. "Hoo. Hoo," the dog whined in deepest sympathy.

Taking one look at her, Sue Veneer was overcome by a grief so intense that she slid off the bed onto the hardwood floor. "I'll miss you. I'll miss you so much," she wailed. Taking Bunny's ridiculously large head in her hands, she rubbed her pointy ears and kissed her big flat face. "But don't you worry. Dennis told me he's found someone to take care of you. Yes! You remember that nice man who came over the other day? You … you …"

But Sue couldn't continue. The thought of leaving Bunny with Joel Eisenberg was almost too cruel to contemplate. "Oh, Bunny. Bunny!" Turning the bulldog on her back, she rubbed her belly and looked directly into her large, all-forgiving eyes. Sue thought about how lonely she'd been—how selfish. And through it all, Bunny had shown nothing but love and devotion for her petty, cross-dressing soul! In Bunny's eyes she was neither a man nor a woman. She was neither a hit nor a flop. She was but one cherished member of the entire human family. In that moment Sue Veneer got what she'd been seeking: the strength to go back to Long Island and take care of her mother. "Thank you, Bunny," she cooed to her animal guru. "Thank you so much."

Tap. Tap. Tap.

Bunny immediately jumped off Sue's lap and ran to the door. Suspecting who might be there, Sue Veneer groaned and reached for another hit of pot. She glanced around the room. The bed was made. The closet was emptied. She had only to give her replacement several last-minute instructions.

Tap. Tap. Tap.

"Coming!"

Pinching out her joint, Sue entered the kitchen and noticed Bunny seated on the floor and panting happily in anticipation. "To each his own," she muttered as she turned the knob and stepped aside to let Joel Eisenberg enter the room. He was wearing the same unbecoming spandex blouse he'd worn the week before.

Sue smiled grimly.

"Is Dennis here?" Joel asked.

"No, but he told me you were coming and he asked me to give you the lowdown."

Ignoring Joel's disappointed expression, Sue gestured to the kitchen counter and began lecturing. "My ride will be here in a few minutes, so very quickly: this is *la cuisine*. It has no dishwasher but it does have this big nasty sink. The counters are wood, which is absolutely ridiculous because they show every spot of grease. I've been trying to get Dennis to cover them for years. He used to clean them with turpentine and a little bit of Lysol. You will use this." Sue reached under the sink and grabbed a small yellow bottle. "Odorless mineral spirits. Guard this with your life!" Before Joel could say anything, Sue had shoved the bottle into his hands.

"The floor, as you can see, is also wood. It needs to be broom swept twice a day, and don't use anything on it except this—Murphy Oil Soap." Sue pointed to the china cabinet. "Don't be fooled," she said. "None of these dishes are as expensive as they look except for there on the top shelf. Under no circumstances should you ever touch that antique chamber pot! Somebody on the Mayflower pissed in it and it's worth a fortune. What else? Oh, yes—the farmer's market in Orleans gets fresh halibut every Thursday...."

"Halibut?"

"Dennis doesn't care for the cod."

"Why are we talking about fish?"

"You don't cook fish?"

"No."

"What do you cook?"

"I don't cook anything."

"Didn't Dennis say you would be making his meals?"

"No."

Sue rolled her eyes at the thought of how carelessly she was being replaced by Dennis. "Well," she concluded, "I guess Dennis will find some other way for you to earn your keep around here. Now follow me."

Sue picked up Bunny like an oversized clutch, marched into the bedroom, and flung wide the closet door. Pulling a trunk into the middle of the floor, she opened it and pointed to a sparkling pile of fabric. "Now, I've cleared everything out of this closet except for these old dresses. Bunny's pedigree papers are also in this trunk, along with her rabies vaccinations. Let me see now. You can keep whatever you like. You're a size fourteen, I believe; luckily some of these skirts have an elastic waistband. Everything else in this room stays as is. Don't change anything. Don't move anything. Your job is to take care of the dog while blending in with the decor. As for my baby, she loves veal but it gives her diarrhea. She will eat her dog food *only* if you sprinkle Parmesan cheese on top. She needs to be walked on the beach three times a day and she'll only shit in the tall grass. And I think that's all you need to know."

Much to Sue's chagrin, Bunny took this moment to drop from her lap, waddle across the room, and sit at Joel's feet. "We're going to be very happy together," Joel cooed. "Budgy. Budgy. Budgy."

Suffering her first pangs of the empty-nest syndrome, Sue bit her lip to keep from crying. "You're moving in when?" she asked.

"Um … tomorrow, I guess."

"Have you ever had a dog before?"

"No."

"But you're willing to make the commitment."

Joel nodded. Sue still didn't trust him.

"The only reason I worry is that last spring Dennis was … ahem … dating one of the houseboys here in town; he moved in to take care of Bunny. He, too, thought he'd be here a while and after they broke up Bunny wasn't walked for over a month. So if there's any chance you're going to want to leave …"

Joel shook his head. "I'm not going to leave."

"Well, just in case, I'll leave you my mother's phone number on Long Island." Finding a piece of pink notepaper in her travel bag, Sue began scribbling. "So are you in love with Dennis?" she asked nonchalantly as she laid the number on the end table.

"It's more complicated than that."

"I'll take that as a 'yes'?"

"The two of us are … well … very deeply connected," Joel explained.

It was time for a serious talk. Sue passed the joint to Joel. Joel hesitated. It had been years since he'd smoked pot. *When in Rome,* he figured, and he put the joint to his lips.

"Tell me then," Sue continued. "How are you two connected?"

"It's hard to explain," Joel replied as he inhaled.

"The only reason I ask," Sue said, looking at him with daggers in her eyes and leaning forward, "is because I love Bunny more than anything else in the world. And if something ever happens to her, I will come back here and kill you."

Joel coughed. Sue continued. "So before you make any grand pronouncements about how long you plan on staying here, let me first prepare you for what your life will be like. As you can see, this room is right below Dennis's bedroom. From experience I can tell you that six nights out of seven you will be awakened in the middle of the night by giggling on the stairway. You will hear the bed banging up against this wall and Dennis getting fucked by someone other than yourself. And there'll be nothing you can do about it because Dennis won't care what you think. You'll be living here only because you are useful. If Dennis does decide to allow you to accompany him to a bar, it will only be because he wants a homely companion who won't be any competition for whatever cute stud he is trying to pick up. On those nights, Dennis will most likely leave you at the bar and go home with whomever he pleases. You will then come back to this room, crawl into bed with Bunny, and wait anxiously for your master's return."

Joel hardly heard a word Sue was saying. Trying to figure out why she was being so negative, he squinted his eyes to see the color of her aura. He added up what he already knew about Sue: her attention to practical details, her love of old songs, her relationship with Bunny. Leaning forward in his chair, he looked Sue in the eyes, ignored her question, and asked, "I'm sorry to interrupt, but I really need to know. Are you a Capricorn?"

"Why the hell would you want to know my sign? Would you like to tell my future?"

"It's just that you seem a little upset."

Sue held up her arms. "I have a better idea," she announced. "Instead of you telling my future, I'll tell yours." With a great flourish, she pressed the back of her wrist to her forehead. "This is what I predict: I predict you will be miserable in this house. I predict that Dennis will never love you. I also predict that you will go on pretending that someday he will. Several times this summer, Dennis will do or say something really sweet to convince you not to leave. On those occasions, you'll start thinking, 'maybe if I'm a good little troll, he'll come downstairs and sit on my face,' or whatever it is you *really* want from him. Deeply connected? He's a tease, you idiot! Why do you think I come to Provincetown every year? To do a show at the Seaview Lounge? I knew I'd never make a dime in that dump! No, I came back here every summer for him. For him! Like a moth to the flame. Only I didn't get burned up. I dried up. I withered away. And you know the real reason I'm leaving? Because I'm sick of cooking for that son of a bitch. I'm sick of cleaning for him. I'm sick of wasting my time. Thanks to him, I lost my looks. I lost my sobriety. I lost my pride. And-when-you've-lost-it-here ..." Sue began bellowing to the tune of "New York! New York!" But before Sue could sing another note, she was distracted by gravel crunching on the sidewalk and a car's headlight illuminating her face. "My ride!" she announced as she dropped the roach on the floor and smeared it into a thin black line. Grabbing her powder-blue flight bag, she leaned through the window and waved to the driver. "Coming, darling!" On her way out the door, she spun around one last time and smiled at Joel. "Have a pleasant evening and, for all it's worth, my birthday is December 23. I was born on the cusp." Then touching her heart, she looked at Bunny, made her a silent promise, and ran out the door.

Chapter Fourteen

Joel blinked several times and looked around the room. *Good Lord,* he thought. *How will I ever blend into this decor?* It was a small, dark room, the kind of chamber in which an aspirant for the priesthood might self-flagellate. On the walls were nothing but an old map of the Massachusetts Bay Colony and a nautical chart of Cape Cod Bay. One faux oil lamp sat on a mahogany chest of drawers, glowing about as brightly as a burnt piece of coal. Across town the bell tower at the Unitarian Meeting Hall began to chime. Eleven bells. *Where was Dennis?*

Flopping down on the straw mattress, he inserted himself in a valley hollowed out by Sue Veneer's bony behind. In spite of the decor, he couldn't have been any happier. He couldn't believe he at last had wound up in the house of his Twin Flame, who also happened to have a really great ass—even better than that of Lucas Allison, who until the week before had been the gluteus gold standard. Brimming with excitement, Joel pulled down his pants, reached for his cock, and was just about to squirt all over himself when Bunny somehow managed to heave all twenty-five pounds of herself on top of him and lay her wrinkled head on his midsection.

"What do you want?" Joel asked.

Bunny cocked her head to the side.

"Do you need to go outside?"

Bunny cocked her head to the other side.

"Outside?" Joel repeated.

Bunny's expression didn't change. Feeling it was time to set some limits, Joel gave the dog a shove and she thudded to the floor. A second later, though, she was back with the same adoring look on her face.

"You really are a stupid ..."

But before Joel could finish his sentence, Bunny's tongue darted out of her mouth and slurped the side of his face. Joel tried to push her aside, but she dug her front claws into his chest.

"Ow!"

He was just about to try to give Bunny another lesson when he heard sounds coming from the kitchen. Click. Squeak. Somebody was coming in the door.

Hoping to lure Dennis into his room, he pulled up his pants and pretended to be asleep. Joel heard Dennis take a plate from the china cabinet. *Any second he'll come into this room and crawl into bed with me.* Joel rolled over on his side; his mind was racing.

Should I tell him that I'm his Twin Flame? And if I do, will we become lovers? Maybe not right away. After all, we live in different cities. Boyfriends, perhaps? But that would hardly describe the intensity of the bond we're bound to have. Fuck buddies? Not quite. Spiritual fuck buddies. We could travel between New York and Provincetown. We'll become an example for other gay men. Maybe we'll go down in gay history like Gore Vidal and Tennessee Williams. Or was it Gore Vidal and Truman Capote? Or maybe it was Truman Capote and Vidal Sassoon....

Joel heard footsteps on the stairs. Could it be that his host was going upstairs without so much as saying hello? His whole body went numb as he listened for Dennis's footsteps on the ceiling above his bed. He heard Dennis walking to the bathroom. Splash. He was turning on a faucet. Click. He was opening a medicine cabinet. There were a few moments of silence while Dennis took his pills, followed by more footsteps, a door being closed, and the headboard of a bed banging against the wall.

Joel pushed Bunny off his chest, ran into the kitchen, and up the stairs. With Bunny padding behind him, he opened the door, peeked into Dennis's studio, and saw what he was hoping to see— a thin line of light beneath the door leading into the artist's bedroom. Joel tapped on the door.

There was a brief pause, followed by, "Come in."

Joel pushed open the door and stepped inside a tiny cubicle containing a big brass bed and little else. And there was Dennis, lying on top of the white covers in blue striped pajamas, reading a manuscript by the light of a nearby lamp. As Joel entered, Dennis laid the pages on his chest, crossed his legs at his ankles, and waited patiently for his new employee to speak.

"Just get home?" Joel asked.

"Yep."

"I must have fallen asleep," Joel lied. "I didn't hear you come in."

There was an awkward pause. If Joel had expected Dennis to be happy to see him, he was sadly mistaken. The artist had just spent the evening listening to Rudy and the rest of the Sphincters mercilessly mocking his new housemate. The jokes had been nonstop and Dennis had come to the sad conclusion that Joel Eisenberg was fated to fill the perennial position of the one person in town that summer whom everybody would enjoy hating. Rudy would see to that. On the other hand, Dennis still needed someone to walk Bunny, so he continued to smile even as Joel sidled into the room and gingerly sat down at the foot of his bed.

"Have a good night?" Joel asked.

"Yep."

"What'd you do?"

Dennis held up the script he was reading. "Well, you were right about some guy coming into my life to help me with my career. Rudy wants me to be in his play."

"Great!" Joel recalled how much he detested Rudy.

"I hope I can remember my lines. Did Sue show you around?"

"Yeah."

There was another awkward pause while Dennis fervently hoped that Joel would leave and Joel fervently hoped that Dennis would invite him to spend the night in his bed. Hoping to break the impasse, Dennis picked up his script and resumed reading. Joel still didn't move.

"So … how's your body feeling since I balanced your energies?"

"Oh … great."

Joel swallowed. His throat was quite dry. "I … I could do a little work on you now."

"Rain check," Dennis replied as he calmly turned a page.

Joel stood up and started backing his way out of the room. Dennis was suddenly afraid he'd been a little too hard on his new employee. "Wait," he said. Joel stopped. "I might need a little help learning these lines."

"Sure."

Joel started back in the room. Dennis held up his hand. "But not tonight. Could you turn off all the lights in the kitchen before you leave the house?"

Joel closed the door behind him and took a deep breath.

That wasn't too bad, Joel thought to himself as he walked back to the Fore 'n' Aft. *Maybe it's a blessing in disguise that Dennis has been cast in Rudy's play. Dennis will need me now more than ever.* Who knew more about dialogue than he did? After all, he'd been to Hollywood. He'd filmed a TV pilot in a major studio. Back in New York he lived only a mile from the Great White Way. There were no accidents in the cosmos, and everything was unfolding just as it should.

Back in his room he masturbated twice before falling asleep, and a few times he was even certain his Twin Flame was thinking about him at the same time and wishing that he had asked him to share his bed.

Dennis Fairchild, of course, was thinking no such thing. As he turned off his lamp, he was thanking his lucky stars that a recent technology stock had earned more than enough money to allow him to take the summer off from painting those damn houses. He was also picturing himself onstage in his sexy Gestapo costume with the tight pants and wondering whether James would take one look at him and beg him to come back. As for Sue Veneer, he was glad she was gone—without all her fancy cooking he might finally be able lose those extra two pounds that had plagued him all winter and spring.

And it was this line of thinking that finally forced him to contemplate what to do about Joel Eisenberg. If he wouldn't be needed in the kitchen, what should he do to earn his keep? Earlier that evening he'd asked Bill Doyle to start sprucing up the yard and building a deck in preparation for the cast party in August. That's how Joel could pay his rent, he decided. He would help Bill Doyle build the outdoor deck; it would keep him outside and out of his hair, and everything would be just fine.

Chapter Fifteen

"Nam myoho renge kyo. Nam myoho renge kyo."

Three weeks later, Bunny opened her eyes and was surprised to find that Joel had already gotten out of bed and begun to chant. Laying her face on her paws, she stared at him adoringly. She loved him when he chanted. She loved him when he ate or slept. It was the smell of his crotch and the piles of dank clothes he left on the floor of the closet. There was something special about his touch, so tentative and yet so strong. There was something tantalizing about how he resisted before giving in and finally giving her a piece of his bagel. Sue Veneer had been OK, but she had to go out every night to do her show, while Joel never seemed to have anywhere to go or anyone he needed to be with. Best of all, whenever Joel walked her down the street, he always encouraged her to sniff other dogs' asses, especially if the owners had big butts and musky crotches. But Joel would never leave her to go home with another man. Joel never left her alone to be with anybody. *That's because he'd rather be with me,* Bunny told herself. *He loves me. That's why it will always be just me in his life. And it will always be me—just me—who gets to sleep with him in bed.*

Joel placed a card on the altar reading DISCOVER WHO
DENNIS IS SLEEPING WITH. He hadn't been allowed to give
Dennis a butt rub for over two weeks, and now he was upset
because Dennis was carrying on an affair so secret that not even
Louis Lustig, the editor of the *Provincetown Poop,* could guess the
identity of the new flame. Two nights ago, Joel had been awakened
by giggling on the steps and footsteps on the ceiling. A yellow
bicycle had been left leaning against the outside wall, and Joel had
resolved to wake up early the next morning to discover its owner's
identity. But by the time he had arisen, the bike was gone. The next
night, the bicycle reappeared, but this time Joel had set the alarm
for seven and was out of bed in plenty of time to catch the intruder
before he could make his escape. It was now almost nine. Joel got
up and peeked out his door into the kitchen to make sure he had a
clear view of the stairs.

"Pghh. Pghh." Bunny was snorting to go outside.

"Not now."

Bunny assumed Joel was playing hard to get. "Pghh. Pghh," she
repeated seductively, rubbing her face against his legs. Joel refused
to move, so she started running around him in nervous little circles. Joel groaned and grabbed the leash from atop the bureau.
"Good god. It's bad enough I have to take orders from Dennis and
Bill."

"Hoo, hoo," Bunny panted happily.

"All right. But we have to be quick."

Stepping into the kitchen, Joel opened the door and pointed to a
nearby hedge. "Go!" he ordered. But Bunny wouldn't budge. Joel
knew from experience she wouldn't move until he actually started
walking with her to the beach. He slipped on a pair of flip-flops and
peered through the kitchen door into the yard, making sure Bill
Doyle wasn't waiting to pounce on him and drag him into another

torturous day of hard labor in the hot sun. He vaguely recalled Bill's telling him that this was the morning he wanted to start building an outside deck for the upcoming cast party, and the last thing Joel needed was to be enslaved by a horny handyman who stared at his *tuchis* every time he bent over to pick up a shovel. For four days he'd managed to avoid the guy; hoping to make it five, he scooped up Bunny, scurried across the yard, and ran down the street to the nearest entrance to the beach. He tossed her in the sand. "Hurry up!" he ordered the dog, who was happily sniffing every blade of grass, looking for the perfect place to drop her precious little turds. "Come on," Joel groaned, anxious to get back before Dennis's mystery date vanished.

Bill Doyle, meanwhile, had seen Joel sneaking across the yard and was quickly getting dressed to follow him to the beach. That first night when Joel had broken their date, he was sorely disappointed, but since then he'd been thrilled to have the astrologer at his beck and call. Bill was quite proud of his skills and anxious to show off what he knew. And Joel looked so damn much like Mitchell, especially from behind, whenever the astrologer had to climb a ladder.

Their first day together had been pleasant enough, working side by side to clean out the gutters. The next day, though, Joel had begun to show an insubordinate streak when Bill tried to give him extensive directions about weeding. Joel had claimed to know what he was doing but as soon as Bill's back was turned, he accidentally ripped out three square yards of periwinkle. When Bill saw the devastation, he remained calm and vowed to give Joel more detailed directions in the future.

The next day he spent a whole hour patiently showing Joel how to paint the window trim in long, smooth strokes. Unfortunately, as soon as Bill went to the store for turpentine, Joel splashed latex paint all over the window, and it took Bill yet another hour to scrape off the astrologer's handiwork. Unwilling to admit defeat, Bill still believed he could make a helpmate out of Joel. Mitchell's ghost, however, had some serious doubts. He tried to warn Bill as he laced up his boots and ran to get Joel.

"There might be a better way of seducing him than forcing him to work in the yard."

"It's his job."

"Are you sure you're not trying to torture him because he might like Dennis better than you?"

"Nah! I'm the kind of guy he needs."

"You know, you did the same thing to me when we bought the house upstate. Every weekend you drove me crazy."

"It was good for you. You were sexy when you worked outside."

"No. I was sexy because I was obeying your orders. Face it. You like to push us around."

"Mind your own business."

Bill caught up with Joel while he was still waiting for Bunny to shit.

"Hey!" he called.

Joel turned and saw Bill coming toward him. *Ah, crap,* he thought to himself as Bill pasted a seductive smile.

"Listen," Bill said, "I was wondering if you were going to be able to give me a hand today?"

"You know ... I'd ... I'd rather not."

"It'll take two of us to saw those beams."

"I've got some writing to do."

Bill's smile started to vanish from his face. Taming Joel would be harder than he'd thought.

"I ... uh ... didn't want to say this, but Dennis told me I could rely on you to give me a hand."

Hearing Dennis's name made Joel bristle with annoyance. "Well, I think I've done enough work in the yard this month. Last week, I spent the whole day painting the trim."

"Actually you spent twenty minutes making a mess. I spent the whole day cleaning it up."

Joel sighed and looked heavenward. Between Bunny's constipation and Bill's unreasonable demands, he'd never get back to the house in time to find out the owner of the yellow bicycle.

"Listen, Bill," he responded with his knuckles planted firmly in his hips, "you and I both know you can do this work ten times faster than me. So why not just save time and do it yourself?"

"I think you're being lazy."

"I'm not lazy. I just have issues about wasting my time," Joel answered, scurrying to the mound of tall grass where Bunny had finally decided to poop. "And I didn't want to say this but the only reason you're hassling me is that … well, I think you have a crush on me." Joel bent down and scooped Bunny's poop into a plastic bag. Bill's jaw hardened into a fearsome scowl.

"Just forget it," he replied. "I'll tell Dennis to find somebody else, and with any luck he'll throw you out of the house."

Bill turned and walked away. Joel panicked. Carrying his little shit purse, he ran after Bill, who was marching back to the house.

"Wait! Wait!" he cried. "Don't say anything to Dennis. Seriously— I'll make some time to help you out."

"I'll do the job myself."

"OK, but just remember, I offered. So if you talk to Dennis, I did offer to help."

Bill turned, looked into Joel's eyes, and saw nothing but his desperation for another man. It suddenly became clear to him. Joel wasn't Mitchell and he never would be. Although Joel looked and acted just his like ex-lover, he had none of Mitchell's sweetness or generosity of spirit. He'd been barking up the wrong tree and now he wanted nothing more than a good stiff drink to fortify himself for the rest of the day. "Don't worry," he called over his shoulder. "I won't squeal on you."

Joel walked to the nearest garbage pail and tossed out Bunny's poop. He felt relieved because he believed Bill to be a man of his word. But he was suddenly feeling sad, too. He hadn't done anything wrong. He'd set his boundaries and been rewarded by being excused from any further yard work. Could it be, he wondered, that even though he wasn't physically attracted to Bill, he'd grown to admire his character and he hated to disappoint him?

Before Joel could ponder this mystery any further, he saw that the yellow bicycle was no longer leaning against the wall: Dennis's fuck buddy had made his escape. Joel ran into the kitchen and looked around to see if he could find any clues. Nothing had been touched.

"Pffgh. Pffgh." Bunny was sniffing something near the steps. Acting on a whim, Joel picked her up and quietly tiptoed up the steps to Dennis's studio. Stopping at the entrance, he looked around. The door to the artist's bedroom was closed and Joel could vaguely make out the sound of the artist snoring.

Sneaking over to Dennis's desk, Joel found what he was looking for. On top of the artist's script for *Shut Your Von Trapp!* was a five-word, misspelled missive scribbled in a shaky hand: SEE U AT REHERSAL. Whoever had spent the night with Dennis was part of the theater company. But who? *A. J. O'Hara who played the Baroness? Ida Dream? The illiterate fool hasn't signed his own damn note.*

"Pffgh. Pffgh." Bunny was snorting as she sniffed the paper. Following Bunny's lead, Joel held the note up to his own nose. The aroma was unmistakable.

Patchouli.

• • •

"You know, Shelly … go fuck yourself!"

Lucas hung up the phone and hyperventilated. He couldn't believe he'd just cursed out the artistic director of the Liberty Street Players. "Damn it!" he said.

It was bad enough that the only musical theater job in New York he could get that summer was with a touring children's theater based in Bedford-Stuyvesant. And that because of his slight stature, he'd been forced to play all the rodents. And that his Rupert the Rabbit in Shelley Levy-Posner's original adaptation of *The Ugly Duckling* had been lambasted in the *Fort Green Community News* as "gratuitously fey." Through all these indignities he'd smiled through gritted teeth, even when it meant smiling through forty pounds of fake fur in ninety-degree heat while being pelted with Raisinettes at P. S. 64 in Brownsville. *The show must go on,* he'd told himself. And all this he'd endured because he'd been promised the role of the Prince Charming in *Cinderella*. But then to lose that role to Jason Posner-Levy, Shelley's tone-deaf eighteen-year-old son. That was the last straw. *Fuck her, fuck her company, and fuck her no-talent son.*

Lucas searched for and found the bag of M&M's he'd hidden in the freezer behind a bottle of vodka. It was moments like this that made him yearn to go back to Provincetown and be close to Oscar. *Oh, god, ours was a love affair like no other,* he recalled. The whole week had been magical, and best of all had been their last night together—a rainy night when they rode their bicycles to the beach, huddled beneath the lifeguard stand, and he'd serenaded Oscar with "There's a Place for Us" from *West Side Story* (the Aretha Franklin version). That had been the night they'd vowed to stay true to each other forever and ever no matter what. Lucas put down his M&Ms and considered calling Oscar to tell him that he wanted to come back to the Cape for the rest of the summer. But he hesitated. He hadn't even the money for a bus ticket. Oscar hadn't called in several days, and during their last conversation there'd been some awkwardness, as though his Latin lover had a secret he wasn't telling.

Suddenly the phone rang. Lucas grabbed it. "Hello?"

"Hey!"

The sound of Joel's voice reminded him that not everything in Provincetown had been magical. They hadn't spoken since that night he'd snuck out of the Fore 'n' Aft. He prepared himself for a scolding.

"How you been?" Joel asked.

"Great!"

"How's the theater treating you? Are you acting in anything?"

"Actually, no. I'm not acting in anything right now." There was an awkward pause. "How are you enjoying being back in New York?" Lucas finally asked.

"I'm not back in New York," Joel replied.

"You're not?"

"No. A living situation fell into my lap and I decided to stay in Provincetown for the summer."

"You're kidding. Wow. I'm so jealous."

"Didn't Oscar tell you I was up here?"

Lucas grew cautious. The last thing he wanted to admit was that when he and Oscar communicated it was primarily for the purpose of phone sex; Joel Eisenberg's name would hardly have crossed their lips. "I ... I haven't spoken to him," Lucas responded.

"That's funny. I saw him today. He says you talk all the time."

"Where'd you see him?"

"In front of the Crown and Anchor. We talked for a few minutes.

He told me how much he misses you. It was really sweet. You know, I've been meaning to call you. I just wanted to make sure you didn't think I was still angry at you."

"Oh? Well … I did think that … a little."

"I'll admit it," Joel continued. "I was a little upset at first that you ran off, but I do have to take some of the blame. I did have some ulterior motives when we came up here."

Lucas was stunned by Joel's vulnerability. "Thanks for admitting that," Lucas replied.

"The point is … well … that it's all in the past and I just want to say again … well … how thankful I am that after all we've been through, that you and I can still be friends."

"Aw. That's very sweet of you."

"And when I was talking to Oscar today … how can I say this? I was really moved at how deeply he cares for you. It's like you know how everybody thinks gay men are so shallow? How we can't be loyal or love each other deeply? It's not true. It really isn't. So after I talked to him, I was so inspired I came home and did your zodiac charts. I did a composite chart for the two of you, and guess what? You two were really made for each other. I've never seen two charts so well matched."

There was a brief pause while Lucas remembered everything he liked about Joel. For all his faults, he was still a brilliant astrologer and not completely untrustworthy. Lucas was even able to recall some of the excitement and hopefulness he felt when meeting Joel, those first few days before the astrologer got all sour and needy. And since Joel had just been so kind to him, it was his turn as a fair and balanced Libra to offer an olive branch in return. "I … I have to admit," he said. "When I first heard your voice, I thought you were calling me up to yell at me. What can I say? I'm really glad you're in my life."

"Friends?" Joel asked.

"Absolutely," Lucas replied.

"So when are you coming back to Provincetown?"

"I have no plans."

"Aw. Come soon. I know Oscar misses you terribly."

"I miss him—and you, too. But I have an audition Wednesday for *Pool Boys on Parade*."

"So come on Thursday."

Lucas creased his brow. It didn't make sense to him that Joel was trying to bring him to Provincetown unless he had a hidden agenda—like Joel wanting another shot at his booty.

"You know," Lucas said with a sigh, "I'd love to come, but, well, I'm embarrassed to say this. I don't even have the money for transportation. I just paid a shitload of bills, and I only have thirty dollars to last me until Monday."

There was another brief pause, this time while Lucas waited to see how much cash his old friend would cough up for the privilege of having him once again near.

Chapter Sixteen

Two days later, Oscar Gonzalez aka Patchouli ran out of his house on Cemetery Road and jumped into his rented van. He was a few minutes late picking up whatever patrons had signed up for his latest business venture, the Provincetown Artist's Excursion, during which for a mere forty dollars, he provided his customers with two small canvases, five tubes of paint, an easel, and some rudimentary lessons in landscape painting. In reality, Oscar Gonzalez knew almost nothing about the subject he was teaching. He still mixed his colors on the canvas and he believed in the kind of free expression that resulted in paintings of blue roses and purple trees, but Oscar's lack of experience in any given field was the last thing that would have stopped him from teaching it to others. He was, by nature, a freewheeling Piscean who, as soon as he achieved anything close to expertise, would immediately abandon that endeavor for something else at which he wasn't any good.

In this regard, being absolutely gorgeous was both a help and a hindrance. There were always some older gay men around who would get him started on anything his heart desired. And there was always another older gay guy around who would flatter him and seduce him into trying something new. By the time he arrived in P-Town that summer, he'd already been a child actor in a Venezuelan soap opera, a dancer in a teenage tango competition, a makeup artist for the most famous drag queen in South America, a hair stylist for rich women in Miami Beach, and a singer of traditional Incan folk songs in an off-off-Broadway show. The idea of becoming a painter had never even occurred to him until Memorial Day weekend, when he'd eaten some psychedelic mushrooms and gone for a bicycle ride in the Provincelands with an art professor from Brown University. This man had convinced him that his true talent was not really acting, but rather translating the beauty of nature into the beauty of acrylics— which, for a beginner like Oscar, would be so much easier than oils.

And this was the main reason Oscar had been drawn to Dennis Fairchild. He'd been eager to know everything Dennis knew about painting, and it was during one of their late-night discussions about perspective that the two men fell into a hot, sweaty embrace. He hadn't wanted to cheat on Lucas, but Dennis Fairchild was every-thing he wanted to be all wrapped up in the body of the sexiest white boy in town. Dennis was disciplined. Dennis was focused. Most of all, Dennis Fairchild was a brand that made money. Their first two nights together, he pumped Dennis for advice. Where should he take his students? How should he advertise? How much should he charge? Strangely enough, in spite of Oscar's monu-mental lack of experience, Dennis was quite sanguine about his chances. His only advice was to flyer shirtless and charge no more than a tourist might pay for an erotic massage. He also counseled Oscar to praise his students extravagantly and to bring a few bottles of chardonnay with him on every excursion.

On this particular morning, though, Oscar was feeling a little shaky. For the past three nights his dearly departed *abuelita* had been coming to him in his dreams and warning him against cheating on Lucas. Not one to discount a message from the spirit world, Oscar was nevertheless uncertain about his future with the young actor. He dearly loved Lucas, but the guy had even less money than he had. It wasn't that Oscar Gonzalez was a gold digger: he just felt that when it came to money, mixed marriages worked best, and at least one half of a gay couple should be loaded with cash. Lucas had been fine as a fling, but long term, Oscar had a hard time seeing it work. *Only time will tell,* he counseled himself as he shifted into second gear with one hand and used the other hand to slip off his tank top. It was showtime.

As he pulled to the curb, he did a quick inventory of who had shown up that day and how many more curious passersby he might corral into his van. There was the older couple from Columbus, Ohio, he'd met at the tea dance. *Eighty dollars.* There was the friend of Aida Lott's, another frustrated fatty sucking down an ice cream cone. *Forty dollars.* There were also three lesbians who might actually believe they'd learn something useful from him. *They might be trouble, but well worth a hundred and twenty bucks.* And finally there was a small man with a bulldog. *The dog looks familiar but ...*

Oh, no! Joel Eisenberg was the last person he wanted to see that morning. This was the man who was once in love with Lucas, and he was probably only there to spy on him and nail him for cheating.

"Good morning, everybody," Oscar cheerfully announced as he jumped out of the van. Sliding open the passenger door, he pulled out his change purse and went to work. "What a great-looking bunch we got here," he chirped as he shoved a couple of twenties into his wallet. Joel, meanwhile, went to the back of the line. He'd tried to speak to Oscar the night before in front of Spiritus, but the Latin Lothario had avoided him like a stale matzoh.

"I hope it's OK to bring the dog," he asked sweetly as he reached the front of the line. "She just hates to be left alone."

"No problem," answered Oscar, determined to appear unperturbed. "I didn't know you liked to paint."

"I got bit by the bug living in Dennis's house," Joel replied.

"Oh, right," Oscar answered, still playing dumb. "You live with Dennis Fairchild."

"You know, you ought to drop by sometime."

"I will do that," Oscar answered without missing a beat.

As Joel boarded, he handed Oscar a twenty and a ten.

"Forty dollars," Oscar corrected him gently.

"The brochure said thirty."

"There's a ten-dollar fee for materials."

"Oh, right. Right."

Joel reached in his pocket and pulled out another ten. Oscar responded by giving him a broad smile and a plastic bag filled with paint tubes and brushes.

As the van pulled away from the curb, Joel grumbled to himself about how much money he'd already spent on Lucas, but he had no other choice. Lucas would be arriving the next day and he wanted to make sure Oscar greeted him with open arms and a stiff erection.

"Our first stop will be the beech forest," Oscar explained as the van crossed Route Six and entered the national seashore. A few minutes later, they pulled into a shady parking lot and Joel was hiking with the others on a trail leading into a leafy oasis surrounded on all sides by sand dunes and scrub pines. Their destination was a large lake in the middle of the forest covered with white lily pads. The lilies had blossomed, the trees were filled with songbirds, and the ground was covered with bright green moss. It was an idyllic spot, but all Joel noticed were the mosquitoes, and he might have gone back to the van if one of the lesbians hadn't pulled a large can of bug repellant out of her fanny pack and doused him from head to foot. With Oscar's assistance, the group set up their easels facing the lake.

In order to avoid the dragonflies, Joel set up his easel on the ridge furthest from the water, where he could observe Oscar flitting from person to person and gushing over every one of his pupil's brush-strokes. It was clear Oscar was trying to avoid talking to him, so out of boredom, Joel threw back his wine and began to doodle. A half hour later he'd painted a white lily, but it looked more like a toilet bowl than a flower.

"Very nice! The next time you can use a color—whatever you feel." Oscar had decided he couldn't avoid Joel any longer without causing comments among his other students. He handed Joel a cup and started filling it with wine.

"I talked to Lucas two nights ago," Joel mentioned nonchalantly.

"You did?" Oscar replied. He was suddenly scared that Joel had already snitched on him.

"He misses you a lot," Joel continued as he sipped his wine.

"I miss him."

"I mean, he *really* misses you." Oscar didn't respond. "Have you spoken to him?" Joel asked as he dipped his brush in water.

"Not in a few days."

"You should call him. His children's theater thing ended. He didn't tell you that?" Oscar was silent. "I wasn't exactly thrilled when Lucas ran off with you that night," the astrologer continued, "but last night I did your zodiac charts, and you two are made for each other."

"You did my chart?"

"Lucas told me your birthday," Joel lied, "and it looks like you two will be together for a very long time." Joel paused just long enough to let what he had said sink in. "The only problem," he continued, "is that you're going through Neptune transit to your Venus."

"Which means?"

"Something's happening to you that feels very good—but it's not real. I think somebody's lying to you." Oscar quietly watched Joel paint. "I also did Dennis's chart," Joel casually mentioned over his shoulder. "His Neptune is right on your descendant."

"Which means?"

"He's the one who's been lying to you."

Oscar swallowed hard. "Why would Dennis lie to me?"

"He wants to have sex with you but he's in love with somebody else. So, if I were you, and I had to choose between Dennis and Lucas, I would choose Lucas."

Oscar's Latin temper suddenly started to simmer.

"You know, this is none of your business. And you're the last person to give me advice. Lucas told me how you give advice."

"I'm sorry. You're right."

Before Oscar could say another word, Aida Lott's fat friend motioned for Oscar to come over and critique his painting. Oscar hesitated. He leaned into Joel and whispered, "Have you said anything to Lucas?"

Joel shook his head.

"Don't say anything, please. OK?"

Joel nodded as he painted. "There's one more thing I need to tell you. Lucas is coming up to see you tomorrow. He just spent his last few dollars buying a bus ticket."

"What time tomorrow?"

"He's on the eight thirty bus. He wanted to surprise you."

"Dios mío."

Oscar got down on his knees before Joel, who continued to paint. "Listen, I just want you to know, I love Lucas. I really do."

"I know," Joel murmured sympathetically.

"Why do I do these things?" he asked himself.

"Pisceans are very romantic and they get swept away so easily. But as Lucas's friend, I'd hate to see him hurt."

Oscar heard his name being called. Looking down to the lake, he saw one of the lesbians pointing to her Styrofoam cup, demanding a refill. Oscar's eyes darted about in their sockets.

"I changed my mind," he whispered to Joel with fear in his eyes. "I need to talk to you tonight."

Joel nodded.

"I need advice. I definitely need advice about what I should do."

"I'd love to," Joel assured Oscar.

"But whatever you do, please do not say anything to Lucas."

Joel nodded and watched contentedly as Oscar scurried over to the lesbian and poured her some wine. Later that day, Oscar drove the entire group to Hatches Harbor where everybody painted lovely little pictures of the lighthouse, most of which got thrown away before the end of the day.

Chapter Seventeen

As Joel got out of the van, Oscar pressed a note into his hand and mouthed the words "eight o'clock." Joel nodded discreetly, but as soon as he could, he ripped open the paper and found Oscar's exact address on Cemetery Road. Lucas had already told him about Oscar's dead grandmother who haunted him from the grave, so he knew it wouldn't be too hard to scare him back into Lucas's arms by making it sound like his advice was coming from the spirit world.

As Joel approached the house with Bunny, he was surprised to see that a big pile of lumber that had been sitting beside the lane earlier that morning was now a raised deck covering the yard between the front and back sections of Dennis's el-shaped house. Apparently Bill had succeeded in getting Blossom Selkow, the loudmouthed bartender at the Vixen, to help him, because there was no way he could have built this patio by himself in only one afternoon. Joel stopped to admire Bill's work as he stepped up onto the deck and approached the kitchen door. He was awed by the handyman's competence but also worried that Dennis had seen Bill working all day without him.

Joel's nervousness only intensified when he entered the house and saw Dennis scrubbing out the sink. The day before he'd asked Joel to clean up everything in the kitchen. "Wow. The deck looks great," Joel exclaimed, hoping to start the conversation on a positive note.

"Yep," Dennis said without turning around.

Joel was devastated, assuming that Dennis's lack of eye contact was the artist's way of showing that he was displeased. "Let me finish that," Joel offered, stepping forward to take the scrub brush out of Dennis's hand.

"I'm done," Dennis curtly replied, carelessly tossing the brush under the sink, turning his back on Joel, and walking up the stairs.

Joel felt a chill up his spine. All his scheming with Oscar would get him nothing if Dennis sent him packing. Joel ran the faucet and filled up Bunny's water dish. At least he'd been taking good care of the dog. Then he paused and tried to decide whether to go up to the studio for a friendly chat with his host. He'd been in the house three weeks and he suspected that this wasn't an ideal time to initiate a conversation with the artist, who usually woke up at noon, was somewhat congenial at lunch, went into funk until sunset, and only really came alive at night. It was now 5:00 P.M.—the putzing hour, when Dennis usually moped around his house, cleaned an old paintbrush, or glumly rehung a painting.

But it seemed to Joel he hadn't any choice. Holding Bunny as a shield, Joel quietly climbed the stairs and crossed Dennis's studio to the bedroom, where he found him seated at the edge of his bed rubbing Bengay into his fingers. His script for *Shut Your Von Trapp!* was right beside him.

"Sorry about the sink. I was planning to do a major cleaning tonight while you were at rehearsal." Dennis winced from the pain in his fingers. "Your joints are acting up?" Joel asked.

"A little."

"Didn't you take your pills this morning?"

Dennis nodded toward an empty container on his night table. "I ran out," he said.

"I could go to Adams Pharmacy later and refill your prescription. You know what else I can do? I can put two pills out for you every morning with your orange juice. That way I can keep track of when you're running low." Dennis winced again. "Here, let me do that," Joel suggested.

Before Dennis could protest, Joel tossed Bunny to the floor, sat down on the bed next to Dennis, and reached for his hand. "There we go. Just close your eyes and relax." Dennis did what he was told and Joel felt immensely grateful and relieved. For the time being he and Dennis were back where they had started, with Joel massaging the artist's hands and feeling like anything was possible between them. "How are rehearsals going?" Joel asked.

Dennis shook his head but didn't answer. After a moment he asked in a pleading tone of voice, "What's my horoscope going to be like the day the show opens?"

"Great. Jupiter will be right on your mid-heaven."

Dennis opened his eyes. "You sure? Because I've got to be good in this."

Joel was taken aback by Dennis's vulnerability. "You'll be fine," Joel said reassuringly.

Dennis pulled back his hand and reached for the script. "Rudy just rewrote the final scene between me and Maria. Tell me what you think."

"You don't like it?" Joel asked.

"Don't tell anyone. But I just don't think it's funny."

Joel quietly rejoiced. There'd been several rehearsals at the house and none of the dialogue had sounded all that hilarious to him, either. He turned to the scene in question, consisting of several pages dutifully lined with a yellow marker. He read it to himself and groaned at the bad puns. "You might be able to make this funny," he concluded.

"Oh, no." Dennis put his head in his hands. "It's terrible, isn't it?"

"It's not that bad. How are you going to play it?"

"You want me to show you? I could use some feedback."

"Sure," Joel replied, always anxious for any opportunity to prove himself indispensable to Dennis.

Dennis grabbed the script and pulled Joel into the studio. He was suddenly vibrant and filled with nervous energy. "I'll play the scene the way Rudy directed me, OK? And you tell me if it's any good."

As Joel studied the script, Dennis tried to relax using the old actor's trick of wiggling his hands and rolling his neck. "Now remember," he said. "I'm playing it different from the movie, so don't be surprised if I get a little rough with you."

"Rough?" Joel asked. He could feel himself getting hard.

"OK," Dennis announced. "Here's the situation. I've just caught Maria trying to escape the convent. We're alone onstage. It's dark. In the movie, Rolf faces down the Captain, but in this version I'm holding the gun on Maria. You're Maria." Dennis grabbed a spray bottle off the desk. "You ready?"

Joel nodded. Dennis pointed the spray bottle at Joel and began to recite in a loud Austrian accent. "I've got you now, you sassy *schweinhund!*"

Joel was temporarily distracted by the force of Dennis's performance.

"Do you see where I am?" the artist asked.

"Oh … yeah … um …" Joel looked down at his script. Conjuring Julie Andrews, he cried out in a proper English falsetto, "Rolf! How did you find us?"

Dennis moved closer and poked the spray bottle in Joel's ribs.

"Sister Helga squealed."

"That Bavarian bigmouth!"

"Did you really think you and those untalented brats could … could … could what?" Dennis asked, needing a line.

"Escape the Gestapo," Joel whispered.

"Let me start again. Did you really think that you and those untalented brats could escape the Gestapo? Say your prayers, my lesbian *Liebchen*."

"Go ahead and shoot me," Joel trilled.

"But before you die, you must kiss me," Dennis demanded.

"I'd rather piss in my spaetzle!"

Dennis moved in, grabbed Joel by the waist, and bent him back over the desk. "I saw how you checked out my lederhosen. Forget about those rotten kids and come away with me. You and I together—our children will rule the world for the next thousand years."

With his heart in his throat, Joel glanced at his script and yelled back at him, "You're barking up the wrong schnitzel."

Dennis pressed himself even closer and snarled, "Do you not yearn for a taste of the master race?"

"Nein!" Joel cried.

Upping the ante, Dennis shoved his fist between Joel's legs. "Do you not lie in bed at night wondering what it would be like to feel the full force of the Reich?" Then he grabbed Joel by the hair and kissed him hard on the lips. Joel might have enjoyed it if Dennis weren't also violently twisting his arm behind his back.

Pushing Dennis away, he cried out with surprising gusto. "You call that a blitzkrieg? Well, you may have rolled over Poland but you ain't rolling over me. Sooner or later we're going to win this war and all you bastards in brown shirts will have to go out and buy some new blouses."

"Now, grab my gun," Dennis whispered.

Reaching out with his free hand, Joel tried to pull the spray bottle away from Dennis. They struggled and were soon within spitting distance of each other.

"Fight me for it," Dennis exclaimed through gritted teeth.

"I *am,*" Joel replied. Using every last ounce of his strength, he finally managed to yank the "gun" away. "Auf Wiedersehen. Pow! Pow! Pow!"

"Ach, du Lieber!" Dennis cried out. Riddled with water drops, he stumbled backwards and died quite dramatically in the middle of the floor. Bunny waddled over to sniff her master's inert body.

"Scene!" Dennis exclaimed, as he pulled himself up and leaned against his desk. "What do you think?" he asked. "The accent? Was it OK?"

Joel appeared to think. "Yeah, sure."

"What about the acting? What did you think of my performance?"

Joel's first impulse was to tell him how sexy he had been as Rolf, but he paused. He relished Dennis's vulnerability and wanted to extend the moment. The artist took note of Joel's hesitation. He put his head in his hands and groaned. "What was I thinking? I can't do this."

"Sure you can."

"No, Joel. You don't understand. Do you have any idea how many people there are in this town who are just waiting for me to fall flat on my face?"

"So?"

"I can't do it." Dennis hung his head and groaned.

"Dennis, you're not impressing me with your self-pity. You forget. I'm the ass-trologer. If I can show my face every day on the street, you can get onstage and recite some corny dialogue. For every person who thinks you're ridiculous, there's going to be one who thinks you're hilarious and three who think you're the sexiest little Nazi they've ever seen. OK?"

Dennis smiled. Joel reached out and rubbed the back of his neck.

"Besides, you just might be able to make something out of this."

"How?"

"By not trying to be funny. As stupid as these lines are, they'll be kind of funny if you play them for real."

"How do I do that?"

Joel gave the matter some thought. "Rudy's directed you to be a cartoon. All I saw was anger."

"Isn't Rolf supposed to be angry?"

"Yes, Rolf is angry. For a reason. It's like you and James. I know you're pissed at him for moving to New Hampshire, but that's only because—I hope you don't mind my saying this—you're still in love with him."

Dennis nodded his head thoughtfully.

"So let's do this again, but instead of playing every line like you're pissed off, play them like you love Maria. And play all the emotions you feel when you love somebody. Passion. Desperation. Need."

Dennis stopped to think and Joel could tell that he'd gotten under his skin. He was intoxicated by the power he felt. Joel picked up the script and scanned a page. "Even though you're holding a gun on Maria, you don't want to kill her. You want to seduce her. You only decide to kill her because she rejects you."

A light bulb went off over Dennis's head. "You're right!"

Joel nodded his head emphatically—if there was one thing he knew, it was the fine line between adoration and the desire for revenge. "Now go ahead," he said. "Use this line to win my heart."

Dennis started to stand up. Joel touched his arm to keep him near him by the desk. "Stay here. Make it intimate."

With a knowing smile, Dennis prepared himself for the challenge. He pushed Joel back on the desk, leaned over him, and spoke in a throaty whisper. "Do you not lie in bed at night wondering what it would be like to feel the full force of the Reich?"

Yes, yes! Joel found himself thinking. *I lie awake in bed night after night thinking about nothing else.*

"Well?" Dennis was asking.

"Wonderful," Joel replied in a reverential whisper.

Dennis jumped up and paced the room excitedly. "Oh, my god. You were right. That's exactly what the scene needed. I need to rethink my entire performance. Fuck Rudy. You've finally given me some direction that makes sense. Thank you," he said, staring gratefully into the astrologer's eyes. Joel realized that this was the happiest moment of his summer.

"Would you like a back rub before we do anymore?" Joel asked.

Dennis looked at Joel mischievously. "You think that would help me relax?"

"It might help me relax."

"It might put me to sleep."

"Then I might have to slap you and wake you up."

Dennis considered the offer and seemed just about to say yes when ...

"Honk! Honk!"

Outside on the street, somebody was calling Dennis's name. "Get your ass out here, you little Nazi!"

Running to the window, Dennis stuck his head out and shouted, "I'll be right there!" He turned to Joel. "I forgot. It's Rudy and some of the guys. We're going to the beach to watch the sunset and light a bonfire."

"Great," Joel replied.

Dennis scrunched his face guiltily. "I'd love to invite you, but the car is pretty full."

"That's OK," Joel replied manfully.

Dennis went into his bedroom and changed while Joel looked out the window and saw the theater director driving a bright red convertible Mustang with two muscular cuties, one in the passenger seat and the other one in the back. Joel had heard that Rudy had recently dumped Keith. Could he and Dennis be double-dating? Joel heard footsteps and turned to see Dennis running across the room wearing a light jacket over his white T-shirt. He stopped as he was about to head down the stairs.

"Thanks for helping me with my lines!" he said. "I'm definitely going to use your direction tonight when we rehearse."

"Great!"

"Oh, and please keep it quiet about directing me. I'll try to make Rudy think it was his idea to play it that way."

"Fine."

Dennis paused. Sensing that Joel would appreciate a reward, he gave him one of his very best smiles. Then, without another word, he ran down the stairs, and Joel went back to the window and looked down just in time to see Dennis running across his brand new deck and jumping into the backseat of the car beside one of the beauties. Rudy made a snide remark that Joel couldn't quite hear, everybody laughed, and the car sped away.

"Pghh! Pghh!" Bunny was rubbing her head against his pants. Joel picked her up and carried her downstairs to his room where for the next two hours he studied Oscar's zodiac chart and carefully planned his strategy for later that night.

Chapter Eighteen

On a typical summer evening, Provincetown is so crowded that it seems you have to wait in line to walk down Commercial Street. Shirtless gay men jostle for space with lesbian couples who get stuck behind straight families with kids. Everybody's crammed close yet oddly, the gay men only see the other gay men, the lesbians only see their friends, the straight couples only see their kids, and the kids only see saltwater taffy and french fries. The only time these different groups see each other is when they accidentally collide, at which point the gay man might mutter to himself, "That fat dyke walks so slow"; the lesbian might grumble, "Those breeders can't control their kids"; and the straight couple might wonder why they hadn't gone to Martha's Vineyard.

Very few of these tourists, however, will ever leave this beaten path and walk three blocks north to an old cemetery where the town has been burying its dead since colonial times. Covering the gentle hills are dozens of wafer-thin tombstones tilting at forty-five-degree angles as though exhausted from having stood there so long. It was right beside this consecrated ground that Oscar Gonzalez

had found an old cottage in the far corner of a Portuguese family's
yard. However shallow Oscar appeared to others, he regularly pondered the imponderables, and the nearness of the graveyard seemed
to spur him to do his best thinking. Tonight, as he patiently waited
for Joel, he was thinking about his grandmother and lighting a
candle in front of a sepia-tinged photograph taken shortly after her
marriage.

Since *abuelita's* death earlier that year, her favorite grandson
Oscar, had draped this portrait in black chiffon and used it like
the Oracle of Delphi. This was the woman who had raised him
after his own father had abandoned the family. This was also the
woman who had found the love of her life with her long-departed
husband, Ernesto, who had died at the age of twenty-five from a
mysterious fever. A tiny woman, she nevertheless had been a strict
disciplinarian with a lethal hairbrush. Most of all she was the family
psychic, completely unafraid of death. And by the time Oscar had
known her, most of her socializing was being done with dead
family members, all of whom had definite opinions about how
Oscar and his older siblings should be raised.

Alma Díaz's most constant advice to her favorite grandson was
to not become like his father, a man who had cheated on his mother
and spent the rest of his life going from one cheap *puta* to the next.
"Once you meet the love of your life, you worship him. This is all
that matters," she had often told her grandson. This explained why
she had come to him in a dream and scolded him for cheating on
Lucas. It also explained why he'd been in a state of constant anxiety
since talking to Joel in the beech forest. He believed Joel had been
sent by his grandmother as some kind of torment to get him back
in line.

"But, *abuelita,* this man is such an idiot. Should I really follow his
advice?" The eyes of the old woman remained cold. "But, *abuelita,*"

Oscar continued, "I am not ready to settle down with Lucas. He has no money. I have no money." Again, the eyes of the photograph were steely. Just then, there was a knock on the door. Oscar glanced at his clock. It was exactly eight and Joel had apparently done his best to be there on time. Oscar ducked out of his loft bedroom and descended the steep stairwell. Joel was already pressing his face against the screen door and squinting. He opened the door and let the astrologer into his parlor.

"You don't live *near* the cemetery," Joel quipped, "you live *in* the cemetery. But that's because you have Scorpio rising."

"Yes, I've been told that."

"Very nice," Joel said looking around but not seeing much in the darkened room.

"It's not too morbid?"

"No, no."

Oscar pointed to a pair of mutilated Barbie dolls sitting on a bookshelf. "Lucky charms to keep away the evil spirits."

"You believe in evil spirits?" Joel asked hopefully.

"Oh, yes," Oscar answered emphatically.

Joel was pleased. This whole thing would be easier than he'd thought. He looked more carefully around the parlor and saw that Oscar had brought the feeling of the cemetery into his home by decorating it in Early Dawn of the Dead. The room was illuminated by a string of skull-shaped Halloween lights. There was also an altar on the kitchen table, on which sat a black Jesus beneath a skeleton-encrusted proscenium. Best of all was a large picture of the Virgin Mary, a hologram that turned into a particularly gruesome Bleeding Heart of Jesus when Joel turned his head from left to right. Apparently Oscar was the kind of lapsed gay Catholic who prayed to go to heaven but decorated as though he would prefer to live in hell.

"I'm so glad you're here," Oscar exclaimed as he led Joel into the tiny kitchen. "And I'm sorry if I was rude to you today. I've just been so crazy."

"You're under some heavy aspects."

"Oh, yes. And I must get your astrological advice. Please, come upstairs."

Joel followed Oscar up some steep and narrow steps, checking out his tight buns as they ascended.

"I was lighting a candle to my grandmother," Oscar admitted as he entered the loft area he'd turned into a bedroom/personal cathedral.

"Wonderful," Joel responded as he looked across the room and saw the photograph of Alma Díaz surrounded by candles and incense. Joel stepped up to the altar and reverently touched *abuelita's* photo.

"She was so beautiful."

Oscar nodded.

"You know," Joel continued, "she's your guardian angel."

"I know."

Joel touched his heart. "I'm so sorry for your loss." Closing his eyes, the astrologer appeared to be sniffing the air. "Her presence is very strong in this room. And she's watching you closely. *Very* closely."

Oscar smiled, unsure whether Joel meant this to be good news or a warning.

On the altar was a piece of paper on which had been scribbled a few lines of poetry. "May I?" Joel asked as he snatched the paper and started to read it.

Oscar grabbed it back. "It's not very good."

"You write poetry?" Joel asked.

"Yes, but I can't write so well in English."

"English isn't good for expressing one's feelings," Joel agreed. "It's good for directions on shampoo bottles. But it's hardly the language of the soul—not like Spanish. Spanish is the most beautiful language of all. I smile whenever I hear it on the subways, on the streets. García Lorca. Márquez. They're my favorite writers."

"Really?"

"If your poetry is as good as your paintings, I'm sure it's wonderful."

This was all Oscar needed to hear. Always desperate for compliments, he changed his mind. "If you like poetry, I'll read it to you."

"Not if it's private," Joel demurred.

"A little."

Joel held up his hand. "Is it about Dennis Fairchild?" he asked.

"Yes," Oscar confessed.

"OK," Joel responded, trying his best to appear reluctant. "But I'm not here to gossip."

"Sit down. Please." Oscar took a large pillow from the bed and tossed it on the floor. Then, grabbing a pillow for himself, he tried to reexperience how awful he had felt when he wrote it. He shook his head; he creased his brow. Joel watched all this and braced himself for the worst. "Now please don't judge me too harshly," Oscar warned. "This poem is called, 'Nose in the Air.'"

"What a wonderful title," Joel replied as he closed his eyes and readjusted his facial expression slightly, from one of spiritual concern to one of artistic appreciation.

Clearing his throat, Oscar began to read very slowly, as though the profundity of what he was saying wasn't only in the words but also in the silences—the vast silences—between them.

You told me the first day we met
that people are always asking you
what are you thinking.
I vowed I would never do the same—

But now that I know you better
I can't help wondering,
What are you thinking?
But what I really want to know is
Could you love me?
Could you love anyone?
You with your nose in the air.

Oscar closed his eyes and bowed his head, a hopeful sign the poem was finally over. Joel snapped himself awake. "You've taken your pain and turned it into something so … beautiful," he gushed.

"Should I read it again?"

Before Joel could say a word, Oscar cleared his throat again and took it from the top. He read even more slowly, just in case Joel had missed anything the first time around.

This gave Joel plenty of time to reconsider his goals. He'd come to this cottage merely to pry Oscar away from Dennis. Once or twice he'd entertained the notion of making a play for Oscar's posterior but he was concerned that diverting a stream of passion might weaken the river of desire currently dammed up and aimed at Dennis. But listening to Oscar's dreadful poem, he began to ask himself, *Why not go for a piece of the poet's* muy bueno *backside?* Oscar did have one of the best bodies in town, and presently his loose jeans were slipping down to reveal the upper regions of a beautifully bronzed and well-toned *tuchis.*

"Well?" Oscar was asking him. He had put down the poem and was looking to Joel for feedback. "Did you like it?"

The astrologer put his fingers to his lips. "You with your nose in the air," Joel repeated reverently. "What a perfect description of Dennis."

Oscar shook his head sadly. "I love Lucas, but there's something about Dennis. I can't help thinking that if he opened up just a little that he could be the one for me. What should I do? It's so confusing."

Joel took a deep breath. "First of all, I want to remind you that whatever happens your soul is still pure and that God still loves you."

"Thank you. Thank you!"

"I'll help you get through this." The two men smiled at each other. Joel pressed his hands together and held them to his heart. Oscar mirrored the gesture as a sign of respect.

"I love Lucas," Oscar confessed. "But with Dennis, I let myself get crazy."

Joel reached out and touched Oscar's arm. "Let's close our eyes now and ask for some healing spirit to enter the room."

Oscar closed his eyes. Joel took a deep breath to center his concentration. "Before we call in our spirit guides, let's focus on different areas of our bodies. First, feel what's going on in your legs."

"This is so hard. I can't stop thinking about Dennis."

"Shh. For now, just breathe into your legs. Your long, muscular legs. Your legs that carry you through life. Give thanks to your legs. Thank your knees for bending. Thank the muscles in your thighs. Your hips. Your buttocks."

Oscar took a deep breath and shifted from side to side.

"Are your buttocks relaxed?" Joel asked.

"I'm still thinking about Dennis. It's driving me crazy. I never should have …"

But Oscar didn't finish his sentence. The two men were silent for a few moments, until Joel's curiosity got the better of him. "You never should have what?"

"I never should have fucked him," Oscar replied.

Joel's stomach knotted. His fingers dug into his knees.

"That's OK," Joel managed to respond.

"Only because he wanted it so badly. He wanted to be bitten. He wanted to be hit. We were on the bed wrestling like two animals in heat. It was awful."

Joel opened his eyes and saw that Oscar had buried his face in his hands. "Why was it awful?"

"Because I knew something was missing."

"What?" Joel asked, finding it hard to imagine what Oscar could have found lacking in the scene he'd just described.

"It was only sex," Oscar answered.

Only sex? Joel asked himself. *Only sex?* For years he had had to hear about hot guys like Oscar having "*only* sex" while he'd been forced to settle for "*only* friendship." Joel suddenly became so angry that he started to shiver.

"Are you cold?" Oscar asked.

"It's the energy in the room," Joel said. "It is very powerful."

Oscar suddenly looked frightened.

"Is it … my grandmother?" he asked. "Is she in the room with us?"

"Yes!" Joel replied, anxious to change the subject.

"What is she trying to say to me?"

Joel thought quickly and began to hyperventilate in preparation for channeling spirits. "Ah-phew! Ah-phew! Ah-phew!"

"What does she want?"

"She wants to talk to you."

"What should I do?"

"Imagine your *abuelita* surrounded by white light. Ah-phew. Ah-phew!"

Just then Joel felt a bolt of energy rushing up his spine, getting caught in his throat, and squeezing itself through his mouth.

"*¡Ay ay ay!*" he suddenly screamed, unconsciously imitating the voice of Yris del Coro.

"*¿Abuelita?*"

"*¡Ay ay ay!*" Joel repeated. He was shaking violently.

"*Abuelita,* it's me. Oscar!" Joel continued to shake. "Tell me, please. Tell me that it's you."

"*¡Sí!*" Joel suddenly cried out in a loud, triumphant voice. "It ees me, your *abuelita*. And I am angry. *Muy* angry." Joel raised his index finger and pointed it at Oscar. "Thees man ... thees painter ... he ees very bad for you. Very, very bad." Now Oscar was beginning to sway back and forth on the floor in terror. "*El diablo* comes to you in many ways, *mijo.*"

"No. No!"

"Thees man. He ees a lost soul. The man who sings. He ees better for you."

"But Dennis and I, we have such passion!"

"Ptui!" Joel spit on the floor. "You are just like your father. He was not loyal to the woman he loved and he went to a dark place. I am frightened for you, my child. Eet ees een the blood. Your father's mother, she was a *puta,* and you are the same blood as she."

"No!"

"Thees artist ees bad. *Muy malo.* I would rather you become lovers with Pedro the peeg farmer!"

"No! Dennis is a good man!"

"You must geev him up."

"I can't. I don't have the strength."

"You must."

"Please, *abuelita,* I must see this man again. And you must give me your blessing. Please!"

"Ptui!"

"*Abuelita!*"

"That ees my blessing!"

"*Abuelita,* no."

Joel glared at Oscar. His spine stiffened. His nostrils flared. He had almost convinced himself he was channeling Oscar's grand-mother, and the transformation was quite exhilarating. As Alma Díaz, he was tall and powerful, and there was nothing he couldn't do. He extended his arms and commanded, *"Ven aquí."*

"What are you going to do?"

He extended his arms again and repeated the command: "Come!"

Joel held one arm away from his side; Oscar crawled over and put his head in his lap. Joel ran his arms up and down the man's back and legs, squeezing his muscles, and patting his behind.

"I miss you so much," Oscar cried.

"I love you, my child."

"I know."

Joel started squeezing Oscar's firm muscular buttocks and Oscar began to moan in what could have been pleasure or pain. Joel was getting more and more aroused.

"I love you, my child, but you must leesten to me!"

"I will, I will."

"You must do what I say."

"I will. Only please do not spank me like you did when I was a child!"

Joel hesitated. This was turning out better than he expected. "No spanking, please!" Oscar repeated. Joel stiffened his spine and gestured for Oscar to lay himself across his lap. "No!" Oscar cried.

"You must be punished!"

Joel reached out and grabbed Oscar by the scruff of his neck. Meeting surprisingly little resistance, he sprawled the handsome Latino over his knees and slapped him hard on his buttocks five times.

"You! Weel! Leave! This! Man!"

"No!"

Joel slapped him eight more times to the rhythm of his words. "You! Weel! Ne-ver! See! Him! A-gain!"

"No! No!"

The candles. The heat of the attic room. The high humidity. Joel was breaking out in a sweat as he pounded Oscar's rear end. The Latino, meanwhile, squirmed and moaned. "Please," he suddenly begged, "please don't pull down my pants!"

"Weel you leave this man?"

"I cannot promise!"

"Weel you?"

"No. No."

What else could Joel do but yank hard on Oscar's low-riding jeans? Without even unzipping the zipper, they slid down his thighs, revealing two golden mounds of flesh. As though trying to facilitate the process, the Latino reached beneath himself, quickly undid his zipper, and pulled his jeans down even further. Joel spanked him several more times and watched the buttocks turn pink. Then he hesitated. He wanted to simply savor the sight of the wonderful tush that had so magically dropped into his lap as though from heaven itself. But Oscar would have none of that.

"Don't stop!" he suddenly growled over his shoulder, no longer sounding like a scared little boy but rather an impatient grown-up who knew exactly what he wanted.

"Is this too hard?" Joel asked in his normal voice.

"You can do it harder," Oscar assured him. So Joel lifted up his arm and let Oscar have another good whack.

"Mmm," Oscar moaned

"You like that?" Joel asked.

"Do it again."

Joel complied.

"Harder!" Oscar demanded.

Joel complied.

"That's great, that's great. Now stick it in."

"What?"

"Fuck me! Quick, while it still stings. There are condoms in the drawer."

With startling speed, Oscar pulled off his pants, pulled rubbers out of his end table, and sprawled belly down on the bed. Joel, meanwhile, fumbled with the foil.

"I ... I can't get this open."

Reaching behind him, Oscar managed to grab the condom, bite open the package, and toss the rubber back over his shoulder, all in the time it took Joel to loosen his belt buckle. The rubber slipped around in Joel's sweaty fingers.

"Don't stop spanking!" Oscar demanded.

While trying to slip on the condom with one hand and spank with the other, Joel stumbled and his knee dug into Oscar's thigh.

"Ow. Too hard. Too hard!" Oscar complained.

Finally getting the condom on right, Joel noticed that his cock was getting limp. To get himself large again, he bent over and started nibbling on Oscar's ass.

"Don't nibble. Hit!"

Joel complied.

"Ooh. That's great."

"Harder?" Joel asked.

"Yeah. Harder. You're great, man. You're great."

The flattery from Oscar had restored Joel's erection.

"Shut up," Joel growled as he spanked Oscar again.

"Now shove it in."

Joel slipped his cock between Oscar's cheeks.

"How'd you know what I wanted?" Oscar asked.

"Oh, god! Oh, god!" It felt so good.

"Punish me, Grandma. Punish me!"

Joel's cock pressed against Oscar's sphincter. It didn't need to press very hard.

Chapter Nineteen

As Lucas turned the corner onto Cemetery Road, it occurred to him that what he liked best about Oscar was his rock-hard masculinity. There'd been moments he'd wished his Latin lover was a little more yielding, but overall he was glad to have found someone so totally dominant in bed. *What a man,* Lucas thought. And when push came to shove, which thankfully it did quite often, he was thrilled to be Oscar's one and only bottom. That was why when his audition for *Pool Boys on Parade* was suddenly cancelled, he couldn't help but take Joel's money and come to Provincetown a day before he was expected. Strangely enough, as he got closer to Oscar's cottage, he started thinking about Joel Eisenberg. Maybe the astrologer had only had the best intentions in bringing him back to the Cape. *I've judged him too harshly,* Lucas told himself as he turned off the street into Oscar's yard. *He really is a nice guy and it's a shame he hasn't been able to find someone for himself.*

With these kind thoughts in mind, Lucas walked around the landlord's house to the backyard where he was suddenly stopped short by a strange, high-pitched, nasal voice. *"¡Chico travieso!*

¡Chico travieso!" It was coming from Oscar's bedroom. This was followed by the sound of slapping and Oscar crying out, *"¡No, abuelita, no!"* Fearing his lover was in some kind of danger, Lucas ran to the door and pushed his way into Oscar's home. Bounding up the stairs, he barged into Oscar's bedroom where the first thing he recognized was the bald spot on the back of Joel Eisenberg's head. The next things he spotted were Joel Eisenberg's fleshy rear end framed by suntanned calves and the calloused heels of somebody lying beneath him. Lucas was so disoriented that his first reaction was, *Thank god Joel's finally having sex with someone.* But then he remembered his own first meeting with this master of deceit.

"Oh, my god!"

Feeling sick to his stomach, Lucas dropped to the floor and cried, "No!"

Oscar pushed the astrologer off his chest, and pulled up his pants. "What are you doing here?" he cried.

But Lucas was crawling back to the stairwell. "Leave me alone!"

"I thought you were coming tomorrow."

"I can't believe this."

Stumbling to his feet, Lucas ran down the stairs and was halfway out the door before Oscar caught him and pulled him back into the room.

"I can explain," he said.

"I don't want to talk to you. You wouldn't even let me touch your ass."

"We were playing a game."

"You told me you were a top!"

"I am, man. I swear!"

"Then why was Joel fucking you?"

"I'm sorry."

"Joel Eisenberg? You don't even think he's attractive. You told me he was ugly."

"No, I didn't."

"Don't you remember? You told me he was a troll."

Joel had also come downstairs, and he was determined not to take anything Lucas said personally. Hearing a lull in the conversation, he slipped quietly toward the door. Lucas turned to him and sniffled, "Joel, wait." Joel turned, but he kept his hand on the doorknob. Lucas looked him straight in the eye. "Did you … did you do this to get back at me?"

Joel shook his head. He hadn't been thinking of Lucas in the least.

"Yes you did. You were trying to hurt me because I wouldn't sleep with you."

"No," Joel insisted.

"It's all my fault," Oscar interjected bravely. "I lost control."

"With *him*? You lost control with *him*?"

"He was channeling my grandmother. And then he started spanking me."

Lucas held up his hand. "Wait a second. You like to be spanked?"

Oscar blushed and turned aside.

"I think I should go," Joel offered.

"No, stay!" Oscar demanded.

"This is between you two."

"No, stay!" Lucas yelled. He turned to Oscar and asked again. "You like to be spanked? Why didn't you tell me?"

"I don't know."

"We were supposed to share all our fantasies with each other."

Oscar stared at the floor. "I'm sorry."

"There's nothing wrong with wanting to be spanked. I love you!" Lucas shouted.

"I love you, too," Oscar whined in return.

"I would have done anything you wanted."

"I … I don't want you to spank me," Oscar responded. "With you I must be a man."

Hearing this, Lucas suddenly snapped. One by one he started throwing Oscar's Barbie dolls at his head.

"What are you doing?" Oscar cried, trying to grab Lucas's arm.

"I hate you!" Lucas yelled as he wrestled Oscar to the floor. A lamp fell off an end table.

"I have to go," Joel interjected timidly. The end table toppled and rolled across the room. Neither Lucas nor Oscar no longer seemed to care whether Joel stayed or went. Pushing through the door, he galloped across the yard and through a hole in the fence. The last he saw of Lucas, he was straddling Oscar's chest, trying to punch him in the face and screaming, "You lied to me!"

At first, Joel felt nothing but relief as he flew through the cemetery. A few seconds later, he felt a breeze on his legs and realized he'd left his pants in Oscar's bedroom. Plopping down on a tombstone, he tried to decide whether to go back for his britches. Why was everything turning out so horribly wrong? he wondered. Lucas would probably spend the night at the Holiday Inn and Oscar would no doubt find his solace in the arms of Dennis Fairchild. And it wouldn't be long before the story of his channeling the spirit of Oscar's dead grandmother would spread through the town like cholera. Joel got on his knees and tried to repent for his sins, but something Oscar had said kept running through his mind. *Dennis likes to be bitten. Dennis likes to be spanked.*

Suddenly Joel realized that as long as Lucas was beating up Oscar, Dennis would be at home all alone. Better still, Joel had just learned a great lesson in fucking and was raring to go. Leaping to his feet, he ran across the graveyard in his underwear. The side streets would be pretty empty and if he stayed in the shadows and pretended to be wearing a bathing suit, he might even make it home without eliciting comments from the tourists. *The trick is to spank him and then stick it in while it still stings.*

"*Nam myoho renge kyo. Nam myoho renge kyo.*" Running up a steep hill toward Bradford Street, Joel started to feel almost guilty for having cheated on Dennis. "Oh, Yris del Coro. You strewed some obstacles in my way. You tested my devotion to my Twin Flame by tempting me with Oscar. But, hey. You test all the true seekers. Buddha gave up his castle. Moses wandered forty years in the desert. Jesus was crucified. What was I to do? Oscar is just so damn sexy."

At the corner of Bradford and Cole, Joel paused to catch his breath. *Oscar is sexy,* he thought, *but not nearly as sexy as Dennis. Oscar has the muscles. Oscar has the profile. But Dennis Fairchild has it where it counts. Dennis has the best tush in Provincetown, the best tush I've ever seen.* Turning onto Commercial Street, Joel nearly collided with a convertible filled with teenagers who hooted, "Nice ass!" as he ran up the street. But he was lost in thought. *In fact, when all the factors that make up tush are added up—size, shape, consistency, and an arrogant personality you just want to fuck the shit out of, Dennis Fairchild has the best tush ever made.*

Entering the yard, he wanted to jump for joy when he saw the light on in the upstairs studio. *I'll suggest we run lines again like we did before. This time when he kisses me, I'll throw him over the desk, pull down his pants, and plug his little Nazi strudel.*

"Arf! Arf!"

Bunny met him at the kitchen door. The damn thing probably had to pee. "Come on. Quick."

"Arf! Arf!"

"Come on! Outside!"

But Bunny had something else on her mind.

"Forget it!" Joel barked. "Pee on the floor!" Stepping over the dog, he ran breathlessly up the stairs and tapped on the door to Dennis's studio. There was no answer so he opened it and peeked inside. The lights were on but the room was empty. The script for *Shut Your Von Trapp!* was sitting on the desk, beneath a half-eaten plate of spaghetti.

Joel's eyes darted around the room. The door to the bedroom was closed. Dennis must have come home from the beach, studied his lines, and gone to bed, where he was no doubt lying awake, miserable and alone. In the few seconds it took Joel to cross the room, he planned his entire life with Dennis. *Now that Dennis knows what a great director I am, he'll want to come back to New York with me and audition for plays. We'll buy a loft in Tribeca. The following year we'll write a two-person play called* Twin Flames. *It will tell the world how much we love each other, how our love had been predicted by my spirit guide, how we were oddly mismatched—how, against all odds, I broke down his resistance through my faith in a Higher Power.*

"Arf! Arf! Arf!"

Bunny had followed Joel up the stairs and was seated in front of Dennis's door, barking up a storm. Suddenly Dennis called out from his bedroom. "Bunny! Shut up."

Joel scooped the dog into his arms. "I got her!" he announced. Skin tingling with anticipation, he reached for the doorknob and paused one last time to relish the moment.

He turned the knob and opened the door.

The shaft of light revealed two heaving figures in the middle of Dennis's bed.

"What the hell!" The man on top turned to see who'd come in the room.

"Oh! I'm sorry," Joel replied.

"Close the fucking door!" ordered Rudy Cantwell, whose scowling face was now clearly illuminated.

"What are you doing?" asked Dennis, straining to see over the broad shoulders of his director.

"I ... I just came for the dog," Joel apologized as he meekly stepped back and pulled the door shut.

Book 2
Passion

Chapter Twenty

Provincetown became famous in the twentieth century both as a birthplace of modern American drama and as a haven for gay culture. Oddly enough, these two things had nothing to do with each other. Eugene O'Neill, thoroughly heterosexual, managed to write his seminal plays here, while literary flamers like Tennessee Williams and Truman Capote generally wasted their time in Provincetown screwing the houseboys, drinking excessively, and vomiting on the streets. What the homosexuals did create was not gay theater but gay entertainment. Lip-synching became the second language of Provincetown, and if one were willing to tuck one's penis and gesture to a soundtrack in front of a Mylar curtain, a few dollars would assuredly be shoved into one's well-padded brassiere by the end of the evening. But Rudy Cantwell had always wanted to change all that. He believed that immortal gay theater should have its place on Commercial Street. When *Shut Your Von Trapp!* opened on August 1, 1997, to rave reviews, his dream of giving gay Provincetown its proper place in history was one step closer to coming true. While the *Boston Globe* and the *Herald* had been kind to the entire production, they'd been ecstatic in their praise of Dennis Fairchild. His performance, according to one reviewer, "stood out as frighteningly sincere amidst the campy shenanigans. If he can simmer in front of a movie camera as he did onstage, could a Hollywood career be far in the distance for this remarkable young man?"

Could it? Dennis Fairchild happily wondered as he leaned against the banister of his backyard deck and gazed with satisfaction at the dozens of well-wishers who had come to his home for the cast party. In spite of his good reviews, Dennis wasn't foolish enough to believe he'd make a living as a thespian on Cape Cod. Even if he were to become the highest-paid actor in Massachusetts, he'd still make less money than a guy who drove a tow truck in Wellfleet. On the other hand, he was hopeful that Rudy Cantwell might soon close a deal with some "money people" and bring the show to New York. At that very moment he was waiting for Rudy to arrive with Dr. Jeffrey Sherman, a rich dentist from Tenafly, New Jersey, who'd loved the show and was allegedly willing to fork over half a million to move *Shut Your Von Trapp!* to the Actor's Theatre in Greenwich Village, where Dennis would be that much closer to Hollywood.

As the artist gracefully fielded compliments, he wasn't unaware of the few dark clouds hovering above his sun-kissed existence. His sex life, for instance, was strangely unsatisfying. His Latino fuck buddy had stopped returning his calls, and Dennis always felt a pinch of jealousy whenever he saw Oscar walking with Lucas. Unbeknownst to anyone, his tryst with Rudy had evolved into a marriage of convenience. After only two nights of being drilled by the well-hung director, Dennis was horrified when Rudy suddenly rolled over in bed and turned out to be an even bigger bottom than he was himself. Their romantic chemistry fizzled, but for the sake of publicity they both decided to masquerade as Provincetown's premier power couple until such time a nasty breakup would garner even more publicity.

Then there was James. Dennis had hoped his ex-lover would show up that night, but when he phoned his mother, Maureen Fairchild of Groton, Massachusetts, she told him that James had gone on vacation to Mykonos with a young man named Chipper who looked "just like you did when you were twenty-one." Dennis prayed his mother had misheard the rumor, something she often did when she was soused. In the meantime he concentrated on hosting what was turning out to be the social event of the season. The Norman Mailers were on their way over; John Waters was in the den chatting with Margaret Cho, who had flown in from LA to perform at town hall; best of all, Michael Cunningham had arrived earlier with a group of his writing students from the Fine Arts Summer Program. One or two of them were quite handsome, so Dennis started to weave his way in their direction. Nose high in the air, he happened to glance at Joel Eisenberg's window and saw the curtain move as though somebody had been spying.

"Yecch, Joel," Dennis groaned to himself. All of his friends either avoided the subject of the ass-trologer or asked him directly why in the world he was allowing such a jerk to live in his home. If Dennis had been a little more honest with himself, he might have answered that Joel was kept there not just to walk the dog, but even more important, to make him look good. As an artist, Dennis was an expert in contrast and scale. Just as in a painting something stands out when placed beside something that recedes, he knew he could make himself appear grand by placing himself next to someone insignificant. Unfortunately, Joel's reputation had taken such a nosedive that this black smudge on Dennis's canvas was threatening to ruin the entire composition. In spite of Joel having helped him with his performance as Rolf, there was no way Dennis could allow him to attend the cast party; Rudy couldn't stand the sight of him. Not having the heart to tell his boarder, Dennis came up with a brilliant compromise. Pulling an old dress, a black wig, and a shawl out of Sue Veneer's trunk, he dressed the astrologer as a gypsy woman, put a sign on his door reading "Free Psychic Readings by Jolina," and suggested that Joel spend the entire evening in his room.

So far that night, the only one to visit Jolina was Lou Lustig, the publisher of the *Provincetown Poop*. It was he who had been peeking through the curtains to see who was attending the party. Joel, still disguised as a gypsy woman, was puffing on a joint and staring at a zodiac chart on his computer screen. Ever since the night he'd found Dennis in bed with Rudy, he'd been smoking pot constantly. Bunny, as usual, was sleeping comfortably on his lap. As had happened with Sue Veneer, Joel's affection for Bunny had grown in direct proportion to his hatred for everyone else in town.

"Disgusting," muttered Lou, who had been a sworn enemy of Rudy Cantwell's ever since the director had poked fun at his weight in one of his shows. "Look at those idiots sucking up to Dennis and Rudy. *Shut Your Von Trapp!*? Ugh. That's about as avant-garde as my ball sack! Those guys aren't artists. They're barely trendsetters. Not that anyone around here can tell the difference. We used to be a working-class artist's community. Now you can't get a chicken salad sandwich without somebody sticking raisins in it. Provincetown's dead. Finished. Give me another hit."

Lou Lustig stepped back from the window and lumbered up behind Joel, who was still staring at his computer screen. "Whose chart are you doing?"

"Nobody you know."

Lou was suddenly suspicious. He was well aware of how Joel used astrology. "You got someone coming for a reading?"

"Uh-hmm," Joel replied, attempting to cover the computer screen with his body.

Lou took another toke and decided he might get more information out of Joel if he plied him with some gossip of his own. "Guess what I heard?" he said as he exhaled. "I talked to George down at Esther's, and Keith Antonelli's back in town. Apparently he's out of his mind on crystal and he's looking for trouble."

"What a shame," Joel answered nonchalantly.

"Yeah. Rudy kicking him out of the show and breaking up with him really did a number on his head. And now that the show's such a big success—my prediction—it's only a matter of time before he shows up at Rudy's and boils a pet rabbit in his kitchen."

"Hmm," Joel answered, not taking his eyes off his computer.

Disappointed by the lackluster response, Lou decided it was time to go. He waddled toward the door. As he was about to leave, he took one last look at his old friend dressed as a gypsy woman, hunched over his computer. The sight broke his heart.

"Can I talk to you a minute?" he began. "How can I say this? Of all the work I did in New York, promoting your career was the thing I was most proud of. So when I saw you were in town this summer, I was thrilled, but …" Lou took Joel's hand, patted it, and looked at him sympathetically. "Are you OK? 'Cause I think you're going nuts."

"I'm fine," Joel answered, trying to take his hand back.

"You're not fine. Joel, ever since you found Dennis in bed with Rudy Cantwell you do nothing but get stoned and walk around town muttering to yourself. You gotta stop."

"Stop what?"

"This." Lou pulled himself to his feet and lumbered to the altar.

Amid the photos of Dennis, the scribbled notes, and assorted pictures of gurus, Lou found what he was seeking: the current edition of the *Bay Bugle* with a half-page photo of Rudy Cantwell and Dennis Fairchild on its cover. Lou picked it up and held it in Joel's face. The headline read "LOVEBIRDS." With a black magic marker, Joel had added bloody fangs to Rudy's face, a noose around Dennis's neck, and the words "NO! NO! NO!" over both their foreheads.

Joel grimaced, realizing he should have done a better job of cleaning up before Lou came over.

"I'm not judging you," Lou Lustig hastened to add. "I like goyim, too. But Dennis Fairchild, he's industrial-strength goyim. He's got a block of ice where his heart should be."

Joel rolled his eyes. "You don't really know him."

"Nobody knows him. With everybody out there blowing smoke up his ass, he's still the loneliest guy in town. Please. Tell me you heard some of what I just told you."

"I heard you."

"Tell me you'll think about it."

"Yeah, I'll think about it."

Somewhat reassured, Lou Lustig crossed the room and pulled Joel out of his chair. The astrologer held his breath and braced himself for a hug, an experience not unlike falling face first into a huge vat of pudding. A moment later, all two hundred and fifty pounds of Lou Lustig had squeezed itself out of the room.

Relieved, Joel sat back in his chair and pressed his fingertips together. Part of him suspected that everything Lou said about his obsession with Dennis was true, but he had no intention of thinking about it. He had far more important things to consider, for what he'd been unwilling to reveal to Lou was that his impending appointment was with none other than Keith Antonelli. He'd seen

Rudy's embittered ex earlier that morning entering City Video with a stack of porn under his arm. On impulse, Joel followed him into the store and lured him over for a reading. Joel completely agreed with Lou Lustig; Keith Antonelli was a time bomb waiting to go off. The trick would be placing him where he would do the most damage and then lighting the fuse.

"Pghh. Pghh." Bunny had awaked on his lap. Joel bent over and kissed her wrinkled face.

"Who's my little good-luck charm? Who is she?" Bunny responded by thrusting out her massive tongue and slurping Joel's chin. "Ooh. Puppy kisses. Who's my little Buddha? Who's my little Buddhalicious?" Joel nibbled on Bunny's ear. The dog snorted with delight. "Isn't Daddy clever?" Joel asked as he started preparing the room for Keith by pulling an extra chair over to the computer. "Now, you sit on the bed while I roll a nice big joint for Keith." Joel went to his bureau and grabbed a package of e-z widers.

"Pghh. Pghh."

"I know. We shouldn't be rolling a joint for a drug addict, but this will relax him and make him more gullible. You know what gullible means? That's what everybody in this town is except your Daddy. So we're just gonna take a little pinch of pot out of this plastic bag. Sprinkle it onto this paper. Here we go. Yes. Yes. Daddy's gonna get Keith nice and stoned so when he gets here, he'll believe anything I tell him."

Bunny padded after Joel and looked up at him with a wide-eyed expression of pure innocence that for a moment made him feel horribly corrupt. Had he really descended as low as to offer drugs to a drug addict? He could convince himself that hastening Dennis's breakup with Jean Paul had done a favor for everyone involved. He could also cast reuniting Lucas with Oscar as a noble sacrifice. But, he wondered, was there any redeeming value in what he was now planning?

Going to the window, he pulled aside the curtain and saw that Rudy had just arrived with a tanned gentleman with radiantly white teeth whom Joel took to be Dr. Sherman, the potential producer. Rudy had his arm around Dennis. They were making a toast. A few muscular guys circled around them. Although Joel didn't know their names, he guessed they were the type of gay men who parlayed their good looks and gym bodies into glamorous careers in the arts. He'd come to loathe this town, where less-attractive men weren't just ignored, they were actually disdained for taking up space where someone better looking could be standing. At the pinnacle of this system were its two reigning monarchs: Rudy Cantwell, with his manly jaw and dark charisma; and Dennis Fairchild, with his blue eyes and pouty lips. Both of them were handsome enough to get laid even if they weren't so successful. Both of them were successful enough to get laid even if they weren't the most handsome guys in town. Individually they were easy to despise, but as a couple, Joel had no choice but to destroy them. Deep in his heart he found the one pure motive for all his actions: justice.

But first he had to straighten up his room. Still wearing the gypsy wig, he snuck into the kitchen and started rummaging in the pantry shelves for a piece of Tupperware in which to store the rest of his marijuana. He climbed a chair, pushed aside a few cereal bowls on the top shelf, and came face-to-face with the antique chamber pot Sue Veneer had warned him against touching. Joel carefully picked it up and examined it, feeling for the moment that he had a lot in common with this piece of pottery. He, too, had been shipwrecked in Provincetown; he, too, had been judged as a useless relic; he, too, had been pissed on again and again.

"You know what I hear," came a sibilant voice as it entered the kitchen. "I hear that Joel Eisenberg actually lives here."

"You're kidding," the queen's friend squealed in response.

"That one's got a borderline personality. I see him coming down the street and I head for the borderline."

"Ha. Ha. Ha," laughed Queen One.

"Ha. Ha. Ha," laughed Queen Two.

"Hey, doll! You on the chair." Joel pulled the wig across his face like a veil and tilted his head toward the two men. "Could you hand me two of those wineglasses?" Joel complied without turning around. "Thanks, darling."

One of the queens took the glasses, leaned closer to his friend, and whispered, "So I hear Rudy's thinking of dropping Dennis for a name as soon as they take the show to New York."

"You're kidding. He got such good reviews."

"They need a star to play one of the leads. That's show business. It was either Dennis or Rudy, so Rudy made sure Dennis would get the boot."

The queens' conversation was suddenly interrupted by an antique chamber pot hitting the hard wooden floor, followed by the gypsy woman, who jumped down and knelt over the pieces while covering her face with her hair. Joel had leaned closer to hear what they were saying, lost his balance, and grabbed the shelf for support. "So sorry," the mysterious figure exclaimed in a breathy falsetto. The two men looked at each other and hightailed out of the room. "Fuck," Joel muttered to himself as he scooped up the priceless pottery, which now consisted of a bowl and a broken handle. It had been a clean break. With a little Elmer's Glue, the handle could be reattached and nobody would be the wiser.

Before Joel could make the repairs, however, someone in a hooded sweatshirt hurried past him into the bedroom. A moment later, Keith Antonelli stuck his head out the door and asked, "Joel? Is that you?"

"I'll be right there," the astrologer replied. "Go in and sit down." Looking both ways to make sure he wasn't being observed, Joel put the broken handle inside the bowl, climbed onto the chair, and gently placed it back on the shelf, with its damaged side concealed against the wall.

Chapter Twenty-one

Keith was pacing back and forth and muttering to himself. "This is so fucked up." He looked a fright. He'd lost twenty pounds, his teeth were discolored, and his dark pupils were the size of pie plates. When he saw Joel enter the room, he started shaking his head. "I'm sorry but I can't do this now. I just saw Rudy and Dennis hugging and kissing in front of everybody. It makes me want to puke."

"Did they see you?" Joel asked.

"No. I don't think so."

"Can I get you something?"

"No man, seriously, it's like a knife in my brain. If I don't leave now, I may hurt somebody. I swear. I'm this close. This close!" He held his thumb and index finger a tiny distance apart and shook them in Joel's face.

"Wait." Joel motioned for Keith to sit next to him in front of the computer. "Here. Smoke this."

Joel lit the joint lying on the desk and handed it to Keith, who flopped into the chair and took a few deep hits.

"Listen, Keith, everything's going to be fine. I've got some good news for you. The truth is that Rudy doesn't really love Dennis. He loves you."

"Look outside. They're so fucking happy together."

"They're just posing for pictures. Here, look at this."

Joel pointed to the computer screen on which there were two circles filled with squiggles and colored lines. Keith leaned closer. "What is it?"

"This circle here is the relationship chart for you and Rudy. Do you see all these blue lines? Blue lines are good."

"Yeah?" Keith asked, intrigued.

"And this circle on the right is the chart for Rudy and Dennis. You see all these red lines? Those are bad."

"Really?"

"Blue lines, good. Red lines, bad."

Keith reached out and touched the screen. "What about these green lines?"

"Forget about those. Just focus on the red and the blue. The point is you and Rudy are meant for each other. But Rudy and Dennis, I'm telling you, they're a disaster."

"So why did he dump me?"

"It was a career move. Rudy gets confused about his priorities. And it's your job to show him that love is more important than anything."

"Is that in his chart?"

"Yes. Here, look at this."

Joel clicked on his keyboard and pulled up another circle labeled "Rudy Cantwell."

"First of all, Rudy is a Scorpio. Scorpios are only really happy when they're in a passionate relationship. And you see this squiggle? That's Venus, the planet of love. You see how close it is to this circle? That's Rudy's sun. He's finally ready to receive what you have to offer, but you have to act fast. Once Venus moves on, Rudy will close up again."

"When's that?"

"Let me see." Joel pulled out his ephemeris and flipped to a page filled with columns of figures. He found what he was looking for. "Tonight. At 3:27 A.M."

"But what about Dennis? I heard they're going to New York to do the play together."

"Can you keep a secret?"

Keith nodded his head. Joel picked up Bunny and started stroking her back.

"What?" Keith demanded impatiently.

"Rudy's getting rid of Dennis. He's going to replace him in the show."

"Who'd you hear that from?"

"A reliable source. If you play your cards right, you could be the one going to New York with Rudy."

Keith sat back in his chair, astounded. "You really think Rudy still loves me?"

Joel took a deep breath and chose his next words very carefully.

"Have you ever heard of a Twin Flame?"

"Is that like … like a soul mate?"

"Soul mate? Phooey!" Conjuring Yris del Coro, Joel made a face like he was going to spit. "You can meet a new soul mate every day on the street. But you only have one Twin Flame and they're yours for all eternity. You and Rudy are Twin Flames."

"Wow! So I knew Rudy in a past life?"

"Absolutely. In your last life he rescued you. Now it's your turn to rescue him."

"Rescue him from what?"

"Dennis Fairchild. Dennis is like a black hole sucking Rudy into the darkness. As his Twin Flame it's your duty to reach out to him and bring him into the light. And if you don't do this—if you don't do everything to reunite your flames—then both of you could go out. Pfft." Joel snapped his fingers in the air dismissively.

Keith looked as if his eyes might pop out of his head. He was obviously reeling at the enormousness of the responsibility Joel had just laid at his feet.

"You're right," he repeated several times in a voice filled with awe. "But how do you know all this?"

Joel pointed his finger toward heaven, smiled serenely, and sat back in his chair.

A few hours later, Bill Doyle had fallen asleep on his couch with an empty tumbler of Scotch on a nearby coffee table. Mitchell Savitt had come to him in his dream and the two men were strolling down a country road surrounded on both sides by lush vegetation.

"Don't give up on Joel," Mitchell was telling him.

"He's a spoiled fucking princess."

"But he can change. You'll see."

The two men came upon a little house made of pink stucco. They walked up to a window and Mitchell pointed inside. "I want you to see the reason why you and Joel have to become lovers."

Mitchell looked through the window and saw a brown-skinned woman breast-feeding a big, fat baby.

"Who is she?" Bill asked.

"Nobody yet. But she could be me. Remember how I always wanted to come back in my next lifetime as a fierce black lesbian and lead a worldwide revolution against racism, sexism, and stupidity? Well this is a coming attraction of the lifetime God has planned for me—but my soul can't move on. Once I become that little girl, my

spirit won't be able to come to you like this. So before I leave you, I
need to know that some other Jew is loving you and keeping you off
the sauce."

"What can I do? Joel's not into me."

"Convince him you can make him happy. Drive him wild in bed."

"I can't do that."

"Sure you can. You're just a little rusty."

The next thing Bill knew, he was lying naked in some tall grass
and Mitchell—also naked—was straddling him and massaging his
chest. His ex-lover's body wasn't the emaciated bag of bones he'd
become at the end, but the thick, healthy man he'd been when
they'd first met. He had Bill's favorite kind of body, an intoxi-
cating mixture of masculine and feminine, a little soft in the belly
and round in the hips, but covered with fur from his collarbone to
his ankles. Mitchell turned and started licking the insides of his
thighs.

"Stop it!"

"You like this?"

"Of course I like it, but you're dead."

"You're still alive." Mitchell took Bill's cock in his mouth. "So
go on, baby, lick it. Lick my big ass. Go on. Fuck me into my next
lifetime!"

Unable to control himself, Bill strained forward and pushed his
face deep into Mitchell's crack.

"Keep licking. You like this? You like my chunky Jew butt?"

"Oh, yeah!"

"The next time you see Joel Eisenberg, I want you to do this to
him. He doesn't know it yet, but this is what he wants. Now make
yourself cum." Mitchell grabbed one of Bill's hands and placed it on
his lover's cock. "Stroke, baby. Stroke."

As Bill pumped, he pushed his face in deeper. His heart beat joyously. The five miserable years preceding this moment disappeared as if they'd never happened. Mitchell had never been diagnosed. Mitchell had never gotten sick. Mitchell had never died.

"Ahh! Ahh!" He was starting to cum. Mitchell pulled away.

"Don't leave me now!" Bill cried.

"Keep thinking about Joel."

"No! No!"

But the idea had already been planted in Bill's mind. All he could see now was Joel stripped naked doing yard work. Joel bending over to pull out a weed. Joel's big ass as he climbed a ladder to paint the trim. Bill felt an explosion in his loins. A cannon shot. He opened his eyes, Mitchell was gone, and his stomach was inundated with jism.

Chapter Twenty-two

"Out of my way, breeders!"

Rudy Cantwell put all his weight onto his bike pedal and barely missed hitting two kids clutching their parents' hands. It was only eight in the morning but Commercial Street was already packed with tourists pouring onto MacMillan Wharf. Rudy weaved his way through this miasma of flip-flops, ugly T-shirts, and sticky hands. Speeding against traffic on the one-way street, he rehearsed what he would say to that little shithead Joel Eisenberg when he pulled him out of bed and pushed his head through the nearest wall. How dare that phony psychic show his face in town and talk about him behind his back. Rudy had eyes and ears in every corner of Provincetown, and he could tell you the exact words the astrologer had used to bad-mouth him to the teller at the Seaman's Bank, the cashier at the army navy store, and the drag queen bagging groceries at the A&P. They'd all squealed, as had Dennis Fairchild, who had informed Rudy that Joel had denigrated his dialogue.

The little fucker has been asking for it all summer long, he seethed, *but this latest broadside is the last straw.* "Eisenberg!" he yelled as he rattled his bike across the lawn and then slammed it against the wall.

Joel jumped up in bed and instinctively pulled Bunny closer as someone pushed his way into the kitchen and pounded several times on his door. "Eisenberg, get up!"

The voice was unmistakable, a weird honk that managed to be unpleasant in two octaves at once. Joel lay back down and pulled the covers over his head, only to have them ripped off a moment later by the angry impresario. Bunny jumped off the bed and ran out of the room.

"Who told you I was replacing Dennis in the play? Was it that fat freak, Lou Lustig? Who?"

"What are you talking about?"

Rudy pushed Joel against the wall and applied some pressure to his throat. "Who told you?"

"Dr. Sherman's friends. I don't know their names."

"What did they say?"

Joel no longer had enough air in his windpipe to speak.

"Listen to me," Rudy growled. "Dennis is staying in the show. So whatever a couple of hissy queens might've said about me behind my back—now you know better. Right?"

Joel somehow managed to nod his head, but Rudy still wasn't satisfied. "So if anybody asks you, what are you going to say?"

"The truth," Joel gasped.

This wasn't the answer Rudy wanted. He pushed Joel even further up the wall. "Listen, fuckface, I've got dirt on you that could send you to jail. You've molested a couple of my friends."

"I didn't molest anyone."

"What about Vinnie Tastone?"

"Vinnie Tastone? I didn't molest Vinnie Tastone."

"He says you did."

Joel gulped. Now he remembered clearly. Vinnie was a weight trainer with enormous thighs who hadn't been amused when he'd removed his drawers and started rubbing his chakras.

"Who else?" Joel demanded.

Rudy counted them off on his fingers. "Danny Phelps. Lee Franklin. Joey DiPasquale." Joel was beaten. Rudy asked one more time. "So what are you gonna say if anybody asks about Dennis?"

"He stays in the show."

"You're damn right. And next time you better think twice before you send some drugged-up mess to my house in the middle of the night."

"Pffgh. Pffgh." Bunny ran in the door and jumped on the bed, followed by Dennis, in a T-shirt and shorts, who pressed his hands against the doorposts and leaned into the room. Apparently Bunny had gone to get the artist and bring him downstairs.

"What are you doing?" he asked Rudy.

"Jolina here did a reading for Keith last night. I don't know what he said but the little jerk came over my house at four in the morning. When I tossed him out, he threw a garbage can through my window."

"He what?"

"I was at the police station all morning. Keith is still in jail."

"Oh, my god!" Dennis responded, barely hiding the glee he felt upon hearing really good gossip. "What did Joel say to Keith?"

"A lot of shit."

"Like what?"

Joel couldn't hold it in any longer. He wiggled out of Rudy's grasp and blurted out in one breath, "I told him Rudy was going to replace you as soon as the show got to New York."

"Shut up," Rudy snarled at Joel.

"He needs a name to get the show produced."

Rudy turned to defend himself, giving Joel just enough time to wrap the blanket around himself, jump off the bed, and run into the kitchen. He got as far as the screen door before he realized that beneath his cover he was completely naked. He turned and saw that Rudy was right behind him.

Like a caged animal, he pivoted to the right, skirted around the table, and again came face-to-face with Rudy. Rudy feinted one way. Joel feinted the other. Rudy dashed around the table and managed to catch the hem of his blanket. He tugged. Joel tugged back. Choosing his physical safety over his dignity, Joel released his cover, ran bare-assed into his room, and slammed the door behind him. Once inside he wedged his naked body between the wall and the door. Rudy ran after him and banged on the door. The china rattled on its shelf.

"Open up, you lying sack of shit!"

"Watch it!" Dennis cried.

Rudy thumped his shoulder against the door.

"Hey!" Dennis yelled. "Cut it out!"

Rudy pushed harder. Joel resisted with all his strength, but he was starting to weaken. "Dennis!" he called out. "I was only trying to help! You can't trust Rudy. I did his chart. He's wants you out of the show because he's jealous of you. You said yourself, he was a lousy director."

Rudy pressed all his strength against the door. It opened a crack and Joel could see his muscular forearm reaching around the door to grab him.

"I said, cut it out!" he heard Dennis yell in anger.

Rudy stopped pushing and Joel heard Dennis yelling at Rudy. "What did Dr. Sherman say yesterday on the boat?"

"I told you."

"Everything? Did he say he wanted to replace me?"

"Yes he did!" Joel yelled through the door.

"Get out here!" Rudy screamed

Joel started to open the door, but this time Dennis slammed it shut. "I never said you were a lousy director," Joel heard the artist exclaim. "Now what did Dr. Sherman say? If you're going to replace me, I want to know now."

Everything got quiet for a few moments as the two men moved to the other side of the kitchen and started whispering. Joel pressed his ear to the door. The next thing he heard was the kitchen door opening and closing. Running to the window, Joel pulled back the curtain just in time to see Rudy riding his bicycle across the lawn and into the street.

Joel's brain was racing. He started to go into the kitchen, but he stopped himself. He suspected Dennis believed his version of the story and not Rudy's. But he knew he had to play his next move carefully. He wanted to show his concern, but if he went to Dennis too quickly, it might look like he was eager to rub in the bad news. It would be better for Dennis to come to him. Throwing on a pair of jeans, Joel turned on his computer and pretended to be absorbed in some crucial business. *Any second now Dennis will knock on my door and ask for advice.*

Any second now.

Joel waited impatiently but Dennis still didn't come, so he got up and listened at the door. Thwack. Thump. The refrigerator being opened and closed. He heard the clank of a milk bottle being removed and taken to the table. Rattle. Rattle. Dennis was opening the silverware drawer and searching for a clean spoon. Joel knew the routine and listened as Dennis picked up a spoon, examined it, and—clank!—tossed it back into the drawer. Joel put his ear to the door again. This time he could hear Dennis sliding a chair over to the china cabinet to climb up and look for a bowl. Joel yearned to step into the kitchen and give him a comforting hug.

Then Joel heard a sudden shout.

He ran into the kitchen expecting to see Dennis sprawled on the ground with a concussion. Instead the artist was standing ramrod straight on the chair, facing the cabinet, and holding something in his hands. "Oh, my god!" he exclaimed in disbelief. Dennis turned. The color had drained from his face. In his hands were the two pieces of ceramic that had once been an antique chamber pot.

"Did you do this?" Dennis demanded, already knowing the truth. Joel couldn't think of any lies so he chose to remain silent. "You broke this, didn't you?"

Joel nodded sheepishly, taking a few steps back. Dennis started to sway and for a second Joel feared he would fall off the chair. He moved closer to catch him, but Dennis held up the palm of his hand like a vampire recoiling from a clove of garlic.

"Do you have any idea how much this cost?"

Joel shook his head. "I was going to fix it …"

"Fix it?" he demanded.

"… with a little glue."

"You can't fix this! It's ruined!" Dennis screamed at the top of his lungs. Then like Charlton Heston in *The Ten Commandments,* he lifted the chamber pot in both his hands, howled like a banshee, and smashed it on the floor.

Chapter Twenty-three

Provincetown had barely reacted to Keith Antonelli's getting arrested for vandalism when word got out that Rudy Cantwell had wreaked his revenge against Joel Eisenberg by chasing him naked through Dennis Fairchild's house and beating him over the head with the artist's five-thousand-dollar chamber pot. Everything about this rumor was an exaggeration except the price of the pot. As for the original source of this story, Joel could once again thank Ida Dream from the Angel Food Deli. Seeing Rudy furiously ride his bicycle onto Dennis Fairchild's lawn, the little black drag queen had slipped out of the store and stationed herself behind the hedges, where she overheard the melee. The story then made its way around town faster than a California wildfire: the one thing bored locals craved even more than hot sex was a hot story, preferably one that included something horrible about their neighbors.

That night, the gossip was making its way around the Little Bar, one of the oldest drinking establishments in town. Built shortly after the American Revolution, this historic shrine to utter dissipation reeked of two centuries' worth of dreams deferred and lives flushed down the toilet. By 1997, the air itself was ninety proof and, if the walls could talk, they would have slurred their vowels and mispronounced their consonants. It was to this den of sorrows that Joel Eisenberg had come to meet Lou Lustig and arrange a ride to the Amtrak station in Boston, where he'd board a train to New York the next day.

It was past midnight. Lou had already departed, but Joel had stayed behind to down another sea breeze. One of the things he dreaded most about going back to Dennis's house was telling Bunny he might never see her again. The guilt of abandoning the dog was producing a hollow sensation in his chest cavity, a heartbreak with which he was completely unfamiliar. It was almost as bad as the rage he now felt for Dennis, who had demanded he never again cross his path until he had come up with the five grand for his precious pot.

"Can I freshen up that drink for you?" With one pinky, Joel slid his glass toward the bartender.

The worst part about his situation was that he now wanted Dennis more than ever. Joel buried his face in his hands. Many years before, he'd seen a horror movie in which an evil scientist had grafted the head of a violent criminal onto his mild-mannered assistant. This twin-headed monster began wandering around town beating up men and raping women. With each foul misdeed, the bad head laughed maniacally, while the good head kept begging, "No! No! Please stop!" And now Joel had become this monster. He could no longer pretend that the part of him that had tried to lie and scheme its way into Dennis's heart was anything other than dreadful. But no matter how much his good head scolded and whined, he would never be able to stop his evil head from wanting to do wrong. The best he could do was drown both heads in vodka and pray to be released from his agony. Joel downed the last of his drink and ordered two more.

When the room began to spin, he decided it was time to leave. Sliding off the bar stool, he felt like the floor was about three feet lower than it had been when he sat down. He staggered and grabbed someone's shoulder for support.

"Watch it, baby." It was Lucas Allison, half carrying, half dragging his lover out of the bar. Oscar was completely hammered.

"Joel, baby. Give me a hand."

The three men stumbled into the street. Joel was only marginally more coordinated than Oscar but they somehow managed to get to the corner without falling.

"I'm glad I saw you before you left town. You left your shorts at Oscar's house."

Joel was suddenly abashed at the memory of how he'd been caught with his pants around his ankles. "I'm really sorry."

"You should be," Lucas replied. "Ever since you fucked Oscar, he wants it all the time. It was OK for a couple of days but now it's getting on my nerves."

"Come on, baby," Oscar slurred as he tried to kiss Lucas. "Fill me up with your love."

"Not now!"

A cab slowly pulled up beside them. The driver was none other than Raymond Hennigan, the concierge from the Fore 'n' Aft, moonlighting to make a little extra money. Lucas flung open the cab door, pushed Oscar into the backseat, and climbed in after him. Turning to Joel he said, "Listen, if I don't see you again, thanks for everything."

Before Joel could reply, Oscar tried to grab Lucas's crotch. Lucas pushed his hand away. "Ugh!" Lucas exclaimed shaking his head. "I love him. I really do—but if he doesn't start fucking me again soon, I'm going back to New York to find someone who can."

The cab pulled away, leaving Joel drunk and alone in the middle of the street. It was one o'clock, the bars had just closed, and their contents had spilled onto the streets and were streaming their way to Spiritus Pizza. Sadly, Joel realized it was time to go home and finish packing. Rubber-legged from the vodka, he stumbled a few steps against the crowd and bumped into Keith Antonelli, who was hopped up on crystal and parading down to the pizza parlor with a group of his druggy friends.

"Hey, Joel!" he cried, giving him a bear hug. "I'm so glad to see you. You're the best. And I'm so glad you told me about Rudy being my Twin Flame. I knew it. I knew there was a reason I couldn't get over him."

"How are you?" Joel asked, a little frightened to find himself face-to-face with his latest weapon.

"I'm great!" Keith said with a manic look in his eyes.

"But didn't you go to jail?"

"Ah, fuck 'em."

'I'm sorry," Joel said. "I'm really sorry."

"For what? You set me straight. You told me the truth. I did what I had to do to keep Rudy's fire from going out. And I'm not done yet. Watch what I do tonight." Keith grinned wickedly and pushed past Joel.

"Wait!" Joel cried, trying to catch up. "Where are you going?"

"I'm going to beat the shit out of Dennis instead. I'll do it in front of the whole town."

"Wait!" Joel yelped. "You can't beat up Dennis!"

"Watch me. I don't look it, but I can fight!"

As they passed the post office steps, Joel was finally able to grab Keith's shoulders and turn him around."

"Don't do this. Nobody wants to see Dennis beat up more than me, but you can't do this. Rudy's not worth it."

"But you said he was my Twin Flame."

"I know but … I exaggerated, OK? I did it because I wanted to make trouble for those guys."

Keith staggered back like he'd been hit in the chest. "You mean Rudy's not my Twin Flame?"

"Maybe he is. Maybe he isn't. So please. You're a good kid. You don't need Rudy. What you need is rehab."

Keith's jaw dropped. Suddenly he grabbed his head and screamed at Joel, "You're evil!" Keith's arms started flailing and several people on the crowded street ducked to avoid being hit. "Get away from me!" he yelled, shoving Joel, who stumbled back and sat down hard in the laps of some boisterous women in work shirts seated on the post office steps and enjoying their pizza.

"What the fuck?" one of them yelled as Joel sat down on her paper plate. "Hey, you!" she shouted at Joel who was trying to stand up. "You owe me a slice!"

Joel turned to see a fierce little female with a gold tooth and a bad haircut. He was relieved to see that he was the larger of the two. "I'm not paying you anything," Joel replied.

"You knocked it down, buddy," the woman said, pushing Joel back.

"Fuck you!" Joel replied, pushing the girl away from him.

"Keep your hands off her!" bellowed a much larger woman who stood up and rushed down the post office steps. This one was a good six feet tall. As drunk as Joel was, he still managed to repeat his Buddhist mantra several times in preparation for being killed. Before any blows were struck, though, someone yanked him back and handed the woman a wad of bills.

"Sorry, ladies," the man said. "I'll make sure he gets home." Joel fell back into the arms of Bill Doyle, still horny from his dream the night before and out for an evening stroll. "You're drunk," he said pulling Joel into the street and hailing an oncoming cab. "How many drinks did you have?"

"Four ..."

"Get in the cab." If there was one thing he'd learned from two decades of living in Provincetown, it was that Jews couldn't hold their liquor.

Chapter Twenty-four

"We have to go to Spiritus and warn Dennis," Joel protested. "Keith is going there to beat him up."

"Don't worry. They all went to a party in Truro."

"Thank god," Joel groaned as he sank into the seat. "I feel awful."

"You gonna be sick?"

"Hopefully," Joel groaned, putting his hands over his face and closing his eyes. At the corner of Court Street, the cab made a sharp right, and Bill grasped Joel's shoulder to keep him from falling over. He found something so adorable about the way Joel looked while trying not to vomit that he decided to forgive him for having been so insulting the last time they had spoken. At the corner of Bradford, the cab made another sharp right, and this time Joel collapsed facedown in Bill's lap.

"Hey, big guy." Mitchell suddenly appeared in Bill's mind. "Tonight's your big chance to nail him."

"But he's practically unconscious."

"Perfect. Remember how you always wanted to have a three-way?

This is the moment you've been waiting for. We'll do this together. Go on. Touch his face."

"But I don't think he can feel anything."

"Nah. He's only pretending to be asleep, but he's thinking: 'If I keep my eyes closed long enough, this big handsome prince is going to kiss me and turn me into a princess.'"

"Oh come on."

"That's what I was thinking the first night we met."

"You slept all the way home in the cab."

"I was only pretending. I wanted to see what you would do. Go on now. Stroke his hair."

Bill did what he was told, and the body in his lap moaned appreciatively.

"I told you he would like it."

Bill could feel himself start to get an erection. Turning over his hand, he let his fingers caress Joel's cheek, but this time Bill's hand was swatted away like a pesky insect. "What was that about?" Bill asked.

"He's playing hard to get."

Bill carefully put his hand on Joel's thigh and, unchallenged, rubbed it up and down for the rest of the trip. As the car stopped in front of Dennis's house, there was a clap of thunder and it started to rain. Heaving Joel's inert body off his lap, Bill pulled out his wallet, paid the driver, and ran around the opposite side of the cab to open the door for Joel. The astrologer tumbled onto the road and landed face first in the grass beside the street. Bill slammed the door and the taxi pulled away.

Trying to pull Joel to his feet, Bill's knees buckled and the two men collapsed into a hedge.

"Pick him up!" Mitchell demanded.

"I don't have the strength."

"Well, you can't just leave him in the rain."

"Where's my Bunny?" Joel gurgled as he tried to disentangle himself from the wet branches.

Bill was relieved to discover that the astrologer was at least semi-conscious.

"She's waiting for you. Upsy-daisy," Bill groaned as he placed his shoulder into Joel's midsection and tried to lift.

"I don't feel so good," Joel groaned.

"Neither do I," Bill said straining under the weight.

"I'm gonna miss Bunny."

"She's gonna miss you, too."

It suddenly occurred to Joel he was being carried across the lawn by none other than Bill Doyle. He'd recently seen him toting large bags of peat moss, so he felt secure that he wouldn't be dropped.

"Thanks," he said.

"No problem."

"Woo! Woo!" Bunny, who'd been desperately waiting for Joel, was scratching at the window screen, whining to get out. "Woo! Woo!"

"My baby!" Joel cried, causing the frantic bulldog to throw her full weight against the screen and burst through the window. She ran across the grass and leaped up to lick her master's hand.

"Bunny. Bunny! Did you miss me?" Reaching for the dog, Joel caused Bill to stumble and they both toppled onto the lawn. "Did you miss me?" Joel kept repeating to his one true friend, who was eagerly licking his face. Suddenly, Bunny darted across the lawn toward Bill's cottage. "Bunny!" Joel cried.

"I'll get her."

Joel slowly pulled himself to his feet and stumbled after them. He stopped at the cottage door. "Bunny?" he called. Joel stepped inside gingerly and walked slowly to the bedroom where Bill and Bunny were playing tug-of-war with a pillow. Half climbing, half falling into the bed, Joel suddenly felt himself being rolled onto his back and being surprised by the sight of Bill's face descending on his own. Then Bill was kissing him, sticking his tongue in his mouth. Having neither the mental capacity nor the physical reflexes to resist, Joel let himself be swept away, as if he'd been hit by a tsunami. Head over heels he tumbled, and when the shock wore off, there he was making out with Bill Doyle, like two high school kids in their parents' basement.

The handyman's ardor seemed inexhaustible, and it occurred to Joel that he might enjoy kissing him back. Waiting for the right moment to leap in, as if he were playing jump rope with the girls, he tentatively slipped in his tongue and started to explore. The taste of the alcohol made his head swim. But Bill was the more aggressive of the two, and there was only so long that Joel could push against the current. His tongue was pushed back and again he allowed himself to be carried away by the sensation of having his head invaded and his mind scrambled.

"Pull down his pants," Mitchell urged.

Bill reached down and began unbuckling Joel's wet jeans. Joel gasped but said nothing as the handyman opened his fly and started fondling his cock. Then he winced.

"Are you sure he likes this?" Bill asked.

"Absolutely. It's just been years since anybody touched him, so he's a little sensitive. Go ahead. Lick it softly." Bill put Joel's cock in his mouth. The astrologer moaned with delight. "Slowly. Don't let him cum. Not for a while."

Joel moaned again.

"Now take off his shoes and socks." Bill did as he was told. Meanwhile, Joel had the sudden urge to pull at Bill's belt, unzip his fly, and lower the man's pants.

"See?" Mitchell said. "I told you he wanted it. Now lift up his shirt and suck on his nipples. Jewish men love to have our nipples sucked. It makes us feel butch, like our mothers." Bill licked Joel's chest, and this time both he and Mitchell began to moan. "Now roll him over and kiss his ears. Quick." Bill did what he was told. "That's right. Now massage his butt." Bill pulled a big bottle of lube out of his night table and squirted some on his hands. Grabbing Joel's buttocks, he rubbed them until they were soft and pliant. "Great! Now get some lube in his hole and finger him." Joel let out another moan, a few notes higher than his last one. "You're doing great," Mitchell whispered to Bill. "Did I ever tell you what a great lover you were?"

"Watch this."

Bill stuck his face between Joel's legs, sucked and licked, and then reinserted his finger.

"Oh, god!" Joel and Mitchell groaned in unison.

"Can you feel this?" Bill asked.

"Oh, yeah. Ghosts have great memories. Oh, god. This is just like old times."

"Oh, baby, I wish this were you!"

"So do I!"

"Oh, Mitchell!" Bill blurted out loud.

"What?" Joel asked.

"Nothing. Nothing."

"Keep it up!" Mitchell demanded. "Don't get distracted. Don't stop."

Bill somehow managed to keep his finger in Joel's hole with one hand while grabbing a condom and slipping it on with the other.

"We're going for gold now! Take your finger out," Mitchell ordered.

"Fast?"

"No. Slow! It feels better. Way better."

"Oh! Oh!" Joel groaned twice, for being fingered felt even better in reverse.

"Now quick. Slip it in while he's still hungry."

Bill shoved his cock up Joel's greasy hole. Bunny meanwhile, who'd been licking Joel's foot, suddenly jumped back as all of Joel's toes curled up in ecstasy.

Chapter Twenty-five

At nine o'clock the following morning, Lou Lustig parked his old Volvo in front of Dennis Fairchild's house, lumbered up the lawn, and knocked on the kitchen door to see if Joel was ready to leave town. Receiving no response, he stuck his head through the window where Bunny had pushed out the screen. Joel was nowhere to be seen and when no one answered his calls, he got back in his car and drove away.

An hour later, Bill Doyle quietly slipped out of bed to pour himself an eye-opener and make his guest some breakfast. At 10:22, Joel opened his eyes and was simultaneously aware of an empty feeling in his stomach and a strange tingle in his nether regions. The angle of the sun coming through the window told him he'd missed his ride to Boston.

At the age of thirty-seven he'd never before been fucked, and except for a little pain and a few anxious moments, he'd enjoyed the experience immensely. Mostly there was that amazing moment when Bill had removed his fingers from his hole and the delightful surprise when something a bit bigger was inserted in its place. It had taken Joel a moment to realize what the new thing inside him was. He'd had the impulse to scream out, "I don't do this. You must have the wrong guy." But the thing had felt so good inside him, not in the least because it belonged to a really nice guy, a man he could trust to wield it in the best way possible. Bill Doyle did everything in the best way possible and now—*nam myoho renge kyo*—he was cooking him breakfast.

"Morning," Bill called from the kitchen, where he was taking a carton of eggs out of the fridge. "I left a T-shirt and shorts for you to wear on the night table. Yours were still damp from last night and I hung them in the sun to dry."

"Thanks," Joel replied, amazed by how thoughtful Bill had been. He saw a bright orange shirt and some maroon shorts, two colors he wouldn't normally wear. Then again, he didn't normally take a cock up his ass, so wearing something different this morning seemed perfectly appropriate. Deciding to shower later in the day, he slipped on the clothes and ambled into the kitchen, where Bill had set a place for him at his rickety old table. Much to his surprise, the room had been cleared of pretzels and half-eaten bags of chips.

"How do you like your eggs?" Bill asked.

"Over easy."

Joel watched Bill carefully fry the eggs. Nobody had ever made him breakfast—not even his mother, who had stocked the kitchen cabinets with Carnation Instant Breakfast and stayed in bed all morning while Joel mixed the concoction himself.

Bill took the spatula and carefully wiggled it under the eggs. The moment of truth, when he would flip them and possibly break the yolk, had arrived. Joel found himself holding his breath as Bill, with the concentration of a brain surgeon, paused to focus his attention. In the blink of an eye, the eggs were successfully turned, and

Joel knew at that moment that Bill cared for him and, if they ever wound up as lovers, he'd be in excellent hands.

"Go sit down," Bill suggested.

Right on cue, two pieces of toast popped up. Bill quickly buttered them, sliced them on the diagonal, and placed them on a plate along with potatoes and bacon. He laid the plate on the table with both hands, and sat down opposite Joel.

"You're going to watch me eat?" Joel asked.

Bill nodded his head. "I ate before." Self-consciously, Joel took a bite and swallowed. Bill was still staring at him. Realizing that Bill was waiting for his approval, Joel said, "Mmm!" and Bill beamed.

"Pghh. Pghh." Bunny had waddled over to sit at her master's feet and wait for her usual share of Joel's meal.

"What are you doing today?" Bill asked.

"Well, I thought I was leaving town," Joel answered jokingly. "But if you keep cooking for me ..." Glancing up, he saw that Bill had grown quiet. Uncomfortable with the silence, Joel asked, "So what are *you* doing today?"

"I've got to meet Marge down at the lumberyard. She wants me to start painting her condo the day after Labor Day. Now that the deck is finished, I can earn a few bucks working around town." Bill paused for a moment and, taking a deep breath, said, "You know, you don't have to go."

Joel didn't know how to respond. His world had been so completely turned upside down. The only thing he knew for sure was that Bill's words had reawakened the strange tingling sensation down below. "Where would I stay?" Joel finally asked.

"You could stay here...." Bill added quickly, "Until you find your own place. I know Bunny would like you to." Joel looked down and saw a soulful entreaty in Bunny's eyes that was not that dissimilar to Bill's. It made him exceedingly uncomfortable.

"Let me think about it," Joel said with uncertainty.

Feeling he might have overstepped himself, Bill stood up and avoided Joel's eyes while he wiped off the counter.

"You OK?" Joel asked, afraid he might have hurt Bill.

"Just promise me you won't leave until I get back and we can talk about it some more."

"Sure. Absolutely," Joel answered, happy to be able to give Bill some reassurance in return for his kindness.

The handyman stepped behind Joel and gave him a hug, kissing him on his neck as he'd done the night before, and said, "I think you're going to find a reason to stay."

"Maybe I will," Joel answered, having an opportunity to act coy for the first time in his life.

Bill pulled himself away. "I'll be back in an hour," he said as he disappeared into a narrow door beside the stove. Joel leaned on the table and pondered. Why had he suddenly grown so uncomfortable when Bill invited him to stay? He thought Bill was a great guy. His tush did lack a little volume, but he could learn to live with that. True, he was a blue-collar worker, the kind of man who hadn't been a part of his family since his ancestors had built the pyramids. But a few days of toiling beside him in the yard had shown Joel how much intelligence it actually took to make a living working with one's hands. Joel had come to like the fact that Bill wasn't an academic, or a social worker, or an actor: the kinds of professions he'd always imagined for his lover. He liked the fact that Bill Doyle was a man who painted houses.

A man who painted houses?

Joel heard footsteps, looked up, and saw that Bill had come down from the attic. He was bending over to kiss Joel good-bye. He had put on a white T-shirt and was buttoning his overalls. "Can I bring you back some lunch?"

Joel looked up in a daze. "What?"

"Lunch."

"I'm sorry. I was just thinking about something else."

Bill went to the door, turning one last time before he left. "You really are a great looking guy," he announced, as he walked out the door and sauntered over to the truck. Joel got up to the window and watched as he climbed into the cab and started the engine.

A man who paints houses?

With the words of Yris del Coro echoing in his ears, Joel brought his dish to the sink and started to wash it. Could it be, he wondered, that Bill Doyle and not Dennis Fairchild was his Twin Flame?

Reeling from this latest possibility, Joel went into the living room and looked around the cabin. Was this the home of the man he'd been searching for his entire life? If so, it needed a little cleaning. And every surface seemed to be filled with photographs—of Bill posing with someone who looked enough like Joel to be his brother.

"This man will be in love with someone else."

Joel suddenly realized that the shirt he was wearing was the same shirt the man in one of the pictures had on. It also smelled a bit musty, as if it had been in storage. Joel walked into the kitchen and stepped up to the door next to the stove. He stuck his head in the stairwell; it ascended to an attic. Climbing a steep set of steps, Joel bent his head and entered a room with a slanted wooden ceiling. There were several bicycles in need of repair, old paintings that Dennis might have cleared out of the main house, and, at the far end of the room beneath a small window, a chest of drawers that had been turned into some kind of altar. On either side of the bureau were clothing racks on which were hanging dozens of shirts, jackets, and pants. Joel stepped forward and looked through them. The larger ones seemed to belong to Bill, but the remainder obviously had belonged to someone else, someone the same size as Joel.

Joel turned to examine the altar more carefully. In its center—where Joel placed his picture of Yris del Coro—was a large framed photo of the man featured in all the other pictures in Bill's house. It was labeled "Mitchell Savitt, 1957–1993." *Mitchell*—the man to whom Bill had called the night before while making love, Joel recalled. Also sitting on the altar was a letter written on several long sheets of yellow legal paper in a shaky handwriting.

I'm writing this letter to help me get through the day. It's all I can do. How can I ever put into words everything I am feeling? All the guilt and all the love because I never realized what a magnificent soul you were while you were alive. You've been so brave these past few weeks. I'm so sorry. If only I could have you back for one moment to tell you how much I love you. I only pray that you are somewhere now where you can hear me and can forgive me. I was the one who should have died, not you. I was the one who messed around. I was the one who wanted more, and now I have nothing but your precious memory and a pain in my heart that I will feel every day that I walk on this earth without you. Oh, Mitchell, how can I ever live without you? What I'm feeling now is unbearable …

Joel dropped the letter on the bureau. He couldn't read another word. The poor man who had made love to him the night before was filled with so much sorrow. Sitting on the bureau was a gift box containing all of Mitchell's things: a ring, a wristwatch, and a pair of glasses. Opening the bureau drawer he found it filled with hundreds of photos at various stages of Mitchell's life. One of them was a picture from when he was a teenage camp counselor, standing with a troupe of boys beneath a banner reading CAMP RAMAH 1972.

This photo looked oddly familiar to Joel; he realized he had the same picture at home. Peering more closely, he saw himself seated among the group of boys, looking every bit as unhappy as he remembered having been that summer.

Mitchell Savitt? Bill's dead lover was none other than Joel's camp counselor from when he had been twelve years old. Joel wracked his brain for memories of Mitchell. He recalled everyone asking him if Mitchell were his older brother because they looked so much alike. He remembered being embarrassed by the comparison because Mitchell had a reputation for being a "homo." There'd been that one awkward conversation on the front porch of the camp dining room during which Mitchell had wanted to act like his therapist and Joel had clammed up. This was the summer when he had first suspected that he was more interested in boys' asses than he should have been, and for the rest of the summer he'd avoided Mitchell Savitt, as though any contact with a gay guy would have resulted in his own penchant becoming a permanent condition—which of course, it had.

So Bill Doyle was still deeply in love with his old camp counselor, Joel thought. A shiver ran up Joel's spine and the room suddenly seemed very small. He tried to imagine his future with Bill. He picked up the letter again and scanned several pages of eternal devotion and unbearable grief. Shaking his head, he couldn't even begin to imagine anyone loving him as much as Bill loved Mitchell. Even worse, he couldn't imagine himself loving Bill back—not in the way he deserved to be loved: completely, and without any reservations.

Suddenly, Joel heard a screen door squeak at Dennis Fairchild's house. Through the window he saw that Dennis himself had stepped outside with coffee in one hand and a pair of scissors in the other. He hadn't thought of Dennis all morning. The artist stretched out his arms and let the sun kiss his face. Then, placing his cup on the railing of the deck, he sauntered over to a bed of daisies growing alongside the house. This morning he was wearing a pair of tan bicycle shorts that, from a distance, looked an awful lot like the flesh underneath. Joel gasped as if he'd been punched in the gut and leaned on the window for support as Dennis bent over to cut the flowers and remained there with his big ass in the air for what seemed like an eternity. Still, it ended all too soon for Joel, when Dennis stood up with a handful of daisies, got his coffee, and walked back into the house. Joel realized that it was Dennis, not Bill, whom he could love every bit as much as Bill loved Mitchell. If he never saw Dennis again, his life would be a living hell.

Joel started to scheme.

So what if I take Bill up on his offer and stay here right in Dennis's backyard? Maybe I can get Dennis to forgive me and invite me back into the main house. Who cares for him more than I do? Who else takes such good care of his dog? Who else could have helped him give the perform-ance of his life? Who else has fingers that can make him moan the way mine do?

Suddenly he felt like the eyes of Mitchell's funeral portrait were peering piteously into his heart. He collapsed into the chair in front of the bureau and held his head in his hands. He remembered the devoted look on Bill's face as he was serving him breakfast, and he imagined how heartbroken he would be if he ever found out that Joel was using him to get back with Dennis. He knew he couldn't do it.

Chapter Twenty-six

A half-hour later, the former child star Tim Valentine was sipping his iced mocha on the outdoor patio of Café Blasé, one of the first restaurants after coming off the ferry from Boston. At the moment he was perusing the *Provincetown Poop* to see what shows he might see that night: *Funny Gay Males* was a possibility; Varla Jean Merman looked interesting; but what he really wanted to see was *Shut Your Von Trapp!* It sounded exactly like the kind of campy play he'd love to star in himself. Tim yearned to do something sexy and dirty—a complete change from Willie Thomas, the wacky orphan he'd played on TV for seven years. *And God knows I need to refashion my image ever since I made that dreadful TV pilot* Wiz of a Wiz *with that completely untalented jinx Joel Eisenberg.* He'd played a teenage superhero who took advice from an effeminate wizard with a lisp and a Lawn Guyland accent. After all six networks turned down the show, he would have fired his manager if only she hadn't fired him first.

But Tim was nothing if not a survivor. The day after Ellen announced she was a lesbian, he jumped on the bandwagon and signed a contract to write an explicit autobiography of his own queer childhood entitled *They All Called Me Mary*. Now all he needed was the right vehicle to raise his visibility within the gay community, the only people who would dream of buying such a book. He was even willing to produce it himself. If he were able to bring an offbeat show with himself in the lead to New York, and acquitted himself even halfway decently, he would get all the press he needed. *They All Called Me Mary* would fly off the shelves and he'd soon be back on the B list.

Shut Your Von Trapp! He loved the title. Taking off his sunglasses to find out where the show was playing, Tim saw someone staring at him from the sidewalk a few yards away. Not sure if he was about to be accosted by a former fan or cruised by a complete stranger, Tim ventured a smile that quickly iced over when he realized the man coming toward him was none other than Joel Eisenberg, his former co-star, the one who had single-handedly destroyed his career.

Stunned by the discovery that he actually had a conscience, Joel had decided to make his escape from Provincetown. He realized that if he were to have any shred of decency left, he'd have to get as far away as possible from Dennis Fairchild's tush. Peeling off Mitchell Savitt's clothes like so much dead skin, he said a quick but tearful good-bye to Bunny and snuck back into Dennis's house to finish packing his bags for New York. Hurriedly stuffing his possessions into a small suitcase, he made a solemn vow to change his ways. The only solution, he believed, was to give up his search for his Twin Flame and devote all his attention to his career. He would heal himself through work.

As he made his way to Macmillan Wharf to catch the next boat out of town, he remembered how much happier he'd been when he was a celebrity. He'd been famous—way more famous than any of these small-town wannabes who'd been making his life so miserable these past two months, he reminded himself. Under what kind of delusion had he been suffering to ever think that Provincetown nothings like Rudy Cantwell and Dennis Fairchild were better than he? He'd show them. He'd once been a star, and he'd become a star again. … It was then that Tim Valentine materialized before him on Commercial Street, as if the universe was reacting to his better intentions by providing him the one man with whom he'd shared the acme of his career, those two magical weeks on a studio sound set making a TV pilot. Showing his pearly whites, Joel made a beeline across the patio of Café Blasé.

"Tim Valentine!"

"Joel Eisenberg!"

"How are you?"

"Great!" Tim replied, mirroring Joel's excitement, but with far less conviction.

"I'm so glad you finally decided to come out of the closet," Joel said.

"Thank you," Tim replied appreciatively.

"Not that anyone ever thought you were straight to begin with."

Tim blinked as he remembered what it was he most disliked about Joel: the man could sometimes be funny, but mostly he was just rude.

"So are you still with the same agency?" Joel asked nonchalantly.

"No," Tim answered with a slight grimace, telling Joel that he'd hit a sore spot. "Why do you ask?"

"I thought maybe they got you your book deal."

"Are you looking for a book agent?" Tim asked, pretty sure that Joel was trolling for contacts.

"No. Just curious."

"Don't you already have a book agent?"

"Not at the moment," Joel answered tersely. Tim saw the dis-comfort in Joel's face and was somewhat glad that he'd just made the astrologer feel worse about his career than Joel had made him feel about his own.

"Beautiful weather," Tim said, taking a deep breath of ocean air.

"It's great here," Joel answered. "I've been here all summer. It's a fantastic place to write!"

"Really?"

It suddenly occurred to Tim that Joel might actually be able to help him. "By the way, have you seen this play, *Shut Your Von Trapp!*?"

Joel nodded and choked slightly. Being reminded of Dennis had introduced some bile into his upper digestive tract.

"Is it any good?" Tim asked.

"It's good," Joel answered for fear that if he'd said anything else he would suffer future repercussions. Rudy's threats were still fresh in his mind.

"Funny?"

"Absolutely. It's very, very funny."

"Is there a part in there for me?"

"For you?" Joel asked, surprised.

"I'm looking for something I could possibly take to New York. I'd like to produce something for a half million or under."

A starring role? Joel wondered. *A half-million dollars?* Maybe he'd been too hasty in thinking the universe had placed Tim Valentine in his path to help him with his career, he thought. The universe had put him there all right, but as his path back to Dennis. *Nam myoho renge kyo.*

"Oh, my god! I can't believe it. There *is* a perfect part in there for you," Joel said excitedly. "Rolf. The teenage Nazi."

"You mean, 'I Am Sixteen Going on Seventeen?'"

"Yeah, but you have to see what they've done with it. Brilliant!"

Joel lowered his voice and motioned with his finger for Tim to lean forward. "And I also happen to know that the director is looking for someone new to play the part. I could take you right over to meet him."

"Wow!" But then Tim seemed to recall something. "I heard the actor playing this part was pretty good."

Joel made a face like he'd smelled a lemon. "He's an amateur. Besides, he's way too old to play a teenager. He's more like thirty-one going on thirty-two. When's you're birthday?" Joel suddenly asked.

"January twenty-eighth."

"An Aquarian. Perfect." Joel leaned forward and grabbed Tim's hand. "This is your year to shine. You know how sometimes life gives you an opportunity that could only be a divine intervention? This is one of those moments."

Tim was a little frightened by the intensity in Joel's eyes. "For me?" he asked.

"Yes!" Joel answered, squeezing Tim's hand even tighter. The young actor nodded. Running into Joel was exactly what he had needed—even if he was starting to lose all sensation in his fingertips.

Just as Tim Valentine was paying his check at Café Blasé, Bill Doyle was rushing back home to see what Joel might have decided about staying with him in Provincetown. He was also eager to inform Joel what had happened to Keith Antonelli the night before. Not finding Dennis Fairchild in front of Spiritus, the drugged-up mess had been dumb enough to pick a fight with Aida Lott and pull off her giant bouffant wig in front of dozens of onlookers. Aida was so enraged that she took her car keys from her purse and tried to blind him. She'd missed his eyes, but she managed to slice the young addict in the cheek, leaving a cut that required eight stitches and an overnight hospital stay.

"Slow down," Mitchell was telling Bill as he turned the corner onto Smuggs Lane.

"I just can't wait to see Joel."

"Listen to me for a second. I just want you to know that whatever happens between you and Joel that, in some form or another, I'll always be near you."

Bill shed a little tear. "I'll never forget you, Mitchell. Never."

"I love you, too, Bill. Forever."

Bill wiped away his tears, climbed out of his truck, and ran into his house. At the front door he saw Bunny looking distressed and he knew right away that something was dreadfully wrong. Entering the living room, he found Joel's note on the coffee table sitting atop Mitchell's shirt and shorts.

Dear Bill,

I'm <u>so</u> sorry I couldn't stay, but I would have missed the noon ferry and there wasn't another one until five. You made me incredibly happy last night and this morning, but I just need to go home to my own apartment and <u>reground</u> myself. In the meantime, please look after Bunny. You are one of the few people besides me who she likes. To me that says a lot. What else can I say but <u>thank you</u>!

I'll call in a few days to see how she's doing.

Love,

Joel

P. S. Thank you <u>so</u> much for breakfast. I can't cook but if you come to New York I'll take you somewhere in my neighborhood.

Bill turned over the note to see if Joel had written anything on the other side. He hadn't even left his phone number.

Chapter Twenty-seven

Three days later the audience waiting to see *Shut Your Von Trapp!* was taken by surprise when, holding a script in his trembling hands, TV star Tim Valentine walked onstage as Rolf. Although the few locals who had come to see Dennis Fairchild were disappointed, they were outnumbered by the fans of Tim's old sitcom, who were so excited that they couldn't help but call out famous lines from the long-canceled show, causing the nervous thespian to break character several times and recite his TV character's tag line: "Hey, poopy-heads. Cut it out!"

Box office for *Von Trapp!* went through the roof, and Rudy demanded permission from the Unitarian minister to add three performances a week in the basement of the Meeting House. Reverend Levitzky initially balked at having to cancel a Noam Chomsky discussion group, but when Tim Valentine donated two thousand dollars to the effort to make their bell tower wheelchair accessible, the clergyperson happily relented.

Gossip quickly spread through the town that Dennis Fairchild dropped out of the show because he'd come down with a mysterious skin ailment—a story that gained credence because he was no longer seen riding his bicycle on Commercial Street. In reality, he'd gone to his parents' house in Groton for a few days and was now sequestered in his studio going over his financial statements, trying to decide whether to begin painting again. In spite of a downturn in his stock portfolio, Dennis still wasn't ready to paint any more Cape Cod houses for the tourist trade. At the moment, all he wanted to do was lie in bed day after day, watching videos of tragic operas. One day, during the second act of *La Bohème,* he actually started to cough. It was only a slight cold, but for the next few days he stayed in his pajamas, kept the curtains closed, and fancied himself with consumption.

Dennis Fairchild wasn't the only one moping about the Smuggs house and its vicinity, however. In the backyard cottage, Bill Doyle was drinking heavily. With Joel Eisenberg gone and no work until autumn, he found no reason to remain sober for the month of August. Upon awakening, he would have an eye-opener; after lunch he would have a pick-me-up; whenever he left the house he would drink one for the road. Happy hour lasted from two to five every day of the week, after which he'd have a couple of cold ones with dinner, and then end each day with a nightcap.

The third sad soul on Dennis's property was little Bunny, who was completely heartbroken that Joel Eisenberg had suddenly disappeared from her life. Convinced that Joel would soon return, she spent most of her day with her head on the windowsill and her nose pressed up against the glass. At night, unable to sleep in the bed she'd once shared with her master, she wandered into the closet and plopped down on a pile of dirty sheets that still held the musky odor of her one true love.

Oddly enough-Bunny was absolutely correct about Joel's imminent return—in fact, he'd never left town. After introducing Tim to

Rudy and extracting a promise from the director to protect his anonymity, Joel had scooted over to the Fore 'n' Aft Guest House, where he could conceal himself and witness events as they unfolded. Taking a chance, he confided in old Raymond, the desk clerk/cab driver, who, for an exorbitant fee, agreed to hide him in a room on the fourth floor beneath a turret facing the street. For a few dollars more, Raymond provided Joel with a hot plate and groceries and surprisingly, the two men got along quite well. Astrologically, Raymond was a mordantly witty Capricorn, and in late middle age he was delighted that most of his peers were finally beginning to find out that life was as difficult and dreary as it had always been for him.

Joel was more confused than ever about which housepainter was actually his Twin Flame. He'd even begun entertaining the possibility that no such thing existed. Nevertheless, he found that he couldn't stop fixating on Dennis Fairchild, and continued to strategize his reentry into the artist's life. The day before Joel was planning to reappear at Dennis's door, the old concierge compassionately invited him to his house for a home-cooked meal and some sage advice about the handsome artist, whom he had known for more than a decade.

A dinner of broiled salmon was graciously served in his one-bedroom condo on the outskirts of town, on the other side of Route Six. From the outside, Raymond's home was just one of many bland townhouses that had been built after 1970 on a strip of land abutting the national seashore. Inside, it featured a lifetime's worth of collectibles, a lot of which were cheap and in bad taste.

"Just a lot of junk. The good stuff, I keep hidden," Raymond declared as he led Joel from room to room. The den was hung from wall to ceiling with seascapes in various styles. The bathroom was wallpapered with posters of many of the great entertainers who'd played in town, including Jim Bailey and Wayland Flowers. There was even a lipstick-stained cocktail napkin signed "Judy" framed carefully next to a swizzle stick. The kitchen counters were covered with garish cookie jars and holiday decorations, as though his grandmother had died and Raymond had claimed all the tchotchkes his straight siblings hadn't wanted. Foremost among these objects was a bright pink needlepoint on the refrigerator that read, "Old Age and Treachery Will Always Triumph over Youth and Beauty." Most intriguing to Joel, however, were the dozen or so Dennis Fairchild paintings that dated back to 1986, when the young artist had first burst onto the scene.

"I hear he hasn't gotten out of bed in four days," Raymond murmured as he opened another bottle of wine. It was eleven at night and the two men were still lingering at the dinner table.

"Do you think it's serious?" Joel asked, truly concerned.

"Nah, the boy's just hiding because he hates anyone feeling sorry for him. He'll just lay low until some other scandal rocks the town. Then he'll turn up on the street as though nothing had happened. My prediction: he'll start painting again, have his most successful show ever, and nobody will even remember he ever wanted to act, including him."

"But Duncan said he's not working on anything."

"Oh, that's just his style—waiting until the last minute to snatch victory from the jaws of defeat. The boy's quite remarkable. I must say I don't blame you for having a crush on him."

"I never said I had a crush on him."

"I won't even respond to that," Raymond said, peering right through Joel. Averting his eyes, Joel took a small sip of wine.

Looking around the room at Dennis's artwork, he asked, "So which is your favorite?"

Raymond adroitly held his Pall Mall and his wineglass in the same hand while gesturing with the other. He pointed to a painting of a house on Conant Street at sunset that was suffused with a saffron glow. "That was the first one he gave me."

"I didn't realize the two of you were so close."

"Oh yes, we were—once. We adored each other. Our tastes were identical and we had a similar attitude about friendships— Realpolitik. Never value people for anything other than what they can do to advance your agenda."

"And what was Dennis's agenda?"

"Well, for one thing, he worked for me. When we first met, the great artist was merely a street urchin, a prodigiously ambitious child with a completely useless degree in art history from Bowdoin College. I hired him as a houseboy at the Mayflower House, but that was when I owned the place."

"Wait. You owned the Mayflower House?"

"That was the decade when my finances were at high tide. Now I couldn't even afford to stay there."

"I can't picture Dennis as a houseboy."

"Neither could any of the guests. But I kept him on because I believed in his talent. I gave him whatever hours he needed and I got him a studio at the Fine Arts Work Center. I also introduced him to Duncan Deeds back when the man had some taste. And ... oh! ... if you think Dennis is gorgeous now, you should have seen him then. He looked like he'd just sprung naked out of Eakins's *Swimming Hole*."

Joel pointed to the pictures. "And this is how he paid you back?"

"That ... and other ways. ... Oh, don't look so surprised. Haven't you figured out yet that Dennis will fuck anyone? He can actually be quite generous with his body.

"I wish someone had told me."

"Your problem is that you want more than his body—you want his heart, and the only way to get that is by breaking it. He only wants what he can't have, and that's why he's still in love with James."

"What was so special about James?"

"Dennis was the sexiest boy in town but James was the sexiest man. Personally, I found him rather dull, but my taste has always run toward mischievous youths. I should have been a priest."

"So why did Dennis and James break up?"

"I believe James gave Dennis very specific guidelines about how many liaisons he was allowed to have outside their relationship, and when Dennis exceeded his quota, James simply left town. I believe he's living now in southern New Hampshire not too far from Dennis's parents."

"What are they like? The parents?"

"He's a corporate lawyer. She's a chatterbox who drinks. If they lived in anywhere but Massachusetts, they'd be Republicans."

The two men continued to converse about Dennis Fairchild well into the night. Raymond encouraged Joel. He coached him like a prizefighter about to enter the ring and shared with him some valuable secrets about what Dennis liked in bed. Unfortunately, as the hour grew later, the old concierge had several violent coughing fits, and Joel began to wonder if his new friend might be very sick. In truth, Raymond was terminally ill and a large measure of his garrulousness came from a heartfelt desire to pass on his wisdom to the next generation of bitter old queens.

"But now I must take you back to your attic," Raymond said, politely ending the conversation. "You have a long day tomorrow. What time are you going to Dennis's house?"

"What time do you think?"

"About noon, I would say. He should be awake but probably won't have left the house. From what I've gathered, he's lying around his studio all day waiting for someone to come over and kick him in his pants. Oh, one last thing," Raymond said, pulling himself from the table and marching over to a hall closet. Reaching deep inside, he pulled out a cardboard box. "I must confess I had an ulterior motive for bringing you here tonight." Opening the box, Raymond pulled out a chamber pot that looked exactly like the one Joel had broken. "Dennis's came from a shipwreck in 1854. This one is from 1837. I suggest you give it to Dennis as a peace offering."

"You're kidding." Joel was flabbergasted. He reached for the chamber pot, but Raymond pulled it away.

"And I'll sell it to you for a thousand dollars less than Dennis paid for the piece you destroyed. I love you dearly but I also have a greedy little nephew who's expecting a large cash inheritance, and I'd so hate to disappoint him."

Chapter Twenty-eight

Raymond was right: Dennis Fairchild hated anybody feeling sorry for him. It was absolutely necessary for him to be the luckiest person in the room, or he'd simply have to leave. The moment Rudy told him he'd been replaced by Tim Valentine, he rode his bicycle home where, except for a brief trip to see his parents, he'd remained imprisoned like Rapunzel, alone on the second floor with his phone off the hook.

The next day at 11:45 A.M., Dennis woke up with a headache. The night before he'd spent a few productive hours in his studio but this day he was still suffering from the week-old cough he had gotten from watching *La Bohème*. Spending yet another day in his pajamas, he decided to watch his favorite opera, *Turandot,* the story of an icy princess redeemed by a passionate and resourceful prince. The ending always made him cry.

After two acts, he padded into his studio to take a look at the painting he had started the night before. During the time he was playing Rolf, he'd taken photographs of Rudy Cantwell and the rest of the Sphincters backstage as they got into their costumes. Finding an exceedingly unflattering picture of Rudy wearing nothing but a wimple and a jock strap, he'd projected it onto the canvas and traced it with a pencil. There was something about staring at Rudy's malevolent mug that moved Dennis to loosen his brush-strokes and use a highly unsettling combination of sickly colors. His collectors, of course, would be shocked by the vulgarity and Duncan would scream bloody murder, but Dennis was too angry to care what anybody thought. "Fuck you!" he muttered to his canvas as he picked up his brush and added some more green to Rudy's teeth.

His fingers were starting to ache. Laying down the paintbrush, he went into the bathroom to find an analgesic for the stiffness in his joints. He rubbed the ointment into his hands like Lady Mac-beth, squeezing and yanking on his knuckles until they cracked. It was funny how Joel Eisenberg had known about his arthritis that first day on the beach—and he'd certainly been right about Rudy Cantwell's capacity for betrayal.

Feeling some relief in his fingers, Dennis placed the tube back in the cabinet, but in doing so, something terrible happened: he saw his face from an unflattering angle. He immediately looked away, but it was too late; the damage had been done. Seen from above, he couldn't help but notice that his face had looked gray and gaunt, as if he had aged five years in a week. Grabbing hold of the sink, he started to hyperventilate. In the middle of his panic attack he remembered what Rudy had said to him the week before. "It's not *just* that Tim has money. He's twenty-two years old. Dennis, as good as you are, you're just too old for the part."

The son of a bitch! He's ruined my summer and there's nothing I can do about it! Dennis stamped his feet on the floor, but stopped himself when a bottle of aspirin tumbled off the windowsill. He picked it up and shoved one, two, three pills in his mouth. He was getting a fever—and he was scared he really was going to be sick. The smell of turpentine wafted in from the studio. He felt nauseous. Nauseous and overheated. His palms were sweating. He needed to talk to someone, but who? In the past only his mother and James had been able to talk him out of his black moods, but he didn't want to talk to Maureen. He was afraid she'd drive all the way to Provincetown to nurse him and then he'd never be able to get rid of her. James, he knew, was probably at the beach somewhere with Chipper, the graduate student from Tuft—the one who looked like he had at twenty.

Dennis staggered into his bedroom and threw himself on the bed. The room was spinning. Rolling onto his side, he grabbed the remote and fast-forwarded to *"Nessun dorma,"* his favorite aria. *If only there were a Prince of Tartary searching for me—a man who could match my icy fire with an icy fire all his own.* Dennis fell back on his pillow and tried to calm himself. He thought he was probably running a fever but he was too depressed to get out of bed to get the thermometer. Why should he even bother to recover? he wondered. He had no real friends. His career was over. Nobody loved him....

"Bunny!" Dennis's ears pricked up at the sound of Joel Eisenberg's voice. The astrologer had just entered the kitchen and was greeting the dog. "Bunny, I missed you so much." Dennis quickly turned off the TV and then quietly shut the door to his room.

Bunny was so happy to see her master she licked every inch of his face and hands. Joel's attention, however, was on whether Dennis was in the house. Clutching the chamber pot he'd bought from Raymond, he started for the stairs. "Stay here, baby," he admonished Bunny. The little dog obeyed but she kept her eye on her favorite master until he disappeared at the top of the steps.

Joel entered the studio and saw that the artist had been painting. Tiptoeing around the easel, he came face-to-face with Rudy's portrait. The style reminded Joel of a Francis Bacon, with bright red blood seeping through the eyes and yellow-green pus dripping from the cheeks. Glancing at the desk, he saw some photos: Aida Lott eating an ice cream cone while stuffing her bra; Ida Dream tucking his penis with a look of excruciating pain on his face. Joel realized that Dennis had the makings of a whole series of wonderfully decadent paintings, work that would take him out of the tourist trade and maybe even get him a show in New York. With this in mind, he approached Dennis's room and tapped lightly on the door.

"Who's there?" Dennis cried out weakly.

Joel's heart fluttered at the sound of the artist's voice.

"It's me. Joel."

"I'm just getting up," Dennis replied with a yawn.

Joel waited a moment and then added, "I brought you something."

After a moment, Dennis called out again, "Come in."

Joel opened Dennis's door slowly and was happy to discover the artist was alone. The shades were drawn and the room was dark except for a small lamp on the night table. Dennis was lying in bed with the covers pulled up to his chin. Joel stepped forward and placed the box containing the antique chamber pot at the foot of Dennis's bed.

"What's that?" Dennis asked.

"Open it."

Dennis pulled himself into a sitting position and reached for the box. His face lit up when he saw what was inside. "Oh, Joel," he said appreciatively, for he could see immediately the quality of the piece. "This is great."

"Is it kind of what you wanted?"

Dennis nodded.

"Dennis, you have no idea how awful I felt about breaking your antique."

Dennis shook his head in disbelief. Holding the pot to the light, he saw there weren't any major cracks or bubbles in the glaze. "Where in the world did you find it?" he asked.

Joel hesitated. "An antique store in New York," he replied. "I just got back this morning." Seeing Dennis was pleased, Joel felt emboldened. "I heard about what happened with Rudy."

Dennis shrugged, trying to appear unfazed, but the effort showed in his eyes. The lack of color in his cheeks indicated to Joel that the artist had been suffering. Part of him wanted to make Dennis feel better, but the better part of him was thrilled. "Can I say something?"

Dennis nodded and Joel sat down on the bed. "It really was a blessing that you got fired from that show. As good as you are as an actor—and I should know because I helped you—as a painter you're a genius." Joel pointed in the direction of Dennis's easel. "Your new painting is absolutely amazing. *Von Trapp!* won't last two days in front of a New York audience. But what you're doing out there could get you a major gallery show in New York. For the first time you're painting what you have to paint."

Dennis sat up in bed a little straighter and Joel leaned closer to him.

"I haven't said this until now because I wasn't sure you were ready, but I happen to know some people in New York who could get you that show."

Dennis rolled his eyes and laughed derisively.

"You don't think so?"

"Who do you know?" Dennis asked.

Joel held up his hand and started counting on his fingers. "Gary Flickman. Natasha Klein. Mimi Schoenfeld."

"Wait. You actually know Mimi Schoenfeld? Of the Schoenfeld Gallery?"

"I did her chart in 1992, and she comes to me every year to do her Solar Return."

"And you can get Mimi Schoenfeld to give me a show?"

"I can if you keep painting portraits like the one out there. You can do a whole series. Paint every one of those ugly drag queens. Mock them all. If there's one thing New York loves, it's dark and ugly."

Joel reached out and touched Dennis's knee. The artist flinched slightly but decided not to protest. Joel took the liberty of gripping him a little tighter. "Dennis. Painting well is the best revenge. And I'll help you. Remember how I helped you with acting? If the whole series is as good as the one out there, I'll get Mimi Schoenfeld to come to Provincetown to see your show."

"Come on. She's not going to come to Provincetown."

"Oh, no? Let me tell you something. When you do a person's chart, you find out a lot about them."

Dennis's face lit up. "What do you know?" he asked gleefully.

"How about the name of the woman she's having a long-term affair with?"

"Mimi Schoenfeld is a lesbian?"

Joel nodded. "And she's in the middle of divorcing her husband so I'm sure she wants to keep it a secret from the judge."

"But you wouldn't blackmail her?"

Joel shook his head and lowered his voice. "Why do you think Jean Paul left the beach so suddenly that day we met? I told him his lover was cheating on him and made it sound like he had to call him right away."

"You didn't?" Dennis replied, feigning shock.

"I don't need to blackmail people to get them to do what I want."

But the artist still looked doubtful. Joel decided to bet the house. "Why do you think Oscar's lover came back to town so suddenly?"

Dennis's smile turned into a frown. Dispatching Jean Paul was amusing, but Oscar Gonzalez was another story. He'd still been very fond of him, and had suffered several twinges of pain when the stud had ignored him at rehearsals and refused his calls.

"I don't know about this," Dennis said shaking his head.

"What's the matter?"

Dennis couldn't answer exactly, but Joel read his mind. "I know what you're thinking—that I'm some kind of psycho with a fatal attraction for you."

"Well?"

"Look, Dennis, I love you very much, but I also know you like the back of my hand. You're an Aquarian. You need to be free. I'm a Cancer. We cling. I know you'll never love me the way I love you. All I want is the chance to be close to you until the end of the summer. For one month, let me be the most important person in your life. Then after the show is a big hit, I'll go home to New York and you can decide if you want to come with me."

Dennis was almost persuaded. Hundreds of men had tried to seduce him in his thirty-one years. It all had begun to bore him, but there was something refreshing in Joel's originality. He didn't entirely believe Joel, but anything would be better than being left alone with his rage and his despair. But there was also the question of whether to take Joel's advice. The series Joel was suggesting would take a lot of work and he didn't have much time if the show was going to open Labor Day weekend.

"I don't know if I can do it," Dennis said, shaking his head. "Painting is too hard. I just want to travel—have fun—"

"You'd be miserable if you weren't making art."

Dennis covered his face with his hands. "I don't have time to do this show. What about the house? What about Bunny?"

"I'll move back in and take care of everything. I'll order out for food. I'll clean your brushes. And when you're tired, I'll give you a little back rub."

Dennis still looked unconvinced, but Joel was determined. Leaning forward, he pressed his lips to Dennis's forehead. "Have you taken your temperature?"

Dennis shook his head.

"Where's the thermometer?"

Dennis nodded toward the bathroom

Joel walked unsteadily to the medicine cabinet. His hands shook as he pushed aside the Celebrex and the Bengay. He discovered a little cardboard box containing an old oral thermometer. Joel sighed—it wasn't quite what he'd hoped to find. Just as he was about to close the cabinet door, however, something else caught his eye. *Could it be?* Joel reached in and pulled out the thin plastic tube. A rectal thermometer. *Nam myoho renge kyo.* All he needed now was a little—yes! Vaseline petroleum jelly in the little square jar. *Perfect!*

Clutching his two treasures, he returned to Dennis's bedroom. Looking up from the bed, Dennis saw what was in store for him. He grimaced.

"These are much more accurate than the oral kind," Joel said, putting on his best nursing face. Dennis looked doubtful, but after a few moments he rolled his eyes, rolled over on his side, and tossed away the blanket.

Chapter Twenty-nine

For the next few weeks, Joel Eisenberg sequestered himself in the studio with Dennis Fairchild and worked side by side with the artist on his upcoming show. Duncan Deeds was hesitant to mount another offbeat exhibition after the financial failure of the last one, but Joel finally convinced him that a visit by the great Mimi Schoenfeld could do wonders for his gallery's reputation. Joel sent Mimi an e-mail asking her to consider reserving Labor Day weekend for a trip to Cape Cod, and it was a happy day on Smuggs Lane when Ms. Schoenfeld responded in the affirmative. She also thanked Joel for including in the invitation her dear friend, one Ms. Delores Tancredo, a captain with the New York City Police Department.

Joel's relationship with Dennis changed dramatically. What had begun as nothing more than lust had grown into one of the most powerful forces in the universe. It was what Jewish mothers feel for their sons, and what Jewish sons later feel for their partners: sexual attraction mixed with the supernatural strength of a matriarch protecting her threatened children. He did whatever he could to help

Dennis. He ordered out for all their meals. He gave him the glucosamine tablets for his arthritis. He made sure the refrigerator was stocked with Dennis's favorite snacks. He came up with funny titles for each painting and, in the week before Labor Day when Dennis was really under the gun, he even mixed the paints, cleaned his palette, and applied the background colors. Several nights a week Joel would be allowed to break out his bottle of massage oil and lovingly rub Dennis's bare buttocks in order to put him to sleep. They'd established certain boundaries: Joel wasn't to touch the artist's cock or finger his hole. But the astrologer didn't mind: Dennis's work required every ounce of his creative juices and he didn't want any spilled unnecessarily.

Joel, on the other hand, was jerking off like crazy. As soon as Dennis was sleeping soundly on the second floor, Joel would run downstairs and masturbate three or four times. In Joel's fantasies, Dennis Fairchild loved to be spanked, adored having his ass eaten, and absolutely craved being fucked. He was so much fun, in fact, that the fantasy Dennis soon replaced the flesh-and-blood Dennis in Joel's mind. Occasionally Joel would bump into the real Dennis in the kitchen, and he would be momentarily surprised that the artist showed no awareness that the two of them had just had sex. The real Dennis was much too absorbed in his work to notice all the wanking that was taking place below him. He did observe, however, that the hand lotion he kept on the windowsill above the sink always seemed to be missing.

But Dennis's lack of awareness could hardly have put a dent in Joel's happiness. He and Dennis were partners now, and Joel fervently believed the artist would never again dream of doing another gallery show without his help. Best of all, thanks to a steady diet of pizza and Chinese food, Dennis started gaining weight, and his magnificent ass got even more magnificent. Nothing excited Joel more than watching Dennis reaching for his third slice because he knew it was only a matter of hours before he'd see that extra cheese rounding out the contours of his bottom. Joel may not have had been allowed to put anything in Dennis's tush, but like Sue Veneer before him, he was completely in charge of what went into the artist's mouth. Except for vitamin pills and the medicine for his stiff joints, everything Joel brought home was as fattening as possible.

But these happy days of summer ended abruptly the day of the Labor Day exhibition. Duncan had done a fantastic job contacting Dennis's patrons, and half the Cape turned out to see what the artist had done. The townies came out in droves and a mob formed in the street outside the gallery. Rudy Cantwell, always eager for some publicity, showed up with his Sphincters, posed before his hideous portrait, and acted as though he'd commissioned it himself. Both the *Provincetown Poop* and the *Bay Bugle* were lavish in their praise. Lou Lustig, previously not a big fan of the artist, wrote that "Dennis Fairchild's harsh lighting and distorted lines recall the German Expressionists. His pitiless portrayals of drag queens can be favorably compared to Picasso, Grosz, de Kooning, and all the other great misogynistic painters of the past. Could it be that *art* has finally come back to Provincetown?"

Unfortunately, Mimi Schoenfeld never showed up and never called. Nor did she send a representative. Nor did any of the art-work actually sell—not a single painting. As Duncan had warned Dennis, nobody wanted to hang a five-foot painting of Aida Lott over the couch or see Ida Dream's crooked smile first thing every morning. As the afternoon wore on and it became apparent that "What Price Beauty?" would be an artistic success but little else, Dennis took to hanging around the refreshment table where three months earlier he had met Joel Eisenberg. Besides needing a few drinks, Dennis wanted to flirt with the waiter, a handsome, young

graduate student named Bennett Hasley (and an old friend of
Duncan's) who was thinking of taking a semester off from Brown
University and spending the winter in Provincetown. Bennett had
that rare combination of good looks and cheeriness that all too often
passed for innocence in the gay community.

Joel grew livid as he watched Dennis picking up the waiter. In a
split second, lust/compassion turned to lust/rage. This was supposed to be the night he collected his reward for being the indispensable force behind Dennis's show. *Is it my fault Mimi Schoenfeld
didn't show?* Joel thought. *Is it my fault the public is too stupid to buy
the art? No! So why should I be punished? It just isn't fair!*

Joel repeatedly tried to interrupt Dennis and Bennett as they huddled in the back of the gallery long after everyone else had left. *There
were other gallery owners they could contact; there were other series of
paintings they could make together.* But Dennis's mind was on something else. As soon as the astrologer finished a sentence, he would turn
his body away from Joel to find out more about Bennett's plans for the
winter. Had the young guy found a place to live? Did he need anybody to show him around town? Had he a place to spend the night?

A few hours later, Joel lay awake in his room listening to
Dennis's bed bang against the wall. A miracle of self-restraint, he
did not march into Dennis's bedroom with a can of turpentine and
set fire to the artist and his new fling.

The next morning, Bennett left to do some souvenir shopping
and Joel went upstairs and found Dennis cleaning brushes in the
studio. Completely unable to hide his desperation, he pleaded for
Dennis to leave with him for New York.

"Don't you understand?" he yelled at the top of his voice. "It's
great that none of these paintings sold. Now we can mount 'What
Price Beauty?' in New York. This show was never about making
money. It was about making history!"

But the artist no longer showed any interest in Joel's plan for his career. For the next few days he did nothing but tan at the beach all day with Bennett and then drink wine and have sex with him all night in his bedroom. Joel knew what he had to do—he'd done it before with Jean Paul. Over the next few days he managed to appear in the kitchen whenever he suspected the young houseguest was passing through. Slowly but surely he was able to gain the young man's confidence.

According to Bennett, Dennis had been exceedingly effusive in his affections, claiming that he hadn't felt that way about anyone in the longest time. Joel hated to burst the young man's bubble but for Bennett's own sake, he said he needed to set the record straight about Dennis's three passionate love affairs that summer alone. He threw in his ex-boyfriend James for good measure. "Now you have to promise me not to tell Dennis what I've told you," Joel whispered in Bennett's ear. "He has the most frightening temper, especially when he's been caught lying."

At first Bennett didn't want to hear what Joel had to say. Gradually he came to believe it, and became increasingly upset at being fooled so heartlessly. The astrologer patted his back as the young man cried on his shoulder. "The best way to get back at Dennis," Joel assured the young man, "is to leave town without even telling him."

Unfortunately Bennett's conscience wouldn't allow him to go back to Providence without first telling Dennis why he was breaking off their affair. After enduring a tearful confrontation at the bus station, Dennis walked home in the foulest of moods, planning how to throw Joel out of his house for good. He wouldn't lose control, like when Joel broke the chamber pot. Instead, he would shun his houseguest until he got the message.

He underestimated, however, Joel's capacity to endure humiliation. When Dennis arrived home from the bus station and went upstairs without saying hello, Joel merely assumed the artist was upset for having lost his fuck buddy. Later, when Dennis avoided him in the kitchen, Joel simply prepared to wait for the storm to blow over. And the next day, when Dennis refused to answer Joel's knock on his door, he increased his resolve to remain right where he was.

Two days passed without a word being spoken between the two housemates until a wet dishrag that Joel had left hanging on the back of an expensive wooden chair elicited a comment from Dennis about Joel's tendency to be inconsiderate. When Joel demanded specific examples, the artist finally unleashed his tongue. With brutal efficiency he listed each and every way Joel had been not only inconsiderate but also malicious and untruthful, ending with, "And how could you tell Bennett I was still in love with James?"

"What are you talking about?" Joel replied.

"Forget it." Dennis reached for a spoon in the silverware drawer. He pulled one out, examined it, and threw it in the sink; it landed with a loud clang. Several more followed. "You can't even wash a spoon," he muttered.

"Excuse me," Joel replied. "Did I miss something, or did you just change the subject?"

Dennis didn't answer. Joel knew he was getting the silent treatment. Reacting in kind, he picked himself up from the table and walked into his bedroom where he stopped short. *I'm a Jew,* he thought. *We don't do silent.* Pivoting on his heel, he marched back into the kitchen. "Do you have something you want to say to me?"

Dennis wiped another spoon on a dishrag and threw it in the sink.

"I may be a little sloppy," Joel began, "but at least I try to be friendly."

Another spoon landed in the sink.

"OK. I did tell Bennett you were still in love with James. But that's because you were leading him on. You were going to hurt him."

Dennis rolled his eyes. Clang.

"Did you hear what I just said?"

Clang.

"You were leading him on, the same way you lead everybody on. You're a flirt and a cock tease and I hate to say it, but you really don't give a shit about anybody but yourself."

Joel noticed Dennis wince. He had drawn blood.

"And that's why you have no friends. You have fuck buddies. You have fans. You have people who work for you, but nobody really likes you. I know you're an Aquarian and this is painful for you to hear, but . . ."

Dennis shook his head, threw one last spoon in the sink, and headed to the stairwell. Turning back to Joel, he said with deadly calm, "I want you to leave." Then he disappeared up the steps.

Joel felt a tingling sensation throughout his entire body. This was the first time he'd confronted Dennis and it felt almost as good as he imagined sex would feel. Flying upstairs, his feet barely touching the ground, Joel ran into Dennis's studio just in time to see the artist enter his bedroom and start looking through his opera videos. Joel planted himself in Dennis's doorway, grabbing both sides of the frame for support.

"Do you have any idea how shitty Bennett would have felt once he found out you were in love with James? Do you have any idea how much it hurts to be rejected? Have *you* ever even been rejected?"

Dennis pulled out his three versions of *Madama Butterfly* and started reading their covers. He'd forgotten where one particular version had been taped.

"But as much as Bennett was falling for you," Joel continued, "it wasn't that hard for me to convince him to leave. He's a smart kid. He was already getting tired of you because you weren't being real. You're not real with anyone because you're not real with yourself."

Dennis stuck the tape in the machine and grabbed two remotes from his end table. Sitting on his bed, he leaned against the headboard and turned on his TV. "It's none of your business," he said.

"Yes, it is. It's my business because every time you sleep with someone it's like I'm punched in the stomach. God, I felt like shit this summer while you slept with everyone in town but me. You shouldn't be having sex with idiots like Jean Paul. You shouldn't be having sex with guys who have boyfriends, like Oscar. And you really shouldn't be having sex with nasty fucks like Rudy Cantwell. You should be having sex with me. This past week, watching you and Bennett was killing me, Dennis."

"That's not my fault."

"Yes, it is. You knew from the beginning exactly what I wanted."

Dennis pressed rewind. The video machine started to make a loud whirring sound.

"Did you or did you not know I had a crush on you when you asked me to live in this house?"

The artist groaned.

"You did! And you invited me anyway. What were you thinking?"

"I thought you'd get over it," Dennis answered with a trace of spite in his voice.

"Oh, god!" Joel cried because, deep down, he knew that Dennis had just told him the truth. "You used me! Do you really think I would have moved in here to take care of your dog if I didn't love you? Do you really think you're such fascinating company that I would have spent hour after hour watching you paint if you didn't have such a great ass? And you know what? If you didn't have such a great ass, none of this would have happened for you. None of it. Your career. This house. None of it. You're an OK talent, but I'll bet you fucked Duncan Deeds to get him to show your work. No. You didn't even have to fuck him. You just flirted with him, like you did with me that first day at the gallery. Well, I'm sick of it! I'm sick of guys like you getting everything while guys like me have to crawl around on our bellies hoping—hoping—we might be able to trick you into bed. OK. I admit it. I tricked you. I tricked you into thinking I was interested in you as a person, because I'm not! It's your tush, Dennis. Just your tush. And if I can't get that, forget it!"

Dennis shook his head and rolled his eyes.

"Please, Dennis! You have to listen to me. Because in spite of everything, I'm still willing to be your friend if you let me set certain conditions. I don't mind you sleeping with other guys just as long as I get mine. And as long as I get mine—"

Just then the video machine stopped rewinding and Dennis got out of bed. He walked over to Joel, whose heart began to flutter. For a moment the astrologer truly believed Dennis was going to thank him for all the wisdom he'd just imparted.

He didn't. Shaking his head, he slammed his door in Joel's face. The next thing the astrologer knew, the door was being locked from the inside and Dennis was yelling, "If you're not gone by tomorrow morning, I am going to call the police."

Go right ahead, Joel thought. Seething with rage, he marched downstairs, picked up Bunny, and sat down at the edge of his bed. Within moments the anger subsided and Joel started to feel numb. A half hour later, the shock wore off and Joel had an awful feeling in his stomach similar to the hepatitis he'd once suffered from eating bad clams. He started rocking back and forth. That helped a little. An hour later it got dark, but Joel didn't get up to turn on his lamp. At eleven o'clock he heard Dennis coming downstairs and going outside, probably to the A-House to find a replacement for Bennett, something he would do quite easily.

Sometime after two in the morning, when Dennis still hadn't come home, Joel got a flashlight and snuck upstairs to the second floor. He'd decided that he simply couldn't live with himself if he went back to New York without getting his hands on Dennis's tush at least one more time. The corrosive rage he felt in his gut was eating him alive and as much as he loved Dennis—he had no other word for it now—the guy wasn't worth dying for. Scanning the night table beside Dennis's bed, he found what he was looking for: a small plate on which he'd earlier placed the glucosamine capsules that Dennis took for his arthritis every night before he went to sleep.

Joel brought the plate of pills into the bathroom, lay the flashlight down on the sink, got on his knees, and twisted four of them apart. He poured their contents down the drain and took from the medicine cabinet several large Benadryl capsules—the ones Dennis took on the nights he couldn't fall asleep. Twisting one of the pills open, he carefully poured its contents into the arthritis capsule. He did this with all four pills.

Returning the plate to Dennis's night table, he took a moment to look down at it surrounded as it was by other small objects that had been left there by the artist. Funnily enough, Joel began to imagine the scene as a still life. The composition wasn't quite right. Joel took away the pen. He took away the remote. He took away all the other items from the night table except the plate of pills. This way, he thought, Dennis would be sure to notice his medicine before he went to sleep. Then he went back to his room. Taking Bunny onto his lap, he began chanting his mantra for good luck.

At three thirty in the morning, Dennis finally came home. Joel listened as he'd listened so many times before. He heard Dennis walking to the bathroom, the seat being raised, the toilet being flushed. Joel held his breath and didn't exhale until he heard Dennis running the faucet just long enough to fill his drinking glass with water.

Nam myoho renge kyo!

Chapter Thirty

The bell at the Unitarian Meeting House tolled ten times. Clutching a bottle of massage oil and a towel, Joel climbed the stairs and put his ear to Dennis's door. He was relieved to hear the sound of his snoring. *Thank god I didn't kill him,* Joel thought as he tapped on the door. Receiving no answer, he quietly entered the room. There he was, lying on his right side, face to the wall in a modified fetal position: his right leg outstretched, his left leg bent toward his chest—his tush in the air and facing toward the door. He had tossed and turned in his sleep: his covers had been kicked away and his pajama bottoms had slipped down, exposing a third of his buttocks.

"Dennis?" Joel said tentatively. The artist didn't stir. The only sound was Dennis's snoring and a seagull squawking in the harbor across the street. Joel stepped forward and lightly touched his back. "Dennis?"

Joel delicately hooked his index finger in the artist's pajama bottoms and slipped them off. They slid across his ass like a sheet being removed from a priceless sofa. And there they were, his old friends, a little larger and whiter than the last time he'd seen them. *Oh my!* Two eyes weren't nearly enough to drink in their beauty. Joel would have needed eyes on every square inch of his body, and even then his thirst wouldn't have been satisfied. Joel reached down and touched his cock. *Ah! The magic of sexual attraction! How is it,* he wondered, *that something as ethereal as light hitting my retina can produce something so coarse and solid as my throbbing erection?* He yearned for time to stand still, with nothing on his mind but the glorious sight of Dennis Fairchild lying naked on a bed. But time didn't stand still, and with each passing moment Joel found himself wanting more. He wanted to touch it. He wanted to spank it. He wanted to hear the sound of his own hand against Dennis's flesh, and he wanted to see the buttocks quiver like the ocean when a strong breeze blows across the waters. Like God in Genesis, he wanted to inject life into his creation. He wanted to fuck it.

"Dennis?" There was no answer. Joel reached out and let his hand hover an inch above his ass. He was so close he could feel heat emanating from his hole. Very slowly he moved his hand up and down Dennis's crack. "I love you, baby," Joel whispered. "If you only knew how much."

Joel closed the door behind him, laid down his towel, and poured some oil into his hand. Looking down at Dennis's ass, he started stroking himself, very slowly because he wanted to prolong the pleasure. He stroked himself with his right hand while his left hand caressed the air above Dennis's flesh. But his brain couldn't coordinate his two hands doing different things, so he wound up spanking Dennis by accident.

Dennis groaned in his sleep and rolled over on his stomach. Lying on his belly, Dennis's ass looked even better. Joel started pumping again, moving around both sides of the bed so he could see Dennis's near-naked body from as many different angles as possible. Every time he was about to cum he stopped, took a deep breath, refocused his sights, and began stroking again. In order to get an aerial view, Joel clambered onto the bed—which was very difficult with his shorts around his ankles.

From above he could see the whole terrain, from Dennis's head down to his toes. He could see how the mountains grew out of the foothills. It was awesome—like the first time Joel had looked out of the window of a plane and seen the Rockies. Only these mountains were more beautiful. They made him want to cum. They made him want to squirt. They made him want to fuck that big ass. "Yeah, fuck that big ass. Fuck you for wanting to throw me out. Who's the big man now? Yeah, who's the big man now?"

"Ah! Ah!" Joel started to squirt a little sooner than he'd planned. Still on the bed, he dropped to his knees and rolled over on his back just in time to shoot all over his chest.

All except for one little droplet that had landed on Dennis's back.

Joel quietly stepped off the bed and wiped his stomach with the towel. Holding his breath, he reached over and, with a flick of his wrist he cleaned off Dennis's back. All done, he started to back away from the bed.

He knocked into the night table. The jar of massage oil hit the floor.

Dennis groaned; Joel hid in the far corner of the room and held his breath. Dennis moaned. "Who?" he asked of nobody in particular. Not getting an answer, the artist got quiet again. Apparently, he'd been talking in his sleep.

Joel waited until Dennis's breathing got regular. Then he bent down with his jism-soaked towel and wiped the sweetly scented oil off the floor. As hard as he tried, though, he couldn't rid the room of the smell of almonds. Taking one last look at paradise, he left the room and pulled the door shut.

• • •

In his room, Joel quickly emptied the top drawer of his bureau into the same suitcase he'd been dragging to the ferry the morning he'd run into Tim Valentine. It was only a matter of time before Dennis woke up and called the police to get rid of him, he knew. This was it. He couldn't keep drugging Dennis forever.

Or could he? The only time Dennis had been truly sweet and kind to him was when he was sick. So why not? Why not give Dennis only three pills next time—three pills a day for the rest of his life, and this way he could keep the artist in a permanent state of fatigue. The doctors would diagnose him with Epstein-Barr, and Joel could spend the rest of his life catering to the needs of his beloved invalid.

But no—there were definite legal penalties for disabling perfectly healthy young men. Joel opened the second drawer of his bureau, took out a pair of jeans, rolled them into a ball, and shoved them into the suitcase. There was no way Dennis would ever be convinced to allow him to stay one second longer, especially when he woke up, smelled the almond oil, and suspected someone had been diddling with him while he was sleeping.

"Pghh. Pghh." Bunny had followed him into the room and she was making nervous little circles indicating she had to go outside to pee. Joel grabbed the leash hanging off the doorknob for one last walk on the beach with his little companion. As he waited for Bunny to finish pissing, he had the most awful ache in his heart. *Is this all there is?* he wondered. *Was jerking off while Dennis was sleeping the be-all and end-all of their relationship?* It seemed so sad. He thought about fucking his ass. *That wouldn't have been enough, either. How strange,* Joel realized. The one thing he wanted most was to kiss Dennis's lips and for Dennis to kiss him back. It killed Joel that this would probably never happen.

Walking back into the yard, Joel bumped into old Flo Johnson, the mailwoman, delivering the morning mail. She was wearing a large sun hat that completely hid her face.

"Here, I'll take it," Joel offered as he held out his hand.

"Just a bunch of bills," Flo sighed as she handed him a small stack of envelopes, "and this." She dropped one last letter in Joel's hand—a large brown envelope framed with red and blue stripes. "Looks like Dennis got a letter from Paris."

As soon as Flo was gone, Joel stepped back into the kitchen and picked at the flap of the envelope; whoever had sealed it hadn't done a very good job. He picked at it a little more: the envelope was half open. Grabbing a knife from the silverware drawer, Joel retreated to his room and cut open the flap just enough to remove the letter, which was written on a piece of hotel stationery and scribbled rather quickly with a black ballpoint pen.

Dear Dennis,

You must forgive me for not making it to your show on Labor Day but I've had to remain in Paris longer than I intended. So sorry. I will be back in the States at the end of next week and I would love to come to Provincetown and experience your art in person. I'll call you as soon as I get back to New York.

Au revoir,

Mimi

Maybe he and Dennis would wind up moving to New York together after all, Joel thought. As for the letter itself, it was nearly perfect; it only needed a postscript. Clutching the note to his chest, Joel flew to his desk and practiced Mimi's handwriting on a piece of scrap paper. He did this over and over, and when he was completely confident, he took pen to paper and wrote the following right beneath Mimi's signature:

P.S. When I come to Provincetown I'd love to see my dear friend Joel, whom I understand is living with you. Don't let him go anywhere, as I'd love to take the two of you to dinner.

Joel slipped the letter back in its envelope, left the mail on the table, and took Bunny to the beach.

September was the best time to be in Provincetown. The water was still warm, and only the locals and the most interesting tourists remained in town. While at the beach, Joel bumped into a charming bird-watching couple from Ohio who'd come to watch migrating warblers. He also met a hairy young man from Montreal who'd come to celebrate Bear Week. When he got home at five in the evening, he noticed the mail had been taken from the table, and he could hear Dennis upstairs watching operas. Keeping his fingers crossed, Joel went to his room to work on his book proposal, and at ten o'clock the two men bumped into each other in the kitchen. They had a perfectly pleasant conversation about the new chef at Ross's Grill and how the local shopkeepers were having a busier fall than usual. The subject of Joel's leaving town never again came up.

Chapter Thirty-one

Two weeks later—five days after Mimi Schoenfeld promised she would call and didn't—Joel lit a candle, picked up his notebook, opened it to a clean page, and started writing. It was ten o'clock in the morning and he hadn't been able to sleep the night before.

Dear Yris,
Why are you torturing me?

What have I done to deserve this horrible anxiety? I haven't slept for three days. There's hot poison churning in my stomach. My thoughts spin round and round without stopping. And I know it will go on like this until Dennis either tells me he loves me or until I learn to forget about him completely. Can't you help me? I'm not stupid. I know he's a cool Aquarian and the only chance I have is to pull back and play hard to get. But, hello—this is me, remember?

Now it looks like Mimi Schoenfeld might not be coming after all, and for the past two nights the phone has rung and it has been James calling Dennis back. I have the horrible feeling that Dennis is frustrated about his career and he's thinking of getting back together with ex-lover. Last night I couldn't stand it anymore. I tried to explain that just because Mimi didn't come doesn't mean she's not interested. But Dennis wouldn't listen to me. He just kept cleaning his paintbrushes as if I weren't in the room.

Every day I love him more and more. My happiness—my sanity—everything depends on his finally recognizing our mutual destiny. Oh, Yris! Please help me. What he wants with James is wrong. It's wrong for him. Wrong for James. Wrong for me. Wrong for the world that needs his art.

Oh, Yris, I think I hate you. I hate you for giving me a challenge I can never overcome. I hate you for making me suffer for no reason. I just hate you. Hate you! HATE YOU!

Certain that his emotional outburst had captured Yris's attention, Joel put down his pen, took a deep, cleansing breath, and sat cross-legged in front of his altar. Sure enough, his spirit guide quickly entered the room and asked him to dictate her thoughts. Turning to another page in his notebook, he wrote:

Stop complaining. You are doing this to yourself.

"What!" Joel cried. "Why would I do this to myself?" Grabbing a pillow from his bed, he pressed his face into it and yelled as loudly as he could several times while Bunny sat at his feet and looked up at him worriedly. Spent from screaming, he threw himself back on his bed and kicked his feet on the mattress. "I did not do this to myself. I didn't. I didn't!"

Bunny jumped on the bed and tried to comfort Joel by licking his cheek, but he lost his temper and pushed her aside. Upset that her master was angry with her, she began nuzzling his face, which enraged Joel even further. Without thinking, he threw her off the bed so hard that she skidded across the floor and hit the wall with a thud. Bunny yelped in pain and Joel jumped out of bed, mortified at what he'd just done. "Oh, Bunny, I am so sorry," he exclaimed as he tried to comfort the dog who, evading his grasp, ran across the room and hid in the furthest recess of the closet. Joel burst into tears. *What's wrong with me?* he thought desperately. *Yris was right. I am doing this to myself. I am driving myself crazy.*

The phone rang. On its third ring, Joel bounded into the kitchen and grabbed it. *Mimi calling from New York? Or maybe James from New Hampshire....*

"Hello," Joel exclaimed, trying to sound composed.

There was a moment of silence on the other end, followed by the high-pitched voice of a woman. "Dennis?"

Joel recognized the voice of the artist's mother. "It's Joel."

"Oh, Joel. I thought you were Dennis. Well, actually, you're the person I most need to talk to."

Joel took a deep breath and settled in for another long conversation with Maureen Fairchild, a blabbermouth of a Gemini whom he'd first met at Dennis's Labor Day opening. They'd quickly become thick as thieves because, unlike her son, Mrs. Fairchild actually believed in his astrological abilities and was desperate for Joel to tell her anything he knew about Dennis. She started each conversation by asking a series of questions but not listening for the answers, after which she gabbed nonstop. "How are you Joel?" she trilled. "And how's our darling little Bunny?"

"Great. Yesterday we found a new trail—"

"And your new book? Tell me. Have you started writing? You have such a gift for explaining astrology to the layman."

"Actually, I'm still working on the proposal and—"

"Have you heard any more feedback on Dennis's show? The people I spoke with said it was just marvelous."

"I bumped into Duncan Deeds and he said—"

"I just think it's so awful that none of it sold. Then again, Provincetown buyers are so provincial. Dennis desperately needs a more sophisticated audience. Do you really think Mimi Schoenfeld will come and see his new work? She will call, won't she?"

"Absolutely ..."

"That reminds me. I ran into James's sister Wendy again and ... oh ... it just keeps getting worse and worse. Are you listening?"

"I'm listening," Joel replied, bracing for more painful news.

"Dennis is talking about going into business with James. Can you imagine? James makes stained-glass windows for churches and synagogues and Dennis is saying he's going to give up painting and help him with the designs. Imagine! Dennis has never shown the slightest interest in stained glass—or religion, for that matter—so I can only assume his real interest is in James. Personally I think James would be insane to even think of taking Dennis back. From what you've told me this month, he's been more promiscuous than ever—and why on earth would Dennis even think of giving up painting and moving to New Hampshire when he's on the verge of getting his first major gallery show in New York?"

"Well—"

"And here's the kicker. You know that he's driving up here tomorrow?"

Joel felt like he'd been punched in the kidneys. "Dennis mentioned something," he lied.

"He says he wants to see us, but it's really just an excuse to drive over and see James. He and Chipper are planning a commitment ceremony for next month, and the only time Dennis can possibly break them up is this weekend because Chipper is away visiting his relatives in Seattle. It's all so dreadful. Dennis isn't in love with James. He just can't stand the thought of James preferring somebody else. He was the same way as a kid. If I gave Joanna a cookie, he'd snatch it right out of her hand. Are all Aquarians like that?"

"Well, they—"

"So, Joel, you're so wise and you have such a gift. Isn't there something we can do to stop him?"

"Maybe there's—"

"I know! Why don't you do an astrological reading for him and tell him that getting back with James would be a disaster?"

"I don't know if that's—"

"No, of course not. Dennis doesn't believe in astrology. I still don't understand how he can be so wonderfully talented with no interest at all in the mystery of the cosmos. Just like his father. You don't know how awful it is to live with a man who …"

As Maureen rambled, Joel noticed that for the first time in days the anxiety in the pit of his stomach had abated … perhaps because he suddenly knew exactly what he had to do. Putting the phone on the desk so he could still hear Maureen's screech, Joel quietly opened the top drawer of his dresser, reached deep inside, pulled out two bottles of pills, and unscrewed the tops. He emptied four glucosamine tablets in his hand, unscrewed them, and poured out their contents.

"Joel? Joel are you still there?" Maureen had actually noticed his silence.

"I'm sorry, I was just thinking," Joel said, picking up the phone. "He won't listen to me and he won't listen to you—but maybe he'd listen to us if we spoke to him together." Joel paused for a moment, hoping Maureen would get the idea to invite him. "I think I need to come up there tomorrow with Dennis," he finally ventured.

Maureen gasped with joy. "Oh, would you? We could do a kind of mini-intervention. It's our only chance."

"Exactly."

"Oh, I'd be so happy if you came. I'm planning a delicious meal and … oh, I just had a marvelous idea. After we intervene with Dennis, could you possibly give me a reading on another matter? It's about Martin. But would he have to be aware of it? Could you get a vibration from an article of his clothing or some such thing?"

"Absolutely."

"What fun! That'll be our plan. Oh, I just remembered. Tomorrow is no good." Joel startled and almost dropped the pill in his hand. "Tomorrow's the night I'm baking a ham."

Joel sighed with relief. "That's all right. I'll eat just about anything."

"Splendid. It's a date. When you see Dennis, make sure you tell him I'll call back later. I'm going to insist that the only way he can come tomorrow is if you come with him. Oh, Joel. Why couldn't Dennis fall in love with somebody as insightful and caring as you?"

"Maybe some day he will."

Joel hung up the phone and silently thanked Yris for yet another solution to his problems. She always came through, but only when things were at their darkest. *Or maybe that's the only time I listen,* he thought, shaking his head.

"Pghh. Pghh." Bunny had emerged from the closet and was scratching at his knee. Joel bent down, picked her up, and, for the first time in days, found it in his heart to snuggle with her. There was still the problem of what to do with Bunny while he and Dennis were away. *Bill Doyle?* Joel had been avoiding the handyman all month—after his abrupt departure, there was the distinct possibility that Bill might still be upset with him. *I'm sure he's gotten over me by now,* Joel thought. He simply couldn't imagine anybody being as obsessed with him as he was with Dennis.

Chapter Thirty-two

A nondrinker living in Provincetown is like an atheist living in the Vatican. You might enjoy the scenery, but you just don't buy what the town is selling. Surrounded by temptation on every street corner, the twelve-steppers of P-Town tend to be an insular and unhappy bunch of guys who eat dinners together, go to movies together, and—when allowed by their sponsors—have sex with one another. Bill Doyle hadn't relished the idea of joining this crowd, but the day after Labor Day he'd tumbled off a ladder while painting Marge Barton's condo. He hadn't been badly hurt, but when old Marge smelled booze on his breath at ten in the morning, she asked him not to come back until he did something about his problem. So while Joel was talking to Maureen Fairchild on the phone, Bill was attending an AA meeting at Saint Mary's Episcopal Church only a few doors down on Commercial Street.

As fate would have it, there was another new member at this meeting: Keith Antonelli, who himself had hit bottom after Aida Lott cut his face with her keys. Keith suffered from so many substance-abuse issues he wasn't sure he'd come to the right meeting—until

Bill Doyle, a man he'd always secretly found attractive, came in and sat across from him at the table. At the end of the session he'd managed to fall in beside Bill as they walked home. "Dysfunctional relationships," Keith announced grandly. "That's my real addiction. The only reason I drink and drug is that I'm looking for love."

Bill nodded. He tried to be supportive of Keith but he found his psychobabble rather tedious. "You don't see Rudy anymore?" he asked.

"Nah. I am so over him. I don't care if he was my Twin Flame."

"Your what?"

"My Twin Flame. That's what Joel Eisenberg told me the night before I got cut. Talk about a dysfunctional relationship. He and Dennis Fairchild. What is that all about? They, like, stayed in the house together all summer?"

Bill shrugged and smiled, although it pained him to do so. The two men walked a few more steps until Keith could see that Bill would soon be turning up his lane to walk home. "So what about you?" Keith asked jokingly. "Are you currently involved in a dysfunctional relationship?"

Mitchell Savitt's name suddenly sprang into Bill's mind as the only man with whom he had any relationship at all. "Nope," he said.

The two men reached the corner of Smuggs Lane, and Keith started biting his fingernails to feign nonchalance. "Well, now's the time to pair up," he said. "Winter's coming and we're all going to need someone to snuggle. Hey, if you're around this weekend, they're showing free movies down at the Holiday Inn."

"What night?"

"Saturday. Wanna come with me?"

Bill imagined himself sitting home alone trying desperately not to drink. "Yeah, sure."

"I'll call you Friday," Keith called over his shoulder as he sashayed east with a little more bounce in his step. He'd purposely worn tight jeans that day for the meeting, and he was happy for a chance to be observed from behind. Bill watched his twenty-three-year-old ass wiggling from side to side and he started to get an erection.

"He's kind of young," Mitchell suddenly warned him.

"I had a feeling you were about to show up."

"He's also a first-class mess. I'm telling you, baby. Joel's the one."

"It ain't happening. I'm trying to get sober—I don't need the drama."

Bill entered his house, flopped down on his couch, and covered his face with his hands. He couldn't get Mitchell to shut up. "Just so you know," his ex-lover added, "I have to move on. I'm getting ready to be that little black girl, and this might be the very last time you hear me inside your head like this."

"Don't say that."

"Haven't you noticed I hardly come around anymore?"

Bill groaned. Mitchell was right. During the month of August when he'd been drinking constantly, Mitchell had almost never appeared. Bill started to sob.

"I'm sorry," Mitchell said.

"Please don't leave me. Not again."

"You'll get over me. You're already starting to forget."

"But I don't want to." Bill bawled even harder.

"Just let it out, baby. Let it out."

Bill cried and cried, and when he was done he felt tired but cleansed.

"One day at a time," he told himself as he threw his head back on the couch. Suddenly Bill heard a voice behind him coming from the door.

"Anybody home?"

Bill turned around and saw Joel Eisenberg with his face pressed against the screen.

"What do you want?" he asked, making no attempt to disguise the anger that had been building inside him all month every time he saw Joel either enter or exit Dennis's house.

There was an awkward pause while Joel wondered how best to respond to Bill's tone of voice. "Is this a bad time?" he asked.

Bill walked to the door to better scowl at Joel, who was standing in the yard carrying a plastic shopping bag and walking Bunny on a leash. This was the first time he'd seen him since he'd made the decision to get sober and he was surprised at how deeply affected he was by the sight of this man. His stomach churned, but he did his best not to show it.

"Just tell me what you want," Bill grumbled.

Joel cleared his throat nervously. "I … was going to ask for a favor." Joel nodded toward Bunny. "I was … um … wondering if you would watch her. I'm going away for a few days and—"

"Where?" Bill interrupted.

"Actually, I'm … I'm driving to Groton to see Dennis's parents."

Bill's stomach did another flip. "So," he began slowly, "you're driving to Groton with Dennis to see his parents and you have no place to leave the dog and you want me to watch her."

Joel nodded his head. "Would you?"

"Pghh. Pghh."

After a moment, Bill sighed and said, "Let her in." Then he opened the door a little further, took the leash, and pulled Bunny into the house.

Joel handed Bill the shopping bag filled with several cans of dog food and some rawhide chews. "I have to warn you," Joel began nervously, "she's been a little weird lately, so don't be surprised if she sleeps all day. She's been kind of listless."

"Maybe she needs a little attention. Right, girl?"

Joel winced at what Bill was implying, all the more painful because it was true. Strangely enough, he had a sudden urge to tarry. "So ... um ... what are you doing this winter?" he asked.

Bill perked up slightly at Joel's interest in him, but he wasn't ready to show it. He took a deep breath as though he were going to talk about something technical. "Oh, Dennis wants me to winterize the mudroom. I'm also thinking of buying a house in Dorchester with my sister and fixing it up."

"Really? Where's Dorchester?" Joel asked, thinking the name sounded upscale and trendy.

"South of Boston."

"Is it a nice area?" Joel asked.

Bill stopped to think. He didn't want to say *working class.* "Lots of kids. People go to work. Backyards."

Joel pictured Flatbush and Hoboken. There was another awkward pause while Joel wondered what else he might ask. "You ... um ... sure you don't mind watching Bunny?"

"No problem. Except ... well, I may have to leave her alone Saturday night. I've got a date."

Joel's head snapped back in surprise.

"Don't look so shocked," Bill replied with a chuckle.

"Who's the date with?" Joel asked, perplexed at how jealous he was feeling.

"Nobody you know."

"Just curious. Well ..." Joel turned to go, but as he did, he got a good look at Dennis's house. The white shingles were glowing pink in the late afternoon sun, but the rest of the yard lay in a shadow cast by the house next door. A warm breeze blew through an old oak tree, and Joel was reminded of all the bad things he'd done that summer and all the bad things he was still planning to do. "Listen,

Bill," he said slowly to the handyman, who hadn't budged an inch from his place blocking the doorway, "I'm … I'm sorry if I've seemed a little distant this past month. Because, well … I think you know I really had a wonderful time the night I stayed here."

Bill blushed and looked at the ground. "You were quite vocal about it," Bill joked, nodding toward the bedroom.

It was Joel's turn to blush. "Yeah, well … anyway, if I left kind of suddenly, it was only because I got a little freaked out about how you seemed to be so attached to Mitchell."

Bill looked at Joel quizzically. Joel pointed to the attic. "I thought it was weird how you wanted me to wear his clothes. After you left, I went upstairs to return the shirt and I saw … I guess you'd call it a shrine."

"Oh, no."

"No, no," Joel jumped in to keep Bill from being embarrassed. "I think it's amazing that you still love him after all these years. I just felt that … well, you did call out his name while we were having sex. And you want to hear something weird?" Joel continued. "I actually knew Mitchell."

"You're kidding!"

"No. I'm actually in one of those pictures upstairs on the bureau."

"How did you know Mitchell?"

"He was my camp counselor when I was twelve."

"That's crazy," Bill exclaimed, although down deep, it almost made sense that Joel and Mitchell, so much alike, would have known each other.

"You want to see?" Joel asked.

Bill stopped to think. On the one hand, he was mortified that Joel had discovered his secret. On the other, he was relieved to have an explanation for why Joel had abandoned him. "Sure," he said. "Come in."

On the way up the narrow staircase, Bill checked out Joel's ass and became nostalgic for the one night he'd been inside it. Reaching the top of the stairs, he caught up with Joel, who'd marched across the room and picked up one of the photo albums. "It's in here somewhere," he said as he flipped through several large pages in which the plastic was starting to crack. On one page the adhesive had worn out and a few photos slid out of the book and fell to the floor. "Here it is," Joel finally exclaimed. "See? Mark Lerner. Bob Levy. Gary Shapiro. We were the Gimmel Group."

Joel handed the album to Bill, who peered at it even more closely. He saw that Joel was the one boy in the group who hadn't even attempted to smile for the camera. "You don't look too happy."

"Twelve years old and gay. What was there to feel good about?"

"Some of these boys are pretty cute."

"If you like Jews."

Bill Doyle turned to admire Joel's face in the light from the window. Joel turned and noticed Bill staring at him.

"What?" he asked.

Bill quickly looked aside and tried to change the subject. "What was Mitchell like back then?"

Joel tried his best to remember. "Mitchell? He was nice. He made a great key chain."

"Did you talk to him?"

Joel paused. "Actually, now that I think about it. There was one time. I never went in the pool because I hated to change in front of the other guys because I had this constant erection. Anyway, Mitchell kind of knew I was attracted to the other guys, so he tried to talk to me one day. I don't remember what he said. I was just mortified that anyone suspected I was gay."

Bill's eyes suddenly started filling with tears.

"I'm sorry," Joel began to apologize.

"I'm just having a bad day," Bill said, starting to weep in earnest. "I just wish you two could have been friends back then," Bill sobbed. "I wish he could see you now. How you grew up."

Joel felt a great urge to wrap his arms around Bill, but he didn't know how to do it without having Bill think he was being seductive. Instead he just leaned in a little closer to Bill and touched his knee. A few moments later, the handyman was wiping his nose with his forearm and Joel dared to put his hand on his shoulder and sweetly say, "I don't remember what he said to me that day, but I do remember thinking that when I got older, I wanted to be just like him." Bill looked into Joel's eyes and saw all the sympathy he craved. Reaching out, he gently grabbed Joel's head and pulled it toward him. They kissed, and for a moment Joel was right back where he was the month before, swept off his feet and going wherever the wave took him.

Then Joel leaned away from Bill. "I can't," he said shaking his head. "It wouldn't be fair."

"Because of Dennis?" Bill asked.

Joel nodded.

"OK. Then you better get going," Bill said, trying not to sound bitter.

Joel then repeated something that had often been said to him—it sounded almost surreal coming from his lips. "I'd still like to be your friend."

"I don't think so," Bill replied, quickly resuming the same stony expression he had before. "I wish I could."

"I understand," Joel said sympathetically.

"Pghh. Pghh."

"You … um … you still don't mind keeping the dog?"

Bill shook his head and Joel bent over to say good-bye to Bunny. "Budgy, budgy, budgy," he exclaimed, hoping to re-create some of the thrill of when they'd first met in the kitchen, the day Sue Veneer had tried to throw him out. "Budgy, budgy, budgy," he repeated. But all Bunny could do was open her eyes, give her master one listless little lick, and then close them again. Feeling like he was making a terrible mistake, Joel stood up to leave.

Bill, meanwhile, turned to face his altar and stared sadly at the large, framed photo of his dead lover. Joel waited on the landing to see if the handyman meant to walk him downstairs, but he remained where he was. "I'll let myself out," Joel suggested. As he descended the steps, he distinctly heard Bill exclaim to nobody in particular, "I told you so."

Chapter Thirty-three

In 1997, you couldn't find a single Taco Bell, Staples, or Target in the village of Groton, Massachusetts. It was a community thoroughly devoted to preserving itself so that Louisa May Alcott might return from the dead in a hoopskirt and not see anything unfamiliar until she reached the Sunoco station at the far edge of town. It was a community in which the VFW considered anybody killed after 1789 to be "nouveau dead" and was loath to list them on their war monument. It was a town where a house had more value if everything in it was original, including the dust, the termites, and the rusty nails popping up from the wide-beam floors.

It was those rusty nails that most annoyed Maureen Fairchild, because she always seemed to catch her stockings when she ran shoeless up the stairs. She hadn't really wanted to live in Groton, but when Martin's father died they'd given up their condo in Concord and moved in with the old witch. Now the matriarch was dead and Maureen wanted desperately to escape this house, as dreary as any Nathaniel Hawthorne could have imagined. She'd wanted to flee to Beacon Hill, but Martin had wanted nothing more than to

grow old surrounded by the same dark furniture that five generations of Fairchilds had been proud to call heirlooms.

Taking another sip of her Bloody Mary, she realized that Dennis
would be arriving any minute with his new friend and she still hadn't
made up their beds. "Bad mother!" she scolded herself as she held
tight to her drink and climbed the stairs to the second floor. First she
stripped Dennis's bed and put on some clean sheets. Then she slipped
through the bathroom to the guest room, on the same floor and
sharing the shower and john. She stripped that bed as well.

Her housework done, she plopped down on Dennis's bed and
contemplated the ideal place to display her son's latest masterpiece,
his scathingly brilliant portrait of Ida Dream. Unfortunately,
Martin would never allow a painting of a half-naked African
American drag queen on the main floor of their home, so it would
have to hang in the attic, right above her work table, where she, too,
had been pushing the boundaries of her creativity, by painting figures very similar to the tortured soul in Edvard Munch's *The
Scream* but set in various area shopping malls.

Maureen had always regretted not taking more time to paint.
Martin's needs had always come first, so initially she'd been relieved
when her husband first started taking horseback-riding lessons,
something that got him out of the house. His riding instructor happened to be a female named Elaine, who was young and trim and a
Capricorn—which, according to Linda Goodman's *Sun Signs,* gave
her a propensity for falling for older men. Maureen had soon begun
to dread Martin's constant comments about Elaine at the dinner
table—how athletic she was, how dedicated she was, how much she
seemed to enjoy grooming her animal....

"Ah, to hell with him! Why should I even care if he's diddling
with a woman young enough to be his daughter? Why am I driving
myself crazy?" Already dizzy from the vodka, Maureen went down

the hall to Martin's closet to find some spare towels for the boys. She had to admit, it would be just like Martin to go for a nice strong girl who could groom his haunches, feed him a sugar cube, and ride him all afternoon. Martin had also been late coming home from work the night before. He claimed to have stayed late at the office, but he could very easily have stopped by the stable for a roll in the hay, she thought. *But he'd never make love in a barn,* Maureen chuckled to herself. *He might soil a perfectly good suit.*

She downed the last of her drink and grabbed a pair of brown towels when she smelled something foul—it seemed to be coming from Martin's shoes. She checked his sneakers and his boots. Nothing. Then she noticed the tasseled loafers he'd worn to work the day before. Turning one of them over, Maureen found that the stitching around the heel contained a thin line of horse manure.

Martin has stepped in it. He's stepped in it big time.

Exhausted from staying out late the night before, Dennis allowed Joel to drive his classic silver Corvette so he could nap and avoid talking to Joel, whose company he barely tolerated. If his mother hadn't insisted on bringing the astrologer, there'd be no way he'd be sitting with the man whose continued presence in his house made his bones ache even more than his arthritis.

Joel, however, felt that the honor of driving meant that Dennis was more dependent upon him than ever. He hadn't set foot out of Provincetown since the middle of July, and the culture shock was making his head spin. He'd forgotten about highways. He'd forgotten about bumper stickers. He'd forgotten that Jesus saved, real men carried guns, and two years at a community college was an achievement worth posting on the window of one's car.

But none of this mattered because the man he loved was sleeping peacefully beside him, his pillow pressed against the window and

his thumb tip pressed against his lips. *How sexy he looks,* Joel
thought. *How innocent.* Like a big dumb baby. Joel's plan was
straightforward. The following morning he would drug Dennis to
make him too sleepy to drive to New Hampshire. And if he wanted
to go the next day, he'd simply drug him again, keeping him mostly
unconscious until James's boyfriend Chipper returned from Seattle.

Joel pulled into the Fairchild's driveway and before he'd even
shifted into park, Dennis opened his door and escaped from the car.
He was halfway up the slate path to the house when Joel saw Maureen coming out the door and offering her cheek for Dennis to kiss.
Dennis started to embrace her but wound up waving his hands in
the air, frowning, and pushing past her into the house. Without
skipping a beat, Maureen flew down the walk to greet Joel. She
reeked of alcohol.

"Joel, darling. I'm so glad you're here. Did you have any trouble
with traffic?"

"We ran into a few jams but it wasn't—"

"You must join me in the kitchen," Maureen interrupted, taking
Joel by the elbow and leading him toward the house. "We have so
much to talk about. Come. Come. Oh, don't look at the garden. It's
gone to hell. I haven't had the patience to weed the damn thing."

Maureen led Joel through a formal dining room already set for
four and into a large country kitchen. Holding tight to Joel's hand,
she hurried him into a laundry room, shut the door behind her, and
leaned on the dryer.

"Joel, I have something to tell you. I've made the most amazing
discovery and I need you to confirm my suspicions. Could I possibly
get you to do a reading for me?"

"Now?" Joel asked.

"No time like the present," Maureen quipped as she reached
deep into a low shelf filled with boxes of detergents and pulled out

a shoe. "Do you remember you said you could read an article of Martin's clothing? Here. What do you smell?" Maureen demanded, holding up a tasseled loafer for Joel, who took a big whiff and almost gagged.

"Horse shit?"

"Exactly! Oh, you're good. You're very good." Maureen placed the shoe on top of the washing machine and took Joel's hand. "Now please, I want you to call your spirit guides or whatever you do and tell me where exactly Martin was when he stepped in it, and, even more importantly ..." Maureen lowered her voice to a whisper, "... who he was with."

Joel looked uneasy.

"Please. For my own peace of mind. I need to know." Maureen stepped back and pointed in the direction of the backyard. "I have been married to that man for thirty-five years and not a day has gone by when I didn't ask myself why I gave up my freedom, my career, my dignity for the life that he wanted." Maureen grabbed Joel by both shoulders. "If you tell me that Martin stepped in horse shit at the stables while fucking his riding teacher, you would only be helping me do what I should have done years ago."

"But ... I don't want to cause you any pain," Joel said nervously.

Maureen shook her head sadly and pressed her hands against her heart. "I'm not saying it wouldn't hurt. But believe me. I am ready to hear the truth."

Joel gulped. Pointing at the shoe, Maureen motioned for Joel to begin.

Realizing he was cornered, Joel closed his eyes and started repeating his mantra. Within seconds, Yris's presence was very strong in the room and he imagined her speaking through his mouth. "I see a man and a woman in a ... it looks like some kind of barn. They're whispering to each other. Now the man is closing the door. And now they're embracing. They're kissing and tumbling to the ground and—"

"Oh, my god!"

Joel opened his eyes and saw that Maureen was holding her stomach and leaning on the dryer. "That son of a bitch!" She started pounding on the washing machine. "Is she fucking him or giving him a blow job?"

"I … I can't see. It's very dark."

"I'll bet she's sitting on it. That's the only way he can get hard." Maureen clutched her stomach and bent over. "Oh, god! I didn't know it would hurt this much."

"I'm so sorry," Joel said trying to calm her down.

"That son of a bitch!" Maureen kept repeating as she stood on her tiptoes and pulled a quart of vodka out from behind a large box of fabric softener. Taking a big gulp, she wiped her mouth with her hand and turned to Joel again.

"Go back. What else can you see?"

"Nothing. It's all dark. The spirit has gone."

Maureen burst into tears and slid to the floor. After a long stretch of weeping, she pulled herself to her feet and staggered into the kitchen. Holding onto the walls and banisters for support, she managed to make her way up the stairs and into her bedroom, where she pulled a large suitcase out of the closet and threw it on the bed.

"What are you doing?" Joel asked, having followed her from the laundry room.

"I've had enough. I'm leaving."

Joel pictured himself explaining to Mr. Fairchild why his wife had left, and Dennis's reaction when he found out it was because of one of his readings. He took hold of Maureen's arms just as she was throwing a brassiere into the suitcase.

"Maureen, you have to calm down."

"I can't," Maureen blubbered.

"Listen to me. The spirits aren't always right. Sometimes they play tricks on us. And even if what I saw was true, maybe she seduced him."

Maureen started shaking her head. "The bastard!"

"That might be true, but you have thirty-five years invested in this marriage. Don't you want to fight for him?"

Maureen nodded her head.

"Say it out loud."

"I want to fight for him."

"Yes. Now listen to me. I can't say this for sure, but all my spirit guides have told me that you and Martin are Twin Flames."

"Is that … is that like soul mates?"

"Phooey. You can meet a soul mate every day on the street, but you only have one Twin Flame. Only one, and it would be a shame to destroy this relationship."

"You're right," Maureen sniffed.

"Tomorrow I'll do a composite chart of the two of you and we'll figure out a way to save this marriage. All I ask is that you get through tonight without making a fuss."

"I can't."

"Yes, you can, Maureen. You Geminis are stronger than you think. You'll get through this and I'll be right by your side. Can you do that?"

Maureen looked up at Joel through her tears and took in every bit of kindness that the astrologer was able to feign. "Oh, Joel. You are the wisest person I've ever met."

Chapter Thirty-four

Joel spent the rest of the afternoon trying to pacify Maureen. He drove her to a nearby pond where they sat in lotus at the edge of the water and prayed to the Original Buddha. When they returned home, he gave her half a Valium and put her to bed for a few hours while he rushed off to the nearest Boston Market to buy some side dishes to go with the ham. Finally, while lighting the two white candles on the dining room table, he said a prayer that they would all get through the evening meal without incident.

Father and son came to the table at eight thirty, each carrying the book they planned to read during dinner: for Martin, a history of the Battle of Bunker Hill, and for Dennis, a large picture book of the great Gothic churches of the Rhine Valley. Knowing that when guests were present Maureen invariably dominated the dinner conversation, they were fairly certain they'd be able to browse through their books in peace. A few minutes later the lady of the house staggered down the stairs and plopped herself in a chair. She was carrying a plastic shopping bag, which she dropped near her feet. Martin said a perfunctory grace, expertly sliced the ham, and passed around the platter. When it got to Maureen, her wrist gave way, the entire ham nearly tumbled off the table, and two slices of pineapple rolled onto the carpet. "Leave it," Maureen slurred.

"Are you all right, dear?" Martin asked, looking concerned.

Maureen simply glared at Martin and started slicing her meat with her spoon. Father and son exchanged knowing glances and for the next half hour conversation was limited to the topic of the number of tollbooths on the Massachusetts Turnpike. Maureen, meanwhile, clumsily tried to feed herself, periodically casting Martin an angry look. In an effort to defuse the tension, Mr. Fairchild turned to his dinner guest and asked him the most basic question he could about astrology: if there are only twelve signs, why aren't there only twelve types of personalities?

Joel glanced across the table at Dennis, who was turning another page of his book. He looked at Maureen, who was now leaning on the table with her face buried in her hands.

"Well," Joel said, realizing he had no choice but to do something he always dreaded: defend astrology to a scientific mind. "It's actually more complicated than that. There's your sun sign, but there's also the signs that the planets are in. You really need a map of the whole sky before you can analyze somebody."

"So you're saying the planets affect our personalities?"

"Actually what we're saying is that there's some mysterious correlation. Whether the planets affect us or not—"

Martin interrupted. "I could almost agree with the concept of the sun affecting us—or the moon. But to say that Pluto, a tiny rock flying through space hundreds of millions of miles away from the earth—to say that this can in any way influence our biosphere, much less our personalities, which we can loosely define as subjective manifestations of the brain's frontal lobe—"

"Oh, Martin, shut up," Maureen burst out, slamming her hands on the table and making the silverware bounce. "You have no idea what you're talking about. Planets are not rocks. They are gods and goddesses. But you'll never understand this because you have no appreciation of mystery. You have no appreciation of feelings. You have no appreciation of anything. So, of course, you don't understand astrology. You never have and you never will, so shut up. Shut up! SHUT UP!"

Martin cleared his throat and quietly announced, "Well, that's one way of looking at it." During the next few moments the room grew very still as Maureen again put her head in her hands, Martin examined an undercooked string bean, and Dennis turned another page of his book. Finally Martin turned to Dennis and asked, "So I understand you're going to see James tomorrow?"

"Yep," Dennis said without looking up.

"Good," Martin declared. "He's a good man. How were you planning on getting there?"

"The 123," Dennis responded tersely.

"There's a better way. Go to Pepperell and take 122 North to Hollis and cut across. Here, let me show you."

"Martin!" Maureen bellowed in exasperation.

"One second," her husband responded testily, as he pulled a fountain pen out of his top pocket and drew a quick map on a piece of scrap paper.

Maureen turned to Joel for support. "He always does this. If there's a useless shortcut, he'll find it and then we all have to suffer."

"Here it is," Martin finally announced, sliding the map across the table and clipping his pen back into the pocket. Dennis reached out to pick it up but his mother grabbed it first, crumpled it, and tossed it across the room, where it landed beneath the telephone table.

"Maureen, what is wrong with you tonight?"

"I don't want Dennis going to see James." Dennis shook his head and turned another page of his book. Maureen turned on him furiously. "Did you hear what I said?"

"Yes, Mom," Dennis answered indifferently.

"You had your chance with him and now you should just … leave him alone."

"Maureen!" Martin cried. "They're going to discuss business."

"Bullshit!" Maureen screamed. "He's going up there to seduce him and I say if he couldn't be faithful the last time there's no way he's going to be faithful now. But maybe that's not his fault. Maybe he takes after you."

Martin winced momentarily, but years of arguing cases before a jury had taught him how to suck it up and maintain a poker face. He turned to Joel. "How's the ham?" he asked.

"Delicious," Joel declared.

"How's the ham?" Maureen asked incredulously. "Should I tell him about the ham that landed on your head?" Maureen turned to Joel and clutched his hand. "It was Christmas," she began with mock sweetness, "the most wonderful time of the year. The week before we were going to open our presents, I found a receipt for a mink stole in Martin's pants pocket. Well, I thought to myself— *lucky me!* There was nothing that I wanted more than a mink stole and since Martin and I were going through one of our many rough patches, I was sure he was trying to make up…."

"Maureen, you're making a fool of yourself!"

"Well. Guess what I got when I opened my present on Christmas Eve?"

"A mink stole?" Joel ventured hopefully.

"No, not even close. An electric can opener!" Maureen pointed a shaky, accusatory finger at Martin. "That son of a bitch had bought the mink stole for his girlfriend."

"Oh, Maureen, that was years ago. Must we talk about it now?"

"All right," Maureen sneered sarcastically. "Let's talk about last night instead. Where were you?"

"I was at the office."

"No, you weren't. You were down at the stables screwing that goddamn horsewoman!"

"I don't know what you're talking about."

"I have proof!"

"You have no such thing."

Martin pushed his chair back, but before he could stand up, he was forced to duck to avoid being hit by one of his tasseled loafers.

"There's your proof!" Maureen yelled. "It was stinking up your closet. Now pick it up and smell it!"

Martin reached for the shoe, gave a brief sniff, and winced. He turned back to Maureen.

"OK. I confess. I did go to the stable last night, but I did not have sex with Elaine. She's thinking about buying the business and she wanted me to check the foundation of the barn."

"Why did you lie to me?"

"Because I knew you'd get hysterical."

Maureen leaned forward and hissed through her teeth. "I have just one thing to say to you, Martin Fairchild: if you go to your riding lesson tomorrow, don't bother coming home."

"You're out of your mind."

"I'm changing the locks."

"Maureen, the lessons are paid for. I'm not throwing away my money."

"Would you rather throw away your marriage?"

"I will not be held hostage by your insane jealousy!"

"Will you promise me never to go to the stables?"

"No."

"Martin, this is your last chance...."

• • •

While Mr. and Mrs. Fairchild continued to fight, Dennis glanced across the table at Joel and rolled his eyes as if to say, "Look what I have to put up with." It was the same look he'd given Joel the first day they'd met at the gallery, when the two elderly women had disparaged his work. It was one of the few times the artist had ever allowed him to glimpse his vulnerability. It melted his heart.

The next moment, Dennis lowered his head and resumed reading, but Joel couldn't stop admiring him. He looked so sweet and forlorn in the house where he had grown up, lit by candlelight and framed by portraits of his ancestors. He glanced at the two battling parents; neither one of them were nearly as handsome as their son, a perfect diamond that had been magically squeezed from their genetic coal. Joel savored how the light made Dennis's hair shine so luminously, how his plump lips were parted just so, how his long eyelashes fanned the air when he blinked. And at the same time he could see the sad little boy who had suffered in this house while his parents fought so viciously. It made him want to take him in his arms and cradle him, to make up for all those years when Dennis hadn't been blessed with a best friend like him—someone who understood him perfectly and could soothe away his pain.

Suddenly, Dennis snapped the book shut, picked up his plate, and left the table. "I'm going to see James."

Maureen spun around in her chair. "I thought you were going tomorrow."

Dennis stopped at the entrance to the kitchen and turned to face his mother. "You're drunk. You were drunk when I got here and you've been drinking all night."

Maureen rose out of her chair and followed Dennis to the sink where he'd begun to scrape off his plate. "I am not drunk. I had a few tiny drinks because I was upset."

Dennis yanked open the dishwasher. "For what it's worth, Mom, Dad is telling the truth. He went to the stables to assess the property. The papers are on his desk."

"Well, that doesn't mean he didn't have sex with her. Joel saw it as clear as day...."

"Joel? How does he know?"

"He did a reading of your father's shoe," Maureen continued. "He visualized the entire scene."

"Mom, Joel Eisenberg is a phony."

"No, he isn't. He has special powers."

Dennis slammed the dishwasher shut and stormed back into the dining room. "What did you say to my mother?" he demanded of Joel with fury in his eyes.

But before the astrologer could think of an answer, Maureen had grabbed Dennis's arm. "Leave him alone. Joel told me the truth, which is more than you or your father ever did."

"Forget it." Dennis tried to head up the stairs but Maureen held tightly to his arm. "Don't you dare go to James's."

"Let me go."

"You'll do just what you did last time. You'll tell James you've been pining away for him all summer. Meanwhile, you've been screwing every guy in town." Maureen suddenly ran to a phone table at the foot of the stairs and picked up a black leather phone book and quickly began thumbing through its pages. "I'm calling James," she announced. "I want to make sure he knows about all the men you've been with this summer. Jean Paul. Oscar. Rudy Cantwell. And god knows how many one-night stands you dragged home from the A-House!"

Dennis cast Joel a brief but searing look of pure hatred.

As for Martin, this latest ploy was more than he could stand. "Maureen," he yelled. "Stop it. Stop it right now."

Hearing her husband's voice, Mrs. Fairchild spun around and flung the phone book at him with all her might. Martin put up his hands to protect his face and the book bounced off his elbow and landed in the middle of the floor. Immediately regretting what she'd done, Maureen dove for it, but Dennis got there more quickly, snatched it, and held it over his head to keep it from his mother. Maureen tried her best to grab it back, but Dennis had longer arms and quicker moves.

"Screw you," she hissed at Dennis. Pivoting on her heels, she strode haughtily from the room and stopped at the base of the steps for one final word to Martin. "I've given the guest room to Joel so you'll be sleeping on the couch." Then she marched upstairs to her bedroom, slammed her door, and locked it.

The dining room was completely silent while all three men looked at the floor. Then Dennis put the phone book under his arm, turned to his father, and said, "I'm going to New Hampshire and I probably won't be back until tomorrow night. Could you drive Joel to the bus station in the morning?"

"Sure thing."

"Also, please tell him that if he's not out of my house by tomorrow night, I'm prepared to take legal action."

"Will do."

"Thanks, Dad."

Without giving Joel even the slightest glance, Dennis turned and climbed the stairs to his room. Joel sat there numbly while Martin returned to his book.

Chapter Thirty-five

A few moments later, Joel stood up. "Good night," he said to Martin.

"G'night," Martin replied without looking up.

There was a bathroom between his room and Dennis's, so Joel quietly slipped inside and heard the artist leaving a message on his ex-lover's answering machine. "James. My parents are driving me crazy. If you want some company tonight, call me back."

There was no telling when James would return the call, so Joel hadn't a moment to lose. Quietly returning to his room, he pulled from his knapsack five sleeping pills disguised as arthritis medicine—one more than he'd used the last time—and carefully laid them on the bathroom counter where he hoped Dennis would swallow them as he had before. Satisfied that he'd done all that he could, Joel went back into his bedroom, closed the door behind him, and fervently prayed to his spirit guide. "Yris del Coro, please. You have brought me this far. Don't fail me now."

Thirty-five minutes later, Joel could hear Dennis's door to the bathroom open and the artist taking a pee. A moment later, Joel heard the sound of the faucet running and a glass being filled with water. *Please let him take the pills*, Joel pleaded silently.

After another half hour of intense prayer—and no sound coming from Dennis's room—Joel went back into the bathroom and peeked through the door into the artist's bedroom. Dennis had fallen asleep in the same blue jeans and work shirt he'd worn to the dinner table. Joel tiptoed quietly into the room and turned off the lamp, so as not to disturb the artist's sleep. That was all he had planned to do. On his way out the door, he turned for one last look.

It wouldn't be right, he told himself. *Once was more than enough.* But Dennis was lying on his back with his legs spread apart and his belt loosened from having eaten too much ham at dinner. As Joel's eyes became accustomed to the dark, he saw that he'd also undone the button of his jeans and his penis was visibly bulging through his fly. Joel's mouth began to water, but he hesitated. He remembered Vinnie Tastone and how Rudy Cantwell had accused him of molesting him. *Still,* Joel thought, *it wouldn't hurt to remove his pants so he can sleep more comfortably.*

Approaching the bed, he carefully grabbed Dennis's zipper and pulled on it very slowly. Click. Click. Click. The fly spread apart like an Easter lily and gradually revealed the complete contour of Dennis's penis straining against his jockey shorts. Joel normally didn't crave cock, but this was Dennis's cock, and he couldn't resist. Hooking his finger under the elastic, he lifted up the waistband, peeked underneath, and caught a glimpse of the head. Dennis snorted and turned over onto his belly.

Joel jumped back. He knew he should flee but he couldn't leave the room. Not while Dennis was rearranging himself on his stomach, moving his butt from side to side, and moaning. Slowly, almost as if Joel's will was controlling them, Dennis's loose pants slipped even further down his legs, unveiling his great big ass tightly encased in a pair of white underwear that reflected what little light there was in the room, so that they appeared to glow from within.

Joel groaned to himself. The artist's tighty-whities looked so damn good that for a few seconds he was tempted not to remove them. But no. Tonight was the night. Joel again approached the bed, cautiously took hold of Dennis's waistband with both hands, and delicately pulled the underwear down around his thighs. *Hello, you big fat babies!* He leaned over and sniffed like a pig seeking truffles, inhaling deeply and rejoicing in how clean they smelled. Climbing onto the bed, he very gently spread Dennis's legs, knelt between them, and said a prayer of gratitude. Placing his right hand on the right buttock and his left hand on the left, he gently parted the cheeks, separating them only an inch. He was going to eat Dennis's ass.

Joel's face began its descent. Two feet. One foot. Six inches. Very slowly it came in for a landing, his tongue dropping from his mouth like the wheels descending on a jet plane. Joel stuck out his tongue and delicately licked the back door to Dennis's soul.

The phone rang.

Joel quickly jumped off the bed and pressed himself against the wall. After the fourth ring the machine picked up. "Dennis," said a deep, masculine voice. "I just got home. Are you there?"

Dennis turned over onto his back.

"OK, kid. You must have gone to sleep. Sorry your parents are driving you crazy, but you'll survive. You always do. I'll see you tomorrow."

"James?" Dennis moaned. Still half asleep and trying to reach for the phone, he knocked it to the floor. This mighty effort seemed to exhaust him. He curled into a fetal position and went back to sleep.

Joel quietly put the phone back on the receiver. If he left Dennis's room now, nobody would be the wiser. The sensation of his tongue on Dennis's ass was imprinted on his brain and he would always have this memory. But he knew he wasn't done for the evening. "Dennis?" he whispered. Dennis didn't respond, so Joel sat down on the bed and rested his hand on the artist's hip. A Yiddish lullaby his grandmother used to sing popped into his mind, so he quietly hummed a few bars. *"Oyfn pripetshik brent a feyerl ... "*

When he was done, he carefully lay down next to Dennis and softly caressed his ear with his lips. Sensing no response, he kissed his cheek. Still not getting any reaction, he gently turned the artist on his back and gazed down at his face. Taking a deep breath, Joel leaned down and pressed his lips against Dennis's.

"I love you," Joel whispered as he kissed first his top lip and then his bottom. At first the artist didn't respond, but then he moaned and started moving his head from side to side as though he were making out with somebody. Sensing a once-in-a-lifetime opportunity, Joel leaned forward and kissed Dennis more passionately this time, opening his mouth and letting his tongue explore the inside of the artist's mouth. For a few moments the Twin Flames were united, and Joel knew that somewhere deep inside the artist's soul there was a part of him just waiting for Joel to make love to him.

Although Joel was aching for more, he didn't want to risk ruining the moment by actually waking Dennis up. Carefully pulling up the artist's underwear and pants, he pressed his lips to Dennis's forehead, whispered, "Good night sweetheart," and quietly tiptoed out of the room.

Chapter Thirty-six

Half an hour later, back in the guest room, Joel had masturbated three times. *So what if he'd been sleeping,* he thought. Dennis seemed to have wanted him as much as he wanted Dennis. All Joel needed was to gradually bring that subconscious knowledge to the surface. *One day Dennis won't require a tranquilizer at all in order to be kissed.* In the meantime, Dennis had to be prevented from seeing James.

Joel jumped out of bed, crossed the hall, and snuck past a sleeping Maureen into the master bedroom. Knowing that Dennis would only take his "arthritis medicine" at night, he rifled through Maureen's medicine cabinet until he found her Valium. Crushing up three pills, he poured them into two empty vitamin C capsules and left them on the bathroom counter where Dennis would be sure to find them. *A couple of Valium might do the trick, especially if they're accompanied by a little note from his mother,* he thought. There were a few outgoing letters on a table in the hallway addressed by Maureen in an eccentric handwriting—not all that difficult to copy.

Darling, Joel wrote very carefully on a piece of stationery he'd found near the phone. *Sorry for all the fuss last night. You did look a little tired at the dinner table, though—so do take a few vitamins before you start your day!*

Having done all he could do, Joel lay down and tried to sleep but was filled with anxiety. He twisted and turned. The clock ticked. Crickets chirped. The electrical wires outside his window buzzed. Unable to stand it one second longer, Joel took a Valium himself and finally managed to fall asleep.

Later that night, Joel dreamed he was watching himself as an infant. He saw himself picked up from a crib and pressed against his mother's breasts. As his face approached the large, pink mounds, he began to drool. *Look at the size of those things,* Joel said to himself. *They look just like a big tush. Is that why I get so hungry for ass?*

"Yes!" His spirit guide had suddenly turned up by his side and was answering his question. "And now that you have become so wise, I can reveal something else. Ten years ago I told you that your Twin Flame would give you his heart. What I didn't tell you then is that you must first give your heart to him. No matter what he says. No matter what he does. You must hold out your heart and make sure that he takes it."

"But who is my Twin Flame? Part of me still thinks it's Bill Doyle."

"No," Yris replied. "It is not Bill Doyle."

"Then it must be Dennis Fairchild?"

Yris shrugged and smiled mysteriously. "This you must discover for yourself."

"But if Dennis is my Twin Flame, how do I make him listen to me?"

"Don't worry. When the moment comes, I'll be with you, and the two of us together will move mountains."

• • •

Joel's eyes snapped open and he found himself under a fluffy down comforter in Groton, Massachusetts. For a brief moment he felt warm and contented, like he'd never met Dennis Fairchild, never gone to Provincetown—like he'd never craved tush. Seconds later, however, Joel remembered where he was and what he'd done the night before. Filled with dread, he rushed to the bathroom and saw that his forged note was still there but that the pills were gone. Expecting to find Dennis passed out on his bed, Joel quietly pushed open the door to Dennis's bedroom. The bed was empty.

Joel heard gravel being crushed in the driveway. He rushed to the window and looked outside just in time to see Dennis backing his car into the street. "He took the Valium and now he's driving," Joel said, groaning. "I might as well have put a gun to his head and pulled the trigger."

Joel ran back to his room and put on his jeans. *Maybe I can borrow a car and follow him,* he thought. Pulling a shirt over his head, he heard a loud thump that came from across the hall.

"Dennis?" It was Maureen calling from her bedroom.

Joel froze. With great trepidation, he crossed the hall, opened the door to the master bedroom, and saw Dennis's mother kneeling beside her bed and trying very hard to stand up.

"Joel, darling. Would you help? I'm so … I'm so tired all of a sudden."

Joel put his hand beneath Maureen's elbow and lifted her onto the bed.

"I woke up exhausted from last night. I took some vitamins but they don't seem to have helped." Maureen flopped back on her bed and closed her eyes.

"Should I call Martin?" Joel asked.

"I ... I called him. He's ... he's with the horsies. He went to see the ..." But before Maureen could complete her sentence, she was fast asleep.

"Maureen?" Joel asked, but there was no answer.

Running to the bathroom, he ripped his note in two and threw the pieces in the garbage. He figured Maureen would continue sleeping until Martin came home—at which point Mr. Fairchild would drive him to the bus station and he'd never see Dennis again unless he acted fast. Running downstairs to the dining room, Joel crawled around the floor. In the corner of the room beneath the phone table was the map Martin had drawn for Dennis the night before. Rushing back to the master bedroom, he peeked inside. Maureen was still sleeping, but her purse was sitting open on the bureau. Silently lifting her car keys from her purse, he ran out the door, slipped behind the wheel of Maureen's bright blue Jetta, and peeled out of the driveway.

The story of Dennis Fairchild and James Van de Hoven would have made a great silent movie: after ten years of an on-again, off-again love affair, they'd exchanged fewer words than one might find in a single crossword puzzle. Their inability to articulate their feelings was part of what made their sex life so steamy. Unfortunately, when they weren't groping each other they were often miserable in each other's company. Dennis didn't want to be controlled, and James was afraid of being abandoned, so they often competed for who could make the other feel more vulnerable while laying less of his own heart on the line. Dennis enjoyed this game of emotional chicken more than James because, of the two, Dennis was the better liar and usually had more to hide. James, on the other hand—an uptight Virgo—was the more traditional, and he'd always hoped that he and Dennis would eventually "settle down and develop a sense of trust."

In the end, though, it was James who became fed up with Dennis's infidelities and broke it off. But three years later, as he was planning a commitment ceremony with someone twenty years his junior, he'd begun hinting to Dennis that he was getting cold feet. Little Chipper had no interest in art; little Chipper left his dirty socks on the floor; little Chipper's friends talked about inane-sounding TV shows James had never seen. James had begun to look back at his earlier love with feelings of nostalgia because, when all was said and done, Dennis Fairchild had the one thing he most prized in a partner: impeccable taste in art. That afternoon while the two men examined James's sketches for stained-glass window designs, James greatly appreciated Dennis's expert feedback.

"This one," the painter said, holding up the paper to catch the light from the window. "The composition is very dynamic."

"It's not too corny?"

"Depends on the colors."

James pondered. He was hesitant to ask the next question because he didn't want to be too dependent on Dennis's opinion.

"What do you see?"

"Something rich. Burnt orange."

All afternoon, James had been feeling a strong resurgence of his attraction to Dennis and the fact that he was right made him even sexier. The two men wandered to a long table near the kiln to see some of the pieces James had just finished.

"Do you still cut the glass yourself?" Dennis asked.

James nodded. Dennis pointed to a large panel hanging from the rafter, a brightly colored abstract. "That one's the best."

James shook his head. "It didn't sell. *This* is what sells." He pointed to a powder-blue lion that looked as if it might have been made for a children's bedroom. "It's for a synagogue in Portsmouth."

"It's hideous."

"It's one of the twelve tribes of Israel."

"Which one?"

"The one with no taste."

The two men chuckled.

"Have you thought about my offer?" Dennis asked casually as he sidled down a long table and sifted through pieces of colored glass.

"You mean about turning some of your paintings into stained glass?"

Dennis nodded. "Duncan thinks he can show them at his gallery in Brewster."

James hesitated for a moment. "Would they still have my signature?"

"Of course."

James looked suspicious. "You wouldn't mind?"

"My last show didn't sell. I don't feel like going back to my old style and I need a way to make money. You can show me how to cut and wrap the glass and we can split the proceeds."

James's heart was beating fast. He'd always dreamed of sharing his business with Dennis. He was almost ready to seal the deal and invite the artist into his bedroom when the memory of Dennis's promiscuity intervened.

"How was your summer?" James asked coyly as he tossed a piece of colored glass from one hand to the other.

"Pretty lonely."

"I heard that you and Rudy Cantwell—"

Dennis shook his head. "Just a rumor."

"Nobody else?"

"Nope."

James cleared his throat. "So if we collaborated, how would it work?"

Dennis started thumbing through a sketchbook James had left out on the table. "You call the shots," he murmured without looking up.

"Really?"

Dennis turned to face James and said in a throaty whisper, "I'll give you everything I got and you can do whatever you want with it."

James moved closer and put his arm around Dennis's waist. "You really hurt me," he whispered back.

"I know, and I'm sorry," Dennis replied. "I swear I won't do it again."

He didn't need to hear anything more. James leaned forward to kiss Dennis, and it was only the sight of a strange, desperate-looking man peeking through his window that kept him from ravishing Dennis on the spot.

Joel had driven to New Hampshire like the devil, guided only by Martin's hand-drawn map and his belief that Yris would tell him what to do once he got there. Mile after mile, his spirit guide sped him on his way. Lights mysteriously turned green as he approached. Street signs popped up just when he needed them. As he passed the post office in the tiny town of Greenville, he looked for an old converted church, and a few seconds later he saw a stone building with Dennis's blue Corvette parked in front. As he got out of the car and approached the church, he noticed a cast-iron cross rising from the steeple on the roof. It sent a momentary shiver down his spine.

He knocked on the door and felt a sickening mixture of excitement and disappointment when James opened it and he saw how handsome he was.

"I hate to interrupt," Joel began breathlessly, saying the first thing that came into his mind. "I wasn't going to come but Dennis's mother ... I didn't know what to do."

James glanced back at Dennis, who was peering past Joel at his mother's Jetta.

"I took your mother's car," Joel continued without skipping a beat. "She gave me the keys right before she went unconscious."

"Unconscious?" Dennis asked suspiciously.

"I was in my room when I heard her fall. I helped her into bed but she fell asleep—or blacked out."

"That doesn't sound good," James said worriedly.

"Did you call my Dad?" Dennis asked.

"I would have," Joel replied. "But I didn't know where he was. Your mother couldn't talk—she was confused."

"She may have had a stroke," James said, growing increasingly concerned. "I think we should call 911."

Dennis rolled his eyes, threw up his hands, and started walking toward the phone. "Let me call her," he muttered without any sense of alarm.

As Dennis dialed, Joel studied the church's interior. It was one immense room from which the pews had been removed. There was a sitting area in the front consisting of an old couch and a few mismatched chairs, and a sleeping area curtained off in the back. The rest of the space was occupied with several work tables covered with colored glass, various steel tools, and a large kiln in the corner. The hooks and chains reminded Joel of the Spanish Inquisition; the oven reminded him of the Holocaust. As for the art itself, it reminded Joel of the kind of cheesy tchotchkes his grandmother would buy in the Catskills and hang in her breakfast nook.

"All this work is yours?" Joel asked politely.

James nodded.

"It's beautiful."

Again James nodded and remained silent. Joel could see why

Dennis was attracted to his strong reserve, and it irritated him intensely. Meanwhile Dennis hung up the phone.

"Any answer?" James asked.

"No."

"Dennis, you better go home and see what's the matter."

Hallelujah, Joel thought to himself.

"I'll go with you," James continued.

Fuck, Joel thought.

James gently took Dennis by the shoulders and looked him straight in the eye. "I don't want you to be alone at a time like this. We'll take my truck."

A few moments later, Joel was glumly following the two lovers outside and watching them climb into the cab of James's pickup. "Follow us!" James yelled out the window as he backed onto the road.

Chapter Thirty-seven

Driving back to Groton, Joel was seized with terror. It was like somebody else's hand was gripping the wheel and that this other person was perfectly capable of steering the car off the road and smashing into the nearest tree. Realizing he needed to calm down, he started chanting. "*Nam myoho renge kyo. Nam myoho renge kyo.*" And as he chanted, his spirit guide filled his heart, not with peace and contentment as she usually did, but rather with a steely determination: "Don't give in to your fear," Yris del Coro whispered in his ear. In the meantime, Joel had lost all sight of James's pickup truck. When he opened the car window to get some air, Martin's map flew right out the window. Tires screeching, he wrenched the Jetta onto the shoulder of the road. Joel cursed as he ran from the car and vainly searched through the grass beside the road. Several cars rushed around the bend and almost hit Joel, who was frantically spinning in circles, not knowing what he should do or where he should go.

Joel got back in the car and sped off in the same direction. A few minutes later he passed a sign indicating that Groton was only six miles away. Ten minutes later he entered the village. Some of the houses looked familiar, but before he knew it he'd exited the town and was back on a country road. He made a U-turn and reentered the village, but again managed to drive entirely through Groton without seeing Dennis's house. It was only on his fourth try—a full fifteen minutes later—that he happened to turn down the correct side street and spot the Fairchilds' house. James's truck was parked in the driveway, right next to Martin's Volvo. Slipping quietly through the front door, he heard conversation coming from the master bedroom.

Joel climbed the stairs with trepidation, and when he entered the bedroom he was confronted by the tableau of Mrs. Fairchild reclining majestically against a mountain of pillows while her husband and son stood protectively on either side of the bed.

She glanced up and gasped when Joel entered the room. She furrowed her brow suspiciously and was about to say something, when her husband stopped her by touching her shoulder.

"Would you mind waiting downstairs for a few minutes?" Martin asked Joel grimly. " I need to talk to my family in private."

Dennis stepped forward. "Dad, I'm going to go now."

But Martin reached out to block his exit. "Please stay, Son. I'd like you to be a part of this discussion."

As Joel started to back his way out of the room, he saw Maureen glaring at him. *She knows what I've done. They all know.* As Joel numbly descended the stairs, part of him wanted to flee Groton and never look back. Another part, however, remembered Yris's words: "Together we will move mountains." *I mustn't give up. I mustn't despair—not while there's the slightest chance I can still make Dennis fall in love with me.*

Realizing that James had to be close by, he walked into the sunroom facing the large backyard. There he was: the mountain in question. Wanting to be helpful in a moment of crisis, he'd gone outside to see if there were any chores to be done; at the moment, he was repairing a fence.

Sucking in his gut, Joel marched into the backyard. "Hey!" he said as he got closer to where James was banging a nail into a tree. "Whatcha doing?"

"Trying to keep out deer," James answered tersely as he pulled on some plastic netting and hooked it to the nail.

Joel watched James pull another nail out of his pocket and bang it into the tree with three expert whacks.

"It really was nice of you to make the trip with Dennis. I guess you've been a part of this family for a long time."

"Yep."

"Martin's a great guy, and Maureen—she's really something. She just loves to meet new people. I think Dennis is the same way. This summer there were so many people coming in and out of his house, I don't know how he kept track of them all."

James cleared his throat.

"Most nights I couldn't fall asleep because of all the people going up and down the stairs to his room. I guess he told you about the play? Rudy was up there almost every night."

James coughed and banged another nail into the tree.

"Anyway, I hear you guys are thinking about getting back together...."

James folded his arms against his chest and glared at Joel. "I don't think that's any of your business," he said angrily.

Joel leaned in closer and put in the most sympathetic expression he could muster. "Look, James, I'm trying to do you a favor. The only reason Dennis wants you back is because he can't stand the idea that you might be happy with somebody else. Whatever Dennis told you, he doesn't love you anymore."

James stared at Joel, dumbstruck. He started to walk away but Joel grabbed his arm.

"Listen to me. Dennis and I lived together the entire summer and for a few weeks I was his only friend. I even helped him paint his last show. I'm going to help get his career started in New York...." James tried to wrest his arm from Joel's grip, but the astrologer wouldn't let him go. "He'll never move to New Hampshire. It would ruin his career. And how long do you think he'll stay faithful?"

"You don't know anything about him."

"Oh, really? Last night he was making out with me."

"What?"

"He was half asleep and he crawled into my bed. I'm telling you, he's a sex addict. He can't control himself." James tried again to pry Joel's fingers off his sleeve but Joel held on with all his strength. "The guy's got a problem. Do you really want to spend the rest of your life wondering at what truck stop he's giving blow jobs? Stay with Chipper. He loves you. He'll be faithful to you. Just nod your head if any of this is getting through."

James's head didn't so much nod as wobble in dismay. "You're crazy!" James said as he shoved Joel away and started heading toward the house.

Joel ran to keep up with him. "Wait! Stop! Can you really make Dennis happy? He wants to be a real artist. He doesn't want to spend the rest of his life making shitty windows to sell at flea markets."

James turned and took a swing at Joel. The astrologer ducked, but the next second James grabbed him in a headlock and was squeezing as hard as he could.

Joel screamed.

Dennis suddenly came running out of the house and grabbed James's shoulder. "What are you doing? Cut it out!"

Joel continued to wail.

James reluctantly released his hold on Joel, who fell back and tumbled to the ground. Breathing hard, he pointed at Joel and yelled, "Next time, I'll break it!"

"What did he say to you?" Dennis demanded.

But James wouldn't answer. Mortified at having lost his temper, and miserable because he suspected Joel had been right about everything, including the quality of his art, he turned away from Dennis and strode toward the house. "This isn't going to work out," he muttered over his shoulder.

"Where are you going?"

"Chipper's coming home tomorrow. I've got to go home and clean."

Dennis followed James into the house, leaving Joel lying alone on the ground. He heard angry voices, a car door slam, tires screech, and a pickup truck engine fade away. A few moments later, Dennis flung the back door open and strode angrily across the lawn.

Joel started to stand up but Dennis shoved him in the chest and he fell back down. Joel tried several times to stand and each time Dennis knocked him to the ground. "Did you drug me last night?"

"What?"

"Did you drug me?"

"No."

"Did you take off my clothes?"

"I wanted you to be more comfortable."

"Were you making out with me?"

"Actually, you were making out with me."

Dennis took a wild swing at Joel and hit him in the elbow as the astrologer tried to block his face. Dennis took another swing, but this time he lost his balance, grabbed the oak tree for support, and cut his hand on the nail that James had just banged in. "Ow! Fuck!" Dennis cried, sucking on his knuckles and dancing in pain.

Joel rushed forward to help.

"Don't touch me!" the artist screamed, hauling off and this time connecting with Joel's cheek. The next thing Joel knew he was flat on his back and Dennis was standing over him looking almost bewildered at what he had done. He hated Joel more than ever— for once again making him lose control. Very quickly reverting to form, he turned on his heels and marched back toward the house.

"Wait," Joel cried, staggering to his feet. "I have to tell you something. We're Twin Flames. We were meant to be together!" Joel followed Dennis through the door to the sunporch, holding up his hands to keep the door from being slammed in his face. Reaching out to grab Dennis, he followed him through the kitchen and the dining room. "Wherever you go, I'll follow you. We can't ever be separated."

When Dennis got to the staircase, he grabbed the banister and yelled upstairs. "Dad!"

Martin answered from his bedroom, "What, Son?"

"Please take Joel to the bus station now."

"Sure thing, Son."

"Please!" Joel pleaded. "Please, don't leave me. Don't ignore me. If you knew how much this hurt, you would never do this to me."

But Dennis was already out the door and marching across the front lawn with Joel in hot pursuit. "Where are you going?" Joel demanded. "Are you going back to James? Wait!"

But Dennis had already reached the driveway. As he grabbed the door handle to his car, Joel remembered the only two words that might still get Dennis's attention.

"Mimi Schoenfeld!" he yelled, and Dennis paused just long enough for Joel to run ahead of him and throw his weight against the car door, preventing Dennis from opening it. The artist tried to shove Joel aside but the astrologer had dug in his heels and couldn't be moved. "Dennis, please. She can get you a show in New York. Don't throw away this opportunity."

Using his last ounce of strength, Dennis was finally able to get a grip on Joel's shoulder and heave him across the lawn. He tried to get back to the car but Joel, crawling on his belly, reached out, grabbed his foot, and pulled him several yards back onto the grass.

"Let go!" Dennis grunted as he fell to his knees and tried to crawl back to the car.

"No!" Joel screamed as he threw himself forward and wrapped his arms around Dennis's thighs. Dennis tried to wriggle free but Joel held on for dear life. An elderly neighbor walking her poodle saw the two men fighting and stopped at the edge of the driveway.

With Joel hugging his legs like a python, Dennis inched toward the car door, reached up, grabbed the steering wheel, and began pulling himself forward onto the seat. Joel's hold was starting to loosen, so he reached forward and grabbed Dennis's belt. He yanked it so hard Dennis's pants slid down revealing several inches of butt crack. Grabbing the stick shift, Dennis managed to pull himself a little further onto the car seat, but with Joel holding his belt, for every inch he pulled himself forward his jeans slipped down the same distance. Seconds later his entire ass was popping out of his pants. Two neighborhood children joined the old lady at the foot of the driveway to see what was going on. They started to giggle.

"Let me go!" Dennis yelled.

"Never!"

"Dad!" Dennis screamed.

Knowing he'd soon be outnumbered, Joel took hold of Dennis's shirt, pulled himself up, and embedded his face in the artist's ass. This would be his last chance to do the one thing he'd always wanted most. Opening his mouth, he sank his teeth into Dennis

Fairchild's left butt cheek and bit down as hard as he could. Dennis screamed in pain; the elderly woman gasped in horror; the children stopped giggling, and still Joel held on with his teeth. He held on while Maureen and Martin came running from the house. He held on while Maureen, in her bathrobe and slippers, wrapped her arms around him and tried to pull him off her son. He held on until Martin crawled across his back, stuck two of his fingers in his mouth, and forcibly loosened his jaw.

Mr. Fairchild did not speak a word the entire way to South Station. It was only when they exited the highway and started weaving their way through the broken streets of downtown Boston that he finally broke his silence. "As soon as you get your tetanus shot, I want your doctor to call mine. Here's his number." Joel took the card and stuck it in his shirt pocket. Huge trucks and buses were rumbling past them, belching diesel fumes and looking like they might capsize at any moment. Martin pulled over to the curb and parked near a sign that read, "No Standing."

"One more thing," he said. "I have no concrete evidence that you forged the note I found in the wastepaper basket, and as long as Maureen claims not to remember what she did last night, you're technically in the clear. On the other hand I have my suspicions, so I plan to ask for a restraining order against you. Do you know what that is?"

"I think so."

"If you ever come near anyone in my family again, I'll have you arrested. And that includes my son. Is that clear?"

"Yes."

Joel started to leave the car, but Martin stopped him. "Also, I don't appreciate being called home from my riding lessons. However, under the circumstances, you might have inadvertently saved my marriage. Therefore, since your actions had some beneficial outcomes—and because Maureen seems to still care for you—I've advised Dennis not to press charges against you for aggravated assault."

"Thank you."

Martin leaned over and opened the passenger door. "Now get out."

Without another word, Joel stepped out onto the curb and joined the throng of people entering the station. This would be the first time since leaving New York that he'd be riding any kind of public transportation, and for a moment he felt like a normal human being.

Book 3
Paradise

Chapter Thirty-eight

At that very moment, Bunny was opening her eyes and looking to see if Joel might have come home. She was still in Bill's cabin—a pleasant enough place—but not where she belonged. Earlier that evening, before he'd left the house, Bill had tossed her a rawhide bone, but Bunny didn't have the strength to chew it. Without Joel, her life had lost its meaning.

Padding over to the window, she stood on her hind legs and looked across the yard to see if there was a light coming from her master's window. Everything was dark there, but she decided to go anyway, just to make sure he hadn't returned. Climbing onto the sill, she jumped through the loose screen into the yard and trotted over to the big house where she pawed at the kitchen door and whined. Receiving no answer, she butted her head against the screen door until it opened. She entered the house, walked into Joel's closet, and lay down in her usual spot on a stinky bag of laundry. The smell of her master comforted her as she listened for Joel's footsteps, wondering if he would ever come back and talk to her sweetly, the way he used to.

Bunny closed her eyes, crossed her paws, and lay her head down on top of them.

All was quiet when suddenly there was a flash of light and something snapped inside her chest. From someplace high above her she heard a voice calling, "Bunny! Come here, Bunny!" It sounded like Joel! Feeling stronger than she had for a long time, she leaped to her feet and ran toward the voice. Up, up, up, she went until she realized her four little feet were no longer touching the ground. She looked to the left. It was dark. She looked to the right. It was dark. She looked down....

Her body was still lying on the laundry bag, looking like she was sleeping. For a moment she was frightened, but she heard the voice of her master reassuring her. "Good girl, Bunny. Good girl." And then she smelled the most wonderful smell. It was heavenly. It was blissful. It was bacon, and it was coming from a corner of the darkness not too far above her head. She wanted to fly toward it, but she was afraid if she left her body in the closet, she would never find her way back home. "Go toward the smell," her master's voice was telling her. Bunny looked back longingly at her body. "No, turn around and go toward the smell."

Eager to obey, Bunny overcame her fear and ran toward the bacon, which now seemed to wrap itself around her. She had all of her energy back, all of her joy. Racing into the darkness, she arrived at the source of all smells.

Doggy heaven, she thought to herself as she became one with the aroma.

Joel sighed in appreciation as he gazed out the window of the bus. His trip from Boston to Provincetown had passed pleasantly enough. The trees were green; the sky was blue; the sand dunes were golden in the late afternoon sun. It was one of those miraculously beautiful days on Cape Cod—at least until Joel stepped off the bus onto MacMillan Wharf and started walking down Commercial Street. "Good god! Were there any houses in Provincetown that Dennis hadn't sketched or painted, any side streets, views of the bay—anything anywhere that wouldn't remind him of the artist?

At the corner of Commercial and Dyer, he stopped, leaned against a mailbox, and started gasping for breath. It wasn't depression or anxiety that had halted him dead in his tracks. It was anger—a red-hot rage that rose up from the center of the earth's core and burned in every cell in his body, and the most painful part was the rage he now felt toward himself. *How could I have been so stupid? How could I have ever thought that someone as mean-spirited, selfish, and cruel as Dennis Fairchild would ever have been able to return my love?*

Keeping his head down to avoid eye contact, he forced himself down the street until he got to Dennis's house. The smell of the kitchen immediately reminded him of the artist, so he held his breath and ran to his bedroom, determined to begin packing. He flung open the closet door, grabbed his suitcase off a high shelf, and slammed the door shut. Opening the top drawer of his bureau, he began pulling out his underwear and socks and throwing them in the bag—but just as quickly he stopped and grabbed his stomach.

Dennis was in the furniture, in the walls—even in the dust—and Joel couldn't fight it any longer. Every cell in his body yearned for Dennis's love. Pressing his cheek against the window frame, he gently ran his fingers along the sill. Wandering into the kitchen, he caressed the counter as tenderly as if it were Dennis's skin. He began to climb the stairs. Entering the studio, he was reminded of the first day in the house. The smell of turpentine broke his heart.

To find the strength to leave this house, he wanted to gaze one last time at the one thing that proved he'd once had Dennis's attention. Kneeling down, he began flipping through a pile of canvasses leaning against the wall. He soon found what he was looking for: the portrait of him Dennis had painted in the brief period when the two of them had actually been close. Joel lovingly placed it on the easel and noticed once again that he'd been painted as if he'd been crying.

"Why are you making my eyes so sad?" he remembered asking Dennis one day while he was squinting at him from behind his easel.

"Because that's the way I see you."

"But I'm not a sad person."

But, of course he'd been sad. *What a fool I've been,* he thought now. Deep in his heart he'd always known he'd never be able to keep the artist. His entire relationship with Dennis had been one long game of kicking a can down the road, all the while knowing that sooner or later he'd have to bend down and pick it up.

A dirty rag was hanging off the easel. Grabbing it, he doused it with turpentine and held it within half an inch from the surface of the canvas. He imagined Dennis coming home and finding his work defiled. The thought gave him a twinge of joy until he realized Dennis would probably be glad to be rid of the painting. There was absolutely nothing Joel could do to hurt Dennis, he knew now, because Dennis had never cared. *I have only myself to blame—and that goddamn voice inside my head that has been pushing me every step of the way.* Shaking his dirty rag skyward, he screamed at the ceiling, "I hate you, Yris del Coro! You're the one who got me into this mess and now you have to get me out."

Joel ran back to his room and threw himself down in front of his altar. Quickly lighting two candles, he tossed a beach towel over his head and started chanting. He chanted with every last ounce of his strength. He chanted like his head were being held under water and he was struggling for air. He chanted so loudly that he was afraid somebody on the street might hear him and call the police. But no matter how loud he wailed his mantra, he simply couldn't chant away that awful feeling in his gut. He let out a bloodcurdling scream and pounded the top of his bureau.

Swinging his arm, he knocked everything off the altar in a single swipe. Candles, prayer cards, and seashells went flying across the room. He was so absorbed with his howling that he didn't realize one of the candles had landed on the turpentine-soaked rag that he'd tossed on the floor. Within seconds it burst into flames along with his dirty sheets, and before he knew it, his entire bed was on fire.

Joel turned and watched the blaze in amazement. For a few moments he simply stared into the flames, mesmerized by the possibility that his spirit guide had answered his prayers, and was helping him get revenge on Dennis by destroying his house.

After their movie date, Bill Doyle and Keith Antonelli had gone to Napi's for dinner and the younger man had begun barraging Bill with horror stories about his former boyfriends and how much he'd learned from being ignored, manipulated, and abused. Bill found it all rather tedious. At forty-seven, he was old enough to believe that wisdom only comes later in life, usually through much greater suffering than anything Keith had experienced. As the younger man prattled on, Bill imagined having to watch this kid stumble through the rest of his twenties; the thought made him want to reach for a drink, so at nine o'clock, rather than risk falling off the wagon, Bill simply told Keith he needed to go home and walk the dog—alone.

Maybe the evening wasn't a total waste, Bill thought to himself as he strolled east on Commercial Street. If nothing else, he'd been forced to think about what he wanted in a relationship. For the first time in days he remembered Mitchell and noticed that his ex-lover had been gradually drifting from his mind since he'd made the decision to be sober. He wondered if what he had enjoyed with Mitchell had been their sense of home. *Maybe what I most want is a man ready to channel all his love into a home and a family.* Bill shook his head. *Could Joel Eisenberg ever be that man?* Joel wasn't the least bit a homebody, unless you counted the way he treated Bunny like she was his only child. For all Joel's selfishness, he had the same Jewish DNA that Mitchell did—a genetic predisposition to sacrifice for members of his tribe, even if at present his entire clan consisted of only one little dog. Bill sighed. Would Joel ever make him a part of his tribe?

"He will soon enough." It was the voice of his ex-lover whispering in his ear.

"Nah," Bill replied. "He only cares about himself."

"So did I … before I fell in love with you."

Bill turned the bend at Washington Street and saw a bright red fire truck parked near his house. Its lights were flashing and several police cars were just arriving on the scene. Bill began to run and quickly realized that it was actually Dennis's house that was burning. Two volunteers were pulling a fire hose down Smuggs Lane and a third was breaking the window of Joel's bedroom. Another was trying to douse the flames with a fire extinguisher. Meanwhile the flames hissed and were spreading from Joel's room to the kitchen, where several aerosol cans under the sink started exploding. He ran up to Joel, who was nervously pacing up and down the lane.

"What happened?" Bill asked.

"I couldn't get to the phone. I went to your house. And by the time I came back … Oh, god! They're going to think I did it on purpose! It was an accident. I swear."

"What happened?"

"I was chanting and ... oh, god! They're going to kill me! Make sure you tell Dennis I called the fire department! I *did* call the fire department."

"Where's Bunny?" Bill asked.

Joel suddenly turned white. "Isn't she with you?"

"I left her in my cabin."

"But I looked for her. She wasn't there!"

Without speaking another word, the two men ran to Bill's cabin, rushed from room to room, and shouted Bunny's name. Suddenly Bill spotted the loose screen on the window.

"Oh, shit! She may have gone to the house! Yesterday I let her out and she went straight to your closet."

"Oh, no!" Joel cried, and the look of horror in his eyes was something Bill would never forget.

"Wait here," he said. Running back to the house, he corralled two firemen and the three of them fought their way through the kitchen door.

Joel dropped to his knees on the wet grass. "How could I have left Bunny to go to Groton?" he kept repeating. The entire house was crackling now, and it felt like it was laughing at him. Soon, a thick black cloud of smoke had obscured the scene. Minutes later, Bill Doyle stepped through it carrying a tiny, lifeless bundle wrapped in a blanket. Joel wailed, "Oh, no!" and covered his face. His life would never be the same. Until that moment, all the stupid, vicious things he'd done had the possibility of being reversed.

Chapter Thirty-nine

Even when Sue Veneer was Dennis Fairchild's housekeeper, she still thought of herself as a queen playing the role of a scullery maid. It was only when she moved in with her mother in Commack, Long Island, that she began to doubt her royal status: there was no question who reigned in that house. Dorothy Hoodwin's desires always took precedence over her child's: they ate whatever she wanted to eat, they shopped wherever she wanted to shop, and the older woman's numerous doctor appointments were unmovable events around which each day was planned. Worst of all, she insisted on addressing Sue as "Kenneth," and she continually reminded her about the two girls he'd once dated in high school as though there were still a chance he might find the right woman and settle down.

One day as Sue was sitting at the ophthalmologist's office waiting for her mother and reading *Redbook,* she glanced at her reflection in the glass door and shuddered involuntarily. She'd become the one thing she dreaded most: an aging suburban spinster with nothing to do all day but nurse a sickly mother who was even more angry and frustrated than she was herself. A week later, Sue was filling her prescription for Tofranil, the most powerful antianxiety drug on the market. Although she'd never had the desire to take pharmaceuticals—she much preferred marijuana and gin—she'd become concerned after having several violent fits, including slapping the dog groomer at PetSmart and knocking down a snotty fourteen-year-old girl for cutting ahead of her at Baskin-Robbins.

Unfortunately, one of the side effects of Sue's medication was that it caused her to gain weight, and she soon found she could no longer fit into her favorite evening gowns. In the following weeks, Sue put on fifteen pounds more and decided to stop taking her pills. Life in Commack soon began to resemble a Long Island production of *'Night, Mother,* with both mother and daughter threatening to first kill the other and then herself.

One fine September morning, Sue was in the kitchen watching *The Rosie O'Donnell Show* because she wanted to see Tim Valentine, who'd recently announced to the world that he was gay. As Sue stared in horror, Tim began performing a scene from his upcoming off-Broadway show, *Shut Your Von Trapp!,* with none other than Rudy Cantwell, her old nemesis from Provincetown. Sue's only consolation was that Rudy gave an absolutely dreadful performance and his idiotic dialogue didn't get a single laugh from the stunned studio audience. Still, she seethed—that miserable son of a bitch had made it on national television and had gotten the shot at stardom that had always eluded her. Unable to control her rage, Sue grabbed the TV set off the counter, lifted it high above her head, and smashed it on the linoleum.

"Kenneth, is that you?" her mother called from her bedroom where she'd been watching the same show.

"It's nothing, Mom."

"Did you drop something?"

"I said it's nothing!" Sue screamed at the top of her lungs.

Just then the phone started ringing.

"Kenneth! Would you get that?"

Breathing heavily, Sue reluctantly picked up the phone.

"Yeah?" she grumbled, fairly certain it was the Catholic Church again asking for a donation.

"Sue, it's Ida Dream. I got your number from the Seaview Lounge."

"What is it?" Sue snarled, assuming that the little bitch had only called to make her feel worse about what she'd just seen on TV.

"Are you sitting down?" Ida said breathlessly. "There's been a tragedy."

"Ida, if this is some kind of a joke ..."

"It's no joke. There's been a death."

Sue leaned against the wall and prepared to hear the news. Some townie had probably drunk himself into the grave, and she looked forward to hearing who it had been.

A few seconds later, Dorothy Hoodwin heard a bloodcurdling scream coming from the kitchen.

"Kenneth?" she called, but there was no answer. Assuming her son had once again burned his fingers on a cookie pan, she went back to watching *Rosie* and didn't bother to inquire further.

Chapter Forty

It was cold and drizzly on the day of Bunny's funeral and many of the local residents who would otherwise have had to cater to Provincetown's tourists found they were able to attend. Gathering at the entrance to Hatches Harbor, they walked quietly half a mile into a pine forest, where a small hole in the sand had been dug by the deceased a few weeks before she died. Among the mourners were Lou Lustig, Blossom Selkow, Oscar Gonzalez, Lucas Allison, Raymond Hennigan, and about a dozen store owners, many of whom kept dog biscuits beside their cash registers for those happy moments when Bunny had trotted in and put her paws on their counters. Bill Doyle had constructed a tiny coffin for Bunny out of plywood donated by Conwell Lumber, and her body had been kept cold overnight in the freezer at Tedeschi's, where Bunny had been a favorite of the nighttime cashier. The handyman had called the Fairchilds in Groton, but none of them had found it necessary to drive down for the service.

The ceremony was quite moving. Reverend Levitzky from the Unitarian Meeting House expressed the profound loss felt by the entire community, and Blossom Selkow gave a more personal eulogy while her German shepherd whimpered and sniffed at the coffin. Later, Blossom joined fellow Jews Lou Lustig and Joel in reciting the Mourner's Kaddish, but the astrologer was too upset to do anything more than mumble a few "amens" at the appropriate moments. For the rest of the ceremony, Joel stood quietly with his head bowed, but when Bill Doyle started filling in the grave, he suddenly pushed himself forward, took the shovel out of his hand, and finished the job himself. The rest of the mourners were a bit surprised to see Joel Eisenberg actually doing physical labor.

After everybody left, Joel stayed behind to collect a few stones from the gravesite as mementos. Bill had promised to drive Joel to the Boston ferry, so he had stayed behind as well. Keeping a polite distance, he watched as Joel put a half-dozen rocks in a large fanny pack strapped around his waist. "Why'd you decide to bury her here?" Bill asked.

"This was where she liked to pee." Joel's bottom lip started to tremble. "She was a good girl."

Bill came up behind him and held his shoulders. "I know."

"She always knew when I was in a rush to get home and she would try to pee faster. She ..." Unable to finish his sentence, Joel began weeping uncontrollably. Feelings of grief that had been buried inside him for years began cascading through his body like a mighty river through a crack in a dam. "She didn't deserve to die ... not like this."

Joel turned and held onto Bill's arms. The handyman knew exactly what Joel was going through. He'd felt the same way after Mitchell died.

"It's all my fault!" Joel said.

"No," Bill said, "it was an accident."

"I killed her!"

"No, you didn't."

Joel looked up and saw Bill gazing at him with kindness. "It must have been so much worse for you. How did you make it through?"

"It was hard."

"How did you keep going—especially when you thought it was your fault?"

"I got through it. I'm still getting through it."

"I can't do it," Joel said shaking his head.

"Yes you can, " Bill answered sweetly, pulling Joel close.

"Don't you see? I thought God was leading me every step of the way. What kind of god would do such a thing? How can I live in this world?"

Bill's heart was breaking, for Joel was torturing himself with the same unanswerable questions he'd been asking himself for years. "Listen, when you get back to New York, call me and, if you want, I'll come down and stay with you."

"No. You have work."

"Seriously, I don't want you to be alone."

Joel wailed even louder and tried to find comfort by pressing himself against the handyman's body. Between sniffles he managed to say, "Mitchell was so lucky to have a great guy like you."

Both men now began sobbing in each other's arms. "We have to go," Bill said through his tears. "The ferry's in half an hour."

"I don't want to leave you," Joel cried.

"Just imagine that I'm with you," Bill said, leaning over and pressing his cheek against Joel's. He really wanted to kiss him, but it didn't seem like the appropriate time. Joel was thinking something very similar and was wondering whether Bill wanted to be kissed. He decided quickly and he knew that Bunny would approve.

Looking up, he pulled Bill's face toward him. The kissing quickly grew more passionate and they were soon feasting on each

other's lips. Toppling onto a soft bed of pine needles, they simultaneously began unbuckling each other's pants, racing to see who
would be the first to get his mouth around the other man's cock.

Afraid they might miss the ferry, Bill sped his truck down Standish
Street and squealed to a stop at the base of MacMillan Wharf,
where a chain blocked the way onto the pier. Joel jumped out and
struggled to put on his backpack. Bill rolled down his window.
"Call me as soon as you get to New York."

"I will."

"No. Call me sooner. Call me from Boston." Joel leaned over for
one last kiss. "You sure you don't want to stay?" Bill asked.

"I don't want to be here when the Fairchilds get here."

"Say the word and I'll come to New York. As soon as I finish my
next job."

"Really?"

"When I say something, I mean it. And Joel. You will get
through this. I promise."

The two men looked deeply into each other's eyes. Reaching out
of the truck, Bill brushed some pine needles off Joel's shoulder.

"Go. You'll miss your ferry." Joel started backing away. "Go on,"
Bill repeated as he started to turn his truck around.

"I'll call you from Boston!" Joel called after him, as he turned
and scampered awkwardly up the wharf with a heavy knapsack but
the lightest of hearts. His faith in God had been greatly restored,
and he found himself wondering if Bunny might have sacrificed
her life in order to bring him together with Bill.

Unfortunately, when Joel got to the end of the pier, the inbound
ferry hadn't yet arrived, and the outbound trip would be delayed.
Hoping to get a definite departure time, he entered the ticket office,

where a sour-faced woman seated beneath a harpoon was reading a romance novel and ignoring him completely. As Joel tapped his fingers on the counter, his postcoital contentment gave way to a series of concerns. Earlier that day, Bill Doyle had told him that Dennis probably would not press for an investigation—he'd simply call it an accident and collect the insurance money. Still, there was no guarantee Joel wouldn't be sued for negligence, and there was also the question of what would he do for a living when he got back to New York. His savings were depleted, he hadn't written a word of his new book. And then there was the matter of Bunny's death. Although he no longer felt quite so guilty for torching the dear little thing, the thought of losing her made his heart ache so badly he could barely breathe.

"Can I help you?" the clerk finally asked in irritation, interrupting Joel's thoughts.

"Oh! I'm sorry. The ferry to Boston?"

"You can wait outside."

"I mean when will it be here?"

The clerk sighed and rolled her eyes. Taking off her reading glasses, she mumbled something snide and pointed one of her blood-red fingernails to a chart hanging on the wall behind Joel. Then she put her glasses back on and went back to reading her novel.

More unsettled than ever, Joel went back onto the pier and wandered around. He wondered if his love for Bill Doyle would continue to shine as steadfastly as Bunny's had for him. According to what Yris del Coro had told him in his dream, the handyman wasn't his Twin Flame. But he was beginning to believe the whole Twin Flame thing was silly, and it would be insane to base his life on a prophecy from ten years earlier. Then again, if he and Bill were to become lovers, where would they live? Joel wouldn't dare show his face in Provincetown again. Would he and Bill be happy living in New York? he wondered. *When he comes home all dusty from a hard day of renovating apartments, will Bill have anything interesting to say? Will we want to see the same movies? Dislike the same friends? Have anything in common other than grief? Even then Bill isn't all that articulate when it comes to expressing his feelings.*

Dennis Fairchild was more withdrawn than Bill, but Joel had never seemed to mind. Dennis's artistic talent had more than compensated for his reticence. And beyond his artwork there was his great house and glamorous lifestyle. And beyond all that—

—there was his tush.

With all the excitement of the fire, the funeral, and the blow job, it hadn't even entered his mind for almost twenty-four hours. Bill Doyle could never keep him down on the farm now that he'd seen the tush. Joel would have given anything to forget it, but Dennis's ass had been permanently tattooed in his memory. It was more likely his arms and legs would suddenly fall off.

Oh god! Joel thought. If it had been Dennis Fairchild who'd just asked him to spend the night, Joel realized, he wouldn't have hesitated. After all he'd been through, was he still just an ass-aholic no closer to finding true love than the day he'd left New York?

"You killed her! You killed her!"

Startled by a loud, screeching voice that sounded somewhat familiar, Joel looked up. While he'd been fretting, the ferry from Boston had pulled up to the dock and an ugly old woman was leaning over the gangplank railing, shaking her umbrella at him and cursing, "You son of a bitch! You killed her!"

It was Sue Veneer in a clear plastic raincoat, a short denim skirt, and a scarf tied around a ratty old wig. Apparently, she'd heard about Bunny and she was coming back to make good on her threat. There were several other passengers disembarking in front of her, so Joel had time to escape. Running further up the pier, he hid behind a stack of lobster traps. He hoped the old hag would get off the ferry, think he had hightailed it in the other direction, and try to find him in town. He planned to slip onto the ferry and be halfway to Boston before Sue knew he had escaped.

Joel held his breath and resisted taking a peek. Suddenly there was a loud clap of thunder and a streak of lightning, and the light drizzle turned into a downpour. *Honk! Honk!* The ferry was starting to take on passengers and Joel longed to board the nice dry boat.

After what seemed like an eternity, Joel felt safe enough to poke his head around the traps and saw to his horror that Sue was waiting for him at the entrance to the gangplank. Her head whipped around and looked right at where Joel was hiding.

Joel quickly pulled back but the jig was up. As he nervously stepped out from his hiding place, Sue Veneer had already reached him was hitting him over the head with her umbrella. "You killed her! You killed her!" she kept screaming. Joel covered his head and backed away.

"It was an accident!" he cried, but Sue was on the warpath.

"I knew it!" she screamed while beating him. "From the moment I saw you, I knew you were evil! You killed her! You killed my baby!"

Trying to flee, Joel ran further up the pier, around a corner, and toward an old wooden building that had once been used for salting fish, hoping somebody inside could help him fend off this insane creature—but the door was locked. He banged to be let in, but Sue was already upon him, grabbing his backpack, swinging him around, and punching him with her fists.

"Murderer! Murderer!" she screeched as she backed Joel closer to the edge of the pier. The rain had now become torrential; there was no longer anybody in sight, and there was nothing behind Joel but a nasty drop into the bay.

"You killed her!" Sue screamed one last time when suddenly her high heel caught in a towrope. She lost her balance and, with a look of sheer panic, she grabbed for Joel. Their fingers almost touched when, with a bloodcurdling scream, she toppled ten feet into the murky waters of Cape Cod Bay.

Honk! Honk! The ferry was making its last call for Boston-bound passengers.

"I can't swim!" Sue screamed as she tried to grab hold of one of the pilings. Joel looked longingly back at the ferry. Then he looked down at Sue struggling to hold onto the barnacle-covered timber. He hadn't asked for this, but the look of fear on Sue's face melted his heart. This was the one person who cared for Bunny as much as he did. He'd already been responsible for one death that week, and his conscience simply couldn't bear another.

"Grab the rope!" Joel yelled, as he threw the towrope into the water. But Sue panicked. She had lost hold of the piling and was being pulled out to sea by the tide. Throwing off his backpack, Joel got down on his belly and pushed his legs over the edge. Holding onto the rope he shimmied down the piling and slipped into the water, which was much colder and choppier than it had appeared from ten feet above.

"Grab my hand!" he yelled.

"I can't reach it!" Sue yelled back.

With the rope in one hand, Joel pushed himself away from the piling and took hold of Sue by the arm. "Take the rope!" he cried.

Sue just gasped for breath.

Using all his strength, Joel managed to pull her toward him. As he was placing the rope in her hand, he was suddenly swamped by a large wave that loosened his own grip. He tried to grab hold of Sue but his fingers couldn't get a grip on her plastic raincoat. Reaching wildly, he grasped at her wig; it came off in his hands.

And then Joel was quickly sinking. He'd forgotten to remove his fanny pack, which was filled with rocks, and the extra weight was pulling him down. Deeper and deeper he sank. He struggled to unfasten the belt, but the damn thing was stuck. His lungs felt like they were going to burst. Finally he broke the clasp, the fanny pack sank to the bottom of the bay, and he started swimming upward with all his might. He thought he was heading toward the surface, but he'd lost all sense of direction and suddenly he banged his head against something. *The piling? A sunken vessel?* His oxygen had given out and everything now was going dark. He was drowning.

No! The fear of death was unbearable. It rose up from the deepest level of his being and enveloped his soul like an inky cloud. *I'm not supposed to die. Not like this. Not without learning what I'm supposed to learn. Not without achieving the things I wanted to achieve. Not without nailing some really great ass....*

But just as quickly as it had overwhelmed him, the terror began to subside. Everything grew quiet. The fear, it seemed, was no longer inside him; it surrounded him like a black sky on a cold winter's night. His problems were over. The life he'd been living was over. The worst that could have happened had already occurred, and for the first time in his life Joel felt absolute peace.

Chapter Forty-one

Joel saw what looked like a distant comet coming toward him: was this the light he'd read about in so many books, the one he'd heard described on daytime talk shows by patients who had flatlined under anesthesia? At first he wanted to run in the other direction, but then he heard a dog barking and a few familiar snorts. It was Bunny! The bright object was actually the dog's happy face, illumined from within like a giant lantern at the head of the Chinese New Year's Day parade. Joel ran to greet her, and the next thing he knew he was inside a corridor filled with light and his face was being covered with puppy kisses.

"¡Ay ay ay!"

Looking up from Bunny, Joel saw Yris del Coro standing before him, her red hair burning bright and sparkling like fireworks. She took Joel by the arm and gently began guiding him through the passageway. Bunny trotted along beside them with a big smile on her face.

"You sent Bunny to get me," Joel cried.

"How else would you have come into the light?"

"This is so amazing. I'm dead, but I'm still thinking. I'm still walking. So everything I believed about the eternal soul was true. Death really *is* an illusion."

"*Cállate, mijo.*"

"I'm too excited to be quiet. I have it all figured out. Everything you told me was a trick. You sent me on a wild goose chase to find my Twin Flame because that's what life is all about. We're all on wild goose chases, lusting after things that don't make us happy and pretending to know things we don't really know. It was all a great big joke and astrology was the biggest joke of all, because it made me feel like there was order in the universe. But there isn't. Isn't that the point of it all?"

"*¡Dios mío!*" Yris exclaimed in exasperation.

"OK. Maybe there's some order. Maybe there's some connection between us and the stars, but its way too complicated for anybody to figure out. The most enlightened thought I ever had was totally insignificant compared with the vastness that surrounds us. Please tell me I'm right."

Before Yris could answer, they emerged from the tunnel of light into an empty silence that was the darkest pitch black Joel had ever experienced.

"I'm scared," Joel said.

"Do not be frightened," Yris replied. "You were very brave just now and so I'm about to give you what I promised to give you ten years ago."

Joel recited his mantra to calm himself down and very slowly the dark silence began to congeal into shapes, like a Polaroid picture developing in three dimensions. First Joel saw some trees. Then a red brick building appeared behind the trees. Then there were actual people strolling about on a bright sunny day. Everybody looked happy and vaguely familiar, as if these were all the people Joel had at one time or another passed by on the street, the ones he'd always wanted to meet if he'd only had the chance. As Joel and Yris walked, the scenery continued to change. Each locale was perfect. First, they were in a shady glen of huge sequoia trees where it was cool and quiet. Next they entered a picture-postcard town with lush gardens, white picket fences, and children playing. Then they arrived at a leafy quadrangle surrounded by ancient buildings made of stone that looked like the Ivy League campus Joel hadn't been able to afford when he was younger. Finally they came to a city, and Joel felt so at home he knew it had to be New York, only the temperature was more like Los Angeles, and the stately old buildings made it look like parts of Boston. They passed through one neighborhood after another, and every block they walked through had inexpensive apartments, groovy people, and a free subway system humming beneath their feet.

"Is this heaven?" Joel asked.

"It's your heaven," Yris replied.

Yris took Joel's hand and they climbed a set of marble steps to what looked like an ancient Greek temple. Once inside, they entered an amphitheater that reminded Joel of a nineteenth-century operating room, with hundreds of people seated around them in steep tiers that climbed to the ceiling. As Joel looked closer, he recognized all his friends and relatives who had passed away before him; they were all smiling and happy, as if they'd gathered together for a joyous occasion, such as a wedding or a bar mitzvah. His four grandparents were in the front row and behind them were his dirt-poor ancestors from Eastern Europe, but they were all cleaned up and quaintly dressed, like extras from *Yentl*. Sitting nearby were his fourth-grade teacher, who'd struggled to teach him long division, and the milkman, who'd always left an extra sour cream on the family doorstep in Brooklyn.

And horsing around in the back rows was his other family—his gay friends who had died young. They were hooting and drinking mimosas as if the seventies had never ended. There were Chuck and Victor from his Transcendental Meditation class. There were Aldo and Kevin from when he'd first moved to the Village. There were Emmett and Vinnie and many more, most of whom at one time or another had generously bared their butts for Joel. Best of all, they all looked as young and beautiful as they had before getting so horribly sick. Most of them stood up and applauded when Joel entered the room. "Hey, girls!" Joel called up to them and waved. They all laughed and Joel felt his heart would burst from happiness.

Suddenly a double door opened at the top of the aisle. A heavenly light illuminated the room and two figures slowly descended to the stage. On the left was an old woman who reminded him of Golda Meir, only without the cigarette dangling from her lips and the weight of the world pressing down on her shoulders. She radiated content-ment and was by far the happiest old Jewess Joel had ever seen.

"Is that God?" Joel asked.

"That's your God," Yris replied.

Descending next to her was a young man who Joel quickly rec-ognized as his old camp counselor, none other than Bill Doyle's ex-lover Mitchell Savitt. Even in this world of strange light, Mitchell seemed oddly insubstantial.

"What's happened to him?" Joel whispered to Yris.

"He's going back to earth to begin his next lifetime. Most of his soul has already left on the journey, but he has one more task to ful-fill up here."

"With me?" Joel asked.

Yris nodded and turned to God, who greeted her nonchalantly, as though she'd just driven there on the Belt Parkway. "Did you have any trouble getting here?"

"No," Yris answered. "Everything worked just like you said it would."

God turned to Joel and smiled. "*Tatele*. My name is God and my job is very simple. All my children should experience a little love in their lives, even if I have to trick them. Here, I'd like you to meet a kindred soul."

Mitchell stepped forward and took Joel's hands. As he looked into Joel's eyes, the astrologer was suddenly reminded of Bill Doyle, and for the first time, he felt regret for something he'd left behind. Mitchell gazed at him tenderly and Joel felt that this near-stranger was able to read his mind, that in fact he could understand him better than anyone else in the amphitheater. His dead relatives in the first row hadn't a clue about the exquisite tortures of being a gay man, and few of his gay friends in the back row would ever understand the delicious agony of being Jewish.

"Long time no see," Mitchell said rather casually.

"You look good," Joel found himself saying. "Your skin looks amazing."

"It's not too translucent?"

"Not at all. By the way, I met Bill Doyle."

"I know. Yris del Coro and I have been working together to get you here. We've been watching your progress."

"So I guess you saw what I did to Dennis Fairchild?"

"Who could blame you? He's adorable. He's just not husband material." The two men chuckled and Joel felt a huge sense of relief wash over him.

"So what's the occasion?" Joel whispered, nodding to the crowd, which had grown silent, like the audience for a play that was about to begin.

In answer to Joel's question, Mitchell looked to God, who nodded her approval. Stepping forward, he wrapped his arms around Joel's body. He didn't so much press himself against Joel's chest as pull himself completely inside. Their hearts merged immediately and every single cell, every molecule, every atom was imbued with the joy of a companionship the likes of which Joel had never known. And then Mitchell opened his mouth and gave Joel the most wonderful kiss. The audience moaned with delight as the astrologer's mind was flooded with rosy beams of light.

Joel was suddenly twelve years old again, and Mitchell Savitt was fifteen, and the two of them were again seated beside the pool at summer camp—only this time neither boy was frightened of what anyone might think of them. As they smooched beside the pool, their souls traveled even further back in time through all their past lives. They were a French farmer and wife. They were an Austrian duchess and her lover. They were two sisters in a rice paddy. They were a mother and a blind daughter. They were an aging father and his strapping son. Two friends in a monastery. Two wives in a harem. Two warriors in battle. They were a blacksmith and his apprentice. Two gypsy clowns. A farmer and his prized ox. A princess and her parakeet. They were two puppies fighting for the same teat. Two ancient trees growing side by side. Two puffy clouds floating across the African sky. They were a lonely planet spinning through space accompanied by her one and only moon. They were two bands in a celestial rainbow. They were the Goddess herself waking from her cosmic slumber and the reflection that she saw when she first looked in the mirror.

Joel opened his eyes and everything had vanished. The amphitheater was gone. His friends and relatives were gone. Everything was gone except for Yris del Coro. "What happened?" Joel asked as if waking from a dream.

"Your Twin Flame has just given you his heart," Yris said, patting him on the chest. "Now you must go back to earth and use it well."

The floor beneath Joel suddenly opened up and he found himself looking down at a blue ocean-covered planet. He and Yris flew toward it, getting closer and closer until a tiny peninsula could be seen jutting out from the corner of a continent. It curved into a bay, and tucked within the curve was a beautiful little town with a long wharf sticking far into the water. Floating near the end of the pier was a brand new sailboat on which an elderly couple was trying to revive the body of a half-drowned man.

"Me?" Joel asked.

Yris nodded her head.

"Do I have to go down there again and be Joel Eisenberg?"

"Only if you want to."

Joel thought for a second. "Yes!" he replied. "Because then I have the subject for my next book. I can teach a seminar and I'll get back on television. I mean, how many people with my communication skills have gone through something like this?"

Yris shook her head. "*Lo siento, mijo*. You won't remember anything."

"None of it?" Joel said angrily. "What's the good of going to heaven and meeting God and my Twin Flame if I won't remember what happened?"

Yris shrugged. "If you choose to return to earth, you'll be stupid, vain, and frightened. You'll make one mistake after another. You won't know what will happen next and you'll barely remember what happened two seconds before."

"You mean I'll be the same as I've always been?"

"Except for one thing." Yris reached out and once again touched Joel's chest. "Maybe you'll feel a little different." Yris del Coro smiled, and that was all the reassurance Joel needed.

"Wait! Where's Bunny?"

Yris pointed up in the direction from which they came. "We'll take good care of her."

"Will I ever see her again?"

But before Yris could answer, Joel felt himself suddenly plummeting, as if he'd just gone over the highest point on a roller coaster. The next moment he was coughing up saltwater on the deck of a boat. A little white dog was licking his face.

"Arf. Arf."

"He's alive!" exclaimed an elderly bald man in white Bermuda shorts and a bright orange shirt.

"Oh, thank god!" exclaimed a white-haired woman looking over his shoulder. "I never would have forgiven myself."

The man put his arm under Joel's back and helped him to sit up.

"Are you supposed to touch him now?" asked the woman as she coddled her Yorkshire Terrier.

"Why? Is he *treyf?*"

Marvin and Shirley Tatelman of Armonk, New York, had been sailing from Boston to Westchester when they decided to duck into Provincetown Harbor to avoid the bad weather. At the end of the pier they'd seen a soggy man in a blue miniskirt yelling and pointing to another man who was floating unconscious in the water. Pulling him into the boat, Marvin recalled his lifeguard training from his boyhood in Coney Island and had performed mouth-to-mouth on Joel until, miracle of miracles, he'd come back to life.

Later that night they were taken to dinner at Bubala's by three gay guys: the drag queen who had summoned them, the astrologer whom they'd saved from drowning, and a third guy who did construction work in town. The drag queen, whose name was Sue Veneer, regaled them with show business stories and afterward took them to a piano bar where he sang the entire score of *Dames at Sea*. They would have plenty of stories to tell when they got back to Westchester.

As for Joel Eisenberg, all evening he seemed somewhat disori-ented, as though he was trying to recall a dream. At the same time, he couldn't help but enjoy the strange sensation he felt in his chest, as if the blood in his heart had been replaced with something cool and fizzy, like seltzer. And when Bill reached across the piano and touched his hand, Joel looked at him as though he had a brand new pair of eyes and his heart overflowed, filling his entire body with happy little bubbles.

Chapter Forty-two

The last person to ask Joel to sign his new book, *Canine Compatibilities: A Star Guide for Loving Your Pet,* was a large, hirsute man in a black leather jacket who'd come in off the street at the last minute. As he placed his copy on the bridge table in front of the author, he stepped back and smiled mischievously. "Joel?" he said. "Don't you remember me? I was always one of your biggest fans."

Joel looked up quizzically. With Mercury going retrograde, he'd had a feeling that some people from his past might show up at the reading. The man's face looked familiar—or rather his features looked familiar—as though someone had taken the eyes, nose, and mouth of an old friend, drawn them on a balloon, and then blown it up to twice its original size. Joel shrugged shamefacedly, so the man pointed his finger at his book and said, "You can make it out to Lucas Allison."

"Oh, my god!" Joel cried. "It's been what … nine years?"

"I know," Lucas said, rubbing his gut. "I'm back in Provincetown for Bear Week."

Joel pointed to Lucas's stomach and blurted out, "Is any of that muscle?"

"Hey, the young cubs seem to like it."

"Young cubs? You *are* a young cub."

"Only compared to you."

"So, you're like a big-daddy top now?"

"Yeah. Ever since Oscar, I like to be the one doing the fucking. Who would have guessed? Hey, I hear you and Bill Doyle are still together."

"Yeah, it's been a while," Joel replied, banging his knuckles on the table for good luck.

"I also hear that old Raymond Hennigan passed away and left you his condo with all of his shit still in it. That's amazing."

Joel was taken aback. "Who told you all that?"

"Ida Dream down at the deli. Do you believe she still works there?"

The bespectacled owner of the bookstore glanced over from the register and signaled that since all the other customers had left she was anxious to close.

"You want to walk me to my car?" Joel asked.

"Sure," said Lucas.

Joel put a leash on his dog—a Frenchie named Bunny II—and accompanied Lucas out onto the street. Although it was only seven in the evening, the late November sky had been dark for hours and the snowy street was nearly empty. Joel took a deep breath of the cool, salty air; he'd been living in Provincetown long enough to state unequivocally that this was his favorite time of year, when the tourists left and the town finally belonged to its residents.

"Have you seen Dennis Fairchild?" Lucas asked.

Joel rolled his eyes and shook his head. "He moved to Paris years ago."

"You're kidding."

"After I burned down his house, the property went up in value about three million dollars because they were able to build condos.

So they sold it and Dennis took the money and followed his dream. He stopped painting and went into business with Jean Paul selling antiques."

"Dennis Fairchild," Lucas said shaking his head. "No matter what happens, that girl comes out smelling like a rose."

"So how's New York?" Joel asked, anxious to change the subject.

"Just a lot of rich kids acting stupid. You did the right thing by moving here. You're what? Forty-three?"

"Forty-six."

"Gay life is like musical chairs. Once you pass thirty-five, the music stops and you just better grab the guy closest to you and sit your ass down."

Lucas and Joel had arrived at Joel's car, a little green Dodge covered with a layer of dirt and salt. The two of them leaned against the hood.

"Speaking of settling down, Bill and I have decided to adopt a little Jamaican girl."

"What? You're going to be a mother? What's her name?"

"Mona. You want to see her picture?" Joel reached inside the car and pulled out a small, framed photo stuck to the dashboard with a magnet. He gave it to Lucas, who beamed delightedly at the face of a chunky brown-skinned girl.

"That was taken three years ago when I first met her," Joel explained. "Her uncle brought her here because her mother died and she had no other family left in Jamaica. When he started working for Bill he needed a babysitter, so I watched her for three summers and ... well ... I guess we fell in love. This winter she's staying with us and this spring we're going to make it legal."

"That's wonderful," Lucas said with a big smile. "I'm so proud of you. Where is she now?"

"She's over at the Meeting Hall rehearsing with the Outer Cape Chorale. She's playing an angel in Handel's *Messiah*."

"That's so great she's singing," Lucas said with a look of nostalgia in his eyes.

"So how about you? Do you ever perform anymore?"

"I never had any talent," Lucas replied. "You only told me I did because you were trying to get down my pants. I've tried that chakra thing on a few guys myself, you know...."

Joel shook his finger at Lucas. "You better careful."

Lucas checked his watch. "Listen, I gotta meet some friends at The Vault, but I'll be here all weekend if you want to meet for coffee." Before leaving, Lucas tilted his head to one side and gave Joel a sidelong glance, a coquettish gesture that reminded Joel that in spite of his beard and his girth, Lucas was still a little queen at heart. "Let me ask you one question?" Lucas said. "That first day I came to your apartment, and you had me spread eagle on the floor, why didn't you fuck me?"

"I didn't think you wanted me to," Joel said, surprised that he had brought up the subject.

"Are you kidding? When we first met, I had you so high on a pedestal you could have done anything you wanted. It was only later that I thought you were a jerk."

"And that took about a week," Joel quipped.

"Less," Lucas admitted. "You know what your problem was, Joel? You never understood that most gay men are bottoms and if you're ready to lay some serious pipe you can have anyone you want."

"Really?" Joel said incredulously. "You really would have fucked me that first day?"

Lucas gave the question some thought. "Probably," he answered, "if you'd asked me politely."

Lucas gave Joel a quick kiss and the astrologer watched as he strutted down the street. He was still a great-looking guy, but his ass wasn't nearly what it had been in the old days. It wasn't bad, but it had lost the shape that had first brought Joel to Provincetown: a perfect sand castle washed over by a wave.

Joel got behind the wheel of his car, took Bunny II onto his lap, and pulled a joint out of his ashtray. He lit up and took three quick tokes, just enough to take the edge off. Mona wouldn't be home for an hour, Bill was visiting his sister in Dorchester, and Joel didn't particularly feel like going home to an empty apartment. He was feeling blue. Except for meeting Lucas Allison, the book signing hadn't been very much fun. His spirited reading of "Housetraining Your Gemini" had gotten some hearty laughs, but the few people who'd shown up were mostly lunatics and losers who were more interested in talking about their own dogs than in hearing anything Joel had to say.

The book will sell, anyway, Joel reminded himself. *My Web site is thriving. There's talk about my getting my own segment on the* Animal Planet. *I have no reason to be depressed.*

Joel drove slowly down Commercial Street. Seeing Lucas again made him think about that pivotal summer. He'd obviously gotten some kind of guidance from beyond the day he'd almost drowned because from that day forward he'd been blessed—or cursed—with the feeling that he and Bill Doyle were simply meant to be together. Unfortunately, after the wonderful honeymoon period was over, he'd discovered that this knowledge in his heart chakra hadn't been received by the rest of his body. As much as he loved Bill, his dick chakra still went wild for men with big asses, and his mind chakra still wondered whether he had made the right choice. The most corrosive doubt of all was whether he'd truly found his Twin Flame. Yris del Coro had grown silent over the years and Joel had begun to suspect that he'd done what Lucas had just suggested: simply grabbed whoever was nearest to him when the music had stopped and sat out the rest of the game.

As he passed by the A-House, Joel considered parking the car and running inside to see if that cute little Aries haircutter from Shear Magic was there having a drink. The kid had seemed interested in getting a reading, and he was one of those hotties who wore those low-cut jeans that could be slipped off his ass without even undoing the belt. Joel started to brake, changed his mind, and kept on driving. Mona would be home in less than an hour and would have to be fed; instead of sex, he'd have to settle for pizza.

Parking the car in front of Bubala's, he left Bunny II in the car, crossed the street, and scurried across the brick patio where he'd long ago been humiliated by Rudy Cantwell. Ever since that night he always put on blinders and stared straight ahead when he entered Spiritus, even on a night like tonight when the place was nearly empty. Joel was so guarded as he approached the counter that he barely noticed two good-looking men seated in the booth behind him. It was only when someone shouted out, *"Mon dieu!"* in a thick Parisian accent that Joel turned around and saw none other than Jean Paul waving him over, and Dennis Fairchild seated across from him and staring glumly at the table. Joel's entire body went numb—the moment he'd been anticipating for almost a decade had finally arrived.

"You promised your mother," Joel overheard Jean Paul whispering to Dennis as Joel tentatively approached the table. Unlike Lucas, Jean Paul hadn't gained an ounce. Dennis, on the other hand, was noticeably plumper—as if he'd gained a pound for every year Joel hadn't seen him. On the table in front of him were pieces of a ripped paper plate that the artist was absorbed in arranging into an abstract.

"We were just talking about you," Jean Paul declared. "We saw in the paper you were reading from your new book. How did it go?"

"Fine," Joel replied, not sure whether or not to sit down.

"We were going to come but Dennis wasn't feeling well."

Dennis shook his head as though wanting to contradict Jean Paul's assertion. His French lover reached across the table and touched his hand. "I think we should tell him."

Dennis nodded slightly and looked aside, so Jean Paul turned to Joel. "Dennis's father died last month. It was very sudden."

"Oh, no."

"We've been with Maureen all this time—she's not taking it well. She forgives you for what you did and she talked about you many times. When we told her we were coming here on business, she said we should find you and ask you to contact Martin's spirit. She still believes you have a special connection."

Dennis rolled his eyes and shook his head.

"No, really!" Jean Paul pointed at Joel and defended him. "He knew all about Charles and the finger bowl. Without him we wouldn't have a business." Turning back to the astrologer, Jean Paul pleaded, "We're staying at the Landmark. If you have time tonight, we can get Maureen on the phone and you can tell her whatever you can pick up."

Joel thought about Jean Paul's request. "I can't do it," he replied.

"But why not?"

"I don't do that kind of thing anymore. Nowadays I write astrology books about dogs because I won't fuck things up if I'm wrong. It's not that I don't have hunches about people. I just can't rely on them and I wouldn't want to say anything to Maureen unless I believed it one hundred percent."

Dennis raised his head and looked at Joel with a glimmer of respect. Joel reached out to him and touched his shoulder. "I'm so sorry about your dad, but I can't contact his spirit and I never really could."

Before Dennis could respond, Jean Paul's cell phone rang. "*Allô,*" he yelled into the tiny receiver. Shaking his head, he snapped the phone shut. "No coverage here. I have to go across the street. It might be Ghislaine calling about her table."

After Jean Paul left, Joel quietly sat down opposite Dennis and wondered what he could say. Finally he opened his mouth and murmured the first thing that popped into his mind. "Your father loved you very much."

"I know," Dennis mumbled, covering his eyes with his hand as though shielding himself from the harsh overhead lighting.

"And I also wanted to say that I did a lot of terrible things back then and for a long time I blamed you. But everything that happened—it was all my fault. I did it all to myself."

Dennis removed his hands from his face and tears were streaming down his cheeks. "I did a lot of rotten things, too. I'm sorry."

Joel had never expected an apology from Dennis, but this was a man who had just lost his father. The Dennis Fairchild seated before him was vulnerable and emotionally available. Joel got an erection.

Suddenly Jean Paul was back at the table. "I need to go to the hotel and get the car. Ghislaine is leaving tomorrow, so if we're interested in her table I have to go to Orleans and see it tonight."

"I'll go with you," Dennis suggested.

"No, stay at the hotel and have a quiet night. I'll call you before I make an offer." Dennis and Joel stood up to leave, and the three men walked outside.

Joel volunteered to drive Dennis and Jean Paul back to their hotel, and they all strolled across the street to his car. Joel cleared away some coloring books and dog toys so Jean Paul could get in the back. Dennis sat up front and was surprised by a little dog jumping onto his lap.

"Oh, my god! It's Bunny," he said as the dog licked his face—something the old Dennis never would have allowed.

"Do you ever paint anymore?" Joel asked as they drove slowly down the deserted street.

"A little," Dennis replied, "but the good stuff never sells."

"Some things never change," Joel moaned, shaking his head.

When they got to the Landmark, Dennis turned in his seat and looked at Joel. "What?" Joel asked

"You seem happier," Dennis said with an uncharacteristic softness in his voice. "More at peace with yourself."

"I am," Joel admitted, although he couldn't exactly say why.

They all got out of the car and Joel put his arms around Dennis for a hug. Sure enough he was thicker than Joel remembered. Although his first impulse had been to simply comfort Dennis for his loss, the artist stood there with no sign of letting go, so—just out of curiosity—Joel let his hands wander down Dennis's body to where his old friend had grown some luscious love handles. He longed to grab his ass as well.

"How long are you going to be in town?" Joel asked. "I'd love to catch up."

"Come on over later," Dennis said. "I'll take you out for a drink after Jean Paul leaves for Orleans."

"Sure," Joel said, forgetting for a moment that he'd have to find a babysitter.

Chapter Forty-three

Joel still had a half hour before Mona got home from rehearsal, so he stopped on Cemetery Road and let Bunny II out of the car for a little run around the tombstones. Just for fun he started pushing his way across the snow-covered graveyard, leaving a trail of deep footprints as he climbed to the highest point in the cemetery. Throwing his arms out wide, he howled at the crescent moon hanging low in the star-studded sky. "He loves me. I was right. Somewhere deep inside he's always loved me. I haven't been crazy all these years."

As he fought his way up the hill, Bunny II struggled to keep up with him by jumping in and out of his footprints like a jackrabbit on an obstacle course. Arriving at the summit, Joel threw himself into a snowdrift beside a mausoleum and stared up at the stars; a moment later, Bunny II jumped onto his chest and licked his face. Each second would be an eternity of joyful anticipation until he saw Dennis Fairchild again.

Suddenly his life during the last few years seemed terribly boring. He was sick of writing about dogs, hanging out with Provincetown kooks, and gossiping with Bill about the nonsense going on in town. He didn't care who was installing an illegal kitchen in his condo. He didn't care who was trying to sell his run-down house for a ridiculous price. He didn't care how many new fire trucks the Board of Selectmen would be buying that year. Joel realized with a sense of horror that, even though he was only forty-six, he'd been behaving more like he was fifty-six: Bill's age. *My lover is an old man and he's making me one, too,* he thought. *But now that Dennis Fairchild is emotionally available, my life will be so exciting.*

He knew he'd have to dispatch Jean Paul, but that would be easy enough—he'd done it before. The trick would be to get Dennis to paint again. *We could take a trip to New York to see my old friends. My Rolodex isn't that out of date.* One of Joel's newest readers was an owner of a gallery on Fifty-seventh Street who was having prob-lems with her miniature pinscher. *She'd be thrilled to give Dennis a shot at selling his work in New York.* The artist could move back to Provincetown and rent studio space from the Fine Arts Center; every night after putting Mona to bed, Joel imagined running over to the studio to give the artist a back rub and feed him pizza while he worked.

Joel pulled open his pants and started rubbing his cock. "Oh, baby! Oh, baby!" he moaned, remembering the way Dennis's love handles had felt. That very night he might actually get his hands on Dennis's big, fat ass. "Emotionally available," Joel kept repeating to himself. "Vulnerable. Hurt. Maybe even a little depressed. How wonderful!"

Joel was coming too quickly. Backing off his fantasy, he let his mind wander to the way Dennis had looked at him in the car. There was something in his eyes that he had never seen before: attraction. *Have all these years of being fucked by Bill finally turned me into the kind of guy who Dennis would love to fuck?* Joel started stroking again, but this time he pictured the artist fucking him. He pictured his own legs in the air, his ass being plowed. He imagined Dennis becoming the top in their relationship. Or maybe they could take turns fucking each other. The two of them would fall madly in love and they'd move back to New York and adopt Mona and …

Mona.

Joel stopped stroking and took a few deep breaths. *What if Dennis didn't want to adopt Mona? What if he didn't even like Mona? What if Bill didn't want to give her up?* How awful! What he'd said to Lucas earlier that evening was true: he and Mona had fallen in love. That first day she'd come into the house that day holding hands with Bill, taken one look at Joel, and beamed with delight. "At last I've found you," her smile seemed to say. Soon after, Joel found himself just as smitten. A maternal Cancer, he loved strapping her into the car seat, cutting her meat into little pieces, singing her songs, and teaching her how to read. Taking care of Mona was never a burden. He felt he had known her for many years and that everything he did for her was like returning a favor for a dear old friend.

And Joel knew Bill loved Mona as much as he did himself; he would often remark that the little girl's smile reminded him of Mitchell's. How could he possibly tear them apart and cause Bill another horrible loss? "Oh, shit!" he muttered several times because he now knew that, even if Dennis Fairchild were facedown on a bed and begging him to spend the rest of his life eating his ass, he couldn't do it—not if it meant losing his family.

Joel's cell phone rang. It was Dennis Fairchild. He let it ring three times before answering.

"Hello."

"Joel?"

Joel took a deep breath, and then blurted out, "I need to tell you something quickly before I change my mind. I know I said I was sorry before, but I want you to know I'm sorry for *everything*. I'm sorry for chasing away your boyfriends, for sabotaging your part in the play, for biting your ass, for drugging you, for burning down your house—but mostly I'm sorry for not respecting you. I was blinded by your tush. So please don't let me come to your hotel tonight. Because if I do, I'll only try to trick you into pulling down your pants. So let's forget about tonight. OK? And if I ever see you again, don't let me anywhere near your tush. Don't let me see it. Don't let me touch it. If I offer to rub your back again, say no! Please! If we're ever going to be friends, I need your help because I can't do this alone."

Joel paused to catch his breath.

"Joel … I … um…"

There was an awkward silence, Dennis cleared his throat, and Joel suddenly knew why he'd called.

"You're canceling, aren't you?"

"I really should go with Jean Paul to check out this table."

"Oh," Joel said, suddenly feeling dryness in his throat.

"But it was great seeing you again."

"Same here."

The two men were quiet for a moment.

"Joel," Dennis said with sincerity in his voice that Joel hadn't known was possible, "even when I hated you, I never thought you were boring. And that's saying a lot, because we both know how easily I get bored."

Joel started to tear up.

"Anyway … Jean Paul's waiting for me."

"Oh. When … when are you coming back to town?"

"Jean wants to do New Year's in Antigua and then we'll be

flying back to France. Wait a second." Joel heard Dennis covering the receiver. A moment later he was back. "Jean Paul says he'd like to come back here for Fourth of July weekend. Will you be here?"

"Of course. This is my home."

"Great."

"So call me when you're in town."

"It's a deal."

Joel hung up the phone feeling like someone had just punched him in the chest. Catching his breath, he began shouting his mantra at the sky. Gradually, he relaxed and was able to start counting his blessings. The moon was beautiful. The stars were beautiful. He lived in an earthly paradise where he could walk his dog on the beach any time he liked. He wrote funny books. He had a few fans. His daughter was a black girl who might grow up in a world in which an orphan raised by queers might change how people think. He loved the way it felt to have Bill's cock up his ass, and that his lover still wanted to fuck him after all these years—even though half the time it was more out of annoyance than anything else. He even loved that he had a hopeless crush on Dennis Fairchild, but—thank god—there was a force in the universe that pulled at his heartstrings even more powerfully than tush.

"*Nam myoho renge kyo. Nam myoho renge kyo.*"

"Pghh! Pghh!"

Joel stopped chanting, picked up Bunny II, and pressed his face into her belly. "And you! I'm so sorry for ignoring you!"

"Pghh. Pghh."

"Because you were the first one to show me love and I'll never forget you. Never, never, never!"

Holding the dog against his chest, Joel closed his eyes and said a prayer for Martin Fairchild—he wished him peace. Then, realizing that Mona would be on her way home, he zipped up his pants, picked himself up, and followed his snowy footprints back to the car.

Acknowledgments

First let me thank my editor, Don Weise, and my agent Eric Myer. Also, this book took a long time to write, so I'd like to thank all the friends and family who have read or listened to portions as they were being written: Ron Akanowicz, Steven Ball, Jesse Cohen, Megan Cohen, Riah Cohen, Doug DeRusha, John Dowd, Lee Floersch, Diane Hamilton, Bela Halmi, Sam Hanser, Rob Hejdak, Alan Klein, David Koch, Erik Kornfeld, Andrew Lawlor, Chris Livingston, Phil Retzky, Jason Ross, Eddie Sarfaty, Andrew Sullivan, and Will Weir. I'd especially like to thank Bob Smith and Michael Zam for their looking over my shoulder as I wrote.

And finally I'd like to thank Michael Stewart, who's stuck with me in good times and bad, and without whom this book wouldn't have been possible.

Tush is dedicated to my father, who spread a lot of joy in the world.